BLOOD AT THE ROOT

Ann Ferguson is Professor of Philosophy and Women's Studies at the University of Massachusetts at Amherst. She has one child, two step-children and one foster child. She is a lesbian, feminist and socialist political activist and currently co-chairs a group of faculty and staff at the five colleges in the Amherst area for peace in Central America.

"**Blood at the Root** takes feminist theory a giant step forward, beyond the constraints of both biological and economic determinism. In this wise and humane book, Ferguson restores human interdependency, love and sex to their central and rightful place in our understanding of the politics of gender. **Blood at the Root** is elegantly reasoned without ever being pretentious, firmly argued without being polemical. I read it with great pleasure, enjoying each insight and grateful for an analytical approach that takes our deeply felt experience – of love, of motherhood, of desire – as the touchstone of theory." – **Barbara Ehrenreich**

BLOOD AT THE ROOT

Motherhood, Sexuality and Male Dominance

Ann Ferguson

London   Winchester   Sydney   Wellington

First published by Pandora Press, an imprint of the Trade Division of
Unwin Hyman, in 1989

PANDORA PRESS
Unwin Hyman Limited
15/17 Broadwick Street, London W1V 1FP

Unwin Hyman Inc
8 Winchester Place, Winchester, MA 01890

Allen & Unwin Australia Pty Ltd
P.O. Box 764, 8 Napier Street, North Sydney, NSW 2060

Allen & Unwin NZ Ltd (in association with the Port Nicholson Press)
Compusales Buildings, 75 Ghuznee Street, Wellington, New Zealand

British Library Cataloguing in Publication Data

Ferguson, Ann
Blood at the root
1. Feminism
I. Title
305.4′2
ISBN 0 04 440445 X

Typeset in 10½ on 12 point Plantin by Computate (Pickering) Ltd
and printed in Great Britain by the Guernsey Press Co. Ltd,
Guernsey, The Channel Islands

Table of Contents

Illustrations

Photographs and captions by Margaret Randall

Between pages 148 and 149

Acknowledgements

This book is the product of many years of sex/affective bonding with socialist and feminist friends, without whose encouragement and feedback it could not have been written. I owe the deepest debt to Nancy Folbre. Our exciting talks gave me many insights into the economic and historical bases of contemporary male dominance. She also tirelessly read and re-read the manuscript, giving me invaluable comments which importantly strengthened the line of argument of the book. Another central aid has been Sam Bowles, with whom I've had many supportive as well as combative discussions on these subjects. Other supportive feedback at different stages was given by Keitha Fine, Meryl Fingrutd, Sandra Harding, Margaret Hunt, Elaine McCrate, Francine Rainone, Richard Schmitt, Tom Wartenberg and Iris Young. The Marxist-Activist Philosophers (MAP) – now SOFPHIA, the Socialist and Feminist Philosophers' Association, helped me revise the key theoretical ideas. The local Feminist Theory Study Group gave great comments on some sections. Bob Ackermann, John Brentlinger and Bob Wolff provided valuable collegial support in an otherwise hostile work atmosphere. Thanks to Margaret Randall for being such an inspiring socialist-feminist and for permission to use her wonderful photographs. A special thanks to Philippa Brewster, my editor at Pandora Press, for her encouragement and valuable suggestions, as well as to Meg Howarth, the copy-editor.

My original and household families have provided a central emotional underpinning to my book project. Thanks to my daughter Kathy, former housemates Connie and Lisa, my parents Bassett and Liz, my sisters Linda and Ellen and my brother John. I owe a special debt to Cathy Buescher for love, emotional support and invaluable technical help with the computer program. Finally, thanks to the international left, lesbian, gay and feminist communities for whom this book was written and to whom it is dedicated. May our dream of a better world come true some day!

PART ONE

Critiques of Theories of Social Dominance

1

Radical Feminist, Marxist and Socialist-Feminist Theories of Male Dominance

The historical paradox of feminism

Advances toward the social equality of women have occurred throughout the world in the 1970s and 1980s. These have included the legalisation of divorce in Italy, the right to maternal child custody and paternal child support payments in Nicaragua and the legalisation of abortion in the US. Though organised feminist movements are strongest in Western industrialised countries, there are also developing feminist groups and organisations in countries of the Third World as well (e.g. Mexico, Peru, India, Nicaragua). The 1985 United Nations' International Conference on Women in Nairobi demonstrated that feminism is truly an international force, though conditions for women, as well as which issues are prioritised by feminists, vary widely, depending on differing economic, social and cultural situations. However, no country demonstrates the particular volatile mix of progressive and conservative tendencies in relation to sexism seen in the US. For, though an advanced capitalist economy does introduce some potentially liberating tendencies into the social formations it is a part of, the resilience of patriarchy in a particular society depends importantly on the particular historical mix of male dominance, classism and racism within each society. Thus, though the model of male dominance I introduce here could be used to analyse the possibilities for the elimination of male dominance in other countries, I shall use the US experience as a case study in this book.

The 1980s is a watershed period for United States' feminists. The American Women's Movement of the 1960s and 1970s which, though it did not succeed in ratifying the Equal Rights Amendment to the Constitution, had enough influence to help

legalise abortion (the Supreme Court Roe *vs* Wade decision).
Other successes for the Women's Movement in the United States
include a tremendous increase in women's access to professional
training (as physicians, lawyers, etc.), implementation of the Civil
Rights Acts of 1964 (including the establishment of federal and
state Affirmative Action guidelines and Equal Opportunities
Commissions to consider race and gender discrimination), rights
for welfare mothers and the comparable worth demands accepted
by some public employers.

In the sexual realm, marriage is no longer a *sine qua non* for
female social success: today, one can be single or divorced and not
judged a total failure as a woman. Premarital sex and non-marital
partnerships are increasingly socially acceptable. Gay and lesbian
liberation has had some success in combating homophobia, thus
widening women's sexual options. It is increasingly acceptable for
women to demand sexual pleasure from men rather than simply
accepting the patriarchal idea that men's orgasms are the aim of
heterosexual sex. Trade unions, universities and some other
employers have formulated policies against sexual harassment at
their workplaces.

However, these positive gains are threatened by a fierce backlash against feminism, as evidenced by the growth of the New
Right. This group's political agenda is based on a Christian
fundamentalism which is explicitly patriarchal. Its priorities
include an anti-abortion constitutional amendment, an attack on
lesbian/gay rights, a virulent campaign on all sexually explicit
material, particularly sex education courses in public schools, and
calls for a return to the male breadwinner/female mom/housewife
family. And though its political strength is not strong enough at
this historical moment to completely eliminate reproductive
rights won by the Women's Movement, it has succeeded in
limiting them, particularly by Congressman Hyde's amendment
which prohibits federal funding of abortions for poor women, the
Reagan administrations's Title 10 executive ruling which prohibits federal funding to family planning centres offering abortion
counselling, information and referrals, and the same administra-
tion's withholding of funds to international family planning agen-
cies which support abortion as an option.

The success of the conservative agenda in the US is evidenced
in another way which impacts negatively on women. The alarm-
ing growth of the American military budget (now one-third to

one-half of total federal expenditure) compared to the stagnation of publicly supported social services (which disproportionately benefit women), the rise of the phenomenon called 'the feminisation of poverty', the absence of a federal child care programme, the massive increase of the pornography industry, the disinterest of much of the younger generation of women in feminist activism (what has been called, misleadingly, 'post-feminism') suggest that the Women's Movement has been unable to alter some of the ideological and material conditions which perpetuate male dominance.

One necessary condition for the advance of American feminist goals has been the increasing sexual permissiveness which began with the Beat, Hippie and New Left movements' challenges to the traditional patriarchal mores of heterosexual marriage and sex for procreation rather than pleasure. This sexually permissive current was further strengthened by the feminist movement's demand for the right to define our own pleasure in orgasms as well as by the rise of the gay and lesbian liberation movements. But the growth of the AIDS epidemic has contributed a severe setback to sexual permissiveness. AIDS has not only created realistic fears about promiscuous sex, but has been used by the Right to argue for a return to compulsory monogamous marriage and an attack on premarital sex and homosexual rights.

Woman-hating attitudes are also present in public reactions to AIDS which unfairly target prostitutes as key carriers of the disease while ignoring the greater likelihood that it is male clients who infect women rather than the other way round. The inexcusable time lag in government aid for AIDS research is racist as well, for Black and Hispanic populations are ten times more likely to be exposed to AIDS as the Anglo heterosexual population, mainly due to the higher incidence of intravenous drug use in poor communities. In short, the public response to AIDS suggests a tendency to scapegoat women, minority races and gay men in a Right-wing backlash against the gains of the American civil rights movement and the sexual radicalism and organised feminism of the 1970s.

How can we explain this paradoxical position of American feminism today? How can the Women's Movement be both gaining and losing against the forces of male dominance? Why are there such opposing tendencies *vis-à-vis* gender equality in our society? And on what theoretical base can feminists organise to challenge the patriarchal tendencies of the New Right in order to promote our own goals? Indeed, how can we deal with disagreements between ourselves as to what constitutes a truly feminist sexual lifestyle?

One of the arguments of this book is that no existing feminist theory, whether liberal, Marxist, neo-Freudian, radical feminist or socialist-feminist, can provide an adequate explanation for the paradoxical position of North American feminism. A central failing of existing theories is that their theoretical analytical concepts either do not allow of sufficient historical specification or else their historical specifications are inadequate to really capture the present situation of women in the US. My socialist-feminist model provides a general analytic category, 'modes of sex/affective production', and argues that specific societies must be analysed as social formations whose forces of male dominance depend on the particular historical combination of the economic and social systems involved. My case study of the US is provided as an example of a historical analysis of a specific capitalist patriarchal society. I do not claim to generalise all of the particular tensions of American patriarchy to all societies, or even to other capitalist patriarchies. Nonetheless, I hope that the general theory of sex/affective production provided here will provide feminist theorists from other countries with a theoretical framework which they can apply to historical studies of their own social formations.

Starting points

I'm a feminist. And a socialist. I'm also a lesbian. And a mother. I am a stepmother of two grown men and a foster mother of another. My teenage daughter is an adopted mixed race child and I am white. These oppositional political identity commitments have given me certain experiences and personal conflicts which motivate and act as a touchstone for a philosophical theory of how motherhood, sexuality and male dominance interact.

I came to my political identities by participation in the civil rights, New Left and feminist movements of the 1960s and 1970s. And just as my own theoretical understanding of the reasons for male dominance have altered with historical developments, so the theoretical paradigms of feminism have developed and altered.

I propose to provide a theory which, as a socialist-feminist perspective, weaves together some of the key insights of radical feminism, Marxism and Freudianism while avoiding some of their problems. In my view, the radical feminists are correct to target the patriarchal social construction of sexuality and mother-hood as a cross-cultural basis for the persistence of male domi-nance. But their theory is both too ahistorical to capture the present weaknesses in the contemporary US system of male dominance and too generalised to account for the differences between women of different racial, ethnic and class backgrounds in this society.

Marxism is superior to radical feminism with respect to its emphasis on historicity. In particular, the historically various social organisations of human labour and its exploitation are central to an analysis of the perpetuation of social dominance. But Marxism has no adequate theory of sexuality and motherhood. Furthermore, both radical feminism and Marxism, in their assumption of a rational self-interested theory of human agency, have too simplistic a theory of social domination and, con-sequently, of the conditions necessary for social resistance.

Finally, psychoanalysis has some good insights about the importance of early childhood gender acquisition and its connec-tion with human sexual desire and sexual orientation. We must accept some of the insights of psychoanalysis to explain the persistence of male domination even when it does not serve the rational interests of men and women to perpetuate it. But Freud-ianism, based as it is in a theory of self formed in early childhood, is too fatalistic. Thus, it fails to understand how the political and social contexts of an adult woman's life, for example participation in a counter-cultural feminist or lesbian community, may provide the possibility for altering her childhood gender and sexual identity. Furthermore, Freudianism, based as it is on an assump-tion of childhood in the historically specific bourgeois patriarchal nuclear family, is too ahistorical to capture the ways in which patriarchy is reproduced in non-bourgeois families in capitalism and in social formations which have different family and economic forms.

My theoretical strategy to incorporate the insights of these three approaches while avoiding their faults is to posit what I call 'modes of sex/affective production' in human societies. These are systems which socially construct 'sex/affective energy', that human physical and social interaction which is common to human sexuality, parenting, kin and family relations, nurturance and social bonding. Just like economic systems, they are historically various. It is in these systems that the male dominance in different forms is perpetuated. Social challenges to male dominance are possible in different societies at different times due to internal conflicts in the system, or else tensions and conflicts male dominance may have with the other forms of social organisation of the society: its mode of economic production, religion, state and legal system.

If we use the theoretical paradigm of sex/affective production, we can make sense out of the apparent contradictory positions of American women today. Though American women are still oppressed by patriarchy, advanced capitalist society has undermined some of these structures and has put us in a position of relative empowerment compared to women of previous generations. Indeed, conflicts between the ideology of individualism and the reality of second-class citizenship for women are partly responsible for the rise of the Women's Movement. Second, though we are divided from each other by racial, ethnic, sexual and economic class differences, we have in common a sex/class connection organised by the sexual division of the unpaid labour of the family household as well as wage labour, the gender bias of the patriarchal state, the mass media and the public/private split of family/household and economy. These two features of American women's lives – that we are relatively empowered and that we share some common oppressions as women across race, family and individual economic class – make us a potentially radical sex/class, although we can only activate that radical potential by dealing honestly with privileges which divide us *vis-à-vis* our other social differences.

Feminist theoretical questions

It is helpful to have an overview by which to compare different sorts of feminist theory. Feminist theories can be deemed successful or problematic to the extent that they can provide answers to the theoretical questions assumed central to the goal of feminism.

Contrary to many of their proponents' scientistic pretensions (we're just after the facts, ma'am!), social theories never develop in a value-free context. Rather, they can be categorised by their most general goals as having conservative, liberal or radical designs on the fabric of the social order: they seek to understand existing social relations in order to preserve, to reform, to destroy and/or to reconstruct them altogether.

Feminist theories are theories of social change. That is, all of them are unalterably opposed to conservatism and desire some minimum change in the social order so as to better accommodate women's rights. However, different feminist theories have different ideals for the future, different analyses of what perpetuates male dominance and, consequently, different strategies of how to challenge it.

Let us compare and contrast the various American feminist theoretical tendencies with regard to how they answer the following six questions:

1 *The origins question*: Can the fact that male dominance exists in so many societies cross-culturally be due to a common origin of male dominance? For example, can it be due to biological differences, strength and body structure, reproduction and so on, or to some common economic, sexual or other interests which motivate men to dominate women: for example, control of children's labour, sexual control or womb envy?

2 *The persistence question*: What causes male dominance to persist in societies with very different modes of production, such as capitalism, socialism, feudalism, slavery or rural independent agricultural production? Does it persist because the conditions motivating the origins of patriarchy still persist, including the male need to control children's labour, women's lesser sexual interest in men than men in women, women's greater maternal bonding with children, male innate aggressiveness or womb envy? Does it persist because men benefit economically from women's subordination in all these different societies, albeit in different forms or simply because of the power of socialised gender differences in early childhood development?

3 *The historical reproduction of patriarchy question*: What are the historically specific causes and structures which perpetuate male dominance in our contemporary society? Is male dominance in capitalist society a secondary phenomenon which is perpetuated because it serves the interests, not of men, but of the capitalist class, as Marxists would argue? Is male dominance perpetuated by unconscious personality structures developed in

the patriarchal nuclear family as feminist neo-Freudians Chodorow, Dinnerstein and Mitchell would argue? Do men benefit
from patriarchy in our society or is it merely an irrational hang-
over from traditional societies and infant socialisation? Are there
ways male dominance is being undermined in contemporary
society and ways it is being re-constructed?

Though the persistence and historical reproduction questions
sound similar, they diverge because thinkers of a universalist bent
tend to emphasise the *continuities* in human history, whereas
historical thinkers tend to stress the *discontinuities*. Radical feminists tend to seize on one universal causal explanation of male
dominance crossculturally, such as womb envy, and to use that to
answer the question of why male dominance persists. Marxists
and socialist-feminists, on the other hand, tend to look for historically specific mechanisms of reproducing patriarchy which
work in a particular economic and social context but may not be
generalisable to others; for example, that women are oppressed in
capitalism because our work in the family creates use value and
not exchange value, thus, in a money economy does not give us
access to social power (cf. Benston, 1969). Historical thinkers
tend to seek for specific answers to the historical reproduction of
patriarchy, and to shun the persistence question as too ahistorical.

One of the paradigms I do not develop in this book is that of
those who term themselves 'post-modernist feminists'. According
to these thinkers, questions about origins and persistence are
illegitimate, for any answers to such questions must assume the
crosscultural plausibility of concepts which assume a contrast
class which is only plausible in some specific historical contexts.
So, for example, basing male dominance on biology assumes a
biological/social distinction; basing it on women's relegation to
the domestic economy presupposes a domestic/public distinction;
tying it to 'modes of production' assumes a distinction between
the economy, or production, and other forms of human social life.
These generalisations, the post-modernists argue, are false
because the concepts used – biology, domestic, economy, production – gain plausibility only in certain social formations (cf.
Nicolson, 1986, Fraser and Nicolson, 1986).

Though I do not propose to give a sustained treatment of the
post-modernist move, I would argue that its strength lies in
specific critiques rather than in the blanket rejection of all theories
with universalist projects and crosscultural comparisons.

4 *The difference question*: Does patriarchy operate similarly across racial, class and cultural differences? Or do contextual differences between women make it impossible to discover a general theory of male dominance? Just how does sexism connect with racism, classism and heterosexism?

The question of difference has been much discussed among all the theoretical tendencies in feminism. Generalisations based on the experiences and structures relevant primarily to white Western middle-class heterosexual women's lives have been questioned by those excluded from these experiences, including non-white, non-Western, working-class and lesbian women (cf. Bulkin, Smith and Pratt, 1984; Moraga and Anzaldua (eds) 1981). Dealing adequately with the difference issue is an important test for feminist theories. However, it does not follow, as some have assumed, that the differences between women make it impossible to come up with some general similarities in the male dominant structures that oppress us.

Dealing honestly with the difference question is one of the reasons why feminists must commit ourselves to an historical and contextual perspective in constructing our theoretical paradigms of male dominance. Otherwise, the differences between women, and the consequent privileges that some women have in relation to others, are consistently overlooked in favour of an emphasis on our commonalities.

5 *The vision question*: Would a non-patriarchal society be achieved by institutions which separate women from men while at the same time giving women economic, social and political power over our lives: for example, lesbian sexuality; single motherhood, including artificial insemination; and separate women's communities which have political and economic self-determination *vis-à-vis* male communities? Should we accept an assimilationist vision of gender equality in which women should strive to become more like men: career-oriented and individualistic? Or should we insist on a reversal of values: men should become more like women: caring, maternal? Is a synthesis of some of the desirable traits of masculinity and femininity in a new androgynous ideal possible? For any of these visions, how would supporting social institutions – marriage, the family, sexual mores, the economy – have to change in order to achieve it?

There are really two sets of questions that should be separated in discussing the vision question. As the contemporary feminist sex debate demonstrates, there may be conflicting feminist sexual moralities about sexual preferences, pornography, etc. But sometimes feminists who share a vision of the ideal society may nonetheless disagree on short-run issues. For example, it is quite consistent to hold that we ought to work for an ideal society which abolishes gender dualism yet hold that, since we are not yet in the position to set up that ideal society, we ought to defend the right of women, as an already constituted gender, to organise autonomously to defend our interests against men. Thus, a visionary morality need not contain the same values as a pragmatic ethics which proposes a moral/political symbolic code of values and political strategies as the means to get us from our concrete situation to this ideal: what I call a transitional morality. I will use these distinctions in discussing the feminist sex debate in chapter ten.

6 *The political strategy question*: What political strategy or strategies are most likely to lead toward the goal of radical social change that would weaken and eventually eliminate male dominance? To answer this question one must have a theory of how social change can occur in systems of social dominance and a theory how the oppressed can best organise to further this change. Views range from the theories of vanguard groups: the working class for Marxists, lesbian-feminists for many radical feminists, vanguard parties in Marxist-Leninism or oppositional cultures as in Black nationalism or lesbian separatism, reformism for liberal feminism and identity politics coalitionism for some socialist-feminist politics.

Some of the main tendencies of American feminist theory are radical feminism, liberal feminism, Marxist-feminism and socialist-feminism (Jaggar, 1983). Neo-Freudian feminism is a perspective that cuts across the liberal and socialist-feminist divide as is sexual libertarian or pluralist feminism in the contemporary feminist sex debate.

Each of these camps tends to focus on some of the above questions more than others and to answer them differently. Furthermore, there are similarities in answers which cut across these camps and differences in details of answer between theorists in each camp.

In the remainder of this chapter I shall review some of the important radical feminist, Marxist and socialist-feminist theories of male dominance in order to assess their strengths and weaknesses in terms of the answers they give to the questions above.

Radical feminism

Radical feminism has been, until recently, the cutting edge of American feminist theory. This does not mean, of course, that its claims have always been judicious, temperate, or even ultimately defensible as originally presented by their proponents. But radical feminism, as the leading voice of the separatist wing of the Women's Movement, has not had to temper its perception of male domination by compromise with other political agendas.

The central feature that has distinguished radical feminism from alternative theories which purport to explain male domination is its focus on male control of female sexuality (in patriarchal marriage and motherhood, control over women's reproductive capacities, and compulsory heterosexuality). While liberal and Marxist feminists target unpaid housework or a sexist organisation of wage work, and the neo-Freudian motherhood theorists pinpoint the unconscious effects of differential gender development in asymmetrical mothering, radical feminists have concentrated on the rational self-interests of men in taking advantage of the biological weakness of women in motherhood (Atkinson, 1974; Firestone, 1970) and the way that the patriarchal construction of masculine and feminine sexuality has limited women's rational choices (Dworkin, 1974, 1981; Firestone, 1970; MacKinnon, 1987).

Early American radical feminism has three characteristics:

1 It tends to prioritise the search for the universal similarities between systems of male dominance cross-culturally over an understanding of their historically specific differences.
2 It tends to adopt a rational self-interest theory of human agency in which men's interests are seen to be in conflict with women's self-interests in patriarchal societies.
3 It explains women's subjugation to patriarchy by a combination of a coercion theory (women are forced to submit to male dominance by men's threatened or actual violence and their control of material resources) and an alienation theory (socialisation into gender roles alienates women from their true, authentic selves and human possibilities).[1]

The first work of American radical feminism, Shulamith Firestone's *The Dialectic of Sex* (1970) developed an important theory of the origins and persistence of male domination. She argues that sex caste, based on women's vulnerability in biological reproduction, precedes economic class as the primary base of all social domination systems. The patriarchal biological nuclear family which women are forced to accept because of our inability to control our reproduction and because of our economic dependence on men when mothering small infants, creates a public/ private split which makes women sexual and economic possessions of men. Firestone's theory claims to stand Marxist historical materialism on its head in order to derive a feminist historical materialism. Unfortunately her theory of origins is faulty because it is too simplistic.

Like Simone de Beauvoir (1952) before her, Firestone assumes that there is an inherent biological vulnerability faced by women because of our reproductive capacities that predisposes us to accept dependence on men (Beauvoir calls it 'immanence') rather than to demand an equal say in determining our own and social values (Beauvoir's 'transcendence'). But this ignores the possibility of female kin networks which could, and on some anthropologists' theories, did, support pregnant and lactating women without reliance on men (Reed, 1973). Indeed, Firestone is inconsistent on the question as to whether the patriarchal family has been a constant institution in human society until the present day, or whether some prehistoric societies (e.g. pre-Hellenic Greece) were matriarchal.

In more recent radical feminist thought, there is a philosophical retreat (Barry, 1979; Daly, 1978, 1982; Dworkin, 1981, 1987) from the view that male dominance is perpetuated through values which are historically socialised in men and women. Rather, the focus on the cross-cultural connection between men's control of women's sexuality and violence against women (cf. also Brownmiller, 1976; Dworkin, 1974) has furthered a belief in a universal set of positive values embedded in 'the female principle' which can be opposed to the negative values of 'the male principle'. This is dangerous because it suggests a biological essentialism that implies that the war between the sexes is inevitable, thus ruling out all but the most unrealistic separatist vision of social change. Ironically, although separatists who hold such views differ in their political beliefs from the Christian New Right, Right-wing theorists such as George Gilder (1973) have essentialist views that are similar to theirs, another reason for questioning this conclusion!

This contemporary American radical feminist tendency has been called 'cultural feminism' by Alice Echols (1983) and Ellen Willis (1984). The term 'cultural feminism' is quite misleading for it suggests that anyone who emphasises the importance of cultural factors in gender identity construction shares the same radical feminist assumptions. This is clearly false: for example, studies of women's and girl's subcultures as centres for both reproduction of, yet resistance to, patriarchy is stressed by socialist-feminist writers in Britain associated with the Birmingham University Centre for Cultural Studies (cf. Women Studies Group CCCS (eds), 1978).

To avoid confusion, then, I propose to call this tendency 'American radical cultural feminism'. This tendency rejects the materialist analysis of early radical feminism. Firestone (1970), Small (1974) and others assumed that women adopt traditional feminine roles in sexuality, marriage and motherhood, not because such roles reflect an innate and superior feminine predisposition such as maternal nurturance, but because rational self-interest in a world where men control more material resources than women dictates that women submit to the patriarchal rules of the game (Willis, 1983).

Today, one tendency in North American radical cultural feminist theory assumes that the biological differences between the sexes inevitably generate cultural differences that are not reducible to rational self-interests. For example, Mary Daly and others have argued that men's womb envy of women's ability to reproduce continues to be one of the motivations for the persistence of male dominance cross-culturally (Daly, 1978). And Mary O'Brien argues that gender reproductive differences make it difficult for men to fulfil a metaphysical need for 'species continuity', guaranteed to women by the natural connection with their offspring. This natural alienation motivates men to set up the patriarchal marriages and public/private splits which allow men to control women's sexuality, to assure their paternity and to perpetuate superior status for the public male realm to compensate for women's natural reproductive power (O'Brien, 1981).

Though I would agree that rational self-interest is not the only factor in promoting male dominance, the American radical cultural feminist explanations, since they are universalist, go too far in the opposite direction. 'Womb envy', after all, may be a rational passion in early human societies where the ability to bear children is important either for minimal survival of the group or for the expansion of labour power. But womb envy becomes irrational in advanced industrial societies where children are not an economic asset but a liability to parents. And indeed, other motivations more in keeping with rational self-interest, for example domestic and sexual services, seem more plausible in such contexts to explain the persistence of male dominance.

Firestone would have rejected emphatically the cultural feminist views on the inevitability of the relation between origins, persistence and reproduction. Rather, Firestone thinks that the availability of contraception and artificial reproductive techniques will finally end the persistence of male dominance that has hitherto assured women's economic dependence as mothers on men.[2] Indeed, the very absence of fixed masculine and feminine essences is what makes Firestone's vision possible: the development of the hitherto repressed androgynous potential of both men and women. This will be possible because the elimination of women's involuntary biological role will allow the gender division of labour in society and family to be abolished in favour of voluntary individual and communal household choices in a decentralised socialist society.[3]

Besides male control of female options for biological reproduction as a factor in perpetuating patriarchy, Firestone cites a psychological mechanism: the power psychology of the patriarchal nuclear family where the father gains more status than the mother as the adult who has power in the public world. Though both boy and girl desire to acquire the father's status, the girl learns that lack of a penis denies her that status. Thus, the denial of social power rather than feelings of biological inadequacy explain 'penis envy', in Firestone's correction of Freud. The hierarchy of gender power is hidden by an ideology of romance in which men mystify and place women on a pedestal so as to make lovable an otherwise socially devalued object. The patriarchal nuclear family also fuels racism and economic classism by presenting the father's power over others as a model for social relationships that becomes generalised in the human psyche.

The problem with Firestone's theory is, ironically, the same as that of the Freudian paradigm she opposes: her power psychology based in the patriarchal nuclear family gives too ahistorical a mechanism to understand all forms of male dominance as well as other forms of social domination. Firestone waffles back and forth between a universal claim that male dominance everywhere is fuelled by a power psychology generated in the patriarchal nuclear family, and a historical point of view that acknowledges that women and children were less restricted in the feudal period because of the lack of the public/private distinction present in capitalist society, the lack of the modern conception of childhood, etc.

Firestone's generalisations about the psychological connections between racism, classism and sexism have been rejected by Afro-American feminists (e.g. Spillers, 1984) who argue that Firestone's analysis ignores the differences between Black and white families in her generalisations about the persistence of a patri-archal power psychology. Her theory that race and class domi-nance is based on a prior gender dominance seems to prioritise feminism over Black and Third world and working-class oppo-sitional movements.

The cavalier disregard of the semi-autonomous bases of racism, ethnicism and classism is a general tendency of radical feminist thought. This tendency is reflected in the political strategy of radical feminism, which tends to promote a separatist Women's Movement based on the commonalities of women across race, ethnicity and class. Though radical feminists are willing to discuss the question of how racism, anti-Semitism and classism divide the women's and lesbian communities (Bunch and Myron, 1974a; Penelope, 1985) they are in general unwilling to make political coalitions with mixed groups of men and women fighting against racism, imperialism or in support of working-class issues (Bulkin, Smith and Pratt, 1984).[4]

There are some advantages to separatist politics: oppressed groups need separate space to gather their energies. Nonetheless, separatism goes beyond the need for an autonomous women's movement when it involves the principled refusal to ever engage in coalitions. For example, some radical lesbian separatists refuse to make coalitions either with gay men or straight women on the grounds that these people are oppressors. Such groups then lose their effectiveness in influencing mass movements, whether it be the Women's Movement, the Black civil rights movement, the lesbian/gay movement or the trade union movement. In part, the problem stems from a theory of identity politics that ignores the problem that both gender and sexual identity, since they are relational not absolute, are only partially separable from race, class or ethnic identity. This issue will be discussed further in chapter ten.

One important contribution of North American radical cultural feminism is its insistence on investigating and theorising how male violence against women is systematically used to perpetuate male dominance. Investigations like those of Brownmiller (1976), Daly (1978) and Dworkin (1974), and Griffin (1979) analyse such practices as rape, footbinding, witchburning and cliterectomy and argue that such tools involve both rational coercion (terror of physical punishment) and irrational constraints (internalised gender identities). The cultural eroticisation of violence against women in pornography and prostitution is considered by Barry (1979), Dworkin (1981) and Griffin (1981). The extent to which socialised masculinity and feminity internalise an eroticisation of male violence against women lends credence to the view that male dominance is not simply fuelled by the rational self-interests of men desiring to maintain women's domestic and sexual services, but connects to irrational anger against women as suggested by the Dinnerstein (1976) neo-Freudian account.

In general, the split between North American radical cultural feminism and earlier radical feminism poses a theoretical dilemma. On the one hand, if we accept a feminist materialism which assumes that women (and men) adopt gender roles out of rational self-interest (as utility maximisers in a context of gender inequality), we can develop a feminist vision which posits the possibility of a society free of gender roles or gender dualism. We can also promote strategies such as woman bonding, autonomy rather than separatism and negotiating with men when this will further our goals. But the 'rational economic agent' theory of agency assumed by the early radical feminists doesn't explain the depths of male violence against women nor the extent to which male dominance persists, because women make choices, for example, of motherhood, of heterosexuality, or in acquiescing to domestic violence against themselves, in cases where they do have other options that seem more in accord with their rational self-interest.

A prime example of how this rational self-interest agent assumption has negatively affected the Women's Movement is the question of lesbianism. The lesbian/straight split occurred in North America in the early 1970s because of two assumptions of radical feminist theory: 1. compulsory heterosexuality is the key mechanism that perpetuates male dominance; 2. any woman can be a lesbian if she chooses to do so, even though this involves renouncing heterosexual privilege. We shall consider the implications of lesbian identity and compulsory heterosexuality more fully in chapter nine. The point I wish to make here is that the assumption that any woman can change her sexual preference is mistaken: it assumes a unified self who is able to change her sexual desires at will in accordance with what is perceived to be her material self-interests.

Though some women may be able to change their sexual identity as adults, we are far from understanding the emotional pre-conditions for this. And in general, since one's erotic and emotional connections are unconscious aspects of self which are not totally under conscious self-control, it is mistaken to discuss the 'choice' of a sexual identity as if it were a simple rational instrumental decision.

There is another anomaly in contemporary gender relations which cannot easily be explained by the rational self-interested agent assumption of radical feminists. Elaine McCrate's thesis (1985) proposes that the increased rate of non-marriage among American women is a mark of our increased economic independence from men due to the existence of more wage labour jobs for women, welfare payments, and so on. Though McCrate's work indicates the importance of women's increased economic bargaining power to explain the increase of divorces, it cannot explain the relative inflexibility of the gender division of labour in parenting and domestic labour. Why, if women have increased bargaining power, are we unable to negotiate a reorganisation of family labour so it is more equitable rather than to opt for divorce? And why do women predominantly become the single parents after a divorce when single parenting is so economically disadvantageous for most who undertake it?

The failure of the 'rational economic agent' model of agency to explain all the features of women's situation today lends weight to the neo-Freudian view that we are constrained by unconscious aspects of feminine gender identity which keep us from making choices in our self-interest. But we must construct a more complicated feminist theory of the self and personal identity than either radical feminism or neo-Freudian feminism to explain how male dominance is being undermined by material changes which improve women's bargaining position *vis-à-vis* men and to take

into account the ways that counter-cultural communities and
feminist networks can counteract some of the more negative
effects of early childhood gender identity.

Marxism

Engels' attempt to explain the origins of male dominance, in the
classic *The Origins of the Family, Private Property and the State*
(Engels, 1972), argues that there was a transition from prehistoric
gender egalitarian matriarchal societies which had communal
modes of production to patriarchal class-divided agricultural societies. But his explanation is riddled with inconsistencies. Engels
argues that it was the possibility of a social surplus of wealth in
men's specialisation, herding animals, that gave them an interest
in controlling women's reproduction in patriarchal marriages so
as to give inheritance rights to men's children rather than, as
matrilineal inheritance specifies, to their sister's children.
    Marxism, like early radical feminism, assumes a rational self-
interest theory of human agency. Engels' argument rests on the
presupposition that when the possibility of economic surpluses
arises in society, both economic class and gender domination arise
simultaneously out of the self-interest of people to exploit others if
this allows them unequal access to wealth. Thus, it is rational for
men to control women's sexuality via double-standard monogamy
in order to control the future labour power of children that will
enable them to amass wealth. But he never explains why men
couldn't do this just as efficiently as uncles controlling the labour
power of their sisters' children under the system of matrilineal
inheritance. Indeed, Engels doesn't consider the strong anthropological evidence that many matrilineal communal hunting and
gathering societies might have been male dominant, which suggests that his economic motive is too simplistic.
    There are more sophisticated Marxist and socialist-feminist
approaches to the question of origins than Engels' early formula-
tion. Gerda Lerner (1986) propounds a version of Claude Meillasoux's view (1981) that women as the biological reproducers of
society were more valuable economic assets in early societies than
men, and hence it is rational for both men and women to acquiesce to the exchange of women, rather than men, as the way to
cement inter-tribal and group economic ties via kin relationships

(cf. also Harris, 1979). Lerner further argues that the first slave societies involved the possession of women who were used to produce children for future economic exploitation, since women can be more easily controlled through sexual conquest and their attachment to children than can unattached male slaves.

On this theory, the 'traffic in women' targetted by Levi-Strauss (1969) and Gayle Rubin (1975) as one of the social mechanisms for the cross-cultural persistence of male domination, has its origins in the social and economic implications of the biological reproductive differences between men and women in the conditions of economic scarcity prevalent in early human societies.

Lerner and Meillasoux's argument, though persuasive, is still too simplistic a theory to explain the origins of male dominance. After all, though it is true that men are less necessary than women if the goal is to reproduce many children to be future labourers (since one man can father children by many different women, but there can only be as many children produced at one time as there are women to bear them), there is evidence that male dominance existed in hunting and gathering societies which required the restriction, not the expansion, of the numbers of children born in order to sustain a viable life style.

My view is that the channelling and control of sexual and nurturant energy is a potential source of conflict in all human societies that must be organised by a system of social relations. Since childbearing is dangerous and wearing on the body, women have a rational interest in restricting births. Furthermore, the close and erotic connection between mother and child that breast-feeding develops acts as an emotional tie that may substitute for sexual interest in other adults, thus cutting men off from sexual connections with lactating mothers. Once we accept the view that human sexuality and associated forms of affection and nurturance are basic material needs which any society must organise to meet, we cannot assume that the social organisation and construction of sex is merely a tool to meet other needs, as Marxism tends to assume.

An alternative sketch of the origins of patriarchy could reject the 'natural stage' theory assumed by Engels and others of a progression from early matriarchal to later patriarchal society. Rather, we can suppose that the biological reproductive differences between men and women initiated the original sexual division of labour in breastfeeding and infant care in most societies that in turn may have set up a conflict between women's erotic attention to children and men's sexual interest in women (Reed, 1973).

This problem could have been resolved in different ways in different societies. Some hunting and gathering societies could subsequently have developed a male warrior class to resolve tribal conflicts over scarce resources. These societies may have resolved their internal gender sexual conflicts by evolving patriarchies in which male warriors asserted sexual and erotic control over wives and children. In some places, such patriarchal warrior societies may have come into conflict with and defeated matriarchal warrior societies (such as the fabled Amazons).

In other places, such patriarchies may have defeated more egalitarian matrilineal settled societies. The evidence offered by Peggy Sanday (1981) suggests that many such early societies could have established a relatively equal gender balance by matrilineal inheritance, the economic and social parity of women and men through a separate but equal gender division of labour, different extended kin networks, and pairing marriages which allowed some leeway for sexual freedom for both partners.

But the likelihood that gender egalitarian societies existed in early human history does not preclude the likelihood that patriarchal societies were able by and large to overcome them by war. In a situation of economic scarcity, patriarchal hunting and gathering societies could have been pressed to conquer more egalitarian agrarian societies when their supplies of large game were depleted. Once having conquered such societies, they could have enforced patriarchal marriage exchanges of women with the conquered tribes in order to solidify their rule and to set up caste or slave societies for further economic exploitation of the subjugated peoples (Kristeva, 1977).

It is clear that there is no final proof of any one theory of origins. Though we can put forth opposing conjectures, what is important to note is that there are various plausible theories which suggest social and historical, rather than merely biological, reasons for the beginnings of male dominance. Thus, it is credible to distinguish the origins question of the initial *causes* of male dominance from the persistence and reproduction questions.

When we turn to the Marxist approach to the persistence question, we find an ambiguity in the basic writings of Marx and Engels on how to construe sexuality and biological reproduction, and thus, the perpetuation of male dominance. Marx and Engels waffle on the question of whether sex is a material need that should be considered a part of the material base of social organisation. In *The German Ideology* (1850) they suggest in one place 'the reproduction of daily life' (which could include meeting sexual needs, producing children, etc.) is co-equal in importance to 'the production of daily life', while in another they suggest that the family, originally part of the economic base of society (i.e. a primary form of organisation to meet material needs), has become part of the superstructure in capitalist society (i.e. no longer a necessary form of organisation to meet material needs). In other places, Marx suggests that sex and procreation, as 'natural' needs, do not need to be socially organised.

In short, classical Marxism is ambiguous as to whether or not sex is an instinct which requires no social organisation, a basic material need whose objects may be variable but whose fulfilment requires social organisation, or a social need created instrumentally to achieve other more basic needs, for example to provide for the procreation of the future labour force. Thus, Marxism has no way of posing the question as to whether there are certain social organisations of sexuality, the production of children and social bonding (which I call modes of sex/affective production) in which men have a material interest in dominating and exploiting women which does not derive merely from the mechanisms that reproduce economic class domination.

As many feminists have pointed out (Eisenstein (ed.), 1979; Flax, 1976) Engels' conclusions about the material base for the persistence of male dominance are problematic. On the one hand Engels articulates the functionalist view that patriarchal marriages, involving double-standard monogamy which controls wives' but not husbands' sexuality, exist in class societies to provide a mechanism for controlling capital accumulation for the ruling class through assured paternity. On this view, ruling-class wives, though they are dominated by their husbands, nonetheless stand to gain by the orderly transmission of private property which sustains them, as the economic dependents of their fathers and husbands.

On the other hand, Engels says in one place in *The Origin of the Family* (1972) that in capitalism, the husband in the patriarchal family stands to the wife as bourgeois stands to proletariat. This suggests that there are two economic systems, capitalism and patriarchy, both of which have their exploiter and exploited classes; and that a woman may be an exploiter in one set of economic relations (e.g. as a member of the bourgeois class) but may be exploited in another (e.g. as a member of the possessed sex/class woman, or wife). Engels' positing of an economic sex/class division within the family and a different economic class system in the wider society shows the possibility that sexism may have its own dynamic, unrelated to its support of capitalism.

Contemporary Marxist-feminists tend to support Engels' first explanation of sexism, that it persists cross-culturally because in class-divided societies the ruling economic class or classes benefit from it. Though both radical feminists and Marxists assume a rational self-interested agent theory of social domination, they disagree about who benefits from male domination. Radical feminists assume men benefit from women's oppression by exploiting their labour and by using the existence of economic class divisions and racism as functional tools to divide women from each other. Marxist-feminists reverse the story and argue that sexism and racism are tools used by the ruling classes to divide men and women in the producing classes against each other, thereby perpetuating class exploitation.

Marxist-feminists, unlike radical feminists, insist that different modes of economic production have different social mechanisms for perpetuating sexism. Therefore, rather than questioning their general claims about class societies and sexism, we should examine their specific historical analysis of how capitalism perpetuates sexism. Since the contemporary debate between Marxist- and socialist-feminists in Europe and the United States hinges on the plausibility of their different historical analyses of the interconnection between capitalism and sexism, we shall evaluate some Marxist-feminist views by assessing their historical analysis of capitalism.

Perhaps the most popular Marxist-feminist analyses of how women are oppressed in capitalism are various versions of the unpaid housework theory: women are oppressed through a sexual division of labour in which they are expected to do unpaid housework. This is functional to capitalism in several ways. Since many women are full- or part-time housewives, women are a 'reserve army of wage labour' who can be drawn in and out of wage labour depending on capitalist business cycles, and can act as strike-breakers in male strikes.

Another functional argument is given by Maria Dalla Costa (1974) who argues that women's childcare and housework are necessary to reproduce the labour power of all workers, male and female, present and future. Thus, women are a particularly exploited segment of the working class. They are not exploited by their husbands but by the capitalists, since their unpaid domestic work is socially necessary to produce the surplus value appropriated by the capitalists as profit.

The idea that sexism is a tool used for capitalist purposes is one type of Marxist-feminist answer to the reproduction of patriarchy question. But there are others that are not quite so mechanistic. Margaret Benston (1969) and Sheila Rowbotham (1973) suggest that women's powerlessness in capitalism is a historical accident: the public/private split in commodity production keeps women's traditional production for use in the home where it is unpaid and undervalued, while men's productive work is moved out of the home into wage labour, hence more highly paid and valued. Once this occurs, women serve as convenient scapegoats: men who are dominated by other men in the hierarchical organisation of wage labour can release their frustrations by having a woman in the home to lord it over.

The problem with the Marxist-feminist view that sexism is functionally connected to capitalism is that it fails to explain the persistence of sexism in other social formations, not merely in other pre-capitalist class societies but in state socialist systems as well. Engels assumed that bringing women into industrial wage labour would provide the preconditions for their economic independence from men and socialism would complete the process by collectivising the tasks of housework and childcare. So far, as Hilda Scott points out (Scott, 1974), this has not happened in any existing socialist country: there is a second shift of unpaid childcare and housework for which women end up being responsible. Radical feminists explain this disparity by claiming that sexism has a dynamic independent of capitalism or socialism: the second shift problem occurs because men are loath to give up their material advantages (more leisure time, higher status, etc.) in order to equalise the unpaid labour of the domestic economy.

Another criticism of Marxist-feminist approaches is their inability to handle racism as a semi-autonomous domination structure. Rather, the standard Marxist analysis of racism in the United States and South America is that it is a vestigial structure left over from slavery (or, in other social formations, a vestige of tribal economic conflicts) which is maintained by capitalists as a mechanism to divide workers, thus increasing their ability to exploit them all (Perlo, 1980; Reich, 1981). A recent New Left criticism of standard Marxist economic theory has argued that the labour theory of value itself is ambiguous on how to understand racism and sexism in wage labour (Bowles and Gintis, 1977, 1986).[5]

In their zeal to defend a simple theory of social domination (economic class oppression) so as to justify a 'unite and fight' political strategy of working-class revolution against capitalism, Marxists have rarely taken seriously the independent effects of territorial nationalism and its consequences for race/ethnicism.[6] Contemporary neighbourhood race/ethnic segregation, and racial and ethnic divisions of labour, are not merely tools by which the capitalist class exploits the working class. They represent a race/ethnicism whose material base lies in territorial separation and control of some peoples by others (Marable, 1981). The race/ethnic history of the Soviet Union and China shows that the question of racial and ethnic control is an issue not simply dependent on the economic mode of production but one with roots in a struggle of dominant racial and ethnic groups to maintain power over subordinate ones.[7]

Socialist-feminist analyses

One resolution of the impasse between Marxist-feminism and radical feminism over who benefits by male dominance – capitalists or men as a sex/class – is the view that both do! Such a theory is a socialist-feminist view which has been termed a dual systems theory (Young, 1981). It assumes that there are two overlapping systems of social dominance, patriarchy and capitalism, each of which has its dominant and subordinate classes and which are in a dynamic interaction of the sort which requires the dominants of each system (capitalists and men, respectively) to negotiate regularly with each other to adjust the combined system to their mutual advantage.[8]

Heidi Hartmann's historical work on what she calls 'the partnership of patriarchy and capital' (1979, 1981) can be considered an attempt to correct the single systems approach of

Marxism, with its ultimate emphasis on the dynamics of economic class, with a radical feminist emphasis on the independent dynamics of gender dominance. Hartmann's theory is an economic dual systems theory of patriarchy. Its advantage over either Marxism or radical feminism alone is that it seems to accord better with the more complicated historical dynamics between class and gender domination. Hartmann's definition of patriarchy, 'a set of social relations between men, which have a material base, and which, though hierarchical, establish or create interdependence and solidarity among men that enable them to dominate women' (Hartmann, 1981a: 14) allows her the theoretical leeway to posit different modes of patriarchy in different historical periods and cultures. It also does not presuppose that the reproduction of male dominance is always centred in male control over women in the nuclear family, as Firestone's work had implied. It does, however, leave unclear what 'material base' Hartmann is referring to in her definition.

Hartmann argues that the institution of the 'family wage' in England and the United States in the late nineteenth century, i.e. a wage large enough to support a man and dependent wife and children, is a historical example of how groups of men colluded across economic classes to preserve patriarchal privileges over women and children that were being eroded in early capitalism by the wage labour of women and children. Male trade unions united to demand a family wage given to the male, and protection laws which excluded women and children from all but peripheral wage labour.

Hartmann's point is that the family wage was not an inevitable feature of capitalist development. Working-class men could have unionised women and they could have fought for equal wages for women and men. Instead they colluded with men of the bourgeois class, who had their own paternal interests in keeping their women at home, and established a system which allowed for the development of the capitalist patriarchal nuclear family (male breadwinner, female housewife and dependent children).

Evidence from the arguments by North American white male trade unionists of the period with respect to the family wage bear out Hartmann's interpretation. The preservation of endangered patriarchal privileges seems to be a clear agenda item as men argued that 'woman cannot serve two masters' that is, capitalists and their husbands/fathers (Foner, 1979)! The family household system, that is, the capitalist patriarchal nuclear family structure set up by the institution of the family wage, allowed most adult working-class men to retain the domestic and sexual services of women they had been in danger of losing in early industrial capitalism when women were drawn into long hours of wage labour. Hartmann's historical analysis makes it plausible to assume that the patriarchal interests of working-class men were a factor in structuring the capitalist wage labour market. Rather than see sex segmentation as a merely functional feature of capitalist development, we are invited to see it as a result of a historical process of adjudication between groups, capitalist and working-class men, with some common and some conflicting interests.

Hartmann's work has been questioned on a number of levels. The criticisms can be organised into four groups: alternative Marxist-feminist explanations of the family wage, different radical and socialist-feminist explanations of the domestic economy and the interactions between capitalism and male dominance, neo-Freudian feminist explanations of the persistence of male dominance and critiques of dual systems theory by feminists concerned with racism.

Hartmann's analysis of racism and ethnicism is problematic. For, as Gloria Joseph points out (Joseph, 1981), the definition of patriarchy seems to suggest that men will collude across class, ethnic group and race to dominate women. But white Anglo-Saxon protestant (WASP) male trade unions did not try to incorporate Black or Irish men into their numbers to enjoy 'the family wage'. A third semi-autonomous system of race/ethnicism is thereby needed to understand some men's exclusion from patriarchal privilege.

Other Marxist-feminist analyses would dispute Hartmann's conclusion that two dynamic systems, capitalism and patriarchy, must be posited to explain the family wage. Theorists like Barrett (1980), Humphries (1977) and Vogel (1983) posit that our contemporary forms of male domination are unintended effects of working-class strategies which were rational and necessary to promote the interests of both men and women, given the historical circumstances in which they were forged.

Michelle Barrett is an Althusserian Marxist-feminist.[9] She argues that what she calls 'the family household system' gets established by an historical alliance between skilled male trade unionists and capitalists. The structure is that which was set up by the adoption of the 'family wage'; i.e. a wage-earning male head and non-wage earning wife and children, and the ideology is that this 'family' is a natural kinship hierarchy which is an altruistic haven of privacy from the competitive, self-interested realm of business.

Barrett's explanation emphasises the accidental way in which the family wage bargain comes to set up the family household system (a structure which I shall henceforth call the capitalist patriarchal nuclear family). She and Jane Humphries (1977) argue that the adoption of the family wage is not a male strategy to maintain dominance over women but a united working-class family strategy to improve its standard of living. Nonetheless, the ensuing social structure creates a new ideology of independent masculinity and dependent femininity that becomes a material force as it becomes a part of the content of masculine and feminine self-identity (and unconscious desiring structure).

Lisa Vogel's (Vogel, 1983) discussion of two contradictory tendencies of capitalism with respect of women suggests a way to see the interaction of capitalist and patriarchal dynamics. Patriarchal forces effectively tip the balance to allow one contradictory tendency to win out over the other. If capitalism did not have both tendencies, there would indeed be a major conflict between the two systems, and no 'marriage' as Hartmann puts it, (Hartmann, 1981a), happy or unhappy, would be possible.

What are capitalism's contradictory tendencies with respect to women? According to Vogel, capitalists tend, on the one hand, to want to bring women into wage labour since female labour is cheap and unorganised. But, on the other, since the capitalist labour process interferes with reproductive and childrearing tasks hitherto assumed by women in the family/household (lactation and infant care) capitalists want to avoid female labour because it is costly to reorganise wage labour so that these socially necessary reproductive tasks can be done (provide maternity leave, childcare, flexi-time work schedules, train others to take mothers' places temporarily, etc.). It then makes sense to argue that at certain historical moments organised working men influence capitalists toward one of the tendencies rather than to another in order to preserve patriarchal privilege.

Though Barrett, Humphries and Vogel have theories which are convincing in some respects, they do not prove their point against the radical feminist position that men as a gender class have independent economic interests in dominating women. Men as a gender benefit from the unequal exchange and control they maintain over women's labour both in the family and in wage labour, even though the institutions by which they have achieved this control may have initially been accidental, or necessary to achieve other goals.

Another set of criticisms of Hartmann centres on the unclarity of the material base she posits for patriarchy. Is it, as Christine Delphy suggests (Delphy, 1984), that there is a patriarchal domestic economy embedded within all male dominant modes of production (from feudalism to capitalism to state socialism) which creates a material inequality for women because of an unremunerated labour exchange with men (fathers and husbands) in this economy? Or, as Nancy Folbre suggests, is the correct way to conceive of the material base of this unremunerated gender labour exchange that it is a patriarchal mode of production of children based on husbands' control over wives' fertility through their control of sexuality in patriarchal marriages (Folbre, 1987)? According to Folbre, the articulation of this patriarchal mode of production of labour power with advanced capitalism has shifted control of women's sexuality and childrearing labour to the state. Since men no longer gain individually by producing children, women have increasingly been forced to carry the bulk of childrearing labour themselves, as evidenced by the rise of divorces, single mother families and inadequate public welfare (Folbre, 1985).

Nancy Folbre and I have argued (Ferguson and Folbre, 1981) that Hartmann places too much reliance on the 'marriage' of capitalism and patriarchy through the late nineteenth-century accord between capitalists and male trade union workers which established the family wage. In fact this bargain has been breaking down in the United States with the increasing wage labour participation of married women in the twentieth century. Hartmann does not sufficiently emphasise the ongoing historical conflicts between capitalism and male dominance that cannot be resolved once and for all by a temporary agreement on a family wage. Indeed, as I shall argue in chapters five and six, the new accords of our contemporary period are weaker in their ability to enforce male dominance than was the late nineteenth-century accord on the family wage.

Even though Hartmann's economic dual systems theory is superior to the reductionist Marxist-feminist explanation of male dominance, it too is ultimately too simplistic in its analysis. This is because Hartmann, like the Marxists, has a theory of the reproduction and persistence of patriarchy which is too rationalistic. If men are indeed patriarchal dominators, why do most women desire them sexually? And why desire to marry and have children? The irrational aspects of motherhood and heterosexuality cannot be handled on the rational theory of human agency Hartmann assumes. Thus, a socialist-feminist perspective must not merely expand to include a tri- or multi-systems approach to social dominance to account for racism and ethnicism; it must also find a way to incorporate a feminist psychology that explains the internal effects of domination and oppression on the selves of both dominators and oppressed.

Problems with the Rational Self-interested Agent Theory

Let us consider problems with the rational individualist theory of human agency (assumed by some early radical feminists, e.g. Firestone, some socialist-feminists, e.g. Hartmann, as well as most Marxists) by looking at Marxist assumptions about human agency. It is ironic that Marxists ultimately maintain a 'self-interested economic man' theory of social domination and revolution. It is paradoxical because many Marxists critique the classical and neo-classical models of 'economic man', that humans are possessive competitive individuals out to maximise their own self-interests. What is mistaken about this view, they argue, is that this is not a universal feature of human nature but a 'second nature' historically and socially conditioned by the competitive market structure of capitalist society. Humans could be co-operative communally-oriented producers with a mode of production, socialism, that did not require humans to develop competitive self-interested attitudes in order to meet their basic material needs.

I have no quarrel with the Marxist critique of bourgeois theories of human nature. But Marxism itself has an economistic view of human nature when it comes to the action of classes in struggle with each other. Marxists characterise human history as a history of class struggles. This is seen as a struggle of classes who as a group act like competitive self-interested agents: the ruling class attempts to exploit the producing classes by imposing an unequal labour exchange that allows them to appropriate surplus labour; and the oppressed classes submit or resist this exploitation depending on the strength of their social resources to do so.

The Marxian emphasis on economic rationality assumes that group behaviour can be understood on the rational self-interested possessive individualist model of human nature. What this ignores are other aspects of human nature which cannot be understood in this way: unconscious libidinal motivations and symbolic definitions of gender, racial, sexual and family identity that motivate individuals.

These aspects of the self are here termed 'incorporative' aspects (see chapter six). While Marx is correct to suppose that self-interest as defined by material and economic structures is one important perpetuant of social domination systems, ultimately his theory of human agency is too rationalistic.

Part of the appeal of both the Marxist and feminist radical re-reading of Freudian thought is the hope of explaining the irrationality of the oppressed groups' submission to social domination by a more complicated theory of human agency and the self. Purely rational self-interested factors alone do not plausibly explain why the German working class accepted Hitler and national socialism (Reich, 1970), nor why independently wealthy women allow themselves to be battered by their husbands.

An adequate feminist theory of male domination must be at once historically specifiable and have a plausible theory of human agency that includes a psychology of human domination. In order to pave the way for such a theory we must consider Freud's theory of the self and feminist and other radical attempts to reconstruct this theory.

2

Freudian thought and feminist appropriations

In the previous chapter I have argued that radical feminist, Marxian and some socialist-feminist perspectives, though they give us important insights about the reproduction and persistence of male dominance, are inadequate with respect to their theories of human agency. Though they capture well the rational aspects of humans in systems of exploitation and domination, they fail to explain unconscious, irrational and libidinal forces that keep both the oppressed and oppressors from re-negotiating gendered, racial and class interaction.

This is where Freud's theory of human nature and society has something to offer feminist theory. Freud offers us a non-unified theory of the self – a split self containing unconscious aspects formed by the social repression of infant sexuality – which can explain both the rational negotiations as well as the irrational submissions of humans operating in structures of social domination. His views of sexuality as a polymorphous drive for bodily pleasure with no innate objects allows us to go beyond the biological determinism of socio-biological theories of gender and sexuality to posit that the objects of sexual desire may be moulded so as to serve the interests of social domination.

Our theoretical task in assessing each of the feminist appropriations of Freud is to find a reconstruction which will explain the irrational persistence of systems of social dominance yet allow for the possibility of social contestation and change of these structures. Neo-Freudian feminists have some good insights on how male dominance is perpetuated but their analyses are too ahistorical. Nonetheless we can historicise aspects of their theories. In particular, we must develop further the insight that the power of the mother, downplayed by classical Freudianism, and the contemporary conflict between aspects of self created by women's work in the family and for wages, create the psychologi-

cal base for resistance to male dominance that has fuelled the
Women's Movement.

There are three important feminist readings of Freud: the
Lacanian reading (Gallop, 1982; Mitchell, 1974; Mitchell and
Rose (eds), 1982; Rubin, 1975); the object relations reading
(Chodorow, 1978b; Dinnerstein, 1976) and the deconstructive
approach (Irigaray 1974, 1977). Lacanian readings are important
because of the emphasis they give to symbolic (and unconscious)
aspects of sexual desire. Object relations readings, on the other
hand, have a different approach to understanding the structure of
the masculine and feminine self. Finally, Irigaray's deconstructive approach is valuable in the way that it forces us to question
the univocal reading of the unconscious that patriarchal authors
like Lacan and Freud give us.

All these feminist theorists have criticised the original bio-
logisms of Freud's theory (e.g. the explanation of 'penis envy' as
due to the girl's acknowledgement of her inferior biological
'equipment', or Freud's 'constancy principle' which privileges
orgasm – 'tension-reduction' – as the biological goal of human
sexuality).[1]

A further objection can be raised concerning the metaphysical
dualism of Freud's theory. Freud sees the human psyche as
involved in constant internal conflict. However, the conflict is
centred around impersonal forces, such as the libido *vs* self-
preservation, the pleasure principle *vs* the reality principle, life *vs*
death instincts. These forces are seen as eternal antagonists rather
than as the sort of forces that can influence, and interact so as to
alter, each other. In other words, Freud's dualism is not dialectical, and consequently is not historical.

Part of the problem is that Freud's theory of the self is not
really a social and relational one. That is, though he grasps the
fact that the human psyche is composed of a number of aspects,
he doesn't see gender identity, for example, as an ongoing process
of conflict and interaction between aspects of a non-unified self
which is constantly re-negotiated by interactions with other
people. Women's consciousness-raising and anti-racism consciousness-raising groups may alter individuals' unconscious,
as well as conscious, desires. An individual's 'id' aspects may
change with adult experience, though the manner in which they
change may be different, and still be in conflict with her conscious
goals, desires, plans and visions.

The lack of a dialectical view on how ongoing social structures can alter the dynamic between id, ego and superego keeps Freud's theory too deterministic and psychologistic to understand the real possibilities for social change that social movements can create. To paraphrase Marx: humans can change their own desires (by putting themselves in different social structures), even if not totally under conditions of their own choosing. As we shall see, none of the neo-Freudian feminist theorists entirely escape this criticism of Freud's theory of self.

A final objection. Though Freud must be credited for challenging the still popular view that motherhood is an asexual experience, his emphasis on a developmental approach to human sexuality suggests that mothers who enjoy bodily contact with their children are unconsciously seeking phallic pleasures with them as a substitute for those sexual interests relating to their own parents that were repressed when they went through their own Oedipal phase.

Such an interpretation bypasses the idea that there is a genuine interest in motherhood because of the sensual and social union it promises between mother and child (Begus, 1987; Weisskopf, 1980) particularly exemplified by the pleasures of breastfeeding. My view of sexuality takes mother love to be a form of sex/affective energy that is neither a substitute for heterosexual intercourse nor a mere acting out of a desire for male power (a 'penis substitute'!).

In ignoring this aspect of maternal sexuality, Freud underestimates a material reason for paternal jealousy of children, the mother's divided sex/affective attention to mate and children. As a result he overemphasises the child's unconscious role in the Oedipal phase, thus underestimating the combined role of paternal repression and seduction in the construction of children's gender and sexual identities.

What these points about maternal sexuality suggest is that Freudian theory, in constructing an explanation of the primacy of the phallus and of heterosexual genital sexuality, has overlooked the subversive power of the mother in the construction of gender and in the construction of compulsory heterosexuality. Though Mitchell and Chodorow's reconstructions of Freud are subject to the same problem, Irigaray points a way to re-appropriate maternal sexuality.

Lacanian feminism: Mitchell and Rubin

Juliet Mitchell (Mitchell, 1974) argues that there are two semi-autonomous domination systems in contemporary advanced industrial societies which perpetuate male dominance: capitalism, the mode of economic production, and patriarchy, the mode of ideological reproduction. For Mitchell, who adopts a Lacanian reading of Freud, patriarchy is lodged in the unconscious via the construction of desire and gender.

Capitalism and patriarchy operate by very different laws. Capitalism perpetuates the ideology of the natural, biological patriarchal nuclear family as the superior form of family and household organisation because women's second shift and unpaid domestic work there is the most reliable, and cheapest, way to reproduce the labour force it needs to reproduce itself. Patriarchy, on the other hand, is perpetuated not primarily through ideological beliefs about the natural role of women in the family, but through the structure of unconscious desires that are tied to gender identity through early childhood experience.

It should be noted here that Mitchell is giving us a structural functionalist argument and, indeed, one which emphasises the economic interests of capitalists while ignoring the economic interests of patriarchs. In this way it contradicts the assumptions of other socialist-feminist theorists such as Hartmann, Delphy, Folbre and myself.

Mitchell presents a Lacanian reading of the development of the self, gender and unconscious desire. The unconscious reproduces patriarchy by constructing the desiring self in two exclusive genders. Children develop a gendered sense of self by learning to define themselves in relation to others in a system of language. Desiring to be the loved one of the mother, the boy learns that 'mother' means the loved one of the other (the father, or the one who is, symbolically, the phallus). Thus, the boy learns that he, as a referent of the signifier, the phallus, can obtain subject status and thus symbolic power (being the phallus, the loved one of the m[other]). But he can do this only by identifying with this 'law of the father' which requires him to renounce the actual mother (the 'lost object a', in Lacanian terms, also the breast) and seeking to be a phallus to a mother-substitute when he is older.

Girls, on the other hand, learn that they can never be subjects in the sense desired (=being desired by the mother) since they are a symbolic lack in relation to what the mother desires (=the phallus). Penis-envy, on this reading, is not desire for the actual organ, the penis, but for the symbolic position it gives one in relation to the mother's desire. The 'normal' resolution of the Oedipus complex for girls, which Freud took to involve translating penis-envy into a desire for a baby, is read by Lacan as a process of identifying with the mother in order to be possessed by, and thus possess, a subject with a phallus (thus, symbolically 'having' a phallus).

Mitchell's Lacanian reading of Freud can explain how it is that women stay in oppressive relations with men even when economic opportunities exist to allow them to become independent of them, and why men continue to oppress women even when they don't need to exploit them in order to get personal services or to avoid unpleasant tasks (e.g. as in an upper-middle class or ruling-class home there are servants to attend to housework). For, if one's unconscious sense of self is bound up with a desire for the other, and this desire involves desiring to be desired by the opposite gendered other, then one is condemned to play the masquerade of whatever society defines as masculine or feminine in order to feel 'truly' oneself and to promote one's unconscious (and deepest) desires.

Mitchell argues that there is presently a contradiction between capitalism and what she calls 'the ideological mode of reproduction' of capitalism (*viz.* patriarchy perpetuated through the unconscious) because capitalism doesn't require kinship exchange of women in patriarchal marriage to organise the economy as did pre-capitalist economies, but the patriarchal unconscious still assumes that men are the desiring subjects who exchange women.

But Mitchell's contradiction is not convincing. For, as long as men have social power over women in any sphere, the gender training of children in the nuclear family will create an asymmetrical patriarchal unconscious, creating men who want to dominate women and women who want to be dominated by men. Thus it is not clear how the cultural revolution she calls for (Mitchell, 1974: 414) is possible. As she and Lacan have conceived of the autonomy of the unconscious, what social change could decentre the unconscious idea of women as the lack who needs the phallus? How, that is, can we even explain the existence of sexual oppositional subcultures (e.g. lesbian-feminism, and non-roled homo-,

bi- and heterosexual mating) which go against such deep structures of the unconscious and the basic sense of self defined in
relation to desire?

Gayle Rubin's 1975 paper 'The Traffic in Women' was a
milestone attempt to combine a universalist Lacanian reading of
gender and unconscious desire with an historical anthropological
approach which would allow for culturally specific differences in
the construction of sexuality, gender, parenting and social
bonding. Rubin maintains that there are three universal features
of systems of male dominance: the incest taboo, the asymmetrical
exchange of women by male kin and compulsory heterosexuality.
Each of these features has a common structure uniting otherwise
very different 'sex/gender systems' (social constructions of
gender, sexuality and kinship). Each of these general structures
creates a situation where women's socially constructed sexual
desires are devalued, where they have fewer rights in relation to
male kin than these have to them, and in which their ability to
bond with other women is limited by male-dominated heterosexual marriages and other features of compulsory heterosexuality.

Rubin's innovative analytic concept, 'sex/gender system', has
been immensely helpful to feminists interested in approaching the
social construction of sexuality, gender and social bonding from a
historical perspective. But Rubin's combination of Lacanian and
Marxian thought does not provide the theoretical underpinning
for a consistent historical perspective.

The problem with both Mitchell and Rubin lies with the way
their synthesis of Marx and Freud reverts to a reductionist
Marxism when the question of social change is raised. Gender,
compulsory heterosexuality and the Oedipus complex all become
'mere' ideological structures that can be consciously eliminated as
soon as their functional connection to the economy is eliminated
with the development of advanced capitalism.

There are several ways in which historical studies throw doubt
on Rubin and Mitchell's approach. The way the Lacanian perspective links heterosexual desire with gender identity assumes a
logical connection between gender identity and heterosexual
identity. But historical studies suggest that the modern concept of
gay and lesbian identity, and the related concept of heterosexual
identity, is not a cultural universal but one that grew out of the
categories of perversion and inversion developed by late nine-

teenth-century sexologists. But if gender identity – one's sense of masculinity and femininity – does not cross-culturally involve an exclusive desire for the opposite sex, then the idea that 'the law of the father' constructs and connects heterosexual desire and gender identity cannot be seen to be a universal mechanism of male dominance. Indeed, Rubin now acknowledges this flaw in her earlier work (Rubin, 1984).

Neither Rubin nor Mitchell can provide us with a convincing vision of a non-patriarchal society nor a theory of social change which will enable us to understand why the Women's Movement has arisen to contest patriarchy or how a feminist alternative could be brought about.

Chodorow's object relations approach

Nancy Chodorow (1978b) and Dorothy Dinnerstein (1976) give us related theories of how asymmetrical mothering in infant care creates different gender personalities whose complementary structures act as an important psychological mechanism to perpetuate male dominance cross-culturally. According to Chodorow, the universal feature of human societies that women and not men are involved in parenting work with infants and young children creates different personalities in males and females. With role models who are present, girls develop a personal identification with their female caretakers and 'ego permeable' personalities which involve a sense of identification with significant others. Boys on the contrary develop 'rigid ego' or oppositional personalities in which they define themselves as different from their significant others. Lacking a specific personal content to read into masculinity since fathers are absent, boys define 'male' as 'not female', and capture their ambivalent feelings for female caretakers by downgrading the feminine.

Chodorow zeros in on the way that asymmetrical mothering creates gender personalities generalisable across cultures. While she doesn't actually say that the consequent different psychological attitudes toward mothering are the key cross-cultural mechanism to perpetuate male dominance, her emphasis implies this. But it is doubtful that the gender differences Chodorow isolates do exist cross-culturally. Oppositional personalities seem to be much more a feature of advanced capitalist societies than

characteristic of men in all cultures, particularly in communal
societies. It is true that evidence is difficult to come by since we
are speaking of unconscious structures of human personality. But
even if we suppose gender-differentiated personalities do exist,
our explanation of male dominance must avoid the single cause
type of explanation Chodorow's account in places suggests.
Rather we should see the different gender personalities and needs
created by asymmetrical mothering as only relevant to the question of female power and male dominance when they are a part of
a whole cluster of other variables, importantly including the way
the institution of motherhood connects to women's position in the
economy.

A problem with Chodorow's 'explanation' of male domination
stems from ambiguity as to the level of generality intended by the
theory. Chodorow proposes to give us an explanation of why
women (and not men) mother. She does this in turn to shed light
on differences in gender personalities, so as to uncover the
psychological mechanisms which perpetuate male dominance.

But why should we suppose that the psychological mechanism
Chodorow isolates, viz. women's need to mother in heterosexual
marriage in order to recreate a triangular mother/child/mate
bond, is essential as an explanation of why women do more
mothering than men in all societies? After all, in many societies
where material scarcity is an issue there are many other explanations of why parenting is valued and why women do the bulk of
parenting.[2]

It is a methodological mistake for Chodorow to think that she
can stretch the metaphorical images of 'a self with permeable ego
boundaries' (the feminine gendered self) vs an 'oppositional sense
of self' (the masculine gendered self) past their primary field of
application – our society. These concepts presuppose our public/
private/split, with the particular types of competitive practices
(market relations) vs incorporative practices (the entwined individual interests and identities of those involved in family/
household systems) characteristic of our society, and more
specifically the male breadwinner/female housewife nuclear
family.[3]

Another problem with Chodorow's theory is how to understand
the interaction of capitalism and the sex-gender system based on
asymmetrical motherhood in perpetuating male dominance. Like
Juliet Mitchell, Chodorow is a Marxist- or socialist-feminist who

wants to join the insights of Marxism and a reconstructed Freudianism. Thus, she has a type of dual systems theory. Though she claims to assign independent weight in perpetuating male dominance both to systems of economic domination, like capitalism, and the patriarchal sex-gender system, in fact the capitalist system ends up being both the moving cause for change and the underlying reason why the patriarchal sex-gender system takes the form that it does.

I disagree with Chodorow's theory because it is static. While I hold that the relation between sex/affective production and economic production is dialectical (hence at times supportive and at times in conflict) her characterisation of the relation between the two systems is structural functionalist: that is, they inevitably support each other.

To set this structural functionalism at work, it is instructive to examine the argument in her paper 'Mothering, Male Dominance and Capitalism' (Chodorow, 1979b). There she argues that the change from feudalism to capitalism created a wage work/ domestic work split which required a change in the ideology of the patriarchal sex/gender system (femininity as passive, non-worldly, dependent, asexual; men as assertive, materialistic, independent, sexual), a change which automatically came about in response to this change in the economic system.

The gender difference in personality structures created by the public/private split she analyses as functioning to reproduce capitalist social relations. So men with oppositional personalities end up treating women with permeable dependent or incorporative personalities as scapegoats for their own alienation in wage labour. And women with mothering needs agree to accept the inferior bargain of unpaid domestic work in marriage, which allows them to be used as an underpaid underemployed reserve army of labour to be drawn in and out of the labour force as capitalist economic cycles make profitable for the capitalist.

Chodorow doesn't conceptualise an independent dynamic to modes of patriarchal sex/affective production. Rather, she assumes that there is an automatic adjustment of all the social relations in capitalism so as to stabilise its reproduction and serve the interests of the capitalist class. But, as we have seen, this begs the question against those like Hartmann who argue that men as a sex/class have interests which at a certain historical point in capitalist development conflicted with one tendency of that development and required a particular historical alliance (the family wage). Furthermore, in my view it is the breakdown of this alliance which necessitates the contemporary re-organisation of patriarchy that we are presently undergoing – that transition to a new male dominant mode of sex/affective production called public patriarchy.

Unlike Chodorow we must conceptualise many sites of the reproduction of patriarchy: not merely family infant care, but also the sexual division of labour of other institutions such as schools and the economy. Doing so gives us a more historical way of periodising systems of male dominance. Rather than merely concentrating on what changes in parenting practices would strengthen women *vis-à-vis* men as her work suggests, we need to speculate about what changes in the relation between parenting practices (the household division of parenting labour) and wider economic and social practices would accomplish this feat.[4]

Chodorow's theory of gender identity underemphasises the importance of same sex bonding, both with other adults besides the mother and with peers. For a girl this means that if there are other strong role models besides the mother who act as caretakers (and/or strong peer networks of friends who take her away from mother), this girl has a better chance of establishing an alternative feminine identification that allows her to separate from mother without having to rely on a heterosexual erotic connection with the father to achieve this. And for a boy, it means that the connection to father and to other men and boys creates a sex/affective bond just as important as his bond to mother for his sense of self. Though Chodorow points to the importance of cultural context in assessing the relative power or weakness gender-differentiated personalities give their owners (Chodorow, 1974), she does not emphasise the point that it is because of the strong same sex bonding of women with women who have relative social independence from men that patriarchy is weaker in such societies.

The need to disparage women to achieve a strong sense of masculine identity should not be conceived as a universal masculine psychological need created by asymmetrical parenting. Rather, such a need is a secondary one which will be stronger or weaker depending on the requirements for acceptance by the father, father/substitute(s) and/or peer male bonding networks. Thus, the psychological underpinning of male dominance is men's initial need to bond with other men in situations where this requires disparaging women, rather than an initial need to disparage women which leads men to bond with men!

What follows from the emphasis on same sex bonding in the childhood development of gender is that the effect of parenting practices on gender can only be seen in the wider social context (extended family or kin networks, isolated family or close knit community, strong or weak peer friendships for the children) in which they are embedded.

When we consider parenting in the United States today, we find that it is very different than the experience of parenting in the 1950s and earlier when women characteristically did not work in wage labour after they were mothers. Now that nearly half of all women with children under eighteen do work in wage labour, we should expect that the gender personality structure of women would be different from that of our mothers, since most of us are engaged in a gender process with conflicting mores, that is, one that demands both that we incorporate our interests with family at the same time as we must oppose our interests to others in wage labour. Indeed, such gender identity conflicts are part of the background conditions for the rise of the Women's Movement, an historical development which cannot be explained on Chodorow's thesis without modification.

Irigaray and a deconstructive approach

Luce Irigaray is a former student of Lacan's who can be seen to pursue Karen Horney's critique of Freud (Horney, 1967), though from a different methodological perspective. As practising psychoanalysts both want to preserve some of Freud's ideas, for example the role of the unconscious and sexuality in psychic disorders and the importance of infantile experience. But both of them argue that Freud underestimates the power of the mother in the construction of the feminine and masculine unconscious. Freud and his follower Lacan overemphasise the importance of penis envy for the female psyche and neglect the equally important womb envy characteristic of the male psyche. For Horney, the power to reproduce children is just as important a desire in young children as is the power to relate sexually to the mother.

Though Irigaray agrees with Horney that identification, and

envy, of the power of the mother creates a differently structured
masculine and feminine unconscious, she disagrees with Horney
in the latter's view, typical of ego psychology, that the ego is an
autonomous force with a built-in heterosexual desire that tries to
negotiate an identity for itself by rational responses to its fears.
Rather, Irigaray agrees with the split theory of self which sees the
ego as an historical product of a conflict between libidinal desires
and the social and material reality of the child. Thus, theorists
must use deconstructionist techniques on Freud's theory of
gender development to point out his masculinist assumptions.

Irigaray argues that Freud was caught up in his own 'specular
logic', i.e. self-reflections about the development of masculine
gender identity, which caused him to distort female gender development (Irigaray, 1974). This led him into the errors of the 'logic
of the same': the assumption that the little girl is the same as the
little boy before the Oedipal stage (Freud actually calls her a 'little
man'!). He can then argue that she perceives her clitoris as the
'same' as a penis, only inferior, thus projecting the male fear of
castration onto the little girl. Even Lacanian readings of Freud
which interpret 'penis envy' symbolically rather than literally, as
a sign of male power over the mother and daughter and hence the
imposition of compulsory heterosexuality onto the girl by the
father, still treat female sexuality and gender construction as a
lack, as merely a negative of the male, because the female does not
have what the mother desires (the phallus, male power).

Irigaray's method is to show that this whole framework of
symbolism of desire and sexuality as focused on the phallus or the
lack of it is a phallocratic symbolism that doesn't capture the
reality of woman's diverse sexual pleasures, not all of which are
genital, unitary or focused on orgasm (Irigaray, 1977). Irigaray
agrees that this phallocratic structure of desire has indeed been
incorporated into the unconscious of both males and females
because of patriarchal structures in the family as well as the power
of what Foucault calls the 'normalising discourses' of psychoanalysis (Foucault, 1978). But she also suggests that the feminine
unconscious contains other possibilities of understanding its
sexuality, hidden from male discourse, that could allow for a
'feminine writing' to decentre the power of the patriarchal
unconscious and normalising discourse.

Some critics have accused Irigaray of succumbing to an essentialist theory of female self and sexuality based on the biological

differences between the male and female bodies. Since women have two vaginal lips as well as breasts, their consequent erotic interests don't centre around one genital like the penis. On this basis, Irigaray argues that our biologically based female sexuality and attendant feminine gender identity is diverse, non-centred and capable of multiple ways of being satisfied. In so opposing, and designating as superior, female over male sexuality, Irigaray seems to idealise the implications of femininity in an ahistorical, non-contextual way.

A second objectionable consequence of Irigaray's analysis is her advocacy of women's language, or what she calls 'womanspeak', a spontaneous language which emerges when women are together but disappears when men are present. This is a fluid, tactile style, as opposed to men's specular logic. As a result it seems contradictory to men, because the meanings are fluid and constantly changing:

> It is therefore useless to trap women into giving an exact definition of what they mean, to make them repeat (themselves) so that the meaning will be clear. They are already elsewhere than in the discursive machinery where you claim to take them by surprise. They have turned back within themselves, which does not mean the same thing as 'within yourself'. They do not experience the same interiority that you do and which perhaps you mistakenly presume they share. 'Within themselves' means *in the privacy of this silent, multiple diffuse tact*. If you ask them insistently what they are thinking about, they can only reply: nothing. Everything. (Irigaray, 1977: 28–9)

Having made such a strong case that patriarchal language is defined by the dualistic phallocentric 'logic of the same', Irigaray here seems to lapse into mysticism. That is, we cannot say anything to men because to do otherwise is a mere reversal of the masculine/feminine dyad supposed by phallocratism. So, to claim that the feminine is superior to the masculine, on the one hand, or to renounce the feminine and become 'honorary' or token men, on the other, ultimately traps feminists because neither path challenges the either/or logic posed by the phallocratic system. But, as Cynthia Freeland points out in her critique of Lacan and Irigaray, (Freeland, 1986) mysticism is not a political but a quietistic stance which ultimately leaves feminists with no power.

To refuse to play the phallocratic language game by itself does not destroy the game!

A third objection to Irigaray's feminist appropriation of Lacan is the consistent ahistoricality of her critique of patriarchy. *Speculum of the Other Woman* (1985) critiques philosophers from Freud to Plato but concentrates on the ideological construction of patriarchy and ignores the historical and material structures of patriarchy which perpetuate male dominance: for example, women's unpaid labour in capitalist patriarchy.

Though it is easy to fault Irigaray's ahistoricality, it is a weakness that we have seen is shared by the other neo-Freudian feminists. However, there is a way to re-read Irigaray's writings which avoids essentialism and quietist mysticism. Irigaray is, after all, a practising psychoanalyst who believes that there is a socially constructed patriarchal unconscious whose desires will act as an irrational influence on women's behaviour as well as men's. Thus feminists need a strategy that will displace the power of the symbols of the patriarchal unconscious. Pointing out that such symbols are not in women's rational interests is not an effective strategy, since a simple rational argument will not work to undo a sense of self built into unconscious desires. But, though a simple reversal of the masculine/feminine dyad is not sufficient to displace the either/or patriarchal logic, a reversal may be at least a necessary psychological strategy to allow the emergence of other forces that exist simultaneously in women's unconsciousness.

The psychological base for this alternative sense of self is connected to love for, and the power of, the mother and other mother figures in one's unconscious life. Irigaray's validation of feminine morphology can be read metaphorically rather than literally, as the validation of an alternate set of values based on maternal as opposed to paternal sensuality. As such, it is not a rational argument, or a defence of women's biological superiority to men, but a therapeutic displacement of one socially constructed structure for another which empowers women.

Irigaray's abstract and philosophical deconstructive approach needs to be supplemented by an historical and empirical study of women's subcultures of mothering and nurturing, such as women's friendships and lay medical practices, women's languages like gossip and women's 'shop talk' which share skills needed in women's work, and women's sexualities: Platonic, lesbian, or promiscuous. (cf. Ehrenreich and English, 1973a; Raymond, 1986).

Toward a dialectical reading of motherhood and feminine sexuality

In this chapter I have critiqued Freud's patriarchal assumptions as well as some of his biologistic views about sexuality. Though the neo-Freudian feminists discussed here share with Freud the weakness that their theories are presented in too ahistorical a fashion, they contain strengths that can be appropriated by a more encompassing theory of historical systems of sex/affective production. In this section I want to touch on two insights which need to be re-interpreted historically: the hidden strengths and values of motherhood, and the radical potential of lesbian sexuality to challenge patriarchal sexual practices.

Chodorow, Dinnerstein and Irigaray all have a radical feminist aspect to their thought in so far as they appeal to a universal women's subculture, based in mothering and underlying patriarchal arrangements, which may be a source of resistance to patriarchal values. Carol Gilligan (1982) and Sara Ruddick (1980) are other feminist thinkers who have assumed the importance of feminine mothering subcultures as a source for non-masculine values, and hence, as a potential challenge to male domination.

Gilligan's view that there is a feminine moral voice different from the masculine moral voice assumed by cognitive developmental theorists assumes a Chodorowian view of how male and female gender personalities are formed. Ruddick, coming from a non-Freudian perspective, has similarly argued that women's nurturing skills and characteristic incorporative sense of self come from the special nature of mothering work which requires that its participants adopt the values of the preservation, growth and social acceptability of particular others: the child(ren). Such an orientation is opposed to the abstract group-oriented submission to authority needed for the male gendered pursuit of militarism and war, and thus accounts for the women's peace movement (Ruddick, 1984).

Such generalisations can be said to be initially suspect as a plausible description of all women, or even of all mothers, cross-culturally, for the same reasons as we faulted the universalist presuppositions of the neo-Freudian feminists studied in this chapter. The economic and social context in which women mother and/or are mothered, including race and class interests, intervenes to determine whether the values of mothering support or are in conflict with other social values (Hooks, 1984).

A dialectical conception of the connection between motherhood and gender would posit that in our contemporary historical period women's unconscious selves are not unified around a self defined with permeable supportive ego boundaries to others. Rather, our unconscious is now split still further by the development of what we can call an oppositional (or self-interested) aspect as well as an incorporative (other-identified) sense of feminine gender.

Most girls and women these days must define themselves in relation to the competitive structures of school and wage labour. Most women, including mothers, work in wage labour in advanced capitalist societies and most secondary schools train girls to develop a competitive sense of self to be future wage labourers. Thus women's gender identity is no longer bound up simply with incorporating with others in nurturant relationships. Our market relations force upon us as well as men an oppositional aspect of self: that defined by competitive, individualistic wage work.

In our contemporary historical context, the contradictory values most women develop from the conflicting social practices of mothering (or mother-training) and the exploitation involved in women's wage-labour work in capitalism are at once a source of alienation, and an alternative way of experiencing the world that can provide a source of residence and a vision of an alternate way of being.

Since most contemporary mothering involves not only self-sacrifice but also a kind of reciprocal pleasure in giving and receiving expressions of love, it is not surprising that co-parenting is an attractive idea for many men as well as women. Furthermore, as we shall discuss later, the curious amalgam of emotional involvement and self-sacrifice (the self defined through its love life) along with individual pleasure seeking which is legitimated in contemporary standards for feminine sexuality holds the key to a more reciprocal re-organisation of sexual practices for men and women, whether in heterosexual or homosexual relationships.

Radical feminist critics of the neo-Freudian feminists have correctly challenged the latters' facile advocacy of heterosexual co-parenting as the way to illuminate gender asymmetry in gender identity and the structures of unconscious desire. Advocating heterosexual co-parenting focuses on an incorporative relation of women with men as the solution for male domination, rather than emphasising the importance of women bonding with other women (Raymond, 1986; Rich, 1980). This solution doesn't allow for lesbian and gay parenting, or deal with the problems of single parents and reconstituted families. In addition socialist-feminist critics (Young, 1984) have pointed out that without changes in the structure of wage labour which create flexi-time jobs for parents and provide full-time child care most couples cannot co-parent for economic reasons.

Though these are weighty criticisms, we can reinterpret Chodorow and Dinnerstein's co-parenting advocacy if we see it, first, as only one part of a utopian vision which requires economic and social reorganisation as well; and second, correct the heterosexist and couple-centred aspects of the vision so as to substitute for the idea of co-parenting a range of feminist co-operative parenting practices, including same sex and non-biological social (chosen) and 'step' parents, as well as single parents with supportive 'quasi-kin' networks. These alternatives will be discussed in more detail in chapter eight.

With respect to the radical potential of lesbian sexuality, Irigaray's work has more to offer than either the object relations approach of Chodorow and Dinnerstein or the Lacanian approach of Mitchell and Rubin. In part this is due to Irigaray's determined emphasis on a non-unified aspectival theory of self. Rather than assume that the feminine personality is created in a way so as to functionally support patriarchy, Irigaray denies that there is just one feminine gendered self:

> Re-discovering herself, for a woman, thus could only signify the possibility of sacrificing no one of her pleasures to another, of identifying herself with none of them in particular, *of never being simply one*. A sort of expanding universe to which no limits could be fixed and which would not be incoherence nonetheless – nor that polymorphous perversion of the child in which the erogenous zones would lie waiting to be regrouped under the primacy of the phallus. (Irigaray, 1974: 31)

Just as there is no one feminine unconscious structured around patriarchally constructed desires, so there is no one feminine self.

Rather there are many aspects of self which patriarchal ideology obscures by assuming that the desire to be a mother, hence the lover of (substitute) father, are what define the feminine self.

Since heterosexual relations are governed by the structure of the patriarchal unconscious in both men and women, Irigaray suggests lesbian-feminist sexual politics as a necessary stage of women's liberation. This empowers women to emphasise other aspects of the feminine unconscious – the power of the mother which is not coded with patriarchal symbols. This allows women to resist the oppressive unity of self imposed by patriarchal logic – that logic which defines women as lack of the phallus. In lesbian relations, Irigaray suggests, women are able to express multiple aspects of self: 'Between our lips, yours and mine, several voices, several ways of speaking resound endlessly, back and forth. One is never separable from the other. You/I: we are always several at once' (Irigaray, 1977: 209).

But though Irigaray suggests a tactical separatism of the Women's Movement she is wary of advocating a lesbian vanguard politics as the solution to the patriarchal structures of the unconscious.[5] For, as she says, 'might not the renunciation of heterosexual pleasure ... involve a new prison, a new cloister, built of their own accord?' (Irigaray, 1977: 33).

To avoid this, women should undertake tactical strikes, discover their own speech and love for other women in a context in which men cannot pit them against each other as rival commodities. The goal is not simply the reversal of the old order, with women superior and men inferior, but, somehow, the smashing altogether of the categories masculine/feminine and presumably the heterosexual/homosexual dyad as well.

How is this smashing of categories to take place? Irigaray does not elaborate. And indeed there is no *a priori* way, independent of an historical analysis of possible countercultural structures and groupings, to answer this question. What we must take from Irigaray and the other neo-Freudian feminists is the importance of analysing gender and sexual symbolic codes as they develop historically, for roles and values encoded in these codes connect to patriarchal structures of the unconscious as well as to bases for feminist resistance lodged there. Only a determined attention to our unconscious oppositional and incorporative aspects of self as well as our rational, instrumental, conscious aspects will give feminists an understanding of what alternate structures are possible to meet our sexual and emotional needs yet resist male dominance.

3

Sexuality and social domination

Before we can develop a historical perspective on the way in which social domination is constructed into human sexuality, we need to ask, what exactly is the nature of human sexuality? The approaches which are prevalent fall into three paradigms. The instinct paradigm assumes that sex is an inborn instinct with pre-given objects and aims. The Drive paradigm maintains that it is a bodily drive (whose objects are learned) for pleasure and/or release from physical tension. The Energy paradigm rejects both inborn objects and drives and assumes that what we call 'sex' is a bodily energy (or energies) which is gathered up and organised into social outlets by contextual social meanings.

My theory of sexuality can be called a Social Energy theory and, as such, uses the energy paradigm of sex. In order to show why I prefer this approach, in this chapter I shall consider each of these three paradigms and their problems in more detail.

The sexuality as instinct paradigm: biological essentialism

Many conservative thinkers hold that sex is an innate animal instinct to reproduce. Such a view allows them to label homosexual sex, exhibitionism and other sexual acts with non-reproductive aims as deviant.[1] Though no radicals can be said to hold such an instinct theory, it is ironic that there is a tendency of radical feminist essentialist thought which can be charged with holding another form of the sex-as-instinct theory, with an important twist: for them (e.g. such thinkers as Mary Daly and Kathleen Barry) innate female sexuality differs in its aims and objects from innate male sexuality, since the former is more concerned with emotional intimacy than mere bodily pleasure, while the latter is concerned with aggressive control of the other (the woman) and a compulsive prioritising of sexual pleasure to the exclusion of emotional intimacy.

With respect to the instinct paradigm, the only difference between such radical feminists and male chauvinist socio-biologists is the precise differences they feel to inhere in male *vs* female sexuality and the positive *vs* negative valuation they place on female *vs* male sexuality. It is instructive, for example, that Kathleen Barry criticises Havelock Ellis for assuming that the male sex drive is inherently sadistic and the female drive masochistic. Nonetheless she goes on to assume innate differences between male and female sexuality which implie that feminists must reject the alienating choices of male-defined sexuality in favour of our own authentic, womanly sexuality. As Barry says,

> In going into new social values we are really going back to the values women have always attached to sexuality, values that have been robbed from us, distorted and destroyed as we have been colonized through both sexual violence and so-called sexual liberation. They are the values and needs that connect sex with warmth, affection, love, caring. (Barry, 1979: 227)

In a similar vein, Mary Daly argues that 'biophilic', or life-giving energy is specific to women, has been repressed under patriarchy by the 'necrophilic', death-loving energy specific to men, and must be reclaimed by gynergy, or sisterhood (Daly, 1978).

Not only radical feminists assume biological essentialist views. The libertarian feminist thinker Janet Schrim defends consensual lesbian sado-masochism (S/M) on the grounds that there is an inherent connection between sexuality, aggression and power hierarchies in the human species as well as in other animal species (Schrim, 1979).

Some defenders of radical feminist thought insist that they are not biological essentialist but hold a social constructionist theory of the gendered sexual values constructed in patriarchy. For example, both Catherine MacKinnon and Andrea Dworkin have argued that the gender sexual roles of man as sadist, master, initiator and woman as masochist, server and receiver are socially constructed. In Dworkin's early book, *Womanhating*, the idea of biological gender is questioned and humans are presented as pansexual and androgynous, a view that she has never renounced, even though her book *Pornography* gives a strong portrayal of male values as culturally sadist and female as masochist. Thus, we can only conclude that, for her, these masculine and feminine values are socially constructed.

Catherine MacKinnon presents an even more deterministic social constructionist view of gender identity's interconnection with sexual identity when she argues that women learn what being a woman means by having the experience of patriarchally constructed sex: 'what women learn in order to "have sex", in order to "become women" – woman as gender – comes through the experience of, and is a condition for, "having sex" – woman as sexual object for man, the use of women's sexuality by men' (MacKinnon, 1982: 531).

Though these social constructionist theories may not technically be biologically essentialist, they are still a form of social essentialism: that is, they assume a social divide between male and female sexual natures which is unconvincingly universal, static and ahistorical. Radical feminists who defend a view of the essential differences between authentic male and female sexuality must assume that all the cultural variations between different types of both male and female sexualities in different cultures are mere appearances, patriarchally imposed to deny women our 'real' priorities. Not only is there no empirical proof possible of this claim, but it seems patronising to insist that women who value promiscuity and physical pleasure in sex over emotional intimacy are 'male-identified', thus dupes of patriarchal socialisation.

Liberal feminists like Alice Rossi (1975) who emphasise the physiological similarities between the vaginal contractions of childbirth, lactation and orgiastic intercourse in order to argue that female sexuality has different instinctual priorities for emotional connection and nurturance than male sexuality have begged the empirical question: Why couldn't such priorities have been learned through socially imposed taboos on mother-child erotic interactions that lead women to channel sexual energy into emotional connections with children and lovers rather than the explicit bodily sexual pleasure?

Not only is the instinct theory unconvincing in its ahistoricity, it also supports the pessimistic conclusion that sex war between the genders is inevitable, since according to it male and female biological programmes differ so fundamentally in terms of our emotional and sexual needs that, without an accepted domination (male over female, or even female over male) there will always be a battle as to what to prioritise. Though the instinct paradigm cannot be decisively disproven – indeed, as Thomas Kuhn has argued, no scientific paradigm can ever be disproved, since anomalies can always be explained away by appropriate tinkering (cf. Kuhn, 1970) – it thus should be rejected on the political grounds that social change activists require a paradigm of sexuality and social domination which allows us to conceive how social change is possible.

The drive paradigm of sexuality

Freudo/Marxism

We have considered Freud's theory of sexuality and male domination in the previous chapter and feminist attempts to challenge his pessimistic conclusions. But there are two strands of Freud's thinking about sexuality that have been used to challenge his own pessimism. One of these, the Lacanian approach as appropriated by Irigaray, is more appropriately considered in the next section as a 'social naming' and 'bodily energy' theory of sexuality. In this section, we shall consider the Freudo/Marxist reconstructions of the Freudian drive paradigm of sexuality by Wilhelm Reich and Herbert Marcuse.

These sexual radicals hold that sexual pleasure is the ultimate measure of human happiness and freedom. They see sexual repression as functioning to maintain class societies, thus serving the rational interests of the ruling classes. In their insistence that the left must deal with the implications of the social dominance infused in our sexuality, the Marx/Freud sexual radicals were, thus, precursors of the contemporary Women's Movement in the view that the personal is the political. However, their own theories of sexual liberation are lacking by contemporary feminist standards.

As we have discussed in previous chapters, Freud put forth the view that sexuality is a bodily drive for pleasure which develops its specific aims and social objects from infantile experience. His hydraulic theory, that sexual libido is like a force pressing for release, suggested the constancy principle of psychic health: that release of bodily tension in sexual orgasm is a necessary condition of psychic health. This led Reich to the questionable conclusion that orgiastic potency was not only necessary for psychic health (Reich, 1973) but could be, if developed in individuals by a radical sex therapy movement, a revolutionary force for undermining the authoritarian personality created by sexual repression which is necessary for perpetuating capitalism (Reich, 1972). Reich's universal linkage of psychic health with regular orgasm is itself an ahistorical claim about the necessary connection between self-respect and sexual satisfaction. Given the malleability of personal identity by historically different social constructions of sexuality and gender this conclusion is implausible, though it may well be a feature of bourgeois societies that create an obsessive connection between sex and personal identity. As we shall see, Foucault argues just this (Foucault, 1978): that the modern 'power/knowledge' generated by Freudianism and the sexologists has been taken over by the bourgeois class as a replacement and amplification of the Judao-Christian hermeneutics of self suspicion as a way to understand, construct and control self and sexuality, and, hence, ultimately populations and races.

Reich challenges Freud's view that sexual repression is necessary for civilisation (Freud, 1961) by challenging Freud's theory of an innate aggressive drive (the death instinct) which must be countered by libidinal energy garnered from a repressed eros. For Reich, aggression and other anti-social neuroses are not original human drives, but occur as the result of the repeated frustration and damming up of libido by sexual repression (Reich, 1973). Reich goes so far as to argue that ego itself, in the sense of personality style or character, is a kind of neurosis, since it offers a defence and a resistance to the free-flowing of libidinal energy (Reich, 1949). Reich's healthy individual is one who has 'orgiastic potency', i.e. can discharge all sexual tension in the involuntary, non-fantasied release of heterosexual intercourse. Such a person has what Reich called a 'genital character', i.e. a kind of anti-character or ego-style which is transparent to the desires of the id.

Reich's ideal person, that with a genital character, should be questionable to feminists for historical and political reasons. However we divide up the aspects of personality, the stereotypically submissive woman in advanced capitalist society is one who lacks as developed an 'ego', that is, the ability to discipline herself in her own self-interest and the ability to distinguish fantasy from reality, as the stereotypically dominant man. But, surely, if having a more developed ego is one of the necessary tools for success in gender conflicts in the competitive individualist society we live in, feminists cannot afford to accept a human ideal which romanticises the loss of the very facility needed to struggle for and negotiate the conditions for gender equality.

Rather, for contemporary feminists, Marcuse's idea of the ego seems more realistic. This is, that a certain amount of delayed gratification is necessary to provide the conditions for an ego which can better control and intervene in reality. This is what Marcuse means by 'necessary repression' and is analogous to the Marxian one of necessary labour: it is an analytic concept which will have different values in different historical situations, depending on the social and individual resources available (Marcuse, 1955). Thus for Marcuse, in all conceivable human societies, there will be a minimum amount of primary libidinal repression necessary for the development of an ego or self-consciousness focused enough to challenge social domination.

Though Reich's ideal of the genital character must be rejected, his analysis of the relation between work, play and sex is ultimately more appealing than Marcuse's. While Marcuse accepts Freud's idea of the firm division between the realm of play (the 'pleasure' principle) and work (the 'reality' principle), Reich questions Freud's pessimism about the inevitable conflict between the demands of the sexual libido and those of disciplined work, on the one hand, and the need to contain aggression, on the other. His own view is that it is only in class societies that sexual repression is required in order to get work done. However, humans are capable of a self-regulating sexual economy in which social labour is compatible with libidinal fulfilment. Like the early Marx, Reich felt that work itself can be desired for its own sake when it is eroticised under the appropriate social organisation of work (socialism). Unfortunately Reich's hypothesis that work can be libidinised without sexual repression is not provable until and unless the ideal socialist society is created.

Reich retains Freud's idea of the necessary biological stages of libidinal development, which leads him to reject pre-Oedipal sexuality (including homosexual interests) as immature. As a result his vision is heterosexist. In this, as in other aspects of Reich's work, there is an ahistorical image of the healthy, genital-oriented heterosexual person which ignores the possibility that sexual and psychic health may rely more on the sexual culture of one's peers than on any necessary organic development. No doubt

Reich's homosexual patients who were trapped in patriarchal
family structures with no alternative household or lifestyle communities available did exhibit neurotic symptoms. But the breakdown of the hegemony of such a family in contemporary society
creates the possibility of psychically healthy (and mature) homosexual relationships.

Reich's theory of the patriarchal nuclear family is that it supports social domination by creating repressive superegos that
encourage women to submit to masochistic relations to male
lovers, and both genders to submit to the authority of father
figures (such as presidents or führers) (Reich, 1974). This analysis
is plausible when Reich locates it historically in the petty bourgeois family in which wives, sons and daughters work in family
businesses subordinate to fathers. He is thus able to locate
fascism's emotional base in the peasant and petty-bourgeois classes
in Germany as opposed to the proletariat proper, whose family
relations are less repressed given the lack of paternal control due
to the anonymity of wage labour (Reich, 1970). Reich also must
be credited with being the first Marxist thinker to take women's
sexual liberation seriously as a necessary tool for undermining
capitalism.

Unfortunately, the plausibility of Reich's analysis of patriarchy
weakens as he waffles between an analysis of an historically
located class-specific patriarchal family and a more general analysis that categorises all families of all classes and ethnic groups in
all class-divided societies as patriarchal in order to contrast class-
divided patriarchal family formations with the pre-class matriarchal age – romantically captured for him by Malinowski's study
of the Trobriander Pacific island society (Reich, 1972). Reich like
Freud is ultimately too concerned with presenting a near universal theory of patriarchy and sexual repression to give us a clear
historically specific thesis.

Though Reich and Marcuse both reject Freud's idea that the
sexual repression typical of the bourgeois family in capitalist
societies is necessary for civilisation, their views of sexual liberation differ. For Reich, a left movement must struggle for socialism at the same time as it develops the countercultural conditions
necessary to undo the authoritarian personality structure created
by the patriarchal nuclear family structure. This will require
radical sex and therapy clinics, and sex education for teenagers
which supports birth control, premarital and other consensual sex

which undermines the sexually repressive patriarchal nuclear family.

Reich's emphasis on sex education and a counterculture which is 'sex-positive' rather than 'sex-negative' is important for the contemporary Women's Movement. However, as we shall see in greater detail in chapter seven, we need a more feminist and historically based idea of sexual liberation to resolve the disagreements between pluralist and radical feminists about just what practices are sex-positive!

Marcuse's *One Dimensional Man* (1964) implicitly rejects Reich's idea of 'sexual revolution' as it is expressed in the view that orgiastic potency creates a democratic personality structure that will challenge capitalism. Marcuse's view is that advanced capitalist society, with its emphasis on creating and meeting consumerist needs of its populace, has created sex itself as a commodity, thus allowing 'repressive de-sublimation'. Thus, not only women, but men as well become sex objects to be exchanged and used instrumentally. What sexual pleasure is derived from the new promiscuity is achieved in an alienated fashion, i.e. by diverting erotic energy that otherwise might be sublimated into critical thinking or aesthetic pursuits. This type of expanded sexuality thus becomes co-opted and does not lead to a true sexual revolution, which for Marcuse involves not merely orgiastic potency but the expanded possibility for sublimated eros as well as the diverse regressive but tabooed pleasures of polymorphous perverse infant sexuality such as oral, anal and S/M interests. Thus, Marcuse, in his later writing, sees the New Left countercultural movements of the 1960s and early 1970s, the hippie, women's and gay liberation movements, as cultural vanguards which demanded not merely a greater quantity of promiscuous sex, but a greater diversity of sexual possibilities. We can remember group sex, the women's movement demand that clitoral orgasms be treated as equally if not more important than vaginal orgasm, homosexual rights and the cultural challenge to masculinity of the hair and dress of male hippies as some evidence for his line of thought.

Marcuse's appropriation of Freud, though like Reich's in its emphasis on the role of sexual repression in maintaining social domination, differs in a number of ways. Though Marcuse is less sanguine than Reich about the possibility of eliminating the necessary social repression of the libido through socialism, he

does, like Reich, hold open the possibility of a utopian moment
that Freud denies. Marcuse does this by introducing the concept
of 'surplus repression' which he contrasts with 'necessary repression' (Marcuse, 1955). Modern industrial capitalism is governed
by the 'performance principle' which subordinates any concern
for the *sui generis* demands of the libido (eroticism) to the goal of
extracting as much surplus value (profits) from workers as possible to benefit the small capitalist class. A socialist reorganisation
of work could reduce repression to the minimum necessary to
guarantee, on the one hand, an autonomous ego-ideal (i.e. a
critical self structure) for individuals and, on the other, the labour
socially necessary for meeting human material needs.[2]

Though Marcuse's analysis rejects the cruder Reichean constancy principle of sexual and psychic health, he does not sufficiently defend his own view that psychic health involves a combination of the release of sufficient sexual tension and the
diversion of libidinal energy into appropriate types of activities
(including sublimation into critical thinking).

I have argued earlier that instinct theory must be rejected
because of its ahistorical and essentialist claims about male *vs*
female sexuality. But a similar charge of essentialism has been
raised against Marcuse as well, for his theory of repressive desu-
blimation implies a universal claim about human nature; that no
matter what social values a society constructs for its members, a
certain quantity of sexual libido must be sublimated into aesthetic
and critical thinking if basic human natural needs and potentials
are to be satisfied and we are not to be alienated. It is implausible
to suppose there is one universal standard which will tell us how
much desublimated sex of which sorts – genital, oral or anal, and
so forth – to balance with what quantity of sublimated aesthetic
and critical thinking for an unalienated human life. A more
plausible approach would assume that alienation is a relational
concept: people are only alienated if needs socially developed in
their societies are somehow frustrated by those same societies.

Thus socialist-feminist theory must historicise the concept of
alienation itself in a way that Marcuse doesn't successfully do. For
even though in *Eros and Civilization* he distinguishes between
necessary and surplus repression, his work on repressive de-
sublimation does not follow this up with a convincing historical
analysis of how this works.

The problem is that Freudo/Marxist syntheses have assumed a

dual system theory of social domination: that class oppression has its base in the economy while sexual repression and male domination has its base in the Oedipal triangle in the patriarchal nuclear family. But though this analysis is somewhat plausible when Reich uses it to analyse Nazi Germany, it is problematic in advanced capitalism where male dominance still persists yet families of the Oedipal type, namely male breadwinner/female housewife households are such a small percentage of the total. While the Critical Theorists' own analysis of the influence of the mass media in advanced capitalist societies seem to suggest a shift in the site of social domination (Adorno and Horkheimer, 1972; Marcuse, 1964) their analysis is not convincing. The suggestion that the passing of the patriarchal nuclear family creates a narcissistic personality (Lasch, 1977) still doesn't explain how the media come to develop such a repressive hold on the creation of needs and personal identities.

Kinsey, Masters and Johnson

In the mid-twentieth century the works of Kinsey, and Masters and Johnson have to some degree countered Freud's emphasis on individual sexual psychology with a sociological yet still physiological approach to sexuality. These theorists still assume that sexuality is a bodily drive which if expressed leads to bodily and psychic health. Unlike Freud, however, they assume that repressive sexual ideology should be countered by a statistical study which contrasts the kinds of sexual behaviours in which people engage in fact with the cultural sexual norms. Kinsey wanted to readjust sexual mores the better to coincide with people's actual 'natural' sexual practices. His studies which uncovered a continuum of homosexual and heterosexual practices among those whose sexual identities ran contrary to such practices led him to create the 1 to 6 continuum scale for measuring degree of homosexual, bisexual and heterosexual interests. This measure legitimated the possibility of homosexual sex.

Since Kinsey assumed the 'natural' aims of sex are orgasm and the mutual sexual gratification of sexual partners, he wanted to drop the sexual double standard that forbade women's premarital sex yet condoned this for men. In these ways Kinsey's work has been used in ways supportive of heterosexual and lesbian women's sexual liberation. Yet Kinsey subtly introduces his own

double standard. He assumes women's 'natural' sexual unrespon-
siveness should be overcome, in large part to allow them the
better to please men. Had he considered the possibility that the
aims of sexuality have been socially constructed via gender
dualism so that most women want emotional intimacy from sex
while most men want pleasure, he might better have been able to
understand women's supposed 'natural' sexual disinterest as a
socially constructed conflict of aims between men and women!

From a feminist perspective, Masters and Johnson can be
credited with defending the uniqueness of the clitoris as an organ
of female sexual pleasure. This move promotes women's interests
against the conservative psychoanalytic establishment's tendency
to take vaginal heterosexual orgasmic sex as the only fully
'mature' and normal form of female sexuality, and is supported
by extensive research on the role of clitoral orgasm in women's
sexual enjoyment even in vaginal sex. Nonetheless Masters and
Johnson also succumb to a conservative functionalism of their
own when they defend the importance of female vaginal sexuality
to preserve the institution of marriage and reproduction. What
seemed initially to be a defence of the right of women to have
different sexual pleasures than men thus ends up as a means/end
argument in which clitoral pleasure is made to serve, ultimately,
the end of heterosexual marriage (Miller and Fowkles, 1980).

The social naming and sex as energy paradigm

On the other side of the divide from those theories which
emphasise the primacy of sex as a bodily drive are those theories
which stress the primacy of the social in the formation of the
sexual. Thus, sexuality is conceived neither as an instinct nor
even as a socially constituted drive, but as a diffuse set of bodily
energies which gets its distinctive characteristics from the way its
specific component energies are socially defined, focused and
organised.

Sex as desire constructed in language: the case of Lacan and Irigaray

Some contemporary readings of Freud, for example that of
Lacan, stress the symbolic and psychological aspects of sexual

desire and effectively ignore Freud's attempts to connect this to bodily effects via the constancy principle. The problems that the Critical Theory tradition has with the assumption that sex is an inherent drive for pleasure and the constancy principle of psychic health are bypassed by Jacques Lacan, whose radical reading of Freud in effect rejects a unified libido theory. Lacan (1982) creates a metaphysical gap between the polymorphously perverse 'partial' bodily drives of the pre-Oedipal, pre-symbolic period – the oral, anal, scopic, and other bodily drives for specific learned pleasures, on the one hand – and Desire with a capital 'D', characteristic of the Oedipal period, on the other. Desire is created when the subject comes to desire to be the desired of the m(other), and realises that this is impossible due to the law of the father which specifies that only the one in the symbolic position of 'having the phallus' (i.e. being the father (other, mate) to the mother) can be this desired one. (Heterosexual) desire is thus created at the same time as the understanding of one's 'position in language', i.e. that one is either a masculine or feminine subject. One learns that who one is is one whose desire of the other can only be obtained by playing the relevant masculine or feminine role. This sexual desire is not based on the physical repression of any genital desires, but on the displacing of all bodily interests, including the partial drives, to the social but impossible Desire of uniting with the desired other by being what the other lacks.

One of the problems with the Lacanian analysis and its feminist appropriation by Juliet Mitchell and Jacqueline Rose (eds) (1982) is that, unlike the Critical Theorists' adaptation of Freud, there is no way to conceptualise what a sexual liberation would be. Rather, it would seem that since sexual Desire is metaphysically insatiable and inevitably bound up with the role-playing of masculinity and femininity, with masculinity the privileged signifier, there are no cultural or personal solutions to counter the sexual power relations between the genders created by Oedipal patriarchal language.

As we have discussed in chapter two, the work of the former Lacanian French feminist Luce Irigaray suggests a bridge between Freudian theories of sexual repression and social naming theories of sex. In her deconstruction of the assumptions of Lacan, Irigaray suggests that the relationship between the signifiers masculinity and femininity can be altered by a revaluing of feminine sexuality beyond the patriarchal Oedipal parameters in

which Lacan insists it must be defined. Though Irigaray like
Marcuse implies that women (and men too) should regress to
pre-Oedipal aspects of self and sexuality involving the power of
the mother, she also implies the necessity for a lesbian-feminist
moment: a tactical strike against heterosexuality that will alter
the social meaning of masculine *vs* feminine in such a way as not
to define these concepts interdependently, or to subordinate the
feminine to the masculine.

Irigaray's deconstruction of Lacan suggests that in important
ways she no longer holds a Freudian concept of sexuality or sexual
repression at all. Indeed, her own descriptions of female sexuality
suggest she has gone beyond the 'sex as drive for pleasure' theory
to a different view of sexuality altogether: that sex is a diffuse
bodily energy not bound up in any one erogenous zone, and that
the domination of women's sexuality comes as much through
misdescription as actual physical repression.

One of the important implications of this line of thought is to
problematise two assumptions of neo-Freudian thought: first,
that sexuality must basically be thought of as a drive for orgiastic
(when 'mature', ultimately genital) pleasure and second, that
male domination of female sexuality has to do with the kind of
sexual repression implicated in keeping women from developing
full genital sexuality. Indeed, it raises the radical feminist question of what sexual pleasure *per se* has to do with women's
liberation.

Symbolic interactionism/labelling theory

The view that sexuality is neither an instinct nor a drive but a set
of bodily energies which get tied together by labelling and socialisation is the view of symbolic interactionism, also called labelling
theory. (Plummer, 1975; Gagnon and Simon, 1973.) For these
thinkers, bodily interests are clearly secondary if not altogether
irrelevant in sexuality. The moving cause of one's particular
sexual interests is determined by how one resolves the issue of
social identity. Sexual desires are totally relative to a social process
of defining what others expect of one as a gendered person and
what counts as 'sexual' for the social group one identifies with.
Learned sexual scripts define what are acceptable sexual desires
(heterosexual, genital, etc.) in normal males and females. Those
who adopt sexual scripts which deviate from these norms (e.g. are

homosexual, have non-genital sexual interests such as voyeurism, S/M interests, etc.) are stigmatised as being not normal. One's sexual and psychic health then turn on one's social definition in relation to peers.

Thus, symbolic interactionists take the same position as Foucault (1978) in rejecting Freud's 'repressive theory' of sexuality: that sex is a bodily given which social forces hold in check. On the contrary, sexuality has no given bodily impetus or force. Rather, our sense of what is sexual is an accidental conjuncture of bodily pleasures with learned social meanings that define these pleasures as sexual. 'Sexuality is nothing but naming makes it so': sexual interests and identities are nothing but a set of social meanings by which one learns one's social identity, i.e. learns to relate oneself to others.

Symbolic interactionism captures something important that the body instinct and psychoanalytic versions of sexuality do not. The emphasis on the social and accidental quality of sexual identities seems to support the perception that infant relations with parents do not necessarily determine the objects or aims of one's sexuality. For example, I had the option to become a lesbian in part because I went to a girls' summer camp where lesbian practices were possible, but I might never have made the break from heterosexuality in adult married life without the cultural intervention of the lesbian-feminist movement. Labelling theory captures the fact that the social definition of self as 'normal' in relation to one's peers seems to be much more important in most teenage girls' definition of themselves as heterosexual than any bodily need for orgasmic release in heterosexual intercourse.

What is problematic about symbolic interactionism is that it eschews an historical approach to understanding why different forms, types and objects of sexuality arise when they do. For example, why is contemporary society so obsessed with sexuality as the key to one's personal identity? Does such an obsession serve historical functions or purposes, such as maintaining capitalist, or male domination? Second, what of persistent gender differences in sexualities? Are these just accidental features of societies or do they have an historical function?[3]

Another problem with the symbolic interactionist approach is that it subsumes the psychological within the sociological. This gives us no way to distinguish group cultural norms (which not all people follow) from individual psychological structures. Feminist theory, as theory seeking to be useful in aiding women to fight for social change, must give us the psychological tools to understand our own individual selves as both historical yet contemporary social constructs. Thus, we need a psychological level of theory that supports feminist therapies that help us as individuals to understand our individual historical unconscious aspects. Our individual childhoods may not be totally determinant of who we are today but they may nonetheless create rigidities, that is, 'sex prints', that help us explain our individual deviance from group norms and/or our greater conformities to them. This individual understanding is one necessary element in an oppositional thera-peutic process that changes us from within in order to confront social domination which is perpetuated both without and within.

This process need not involve one-on-one individual therapy. Some can achieve understanding and change by interactive femin-ist friendships (Raymond, 1986). Most women will also require some level of more generalised group understanding of the sort that successful consciousness-raising groups provide. These allow an emotionally charged critique of our more general (and con-temporary) socially engendered aspects. A similar technique can be used to understand and change internalised race/ethnicism and classism.

A final criticism of symbolic interactionism is the problem of consistent relativity. As a consistent but ahistorical relativism, symbolic interactionism can offer us no utopian moment. What is sexually liberating, healthy, equal, etc. is all entirely relative to whatever definition is taken by the group with which one identi-fies. Thus symbolic interactionism cannot by itself satisfactorily answer the feminist demand for a vision or visions of liberated sexuality and gender.

Foucault's 'power/knowledges'

Foucault is perhaps the most well known representative of the 'social naming' paradigm of sexuality, social construction and social domination. Foucault appropriates and modifies the social naming theory for his own purposes. While he accepts the label-ling theorists' position that sexuality is a diffuse set of bodily energies and pleasures socially constructed together by naming them all as sexual, Foucault historicises and adds to this line of thought by arguing that modern 'normalisation' techniques of the social control of sexuality have supplanted the earlier forms of social control connected to marriage alliances (Foucault, 1978). For Foucault, psychoanalysis is only one example of the modern 'power/knowledges' of bourgeois human sciences in an interconnected net of discourses, social methods and physical techniques which are used to gain 'bio-power', i.e. control over populations and their reproduction. These techniques give their practitioners – prison and legal officials, social workers, psychiatrists, teachers, army officers and parents – special powers over others via categorising their behaviour as abnormal and then using the combined techniques of reason, incarceration and other physical techniques to 'correct' these behaviours (Foucault, 1977a).

Foucault explores the genealogy of psychoanalysis as a power/ knowledge in *The History of Sexuality, volume 1 (The Will to Know)* (Foucault, 1978). His view is that the modern idea of childhood sexuality and sexual identity as most central to personal identity are ways of thinking about and regulating one's body practices that have been created by modern sexology. These labellings of inversions, perversions and 'normal' development are used in psychoanalytic therapy to actually focus the diffuse bodily energies of its patients into specific sexual desires in relation to tabooed parental objects. Thus, psychoanalytic discourses about sex actually create, produce and intensify sexual energy, often through colluding in tabooing and suppressing it.[4]

Those within this reconstructed 'Oedipalised' family who do not accord with its theory of sexual health (e.g. hysterical women, masturbating children, homosexuals and other perverts) are at once labelled as abnormal – thus being created as potential clients – and controlled by therapy to 'alleviate' the sexual and personal anxieties and frustrations thus created.

Foucault's vision of how power operates in society is based on a Nietzchean view of human nature: every individual has a will to power over others. Individuals are always involved in strategies for increasing their power over others at the microlevel of society, some by developing or applying socio-physical techniques, others by discourses which normalise and empower them *vis-à-vis* others. The whole of the human scientific establishment (state, university, schools, research centres, hospitals, prisons, etc.) operates according to rules, techniques and theories which always inextricably link the will to power with the will to truth.

Foucault's nominalist thought can be contrasted with the struc-

turalist and totalistic aspects of Freudianism and Marxism since
he denies their presupposition that power is based in some mono-
lithic structure or structures (the economy, the family, a dual
systems perspective, etc.) Instead, he aims to substitute a 'genealogy of the present' consisting of history of conjunctures of
discourses and techniques which may accidentally turn out to
provide the preconditions for developments which are instrumental in bringing about others.

An example of this is our contemporary understanding of our
sexuality as essential to our personal identity. This connection
was developed by the bourgeois class in its concern to control its
own sexuality. However, though the strictures against masturbation and for men to maintain sexual purity develop along with
sexologist characterisations of some sexual behaviour and objects
as deviant and sick, the consequent repression of sexuality should
not be understood as a self conscious technique developed by the
class to control itself and the working class, the better to develop
capital accumulation and support capitalist domination. Instead,
the bourgeois view of sexuality is adopted as a way to affirm
themselves against the aristocracy by developing a distinctive set
of discourses and techniques to regulate their own sexuality. And
only after these techniques are developed in the pursuit of one
goal do they then become helpful in being applied as techniques
to dominate another class. As he says:

> Let us not picture the bourgeoisie symbolically castrating itself
> the better to refuse others the right to have a sex and make use
> of it as they please. This class must be seen rather as being
> occupied, from the mid-eighteenth century on, with creating
> its own sexuality and forming a specific body based on it, a
> 'class body with its health, hygiene, descent, and race: the
> autosexualization of its body, the incarnation of sex in its body,
> the endogamy of sex and the body'. (Foucault, 1978a: 124)

Subjects, that is, socially create and produce by their own discourse (itself often accidentally developed) their own sexualities,
and mould and shape their own bodies and desires as well as those
they otherwise wish to control.

Furthermore, power is never absolute even at the microlevel,
for it always generates resistances. Thus, there are no pure
victims: prisoners, women, gays, colonised races and other popu-

lations targetted as deviant tend to engage in individual or cultural resistances to the dominant power/knowledges.

A feminist concept of sexual liberation using a Foucaultian perspective rejects the sexual vanguard counterculture theory of Reich and Marcuse. What these amount to is simply the valorisation of the hitherto stigmatised pole of a given set of patriarchal dualist oppositions (marriage/non-marriage, coupling/cruising, reproductive sex/pleasure sex, men/women, heterosexual/homosexual etc.). Foucault would argue that the simple reversal of values in a dualist polarity never ultimately overcomes the logic of social domination – instead it merely generates new 'normalisation' techniques.

Gayle Rubin's latest work (Rubin, 1984) takes up Foucault's line of thought by criticising any sexual ethics which creates 'hierarchies of sexual value'. Thus, feminists must resist the normalising techniques of psychiatry, the church and the state which have put married, heterosexual, reproductive activity at the top and despised sexual castes – homosexuals, transsexuals, fetishists, sadomasochists, sex workers and man/boy lovers – at the bottom. But we must also reject the reverse strategy of radical feminists who create a vanguard of lesbian-feminists at the top and stigmatise straight women and sexual minorities like S/M and man/boy lovers. For Rubin and for Foucault, the feminist left must create an alternative 'power/knowledge' of its own emphasising the claims of 'bodies and their pleasures' rather than preferred sexual identities. Rubin's 'democratic' sexual morality would valorise consensual sex for pleasure and refuse line drawing concerning the objects of sexual interest, so as to respect the rights of what she calls 'sexual minorities'. Such a discourse allows us to substitute the concept of diversity for that of perversity and to be truly pluralist in our approach to sexual possibilities (cf. also Weeks, 1985, 1986; Sawicki, 1986).

What are the implications of Foucaultian thought for feminism and for strategies for sexual liberation? There are a number of implications, some of which are salutary and others problematic. On the positive side, the Foucaultian critique of psychoanalysis has yielded a number of insights for feminism. For example, challenging the mystique of the Freudian theory of the Oedipal incest wish has allowed feminists and others to insist on uncovering a 'subjugated knowledge' denied by Freudianism; that is, the reality of incestual father/daughter seductions as a mechanism of patriarchal domination bypassed by Freud when he substituted the infant wish for the reality of parental seduction in his theory of hysterical neuroses (cf. Begus, 1987; Herman, 1982; Masson, 1984).

Another positive aspect of Foucault's emphasis on historical discontinuities in the specificity of power/knowledges. Such an approach directs feminists seeking to understand differences between women to look for historically specific discourses and social techniques which privilege white women over Afro-American women, middle-class women over working-class women, and heterosexual women over lesbian women. For example, though white bourgeois women in the United States were defined as asexual and physically frail by nineteenth-century religious and medical discourses, Afro-American women were defined as physically strong and excessively sexual by other discourses: those which sought to justify slavery and those in the eugenics movement who argued for sterilisation of the inferior races (Aphtheker, 1983; Davis, 1981; Gordon, 1976). Thus, to understand and deal with social privilege requires studying the way that historically specific power/knowledges have both oppressed some women yet given them social privilege *vis-à-vis* other women at the same time. Such specificity counteracts the tendency to jump to the totalising generalisation that all women are equally oppressed by patriarchy (Sawicki, 1986).

A problem with Foucault is that his consistent relativity affords the Women's Movement no clear way of choosing either a vision or a strategy of sexual liberation. Foucault hints that oppressed sexual groups need to construct alternate power/knowledges which allows them to prioritise

the claims of bodies, pleasures and knowledges, in their multiplicity and their possibility of resistance . . . The rallying point for the counterattack against the deployment of sexuality ought not to be sex-desire but bodies and their pleasures (Foucault, 1977a: 157).

But what if different poles of the Women's Movement construct these power/knowledges differently? For example, while Gayle Rubin wants to include in her coalition of oppressed 'sexual minorities' consensual S/Ms and man/boy lovers, Andrea Dworkin and Kathleen Barry argue that such practices are not those of oppressed minorities but of those who perpetuate patriarchal power by their participation in non-reciprocal and degrading sex.

The problem of constructing alternative power/knowledges is that a line must be drawn between sex feminists want to call politically correct and that which is incorrect. A consistent relativism gives us no way to draw this line, and though feminists on both poles of the sex debate would probably agree that some groups are not oppressed sexual minorities but sexual criminals/perverts (e.g. rapists, fathers who commit incest, etc.), the power/knowledge of Gayle Rubin which creates as its minimal condition consent is quite different from that of Barry, Dworkin or Griffin who want reciprocity which they feel is impossible within the structures of sex roles which stem from patriarchy.

Part of the problem with thinkers who flirt with relativism, like Foucault and the libertarian/pluralist feminists, is that their supposed 'objectivity' about the relativity of values is itself suspect. So, even the archaeological and genealogical historical methods espoused by Foucault contain implicit value presuppositions. In insisting on approaching history with the assumption that it contains major ruptures, or discontinuities in the type of social power structures present in different ages, Foucault may be begging the question against a radical feminist analysis which is interested in the continuities of the social techniques of male domination (cf. Daly, 1978; Leghorn and Parker, 1981; Raymond, 1986; Rich, 1980). Furthermore, even if there are important discontinuities in techniques of social power, a gay male historian like Foucault cannot be trusted to have got the periodisation of these 'epistemic ruptures' correct, as his main concern has not been with understanding structures of male domination.

In sum, the Foucaultian perspective contains the classic self-referential paradox of relativist theories. Either Foucault is creating his own power/knowledge with its own values (e.g. radical pluralism) which he cannot give good reasons to support against an opposing power/knowledge of radical feminists, or else his position is disappointingly apolitical, for it gives us no more general standpoint from which to judge sexual practices by the content and structure of the social relations involved in them.

A similar flaw can be seen in Rubin's Foucaultian argument. The hidden presupposition of a pluralist power/knowledge endorsing a 'democratic sexual morality' is that consensual pleasure empowers, whether or not one partner has more options or greater control than the other. But this does not take account of the fact that sexual practices are embedded in social structures like age, gender roles and economic power which tend to give one partner greater control over the other. Surely there has to be a way to conceive of sexual liberation which can allow us a qualitative vision of sexual reciprocity that relies on more than just consensus in its assessment of the potential values, disvalues and risks of sexual practices.

Deleuze and Guattari

The French theorists Deleuze and Guattari develop a 'social energy' paradigm of sexuality that, though it is similar in important respects to Foucault, differs in that it emphasises the material aspects of sex as socially constructed, thus allowing us to draw an appearance/reality distinction between the hegemonic Oedipal sex of patriarchal capitalism and the reality of sex as a polymorphous perverse objectless bodily energy. I believe that their theory, suitably modified, can allow us an historical analysis on which to develop a theory of contemporary sexual alienation as well as a vision of sexual liberation.

For Deleuze and Guattari, desire is not a lack, *à la* Lacan, or a drive seeking release/satisfaction, *à la* Reich and Freud. Rather it is a bodily energy which is gratified in the act of being expressed, and socially moulded into different forms of 'desiring production' (Deleuze and Guattari, 1977). Deleuze and Guattari, like Foucault, criticise the presumptions of Freudianism to have discovered the universal 'stages' of human sexual development (oral, anal and phallic). Rather, they argue, the discourse of Freudianism just reinforces the patriarchal nuclear family structure which insists that 'mature' sexuality be coded as genital and as focused on incestuous Oedipal concerns (Daddy–mommy–me).

For Deleuze and Guattari, orthodox Freudian psychiatry colludes in reinforcing the patriarchal nuclear family, itself a functional necessity to contain the otherwise schizophrenic tendencies of modern capitalism to 'de-territorialise' sex. Thus, social liberation requires such a de-territorialisation, i.e. a refusal to centre sexual interest around a specific human genital other or to see oneself as the type of subject that can or wishes to 'possess' a particular human being.

One unfortunate implication of Deleuze and Guattari's theory is that they come perilously close to justifying the decentring of selfhood altogether as a revolutionary ideal. That is, if Oedipalised sex is what stabilises capitalism by creating selves fixated around genital sexual possessive relations with others, then radicals should support the decentring, indeed, the unhinging of selfhood altogether as a way to break down this stabilising structure for capitalism. Hence their chapter on 'Schizanalysis' seems to advocate schizophrenia as the solution to race, gender and class inequalities!

Deleuze and Guattari's use of language in describing sex as a bodily energy that is not a drive is wonderfully instructive in reminding us that sex is not 'all in the head'. They too, in their way, are seeking, like Irigaray, to displace the Lacanian and Freudian emphasis on gender games and genital sex as at the centre of sexual desire. But in emphasising the materialism of sexuality, they treat its sociality as merely an artificial aspect. They have inadvertently become trapped in a dualism that leads them to emphasise the bodily aspects of sex to the exclusion of the desire for social connection that, it can be argued, is equally an aspect of sexuality.

Conclusion: we need a better social energy theory of sexuality

My own approach accepts the idea that sexuality is one type of social and bodily energy (sex/affective energy) which is historically constructed. But it is a dualist error to suppose that it is originally more bodily than social, as do the drive theorists, or more social than bodily, as do the social naming theorists. Rather, humans are basically both social beings and bodies, and our sexuality is a bodily yet social energy to unite with others. Since it is neither an instinct nor a drive with one particular aim (e.g. bodily pleasure), we cannot think of an ahistorical 'authentic' human sexuality that has been alienated by social domination or sexual repression as do Marcuse, Reich and Deleuze and Guattari. But this does not mean that there is no objective base for a feminist critique of our contemporary construction of sexuality.

An historical rather than a universal test of alienation is given in chapter seven, which shows how the social contradictions in our current socially produced sexuality relatively empower women to demand a feminist sexual liberation historically specific to our time and place.

PART TWO

The Theory of Sex/ Affective Production

4

Sex/affective production

Love, sex and work – these are the places in which radical feminists, Freudians and Marxists, respectively, have sought the creation and perpetuation of male dominance. In previous chapters we have seen that each of these approaches, though insightful, has been too simplistic to provide a theoretical structure which can capture the persistence of male domination as well as the historical changes and conflicts in gender roles and expectations many of us have experienced in our lifetimes. The project for this chapter is to outline a theoretical approach which can combine the insights of these three approaches in a way that can do justice both to the changing history and to the underlying continuity of male dominance.

In order to understand the philosophical implications of positing sex/affective production, we must consider what follows concerning the nature of sexuality, love and social bonding, and the role of human labour in their construction. Only after doing this can we understand how contemporary changes in human gender, sexuality and affectionate relationships have created a crisis in the reproduction of male dominance.

My central theoretical claim is that there are historically various ways of organising, shaping and moulding the human desires connected to sexuality and love, and consequently to parenting and social bonding. It is in part through these systems that different forms of male dominance and other types of social domination are reproduced. These systems, called here systems of sex/affective production, have also been called desiring production by Deleuze and Guattari (1977) and sex/gender systems by Gayle Rubin (1975). I use a different technical term than these other writers for two reasons: first, the theories of self, sexuality and social bonding assumed are different, and second, these authors use their terms to define a realm of social organisation which they mean to contrast to the workings of the economy. I would argue, on the contrary, not only that every economy has as inseparable components, desiring and gendered relations, but also that the 'dual systems' of Deleuze and Guattari and Rubin (e.g. slave, feudal or capitalist production *vs* desiring production or the sex/gender system) conceptualise a split between family or kinship relations and the economy which is better conceived (in advanced capitalist societies) as two semi-autonomous sexual economies, each with its desiring and gendered production, one centred in the household and one in capitalist production.

From the fact that every known human economy is gendered and desiring, it doesn't follow that economic priorities completely determine the specific form of sex/affective production in that economy. It does mean, however, that there are some minimal functional connections between them. For example, class-divided economies require some authoritarian form of sex/affective production; a democratic form of sex/affective production, for example the democratic socialist model described in chapter eleven, would undercut the worker acquiescence to the expropriation of surplus labour that is necessary for the perpetuation of class-divided societies.

The production of sexuality, bonding and affection

The concept of sexuality embedded in the notion of 'sex/affective energy' differs from the Freudian concept. While Freud privileges the bodily function of libido to relieve tension (a body drive theory of sexuality), the theory espoused here is a 'social energy' theory of sexuality. That is, sexual or erotic interest in others is presumed to be but one type of emotional or social interest in them. Sexual energy is merely one form of a social yet bodily based desire to unite with others, i.e. to incorporate oneself with a loved other (Hartsock, 1983).[1] Thus, affectionate attachments and friendships of the Platonic sort, maternal and paternal love, kin tie and social bonding with work mates or with a community of identity (religious, ethnic, racial, class-based) are all forms of sex/affective energy.

Sex/affective energy has no particular 'natural' objects or bodily functions. Although orgasmic sexual activity may indeed relieve bodily tension, this cannot be construed to be the natural aim of such processes as Freud and his followers suppose. And, although I have described sex/affective energy as involving a desire to unite with social others, this should not be conceived as a natural aim or goal inherent in sexual and affectionate activity. Thus, my point that all social constructions of sex/affective energy involve a desire to unite with social others is a general empirical, rather than an *a priori* or definitional claim about the 'essential nature' or inherent purposes of sexuality. The point is that all known human social constructions of sex/affective energy create the social desire to unite with others as the key focus of this energy. Thus though sex/ affective energy is so mouldable that it can be directed toward either exclusively bodily or social aims or both, its immense potential for solidifying human groups has always been harnessed to motivate people to engage in the other sorts of human labour necessary to meet human needs.

Though orgasm is a healthy release for body tension, orgasm *per se* does not indicate emotional health, or the optimal satisfaction of sex/affective desire. Rather, we require a historically based vision of what constitutes bodily and emotional health in sexual and affectionate interactions. I shall argue in chapter seven that in advanced capitalist societies which have developed in individuals a self-identity based on a notion of democratic individualism, the model which will best resolve the desire to enjoy sexual pleasure as an end in itself as well as the desire for individual equality is a social construction of sexuality and affection which values reciprocal (free flowing sex/affective energy) rather than solely hierarchical (uni-controlled and directed sex/affective energy).[2]

The notion of sex/affective energy developed here assumes that sex/affective interests can be as fully satisfied (hence as healthily expressed) by Platonic as by orgasmic interactions. Since sex/ affective energy has no natural objects, interests or stages of development, humans must organise a social production of this energy by channelling it into socially presented objects and aims. And what counts as personal and sexual health can only be determined by examining the historical social expectations built into the particular mode of sex/affective production and the ways that the system allows their frustration or achievement for specific groups of people.

The social energy theory of sexuality, in not privileging orgasm as the ultimate (deepest) aim of all human attachments, can better understand the way in which Platonic friendships and gender bonding around work are as direct an expression of sex/affective energy as is explicit sexual intercourse. As a result, we have a better understanding of how the sexual division of labour in patriarchal societies allows for an expression of homosexual attachment between men and between women. Any challenge to this division by feminists is thus an immediate threat to the flow of male-bonding sexual energy; and such an intervention by feminists into the chummy clubs, workplaces and board rooms where male bonding has traditionally held sway will be resisted unconsciously even by men who are consciously non-sexist. For this reason, some of the self-aspects of even non-sexist men will make them adversaries to feminism (as will indeed some of the self-aspects of women!).

If homosocial sex/affective energy is potentially as strong a bonding force as heterosexual sex/affective attachments, it becomes clearer why all systems of patriarchal sex/affective production must establish systems of compulsory heterosexuality which deal with the potential conflict between same sex bonding and heterosexual bonding (cf. Hatem, 1986). Since compulsory heterosexuality is necessary to ensure the reproduction of the next generation in a form in which male dominance will be preserved, both male and female homosocial bonding must be restricted so as to require an attention to the propagation of the species through heterosexual unions and kinship or other social arrangements which distribute responsibility for the economic and social support of children. Beyond this, however, many forms of male bonding, including institutionalised homosexuality, are compatible with the preservation of male dominance. But female bonding, as a potential threat to the preservation of male dominance, must either be subordinated to the primacy of hierarchical heterosexual unions, or defined socially to be of such a different category (e.g. spiritual not erotic, as in nineteenth-century women's friendships) as not to challenge the social primacy of patriarchal heterosexual unions.

Thus, it is not only by demanding entrance into workplaces hitherto reserved for men that feminists threaten masculinity and male homosexual flows of sex/affective energy. In their heterosexual sexual encounters, men's masculine identity is threatened by feminists who demand reciprocity rather than male hierarchical control of these interactions. Furthermore, feminist bonding with other women challenges the priority that patriarchal sex/affective production systems insist that women place on their heterosexual relations, whether with husbands or lovers. The expansion of the Women's Movement threatens the ability of heterosexual men to achieve orgiastic sexuality without major changes in their masculine identity.

There are two aspects of a man's gender identity which may be threatened in ceding sexual reciprocity to a woman lover: that associated with his individual, traditional (i.e. formed in childhood) sense of male prerogatives and characteristics, and that associated with his contemporary peer reference groups. For the man who has no network of male friends who are actively engaged in a countercultural anti-sexism, feminist demands for reciprocity threaten both aspects of masculine gender identity. Such a man stands to forfeit not merely his superego/childhood sense of masculine success, but also that homosocial sex/affective energy reflected in bonding with his contemporary male peers.

The gender division of labour crossculturally has created women's subcultures in patriarchal societies. These subcultures, created by common work – in childbearing and rearing, in mediating human relationships via informal kin negotiations and friendships, in sharing work skills and in separate women's religious and living communities (Raymond, 1986) – create strong sex/affective bonds between women.

These bonds of work and friendship operate as a powerful force because those involved resist giving up the social union involved. This can operate as a conservative force for retaining patriarchal arrangements under conditions where a challenge to male dominance is only thought possible on an individual level. Thus, in periods of stability for patriarchal arrangements, a woman who resists patriarchy by an individual challenge to the gender division of labour may risk the loss of her comfortable women's cultural networks. A feminist friend of mine, when asked why she was in training to be a nurse rather than a doctor, said that since she wanted to work with women, nursing was a better choice of career since there her co-workers would be women while in doctoring they would primarily be men. Similarly, women of the New Right see contemporary feminists as those who wish to give up traditional feminine values and women's networks by doing men's work and adopting masculine values, thus risking the loss of their common work and regular association with other women.

Though the Women's Movement has shown that there is a way in contemporary society for women to give primacy to women's networks while still challenging the gender division of labour, the reconciling of the desire to retain one's sex/affective bonds with women and yet to challenge male dominance is only possible under certain sorts of historical conditions – those in which the institutions which reproduce male dominance are themselves in crisis or change.

The social energy theory of sexuality revises Freudian presuppositions as to how social repression works. If sex/affective energy is conceptualised as a social bodily energy, on the one hand, yet not a bodily drive subject to the constancy principle on the other, an important feature of sex/affective production noted by anti-Freudians Foucault, Deleuze and Guattari can be explained. This is that the social repression of sex/affective energy, by forbidding certain objects, persons and activities as legitimate objects of interest, does not eliminate but, in fact, actually increases the sexual interest of these objects, persons and activities. Dyadic oppositions between good or legitimate objects, persons and activities are contrasted with tabooed objects in a symbolic coding process that not only does not reduce or dam up sexual energy, but which actually increases it. Things called 'bad' and tabooed, by that very act become of sex/affective interest. Thus, when social repression restricts self-identification with some of the invested objects in the field of the symbolic code, it not only creates some of the sex/affective energy connected to these objects, it then channels some of this energy by displacement onto forms considered more socially acceptable: affection, disgust, Platonic bonding and so on.[3]

This feature of sex/affective production, that tabooed objects increase erotic interest and yet are displaced from self-consciousness, shows the manner in which historically created sexual symbolic codes can enter materially into the creation of sex/affective energy, creating not only social objects for sex/affective desires but also different levels of intensity of interest, depending on the contradictory messages presented by the dominant sexual symbolic code. Any base/superstructure treatment of sexuality in which 'body' interests or functions are seen to be more central than 'social' or 'ideological' ones must thereby be rejected.

Modes of sex/affective production

If sexuality is a social bodily energy, then it is a product which has to be socially produced. And if sex/affective energy includes all forms of social bonding – not just sexual interactions but parent/child ties, friendships, work and ethnic/national bonds – then the forms of human organisation which a society develops to meet the human material needs for such connections will be as important in understanding those societies as their economic systems.

Every society must have one or more historically developed modes of sex/affective production to meet the key human needs – sexuality, nurturance, children – whose satisfaction is just as basic to the functioning of human society as is the satisfaction of the material needs of hunger and physical security. Thus, sex/affective production systems are both like economic modes of production and functionally part of such systems. They are like them because they are human, and historically various, modes of organisation that both create the social objects of the material needs connected to sex/affective energy and also organise the human labour necessary to achieve them. They are functionally a part of such systems because in organising human sexuality and the social bonds of parenting, they also manage and produce children, a task which is a necessary feature of any economic system. In addition, in organising the sex/affective aspects of the work bonds of the workforce in the economic system, they provide the necessary co-operative aspect of human labour power without which humans could not engage in collective economic activity. Finally, the sex/affective production system of a society structures either equal or unequal exchanges of sex/affective energy between the participants, thus establishing one base for either social hierarchy or equality between them.

While sex/affective production systems are analogous to economic systems in some ways, they are disanalogous in others. One important way in which they are disanalogous is that since their main function is to produce human beings rather than material products and services for human consumption and distribution, they rely more centrally on non-rational symbolic codes that are constitutive of personal identity than do economic systems, which rely more on structures which define the rational self-interests of actors within them. Sexual symbolic codes will be discussed further in the next section.

One way to characterise the interdependence between relations of sex/affective production and the economic system as a whole is to use the concept of a social formation. A social formation is a system of production in use in a particular society at a specific time that may contain within it several different historically developed modes of production. An historical example of a social formation is the combined capitalist and slave modes of production in the United States before the civil war from the seventeenth to the nineteenth centuries. Our present US economic system can be thought of as a social formation consisting of capitalist, patriarchal and racist modes of production. It has a co-dominant set of relations: 1) those between capital and wage labour; and 2) those between men and women in patriarchal sex/affective production. It also has a subordinate set of class relations characteristic of welfare state capitalism, that is, the existence of a class of institutionalised poor, those subsidised by the state on welfare or unemployment. Its racial divisions of wage labour and its general separation of the races into different living communities creates a set of economic and sex/affective domination relations between the white dominant race and subordinate non-white races. Finally, the dominant mode of capitalist production is that controlled by multinational corporations, while a small subordinate sector of capitalist production involves small family businesses (the traditional petty-bourgeoisie).

An argument for the claim that male/female social relations are co-dominant with other social relations of production is the universal presence in all societies of a sexual division of labour and thus culturally defined male and female roles children learn as part of their social identity. Each society has a 'sex/gender system' (Rubin, 1975) – what can be called a sex/affective production system – which organises all material work and services by defining what is culturally acceptable as man's and woman's work. It also organises nurturance, sexuality and procreation by directing sexual urges (in most societies toward heterosexual relations and non-incestuous ties), by indicating possible friendships and by defining parenthood roles and/or kinship ties and responsibilities.

Patriarchal relations have persisted through different modes of economic production, including socialist modes of production such as those in Russia, China and Cuba. The development of different modes of production has meant that the content of the sexual division of labour will vary; for example, in some modes of sex/affective production and social formations men work for wage labour and women do not, while in others, such as feudalism, neither men nor women work for wages. Other relations of exploitation will vary as well, depending on which groups in addition to male heads of families (feudal lords, slave owners or capitalists), benefit from the women's work in reproducing labour power in the family.

A key distinction between the socialist-feminist idea that systems of male dominance are lodged in different modes of sex/affective production and the radical feminist idea that male dominance is lodged in men's crosscultural control over women's sexuality is that the former approach emphasises the importance of historical specificity in a way that the latter does not. Radical feminist theory does not distinguish between structural analytic principles that are constant to all systems of male dominant sex/affective production, middle level categories which describe certain historical forms, modes or systems of sex/affective production, and particular social formations and the particular ideological contents of specific historical sex/affective codes. According to my approach, the first are principles that describe the general functions that social structures must serve to maintain male domination, the second describe specific social mechanisms which reproduce male dominance in certain types of social formations and the third describe concrete structures and sex/affective ideals which shape gender relations in a particular society.

Two structural analytic principles of systems of patriarchal sex/affective production are that there be a gender division of all or nearly all social labour and that there be different gender roles in sexual interactions. Together these principles create what can be called 'gender dualism'; i.e. typical masculine and feminine personalities which have different skills, values and interests because of their work and sexual training. Such a gender structure not only supports the ideology of the natural complementarity between the sexes; it also reproduces itself by creating two polar human personalities which cannot do the work of the opposite sex.

As an example of the ideological force of gender dualism, consider how many women in my generation were warned by their mothers that male sexuality is a driven, aggressive force that could not be controlled once it was put in motion. And that since women's sexuality is, and should be, more emotional and less physical in its direction (cf. Barry, 1979), women are to blame if we fail to restrain male sexuality!

Though the content of masculine and feminine sexuality changes in different modes of sex/affective production, gender sexual dualism perpetuates a taboo against the ideal of sameness and reciprocity in sex/affective encounters, which in general facilitates the acceptance of dominant and subordinate roles in these areas, thus supporting the patriarchal control of women by men.

In general, by preserving homosocial work situations, the sexual division of labour meets the condition of ensuring that male bonding be preserved in order to preserve male power over women. A further necessary condition, however, is to channel the consequent female bonding so that it supports male dominance rather than creating women's subcultures which can come to act in opposition to it. In most kinship based societies this occurs by the 'traffic in women' (Rubin, 1975), i.e. the fact that female kin must subordinate their primary bonding with female kin of origin to a heterosexual marriage tie, to ties with children (who lack social power), and often to husband's kin who owe their primary loyalty to him rather than to her.

Male bonding requires both the material condition of an ongoing flow of sex/affective energy between men and the ideological rationale that there is a natural complementarity between men as sexual dominants and women as sexual subordinates which excludes the possibility of eliminating gender divisions and hierarchies. This requirement in turn yields the structural analytic principle of compulsory heterosexuality which requires that sexual dominants relate sexually primarily to sexual subordinates.

The vast majority of human societies which have institutionalised forms of homosexuality have done so by requiring homosexual partners to adopt masculine and feminine gender identities and, consequently, what we today would term 'butch-femme' roles in sexuality (Rubin, 1975). Such a finding only strengthens the idea that there is a functional connection in most societies between patriarchal gender roles and compulsory heterosexuality, for even homosexual relations are required to operate by the natural complement ideology of compulsory heterosexuality which requires gender roles (Ferguson, 1977).

Though many patriarchal societies have had institutionalised forms of male homosexuality, these relationships have also acknowledged the force of the sexual dominant/subordinate rule. They have done this in two ways, each of which can be described, via middle level concepts, as different modes of sex/affective production. What we can call hierarchical homo- and hetero-patriarchies are those societies which, besides dominate/subordinate hetero-relations, legitimate only male relationships between socially superior and inferior males, such as man/boy love, or relations between members of superior or inferior classes, castes or racial/ethnic groups. Foucault's study of the rules of homosexuality in ancient Greece (Foucault, vol. 2, 1985) and Weeks's look at the fascination of the nineteenth-century British male aristocracy with working-class men (Weeks, 1981) provide two examples of the workings of hierarchical homo- and hetero-patriarchies.

Another middle level type of sex/affective production is equal male homo-/unequal hetero-patriarchies. Such a structure occurs in those societies which allow for egalitarian homosexual relations between men but which heavily repress female homosexual relations. At the same time these societies support the sexual dominant/subordinate rule for heterosexual relations, for example by practices in which older men marry much younger women, and/or women are denied property or choice of marriage partner. Mervat Hatem provides a fascinating study of the conflict between eighteenth- and nineteenth-century Egyptian society organised in this way and French and English imperialists whose sex/affective codes limited homosexuality completely. This difference in sex/affective production systems created a problem for maintaining the male bonding required between the ruling Egyptian class and the Europeans (Hatem, 1986).

Equal male homo/unequal hetero sex/affective production intensifies sex/affective energy in its genital forms around male-male and male-dominant heterosexual encounters. Since these systems usually also insist on virginity for women until marriage, women who have not been able to experience any other use of their sexuality can be 'put in thrall' to a dominant man (cf. Freud, 1918). Lesbian relationships must be repressed in these systems because, in conjunction with the female sex/affective bonding which occurs in the gender division of labour, they could provide a base for a serious challenge to patriarchy.

Though nineteenth-century England and America may seem to be anomalous patriarchal societies because close women's friendships, ones which in many cases were sexual, were tolerated (Faderman, 1981), in actuality these relationships were tolerated because they were not seen to be sexual at all. Thus they were not a challenge to the primacy of male dominated heterosexual relations. Because of the Judaeo-Christian ideology that the natural purpose of sex is reproduction, it is true that such societies have always restricted both male and female homosexuality more than other societies, such as Greece and some middle Eastern cultures (Hatem, 1986). Nonetheless, the nineteenth-century British and American exception to the Judaeo-Christian rule can be explained by the presence of a Victorian ideology which insisted that women, unlike men, are essentially asexual and spiritual while men are essentially sexual and materialistic. Thus, close male friendships were suspect while women's friendships were not. Such women's friendships, occurring as they did in the absence of the sort of lesbian subculture we have today, were no real challenge to the persistence of patriarchal marriage institutions nor to continued male dominance in the public spheres of the state and the economy. Thus, these patriarchal systems, like those of medieval Europe and puritan colonial America, are cases, at the middle level, of what we can call restricted homo/hierarchical hetero-patriarchies.

There are other differences between patriarchal systems of sex/affective production which can be captured by another set of middle level categories: those which indicate differences in the structures of male-dominant heterosexuality depending on the type of kinship system, or other social form, in which they are based. In the following chapter father and husband patriarchies will be distinguished from public patriarchies to highlight some important differences.

One example of the different ideological content of the sexual symbolic codes of US nineteenth-century husband patriarchy and twentieth-century public patriarchy is evidenced in the shift between nineteenth- and twentieth-century notions of masculinity and femininity, and the contemporary confusions as to what constitutes a sexual identity: Is being a sado-masochist a deep structure of identity on the level with being male or female, or gay or lesbian? What about being bi-sexual, or celibate?

Woman the chaste mother and man the id, woman the possession, man the possessor – these were the ideological terms of the sex/affective code characteristic of Victorian and American capitalist husband patriarchy. These have been replaced by woman as vagina, man as stud, woman the manipulator, man the manipulated, as the ideological terms of the present sex/affective code of capitalist public patriarchy. The differences and conflicts in these historical sex/affective symbolic codes will be discussed in more detail in the next chapter.

Sexual symbolic codes and social domination

Particular modes of sex/affective production work by the creation, displacement or reversal of a sexual symbolic code. Such codes function to allow persons to distinguish self from other, and one's group of identification from other socially superior and inferior groups by providing normative standards by which to classify good, thus self-related, behaviour from bad, thus other-related, behaviour.

It seems to be a general feature of human societies that there are social divisions (gender, age, kin, social class, religion, race) which allow an individual to identify with one group and to distinguish self from other groups. Various writers have speculated that the persistence of such social divisions mirrors a universal psychological dynamic which individuals must face in developing self-consciousness: the conflict between a need for autonomy, on the one hand, and social recognition or incorporation within a group, on the other (cf. Adam, 1978; Benjamin, 1980; Flax, 1978; Hegel, 1894; Lasch, 1984; Sartre, 1956).

Whatever the origin of the conflict between self and other, sex/affective production systems perpetuate social domination by creating and maintaining a set of sex/affective desires, and a set of norms to regulate them, which maintains a self/other dichotomy and hierarchy in which there are dominant and subordinate roles. These roles are not merely perpetuated by individual internalisation of economic class, racial, ethnic and gender identities and desires in childhood. They are also supported by the structures of other social practices, for example, the form of organisation of parenting, of the economy, of neighbourhoods and households, and state laws. These latter legitimate, forbid, empower and otherwise sanction certain forms of interaction for people depending on their status *vis-à-vis* the sexual symbolic codes – male or female, white or non-white, adult or child, rich or poor, married or single, straight or gay.

Male dominant sex/affective production systems involve two major components: material forms of domination, for example, the male dominated nuclear family and sex-segregated wage labour, and sexual symbolic codes (normative regulations and oppositions, like the sexual double standard, heterosexual romantic love and normal/deviant sexual oppositions) (Escoffier, 1985). These sexual symbolic codes use polar oppositions like married woman/prostitute, mother/lesbian to divide women from each other, thus reducing the sex/affective energy and interactions between women.

Obviously 'mother' and 'lesbian' are not true oppositions in the sense of being mutually exclusive, as I, a lesbian mother, can attest! But it is surprising to note the range of social forces that contrive to convince women that the two categories are mutually incompatible. This is obviously a function of our historical form of compulsory heterosexuality: if women can be convinced that motherhood, which most women want, requires heterosexuality, they will not think lesbianism a possible option for themselves. A woman in my community went so far as to complain that it wasn't fair that I, as a lesbian mother, hoped my daughter would decide to have children that would, of course, be my grandchildren. Since I had not put in the self-sacrifice necessary to preserve my heterosexual marriage, she thought I did not 'deserve' grandchildren!!

The general good woman/bad woman oppositions mentioned above are supplemented by racist sex/affective production systems which further divide women by white/Black or non-white classifications. Though racist and classist systems have their own separate logics for reproducing themselves which are not simply dependent on male dominant sex/affective systems, they often act in concert to maintain existing social hierarchies in all three areas.

If straight women can be divided from lesbian women, married from single (and virginal) women, chaste women from prostitutes, white from non-white women, women lose the understanding that we are all part of a meaning-system in which each negative category of woman stands for a use of sexuality that in some ways represents a challenge to the patriarchal control of women. As Jan Raymond puts it, virgins, nuns, lesbians, women living with other women and prostitutes all represent 'loose women', women not defined in relation to, and dependent on, men. They thus challenge the symbolic code of 'hetero-reality', i.e. that woman should exist for man (Raymond, 1986).

There are two major approaches to understanding sex/affective symbolic codes: the transcultural, universalist approach and the historical constructivist approach.[4] Although these approaches are usually opposed, there is a way to borrow insights from both traditions that is important for feminists to pursue.

The transcultural, universalist approach is characteristic of radical feminism (Daly, 1973, 1978, 1982; Dworkin, 1981; Griffin, 1981; Hartsock, 1983; Raymond, 1979, 1986). It assumes that the symbolic value systems of all patriarchal societies are characterised by a dualist polarity between the forces of good (superiority) and the forces of evil (inferiority). This universal symbolic code is both patriarchal and racist in its association of good with masculinity, heterosexuality, whiteness (or chosen race), the dominant economic ruling class, culture, reason and mental, sexual, etc. control. The evil or inferior is associated with femininity, homosexuality, black or minority races and/or religious groups, subordinate classes, animality or the 'natural'/body, and sexual promiscuity. A quote from Paul Hoch (Hoch, 1979: 45) summarises these dualistic connections:

The conflict between hero and beast becomes a struggle between two understandings of manhood: human vs. animal, white vs. black, spiritual vs. carnal, soul vs. flesh, higher vs. lower, noble vs. base. These all correspond to the basic moral dichotomy that was assumed in order to provide legitimacy for the first hierarchical societies: the superior morality and manhood of 'civilized' and 'noble' upper class white heroes (who monopolize the functions of the soul and mind) in contrast with 'barbaric' and 'base' lower class villains (consigned to the merely animal realms of the carnal and the body). Similar dichotomies of heroes vs. villains, good vs. evil and light vs. dark were invoked to justify the struggle of Christian against infidel at the time of the Crusades; and, later, of colonizers against natives, cowboys against Indians, Texans against Mexicans, and Yanks against Communists in Vietnam.

Though Hoch inexplicably ignores the way the gender distinction between masculine and feminine is at the base of the dualist construction of 'manhood', radical feminists have been more explicit in drawing the connections between sexist, racist and classist dualisms. For example, Susan Griffin connects the dualist race/class dichotomous mind with the male chauvinist mind and argues that they are really identical:

> For the pornographic mind and the racist mind are really identical, both in the symbolic content and in the psychological purposes of the delusionary systems they express ... Through these systems of thought, the mind learns to deny the natural part of its own being. It learns to project this denied part of its own being onto another, playing out against this other its own ambivalence toward the natural self. So a woman is hated and loved, ridiculed, sought after, possessed, raped. And so, also, the black or the Jew is captured and brought into slavery, or exiled; owned or dispossessed; humiliated, excluded, attacked, and murdered. (Griffin, 1981b: 158)

Many Black nationalists have developed a universalist analysis of white Western racism that parallels radical feminist treatments of patriarchy. W.E.B. du Bois (1961) speaks of a 'double consciousness' that Afro-Americans must adopt to protect their basic self-respect (good in relation to the Black community, bad or inferior in relation to the white). The consequences of racist dualism on the internal self-definition of oppressed minorities is documented by Franz Fanon in *Black Skins, White Masks*:

> In the white world the man of color encounters difficulties in the development of his body schema. Consciousness of the body is solely a negating activity. It is a third person consciousness ... 'Mama, see the Negro! I'm frightened!' Frightened! Frightened! Now they were beginning to be afraid of me. I made up my mind to laugh myself to tears, but laughter had become impossible ... I was responsible at the same time for my body, for my race, for my ancestors. I subjected myself to an objective examination, I discovered my blackness, my ethnic character- istics; and I was battered down by tom-toms, cannibalism, intel- lectual deficiency, fetishism, racial defects, slave-ships, and above all else, above all: 'Sho' good eatin'. (Fanon, 1967: 110–12)

While this universalist critique of hierarchical dualism in our gender, racial, class and sexual symbolic codes may provide us with an understanding of the most general dichotomous structure that operates to define polar and oppositional positions in social practices, it misses their changing historical content and the consequent challenges to the dominant symbolic codes by oppositional codes. Therefore, it tends to portray a static and unchanging structure to gender, race/ethnic and class identities.

Even a cursory look at the history of sex/affective symbolic codes provides a very different picture. For example, 'good woman' in nineteenth-century European and American dominant sexual codes was equated with asexuality and spirituality. There was no concept of lesbian identity which could suggest that women could have sexual feelings toward each other. Close women friendships, even companions that lived together, were not stigmatised as they are in today's society (Faderman, 1981; Smith-Rosenberg, 1975). Thus, a direct challenge to the nineteenth-century patriarchal sex/affective code did not involve the same actions as it does today. Indeed, women dressing as men were much more of an immediate affront to the historically specific codes of masculinity and femininity than exclusive socialising with women – a situation which is nearly reversed today. To understand how to challenge our historically specific patriarchal (and racial) sex/affective codes, we must rely on more than generalisations about the dualist categorisations of the patriarchal (and white racist) minds.

There is a similar shift in the historical content of racist schemas. While nineteenth-century stereotypes of Afro-Americans in slave society supposed them to be animal-like beasts of burden, twentieth-century welfare state stereotypes suppose them to be non-working parasites (welfare mothers) and criminals (unemployed Black men and youth). The general feature that has remained constant through the shift from nineteenth- to twentieth-century racism is the view of minority races as super-sexed (Black women as promiscuous whores, and Black men as rapists of white women). This racial sex/affective structural analytic principle creates fear and jealousy which serves to divide white women from Black women and men, thus allowing white men to control all these subordinate groups. (For more on sexual racism, see Aphtheker, 1983; Carby, 1986; Cleaver, 1968; Firestone, 1970; Stember, 1976).

Sex/affective labour

One of the conceptual problems in conceiving of sex/affective
production on the model of economic production is that it implies
that nurturance, social bonding and sex are human material needs
which, since they must be produced, involve work. This may
seem counter-intuitive. After all most people think of sex as play,
or leisure, not work, with the obvious exception of paid prostitution. And though mothering is thought to involve some work
such as nappy changing and feeding, there is a question as to how
much of it is 'real' work because of the difficulty of drawing an
objective line between what is required (or socially necessary) and
what is leisure. For relating to a child out of love often involves
things one does with them for one's own enjoyment as well as the
wellbeing of the child. So if there is no way to decide what amount
of mothering energy is socially necessary for the wellbeing of the
child, how can we decide when mothering activity is leisure and
when it is work?

Part of the peculiarity of classifying mothering as work disappears if we note that there are similar problems of drawing the
line between work and leisure for all types of social production
that are pre-capitalist. That is, when goods and services are
produced for use rather than for sale, it is often harder to decide
which activities are socially necessary (hence part of a social/work
exchange) and which are extraneous. A farm family may require
that the wife put by some of the farm product for later consumption by canning it. But was it really necessary for her to can forty-
two jars of string beans?!

Similarly, a middle-class family may feel it socially necessary
for their small child to be read to every night to develop conceptual skills and an interest in reading necessary to do well in an
advanced industrial society. But how much reading is necessary?
The husband may particularly resent this activity on the part of
the wife if it noticeably interrupts nurturance he'd like to get after
his hard day's work. This connects to what we might call the
'mediation problem' of women trying to balance the sex/affective
needs of children and husband/mates, something that will be
further discussed in chapter eight.

Nancy Folbre has developed a model for comparing unpaid
housework and wage labour to give an overall assessment of the
equality or inequality of the gender exchange involved (Folbre,

1982). She distinguishes between work and leisure in unpaid household activity by referring to market equivalents and contextual expectations. So, if American childcare in the average middle-class childcare centre contains certain features, these can be said to be elements 'historically and morally' necessary to the reproduction of children in the middle class. Thus, housewives which do this work at home can be said to be doing work of comparable value. Similarly if a certain amount of sexual activity is the norm for married couples in a certain historical circumstance, then roughly that amount can be said to make life minimally sexually satisfying for those involved and thus to involve socially necessary labour.

If this way of dividing work from leisure is granted we have a theoretical model for how a patriarchal economy operates as an overlap between household and capitalist economies in our society. For if the total labour hours that women put into wage labour and unpaid sex/affective production are compared with those of men, it is clear that in all but the capitalist class[5] and countercultural family households women do more total work and receive fewer goods and less leisure than men, thus allowing men to appropriate a social surplus of goods, sex/affective labour and services from women.

It should be noted that such a way of dividing work from non-work involves two assumptions. First, there is the underlying assumption that work is activity necessary to meet basic human needs. This can be true even though the amount, objects and form of these needs (e.g. for orgiastic sex, affection and social bonding) varies in different forms of sex/affective production. Thus, we must broaden the underlying philosophical assumptions of Marxist materialism to suppose that the needs for social union involved in sex and nurturance are just as basic to human survival as eating, being clothed and having a roof over one's head. Though it is hard to establish this sort of claim empirically since there are such diverse ways in which societies allow people to meet their social bodily needs, some evidence of the thesis is that human babies require a minimum amount of affection in order to survive. Studies of orphans and autistic children support this claim.

We tend to think of work as activity which is unpleasurable, coerced or done merely instrumentally. But this attitude only mirrors the alienated conditions of wage labour under capitalism and not even all of that. Many people find ways to enjoy their work for its own sake anyway, particularly professionals who are writers and teachers. Such people might have just as difficult a time as a devoted mother in drawing a line between the necessary and non-necessary aspects of their work-related activity. As a feminist philosopher, am I working or playing when I read a feminist novel before sleeping?

It is consistent to hold that sex and nurturance are necessary human needs, that activity connected to achieving them is work, yet admit that what counts as satisfying these needs is historically relative.[6] Just as the poverty line and what counts as a minimum standard of living has been constantly rising in advanced capitalist countries, so the standard of what counts as an acceptable hetero-sexual sexual exchange has changed since the nineteenth century.

While the United States' Second Wave Women's Movement in the 1960s inaugurated a demand for equal access to orgasms for women in heterosexual interactions that had been absent previously, so the standard of what counts as an equal sexual exchange is presently under reconstruction among feminists today. Thus, one pole of the Women's Movement (the pluralist feminists) tends to hold that consensual sex focused on the goal of orgiastic bodily sexual pleasure for both (or all) partners is the mark of equal sexuality. The other pole, radical feminism, privileges the importance of equal initial power and choice (lack of domination) and expanding the depth of emotional intimacy for both partners. Whatever standard comes to be accepted by the majority will be (and it may well be a balance of both concerns) our future measure of sexual equality and the way we can distinguish equal from unequal sexual relations.

A second reason for characterising sex/affective activities as work is to acknowledge their centrality as a component of human identity and sense of self. The work/play distinction marks what society takes to be central features of one's social identity: what one does for a living (ones' work) connects to one's social status as well as one's social class, while what one does for leisure is thought to be an incidental or accidental aspect of one's identity. It is therefore important to categorise as work those activities women do at home which meet basic human needs. Not to do so keeps exploitation and domination relations in sex/affective production at home from being visible and thus perpetuates women's lesser social status.

The importance of seeing parenting as work is particularly important to understanding a contemporary shift in modes of sex/affective production. Delphy (1984) argues that a male-dominated family household economy persists after divorce in single mother-headed families. This s so for the vast majority of single mothers who are paid little c no child support and end up being saddled with the bulk of direct and indirect (breadwinner) parenting work. Thus, in many single mother families, male exploitation of women's sex/affective parenting labour actually increases although they are absent as husbands and fathers! This is a central structural feature of parenting under our contemporary system of public patriarchy.

The sex/affective labour that women do for wages and in the family has a distinctive character. By and large it involves mediating and nurturance skills that encourage women to identify with the interests of children, husbands or lovers, clients, patients and customers, thus making it difficult for women to take an oppositional stance of the sort necessary to acknowledge one's involvement in an exploitative exchange of labour. Thus, unlike the Marxist analysis of exploitative labour, a feminist approach must take account of the content of some gender labour, in particular that labour which involves sex/affective labour, and the way that it shapes women's perceptions of self and interests differently from men's. We can then distinguish between male and female sex/affective labour (gender labour) by both its contents and its social relations.

David Alexander (1987) has categorised four common clusters of skills of women's gender labour at home and in wage labour. These are physical maintenance labour, personality labour, nurturance labour and sexual labour. The skills of, and a gender identity interest in, all four types of labour are initially taught to women in the capitalist patriarchal forms of the family to meet the sex/affective needs of husbands, children and other kin there. Thus they can all be seen as species of sex/affective labour practised primarily by women and not by men.

By 'physical maintenance labour' is meant the direct care of people's bodily needs connected to physical health: feeding, cleaning and maintaining bodies and nursing the sick – babies, old people and patients. 'Personality labour' refers to skills of mediation learned to negotiate conflicts between family and kin members. 'Nurturance labour' refers primarily to the psychologi-

cal skills needed in mothering children and men: the ability to
listen, give advice about personal problems, help uncover,
process and resolve emotional conflicts. Finally 'sexual labour'
refers not only to explicit sexual servicing of men by women, but
flirting, physical appearance and other behaviours symbolically
coded as feminine sexual messages to enhance men's sense of
masculine self-worth.

Alexander argues that these skills are required to a greater
degree in women's wage labour occupations (secretary, waitress,
executive assistant, sales, elementary and secondary school teachers) than in men's. Furthermore he find these skills and services
more demanded when a workplace is extremely sex-segmented (as
when all or most waitpersons are women in a particular restau-
rant) than when the workplace involves mixed sex labour. Not
only are sex-segmented workplaces more exploitative from any
worker's point of view regardless of gender (less unionised, less
workers' control over the process of work, less security, etc.),
they are also more male dominant (more sexual harassment,
topdown authority wielded by male bosses and supervisors, etc.).

Though Alexander points out some ways in which women's
non-waged work in the home has simply been transferred to wage
labour, he does not think that the 'extension' thesis (the view that
women's work in the home is simply transferred with similar
content to wage labour) is in general valid because of the historical
exceptions given by Davies (1979).[7] Here I part company with
him, for I would argue that the extension thesis captures an
important truth: that in general wage labour, like household
labour, consists of the material contents and sexual symbolic
codes of gendered sex/affective labour. The exceptions show only
that women may sometimes accidentally be assigned work not
initially connected with gender labour in the family, often for the
simple reason that as an already oppressed group they are easier to
exploit than men. When this happens, however, as in the switch
from male to female secretaries, the work usually takes on the
additional sex/affective implications of gender labour in the home
(cf. Weinbaum, 1983). When occasionally men come to dominate
a type of wage labour hitherto done in the home by women (e.g.
chefs), the social meaning of the work alters in keeping with the
symbolic codes for gender labour. Thus, male chefs are not seen
to be nurturing their customers by providing them with a loving
and basic material service; rather, they are showing their culinary

skills (in implicit competition with other chefs) in creating an aesthetic taste delight thought of as a work of art! Cooking seen as serving others has subtly shifted to a professional skill that in no way implies the subordination of the one providing the service.

The operation of the extension thesis of gender labour is the functional way that patriarchal sex/affective production in conjunction with the capitalist system both reproduces itself and alters the development of the capitalist labour process in so doing. Women thus become more docile workers in both systems since their sex/affective labour, whether paid or unpaid, directly and indirectly serves men, as lovers, co-workers or capitalists, by catering to their need for masculine authority and by providing them with more control over and benefits from sexual, nurturant and economic exchanges.[8]

Conclusion

This chapter has presented the theoretical concept of a sex/affective production system, described the attendant concepts of sexuality and work assumed by the theory, and distinguished between the universal and historical aspects of sex/affective production systems. In the next chapter we shall demonstrate in more detail how the use of such a theory helps us to locate different modes of patriarchal sex/affective production in US history.

5

US patriarchies, past and present

In order to demonstrate the explanatory power of the claim that different forms of male dominance are grounded in different modes of sex/affective production, I want to contrast our contemporary system of male dominance, capitalist public patriarchy, with the modes of sex/affective production which have been co-extensive with earlier phases of capitalist development: capitalist father and husband patriarchy respectively. Though pre-capitalist societies can have their own forms of father patriarchy, modes of sex/affective production differ from capitalist social formations since in the former economic production is centred in family and kin networks. In pre-capitalist societies kin relations not only organise parenting, sexual and social bonding relations; they also organise the economy itself.

In all human systems of sex/affective production to date marriages have been the primary means to define the sexual, parenting and work exchanges between women and men. In patriarchal sex/affective production systems the terms of marriage (asymmetrical kin exchange of women, male ownership and control of property and economic resources, and male control of women's sexuality and reproductive decisions) are one important base for male dominance. Women in pre- and early capitalist patriarchal societies have a legal and social position in the family similar to slaves. Though some women, and slaves, may be well treated, wives have little if any legal rights or guarantees (Leghorn and Parker, 1981).[1]

Many family historians (Aries, 1962; Shorter, 1975; Stone, 1977) have suggested that there was a shift in internal family relationships in the transition from feudalism to capitalism. Though aristocratic, craft and peasant families all had somewhat different organisations, they shared one important feature that families in contemporary capitalist systems do not. This is that

relations between the generations were more formal and hierarchical than they were intimate and affectional. The concept of
filial obligations, the obedience children owed their parents and
the economic/political alliances or services they could provide for
them, stood in place of our modern notion that parents and
children should share love and intimacy between each other.
Some family historians have found the difference so striking as to
categorise the modern family as the 'sentimental' family, and to
connect modern notions of romance in marriage with those of the
special intimacy and love between parents and children.[2]

It can be argued that such differences in the institution of the
family connect to different modes of sex/affective production and
different social formations. A feudal economy (as a middle level
category) is a system of production for use in which peasant families are the producers for themselves and the families of the
nobility. Particular feudal social formations, such as Western
Europe from the fifth to the twelfth century, involve other
exploiter economic classes, e.g. the Catholic Church priesthood,
and other subordinate classes, such as soldiers and servants. Patriarchal feudal sex/affective production consists of the differing
patriarchal relations between men and women in two or more subordinate modes of the social formation; for example, the peasant
family, the aristocratic family, the monastery and nunnery. These
families, although they differ from each other, are more similar
than the bourgeois 'sentimental' family characteristic of middle
and advanced capitalism, in that they involve formal rather than
sentimental relations between family members.

In my view, the shift from the formal to the sentimental family
form coincides with the shift from one mode of sex/affective
production to another: that is, the shift from father to husband
patriarchy. The interpersonal dynamic between parents, children
and mates will obviously be different when affectionate connections are present, and valued, or absent; when they are exclusive,
as in the nuclear family, or not exclusive, as when children are
cared for by wet nurses, nannies or extended kin networks.
Sexual intercourse to produce heirs will have a different dynamic
when children (and sexual energy between partners) are valued
for their own sakes rather than simply for instrumental reasons.

There have been three main periods of male dominant sex/
affective production in the history of the United States from the
colonial period forward. Each of these periods involves a different

sort of patriarchal relationship between men, women and children and each of them has its different basic mechanism for maintaining male dominance. In the colonial period, father patriarchy was reproduced by fathers' legal and economic control of children's marriages and inheritance through family property vested in sons, not daughters. In the romantic Victorian period, husband patriarchy was reproduced by the institution of the 'family wage', which was vested in husbands who were the family breadwinners.

Our contemporary form of male dominance in advanced capitalist societies differs from pre- and early capitalist forms because the male control of women in family kinship networks, importantly weakened through capitalist development (Mitchell, 1974; Rubin, 1975), now requires more subtle and extensive reinforcement by state welfare regulations and media influence. Thus I follow the lead of Carol Brown (1981) and term our present period 'public patriarchy'.

Public patriarchies are modes of sex/affective production characteristic of modern industrial states, whether they are capitalist or state socialist societies. In public patriarchy, men still have control over women in many family situations through an unequal division of family waged and unwaged labour (the so-called 'second shift' problem of working mothers), through domestic violence and through the relative power in family decision-making that their higher paid wage labour brings. Nonetheless, the primary social mechanisms of control over women now lie not in the direct power of men in the family but in the public mechanisms of the patriarchal welfare state. These include the gender segregation of wage labour, state controls over women's physical and mental health and biological reproduction, and the exploitation of all mothers' unpaid childrearing labour (Folbre, 1985). Another aspect of patriarchal sex/affective production in contemporary capitalist social formations involves the mass media's gender stereotyping and sexual objectification of women in a context of sexual consumerism. Let us consider each period in greater detail.[3]

Period 1: father patriarchy

Most of feudal Europe and the European settlers in the colonial US were organised by father patriarchies. Father patriarchies are modes of sex/affective production coextensive with feudal and independent rural modes of economic production. In such societies fathers exercise coercive control over the resources of the family economy (itself the only available source of income other than the army or the church) available to their children. Households are usually not nuclear but extended in two senses: first, they may contain the older generation relatives and unmarried relatives; second, they may contain servants and apprentices, usually young relatives 'put out' from their family of origin to learn a trade.

In such extended family households, some class relations were often internal to the household: the father was the master not only to his own children and wife but to indentured servants and young apprentices. In the South under slavery, his situation was even more despotic, since he had slaves over whom he had complete sexual and reproductive control.

The father in the father-patriarchal household owned the family property and dispensed it at will to his children, the land to sons and a lesser dowry to daughters. The father was the religious/moral head of the household. Children needed their father's permission to marry and were completely dependent on his largesse in inheritance. A woman's sexuality was controlled first by her father, then by her husband or male relatives if she remained single.

Although a small artisan class grew with the rise of commercial capitalism and urban centres, which afforded men of the subsumed servant class an escape from patriarchal domination in the rural family household, it was not possible for a woman, regardless of economic class, to have any economic independence unless she was a widow and could take over her husband's trade, business or land.

In seventeenth-century New England, the particular social formation of Puritan father patriarchy makes a fascinating study because there are indications that even though mothers did the major part of childrearing, they had less power over mothering than did their descendants in nineteenth-century New England households (Stewart, 1981).[4] Not only did Calvinism hold suspect an intense mother/child bond because of the mother's assumed greater susceptibility to bodily sin than the father, there was also the pervasive practice of 'breaking the will' that was practised on children, usually by fathers, at the age of two to three years old: a practice that would also tend to weaken the mother/child bond (Demos, 1970). Of course, we may conjecture that not all of the attempts to break the mother/child bond were successful in Puritan society. Erikson (1966) has suggested a fascinating psychoanalytic interpretation of the Salem witch trials which sees both witchcraft practices and the denunciations of witchcraft in these trials as a subversive resistance by women against patriarchy.[5]

Father patriarchy is still characteristic of some families, particularly ethnic, religious and racial minorities, in rural production today. For example, Celie in Alice Walker's *The Color Purple* (1982a) was given in marriage without her consent to Mr Albert by her step-father. Celie and the older generation in her family assume that her father and husband have a right to control her sexuality and reproduction (including removing Celie's children for adoption without her consent). The patriarchal double standard assumed by Albert, however, allows him to bring his mistress to live in the house with his wife while the latter is not allowed the opportunity for any other sexual liasons.

Period 2: husband patriarchy

Major shifts in maternal childrearing practices, changed attitudes toward childhood, the elimination of the system of putting children in other families as apprentices and the shift from arranged to voluntary marriages mark the change from father to husband patriarchy. Husband patriarchy is characterised by a public/private split between home and capitalist production, by mostly nuclear households with wage-earning or entrepreneurial husbands, and non-wage earning housewife wives/mothers and children.

American society witnessed such a transformation after the American Revolution and through the Jacksonian period for bourgeois families, and somewhat later for working-class immigrant families. Though slavery in the South was preserved as a pre-capitalist enclave, the shift from rural production and commercial capitalism to industrial capitalism was rapidly occurring during this period.

There are several reasons to believe that the shift from father to husband patriarchy marked a decisive shift from one mode of sex/affective production to another. In particular, the shifts in the ideology and practices of motherhood, childhood and the norms for masculine and feminine love, marriage and sexuality/ reproduction are striking. These shifts created a separate sphere of 'women's work' and expertise in the home. Women's work was accorded a social value not present in father patriarchy. The First Wave Women's Movement is evidence that women were not loathe to use this improved status to seek liberation from male domination in reproduction, the economy and other areas hitherto socially controlled by men.[6]

Capitalist development undermined the system of father patriarchy by providing jobs in wage labour for children who wished to escape parental control over economic resources. Thus, fathers' ability to control children's marital decisions was weakened. The corresponding ideology of possessive individualism (MacPherson, 1962) displaced the earlier feudal organic world view of natural purposes in which the natural female role of biological reproduction was to be controlled by male authorities in arranged marriages rather than being freely chosen.

Progressive individualism emphasises the value of the individual's voluntary contractual decisions over tradition or biology. This suggests that marriage for love is preferable to arranged marriage. The ideology of romance develops as men's and women's work becomes so separate, given the division between the domestic and waged work spheres, that men and women of the propertied (bourgeois) classes can only develop a mystified (and idealistic) idea of what each other are like!

A new ideology of motherhood and sexuality came into existence in American history during the 1840s: the 'moral motherhood' and 'cult of domesticity' paradigm (Ryan, 1975). In this ideology, which, as we shall see, did not refer to all women, women were no longer conceived as inferior helpmates to men. Rather, women were 'moral mothers'. The domestic world was now conceived as a separate sphere and motherhood as a chosen vocation, one that required specialised skills: moral perception, intuition and emotional connection. Men could not achieve these skills, for they were constrained to act within the public sphere of the capitalist market place. This required that men develop the skills necessary to survive there: egoism, individualism, cunning and immorality. Instead of natural mothers who subjected themselves to the superior moral authority of men (the ideology of father patriarchy), women had become the chosen mothers, the moral and spiritual superiors of men in the protected sphere of the home.

Corresponding to the change in the conception of motherhood was the creation of the modern conception of childhood as a fragile time of growth and immaturity sharply distinct from adulthood. Philippe Aries (1962) and other family historians argue that this idea arose first in the late eighteenth and nineteenth centuries in bourgeois homes with a sharp separation between the public world of men's work and women's private domesticity. A new emphasis on the importance of the maternal care of the biological mother for the moral growth and physical health of children developed, but only after extensive educational campaigns which were necessary to challenge the prevalent practice among the gentry of sending children out for wet nursing (Badinter, 1981).

In husband patriarchy not only did women gain immensely in status compared to father patriarchy, they also increased their power to control their sex/affective relationships. While the First Wave Women's Movement is one sort of evidence of women's increased expectations for legal, social and economic equality, Daniel Scott Smith (1974) also suggests that the sharply limited fertility rates of bourgeois women in the nineteenth century mark what he calls 'domestic feminism', i.e. women's increased control over reproductive sexuality.

From the sex/affective production paradigm, we can further develop Smith's insight about women's increased power *vis-à-vis* men in reproductive control. The reduced fertility rates for bourgeois women suggest that women had gained power over reproductive work compared to their situation in father patriarchy. For reducing fertility increased their control over mothering work. Reduced fertility not only means less risks of maternal mortality, but the possibility of increased attention to each child.

The public/private sexual division of labour in the bourgeois nuclear family creates a conflictual 'sex/affective' triangle in incorporative commitments for mothers that is not present for fathers. In capitalist patriarchal societies it serves mothers' interests to favour sex/affective relations with children over those to mates/fathers, for these latter do not have the possibilities for mothers' control and/or egalitarian exchanges that the former do.

Thus, mothers have an interest in supporting the new ideologies of motherhood and childhood, for they legitimate the increase of sex/affective energy between mother and child at the expense of sex/affective energy between father and mother, thus giving women increased bargaining power in sex/affective power relationships.[7] If women are seen primarily as mothers yet naturally uninterested in sexuality for its own sake, then it is justified for women to try to regulate men's sexuality, and their own reproduction, so as to enhance both the increased quality of each existing mother/child relationship by holding down the numbers of children, and to emphasise the greater importance of emotional intimacy (involving skills in which women are taught to excel) over genital sexuality (men's goal) in mating relationships.

The women's social movements of the late nineteenth century used the moral motherhood/asexual woman ideology to demand changes in public and private sex/affective power relations between men and women. The voluntary motherhood and social purity movements used the notion of the morally pure, asexual woman to insist that sexuality should be controlled by women not men. As Linda Gordon has pointed out (Gordon, 1976: ch. 5) this was not necessarily because advocates of social purity were opposed to sexuality *per se*. Rather, they argued that sexuality needed to be controlled by women in order to bring men under the same standard of sexual morality as women, thus eliminating the double standard. Not only was this designed to allow women to control the timing and frequency of genital intercourse so as to give more control over private reproductive sexuality. Further, since male sexual promiscuity was conceived to be the source of female prostitution, women's superior moral control over sex was also hypothesised to be an essential part of the campaign to eliminate women's public sexual slavery in male-controlled prostitution.

The nineteenth-century emphasis on women's spirituality and Platonic friendships over their sexual loverships was a reversal of the priorities most heterosexual women today place on sex/affective relationships. But this was not necessarily against women's sex/affective interests, given the strength of husband patriarchy at the time. Rather, given that heterosexual genital relationships were usually unsatisfactory (no sex education and little communication between men and women because of the great differences in their work worlds), it is not surprising that the affectionate relations that women had with other women most often involved higher levels of erotic energy than did relations, whether genital or affectionate, with men (Faderman, 1981; Sahli, 1979).

Again, as we have argued, the primacy of the mother/child bond over the heterosexual couple bond in bourgeois families involved a similar concentration of sex/affective energy. Thus, we need not assume that Victorian women's lives were devoid of sex/affective gratification in comparison with colonial or contemporary women; nor that women had 'given up' sex in order to get control of mothering. As feminists have argued in criticism of Freud's theories, close maternal relationships, involving breast feeding and physical affection, are intensely sexual (Begus, 1987; Rossi, 1975; Weisskopf, 1980). Only male theorists obsessed with heterosexual intercourse as the goal and aim of human sexuality and ignoring the breast as an erogenous zone for women could suppose that the incest taboo actually succeeds in preventing sexual exchanges between mother and children (although it does create guilt about these exchanges!).

American bourgeois women in the post-Jacksonian nineteenth century may have gained power in sex/affective production compared to their ancestors in earlier father patriarchy by emphasising non-genital but intensely erotic and affectionate relations with children and other women. But in changed historical conditions it also seems true that the twentieth-century sexual revolution, particularly the lesbian-feminist validation of explicit sexual relations between women, contains a radical potential for increasing women's power and control in sex/affective exchanges. This is true even though much of the theory and practice of sexologists and advocates of sexual freedom have been male-dominant (Campbell, 1980; Jackson, 1983; Jeffreys, 1985; Simons, 1979).

Class and race differences in motherhood and sexuality

The romantic/Victorian ideology of moral motherhood was a tool used by northern, white, middle-class Protestant women to aid in the transformation of sex/affective production from father to husband patriarchy. It was the development of a new ideology that increased their power over the production and distribution of sex/affective energy so as to raise the relative quantity of sex/affective energy they received from children and homosocial networks. But by the end of the nineteenth century, the moral motherhood ideology was almost universally accepted by white working-class families as well. This was ironic, since the emphasis that the romantic/Victorian ideology placed on women being at home where their standards of sexual purity could be enforced on husbands legitimised sexual violence and harassment against working-class women who were forced, for economic reasons, to work outside the home.

For Black women the moral motherhood ideology has two dimensions of racist control: the background of slavery and economic necessity. The historical background of slavery in which Afro-American women were raped by white owners in order to produce more slaves created the material base for a racial-sexual stereotype of Black women as bestial and sexual. Motherhood for them was not, like that for 'full' (white) humans, a chosen career, but a natural, involuntary process as it is for all beasts of burden. The image is created of Black people mating (and being bred) like dogs.

Under this stereotype, Black women could not be expected to be moral authorities like white mothers. Rather, they could care for the white mistress's children under her moral supervision. Thus Black women as mothers are seen as servants caring for white children rather than mothers in authority caring for their own children.

Thorstein Veblen provides one explanation for working-class acceptance of the bourgeois moral motherhood ideology (Veblen, 1973). This is that the ability of a man to support a woman in 'conspicuous leisure' (i.e. as a non-wage working housewife) becomes a mark of masculine as well as class status. Heidi Hartmann, as we have already seen, provides a more materialist explanation (Hartmann, 1979, 1981a). Nineteenth-century organised trade union movements led by skilled male workers attempted to create a family wage in order to protect their challenged interests as family patriarchs. A family wage which allowed a husband to support a non-wage earning wife and children performed two functions of patriarchal control: it cut competition from non-unionised women wage workers and it allowed men to keep their wives at home to provide personal services not so easily forthcoming when women have to deal with the problem of the second shift.

Though Hartmann overemphasises the effects of 'family wage' bargains (which were never generally achieved by all sectors of the working class) we can see these agreements as indeed 'bargains' struck by male capitalists, upper-middle class women reformers and skilled male workers, which served each group's interests. The capitalists gain because their new concern to reproduce a skilled labour force led them to emphasise public schooling and home childcare for children, care most economically provided free by working-class mothers. Skilled male trade union workers get to keep their wives at home to preserve their patriarchal privileges over them. And upper-middle class women reformers protect the sacred sphere of women in the home, and their increased informal sex/affective power there, by promoting the ideological function of mothers protecting children under their care.

It is important to note that contemporary changes in the married women's wage labour force have changed the historic dynamic in which women could in fact gain power as mothers by remaining home with children. Working-class white women historically did gain power as mothers by the institution of the family wage and protective legislation, but they also lost the power that being economically independent/less dependent on men brings to women who are waged. Black women, however, never gained any power from family wage legislation, for Black men were largely excluded from unions (Joseph, 1981). So Black male unemployment and low wages was and is one of the reasons so many Black married women worked and work in wage labour.

The development of capitalist public patriarchy

Four important developments have occurred in twentieth-century advanced capitalist societies that have broken the hegemony of husband patriarchy and created the transition to capitalist public patriarchy.[8] These are: the development of consumerist capitalism and the joint wage-earner family; a relative transfer of power from individual husbands over wives to male professionals (doctors, therapists, social workers) in the welfare state and to women's male bosses in wage labour; the rise of single mother-headed and other alternative households; and finally, the new sexual consumerism (the so-called 'sexual revolution'), including mass production of birth control devices and man-made reproductive technology, a new symbolic code of sexual categories and possibilities, and mass media use of gender and sexual images.

Consumer capitalism and the two pay cheque family

Advanced capitalism has developed a so-called labour aristocracy of privileged workers in the first world countries of the US and Europe, built on the colonial and neo-colonial exploitation of third world countries. Through union struggles, many (mostly white male) American workers come to have relative security and some government protection for collective bargaining rights. Corporations seeking new markets create mass advertising and create new consumer needs (cf. Ewen, 1976). These new standards of consumption, many of which become materially necessary under new conditions of work – for example, suburban housing and no mass transportation require workers to own cars – then put pressure on women, already temporarily drawn into the waged workforce during the two world wars, to work part- or full-time in wage labour to allow families to increase their consumer spending.

The two pay cheque family has displaced the old capitalist patriarchal nuclear family (CPNF) of male breadwinner, female housewife and dependent children characteristic of husband patriarchy. Indeed only from 10–15 per cent of family households at any one time exemplify the old CPNF form. But the new joint wage-earning family has undermined the family wage bargain struck in the late nineteenth century without, however, liberating women from male control and exploitation. Rather, the new second shift problem of how to handle childcare, housework and wage work creates a new level of material exploitation of women.

Though capitalist development has removed many of the tasks associated with mothering maintenance work under husband patriarchy from the home (e.g. sewing, mending, cooking, gardening, nursing children and old people are tasks for which commodities or services available for money can be substituted), these same tasks are now being done mostly by women in sex segregated wage labour (and often still in cottage industry) for low pay and in non-unionised situations. Furthermore, as Ehrenreich and English (1979) note, the rise of the male-dominated medical profession in the late nineteenth and early twentieth centuries diminished the control women had in health care and childbearing (by eliminating midwifery and substituting impersonal male doctors in hospitals under alienated conditions: Rich, 1976). Child nurturing and mothers' power to teach (and create) children in their own image are weakened by the power of the public schools to undercut parental authority.

Another source for the undermining of the CPNF which has been particularly noticeable in the transition of American family life from the 1950s to the 1980s is the increasing disillusionment of middle-class men with this lifestyle. Barbara Ehrenreich argues that the development of the playboy mentality began with the beat movement of the late 1950s and continued through the 1960s (Ehrenreich, 1983). According to Ehrenreich, the so-called sexual revolution of this period, as well as the 'human potential' movement which followed (i.e. various forms of pop therapy) are all expressions of the flight from commitment of men who, in a consumerist society, no longer wanted to be saddled with the maintenance of a housewife and children. The increase in divorces, later marriages, and more second and third marriages are obviously developments that add to the increase of women's wage labour and the development of the two pay cheque family.

Mothers and children in public patriarchy

Although public patriarchy is in some disarray with respect to sexual symbolic codes, with respect to children there is a new accord between capitalists and political male elites that has displaced the 'family wage' accord characteristic of husband patriarchy (Hartmann, 1981a). This accord, which gives women greater power over our sexuality and our children at the expense of less economic support from men as husbands and fathers, was fuelled by the change in the status of children characteristic of consumer capitalism.

Carol Brown (Brown, 1981) argues that children have become an economic and social liability rather than a benefit to their parents.[9] In this context, created by public schooling and child labour laws, men gain by shifting the financial and labour burden of children onto mothers. Thus, what seems to be an advance or a victory for women, the change from 'father right' characteristic of nineteenth-century divorce law to the 'mother right' typical of twentieth-century cases, is in actuality a breakdown of paternal obligations toward children. Women have won a 'right' to child custody that merely guarantees an added unequal burden compared to fathers: not only bearing the total burden of the sex/

affective work involved in raising children, but in addition being 'the breadwinner', if only via welfare payments, as well.[10] Increasingly, the production of children has become a public not a private investment (Folbre, 1985), but one for which society (particularly men and single women) refuses to pay a reasonable share of the costs or to allow the majority of the primary producers (mothers) reasonable pay or good working conditions (cf. also Delphy, 1984)!

One of the most striking effects of the rise of single motherhood in the United States, combined with the patriarchal division of wage labour and minimal welfare, health and childcare services for low income families is the feminisation of poverty. Over one half of poor families are headed by women, while half the children in single mother families and 68 per cent of Black and other minority families are poor (Ehrenreich, Stallard and Sklar, 1983). This shows the combined sexist and racist effects of white supremacist capitalist patriarchy.

Many of the single mother families are newly poor: women who have lost their economic class standing because of divorce (Sidel, 1986). This is further evidence of the way that women's economic class standing is dependent on their sexual and marital services to men, and shows how capitalist public patriarchy, by creating children as public goods but refusing to take public responsibility for them and their caretakers' needs, ends up creating a new sex/affective production system which is exploitative to women in impersonal rather than personal ways. For single mother households, no longer is the father/mate in the household demanding personal and sexual services. But then the woman is forced to shoulder the double burden of breadwinning and childcare with no personal help from the man, and minimal (if any) state help.

The economic and social developments of advanced capitalist patriarchy have importantly changed both the scope and the meaning of parenthood. In pre-capitalism and early capitalism, children, though they may have been an economic responsibility when very young, soon began to repay the labour invested in their care as they became involved in productive work and/or were used in marriage alliances to enhance the general fortunes of their family of origin. In advanced capitalism, on the other hand, children have become commodities. That is, they no longer can be expected to contribute much if anything toward the economic upkeep of their parents.

In addition, parents of all classes find their parenting responsibilities extended to cover a new economic and psychological stage of development which public schooling and child labour laws has created between childhood and adulthood: adolescence. The parameters of adolescence stretch from puberty (when most young people in the pre-modern period would have been married or away from families of origins as servants or apprentices) to high school graduation and beyond for children of the middle class and above who are in college. It is a state of 'infantilised' economic dependence on parents which is highly contradictory. It is contradictory since young people are treated as if they are consuming adults by the mass media yet are forced to be economically dependent because of school requirements and age and minimum wage restrictions on full-time wage labour.

Sexual consumerism and the 'sexual revolution'

The increasing acceptance of premarital sex, a climbing divorce rate, a greater permissibility for 'nice' women to be engaged in sex outside of marriage, some acceptance in liberal areas of lesbian and gay sexuality, a proliferation of sexually explicit material for popular entertainment and relatively easy access to some form of artificial birth control have led many to suppose that there has been a sexual revolution which has benefited both men and women by allowing for freer sexual expression and self-determination than in societies characterised by family patriarchies.

However, this so-called sexual revolution has had contradictory results with respect to increasing women's sexual power and self-determination *vis-à-vis* men. Though these changes have provided new opportunities for feminist countercultural networks and alternative sex/affective family and household forms, men can also be seen to be consolidating power over women in other ways.

Much feminist debate has centred around the proliferation of sexualised images of women in the mass media, not only in sexual advertising and in male-directed pornography of all sorts, but also in such sentimentalised literature as the female-directed Harlequin romance (Snitow, 1983). This debate will be discussed further in chapters seven and ten. My view is that these images of women are on the whole sexually objectifying and, therefore, supportive of a collective, impersonal, male control of women's bodies. This is, indeed, one of the important sources of the public patriarchal ideology of women as men's sexual possessions even outside of marriage. Nonetheless, there are contradictions in the media messages, some of which express women's resistance to male domination and others which empower women (Modleski, 1982; Webster, 1981).

Within the nuclear family context itself, the sexual revolution may have increased the sexual satisfaction afforded to women but at the expense of their power to say 'no' as well as their power as mothers. The late 1920s and 1930s saw the popularisation of Freudian ideas through the development of a new liberal ideal of the 'companionate marriage' (Simons, 1979). This involved a new domestic ideal of 'mom' as sexy housewife. Mental health within the family required that mothers balance their affectionate involvement with their children by an equally intense, sexually intimate and affectionately involving relationship with their husbands. Women who attempted to resort to nineteenth-century methods of controlling sexual intercourse by resisting husbands' advances could now be labelled 'frigid' and 'castrating women'. Women who preferred the company of their children to that of their husbands were 'narcissistic', had 'separation problems', were causing sons to become homosexuals by tying them to their apron strings, and in general were damaging their children's health by excessive 'momism' (Ehrenreich and English, 1979). Finally women who prefer homosocial friendship networks to social time with their husbands, a practice taken for granted in the nineteenth century, can now be stigmatised as 'sexually repressed', or even worse, as lesbians, a concept which didn't exist in the nineteenth century (Ferguson, 1981b; Jackson, 1983; Jeffreys, 1985; Weeks, 1979, 1981; and cf. chapter nine).

Nonetheless the ideas that women are also sexual beings, and that heterosexuality is learned, not innately given, have been used to create greater sexual autonomy by women in contemporary American society. The assumption that heterosexuality is inevitable due to the need to produce children for material survival is no longer plausible in advanced industrial societies. This, plus the increased availability of birth control devices, allows women of all classes greater reproductive control and has also created a change in the sexual symbolic code: the concept of sexuality becomes functionally separated from the concept of procreation. This not only legitimates the idea of sexuality for its own sake – sex for pleasure not for babies – it also makes lesbians and gays importantly a cultural vanguard of this new attitude toward sex (Altman, 1983).

The new attitude toward sexuality and reproduction has increased women's autonomy in the United States more than other capitalist industrialised countries such as England, Ireland and Italy where the Church and the patriarchal family are more firmly entrenched. Perhaps this is a product of a nation primarily of immigrants with more mobility from families of origins and consequent increased individualism, and the greater consumerism that great American wealth allows even to members of the working class. Whatever the reasons Americans in general now have a freer choice with respect to whether they want to engage in marriage itself, and a greater initial bargaining power when entering into marriage. Lesbian subcultures have allowed women to escape from personal control by male kin and lovers (cf. chapter nine). The possibility of wage labour jobs and welfare payments that will economically support women have allowed women to divorce men and to obtain increased possibilities for personal autonomy and sexual satisfaction in their subsequent relationships.

Though women's sexual and reproductive autonomy has been importantly increased in US capitalist patriarchy, the situation is still a contradictory one for women. One can analyse the massive increase in the male pornography industry in the US from the 1970s to the 1980s (from 5 million to 5 billion dollars) in two different ways. Either one can see it as a relatively benign male fantasy 'backlash' to the increased sexual autonomy of women (Soble, 1986) or else as a determined attempt by male chauvinists to sexually objectify women so as to legitimise sado-masochistic gender roles in heterosexual sex (Dworkin, 1981; Dworkin and MacKinnon, 1985; MacKinnon, 1983, 1987).

Though it cannot presently be proved which of these two analyses is correct, the sexual symbolic code as presented in the public media is clearly a site of contestation, with sexist images in male pornography, sexual advertising, romance and family TV shows alternating with the strong feminist images of such rock stars as Tina Turner, movies with strong heroines such as Sigourney Weaver in 'Alien' and androgynous male images such as Michael Jackson. In addition, the New Right's attempts to regulate pornography so as to curtail all sexually explicit images of women can be seen as an attempt to circumvent any of the gains in sexual autonomy by women by reverting to the Victorian asexual image of women.

What such contradictory impulses show is that capitalist public patriarchy, lacking as forceful a male power over women as those systems of private patriarchy based on male control of women in the family, is in a perpetual crisis with respect to male control of sex/affective production via sexual symbolic codes. Women's increased bargaining power in some economic aspects of our lives in advanced capitalist societies has unravelled the automatic recreation of patriarchal compulsory heterosexual desire (and its attendant sexual symbolic codes) in the family. The old concept of any unattached woman as 'loose' (whether a spinster, divorcee, lesbian or prostitute) has lost much of its social stigma and power to keep women in line. Consequently various male elites (from the New Right patriarchal networks to the more liberal male-bonding circles of mass media image producers and users) do not agree on how best to draw the symbolic line between 'good' and 'bad' women that can maintain the hierarchical flow of sex/affective energy from women to men on male terms. From this it does not follow that male-produced sexist media images of women have no power: what it shows is that feminists have a unique historical opportunity to influence the creation of sexual symbolic codes to undermine male dominance if we can take advantage of the disarray in patriarchal sex/affective production.

Conclusion

We can conclude that the relative bargaining power of women *vis-à-vis* men in American public patriarchy presents a contradictory situation. Women have both powers and vulnerabilities. In contrast to modes of sex/affective production based on family patriarchies, women in public patriarchy tend to have more gender power to the degree that they are sex/affectively unattached to the family institutions of marriage and motherhood. Thus, though there are still some upper- and middle-class women who gain economic privileges through their marriages to wealthy men, such a choice by itself is no longer so obviously in the best economic self-interest of women.

That it is no longer so obviously in the economic self-interest of

women to marry has undermined the material base of the patriarchal sex/affective code that women should be subject to male
sexual desire rather than sexual actors in our own right. As such,
it has been one of the sparks of the second wave Women's
Movement. On the other hand, the increasing influence of the
fashion industry and mass media on sexual consumerism continues to support the patriarchal status quo by re-creating gender
stereotypes of man as sexual consumer, woman as consumed
object. These pervasive images come to fill the empty spaces of
sexual desire vacated by the breakdown of the 'companionate
marriage' ideology discussed earlier.

Though Catherine MacKinnon overstates the case by lumping
all media gender stereotypes in with male pornography (MacKinnon, 1987), there is an important way that gender media images
have become an essential for heterosexual sexuality. Since the
capitalist patriarchal nuclear family has given way to a raft of
alternative family forms, another material base is required to
perpetuate the heterosexual 'masquerade' of the innate attraction
between men and women (Lacan, 1982). Since the contents of
heterosexual desire are socially learned and there is no longer a
hegemonic patriarchal family to provide the content of masculinity and femininity, there must be some other social arena which
teaches males and females what the opposite sex desire from
them. Thus, fashion and media images, once merely the perpe-
tuators of images generated by the patriarchal family, have
become the semi-autonomous social arena in which sexist and
heterosexist desire are constructed.

However, since the images that are constructed contain some
which are empowering and some which reproduce male dominance, women (and men) have the opportunity to discount the
oppressive images, particularly if we have sex/affective peer networks, in adolescence and adulthood, which provide us with a
means of escape from the patriarchal moulders of sexual desire.

This chapter shows that positing modes of sex/affective production can periodise American history to pinpoint different
mechanisms reproducing male dominance in those periods, some
of the historical forms of resistance to that dominance and some
possibilities for ongoing resistance today.

6

Women as a new radical class in the United States

In previous chapters it has been argued that we must develop the concept of modes of patriarchal sex/affective production and, more specifically, see our present society as a capitalist public patriarchy in order to understand our contemporary form of male dominance. This chapter will expand further on the implications for the revolutionary agency of women today. To do so, we must develop a philosophical theory of the self that can both account for the effect on individuals of social systems of oppression and posit the historical conditions under which people who are dominated by such systems are able to radically challenge them.

Such a task requires a discussion of social domination and resistance. I shall present a 'tri-systems' theory of the semi-autonomous yet interdependent workings of racism, patriarchy and capitalism in contemporary US society which incorporates yet tries to go beyond the insights of classical Marxism, Freudianism and radical feminism. The standard Marxist idea of an exclusive class position for each individual no longer captures the complicated and contradictory reality of productive relations in racist capitalist public patriarchy. Rather, there are at least four different historically developed class relationships that can characterise a person at the same time: race class, sex class, family class and individual economic class. Given the appropriate historical conditions, an individual's subordinate class role in any one of these aspects can serve as the material base for personal development of revolutionary agency. The chapter will conclude by arguing that women in capitalist public patriarchy are in the appropriate historical conditions to develop into a group with revolutionary agency.

The self, personal identity and aspects

According to the theory developed here, human selfhood as well
as sex/affective desires are not fixed givens. There is neither a
single focus for bodily sexuality nor a unified self which can be
seen to 'lack' certain others. Freud is correct to suppose both a
polymorphous perverse sexuality and a split self, with layers of
conscious and unconscious desires, many of which are in conflict.
One's sense of self is, as he thought, importantly relational: one is
defined by one's desires which in turn relate one to desired
objects. The repression of sexual desires and interests in childhood does not eliminate them but pushes them into the
unconscious, thus creating a split self, with both conscious and
unconscious aspects.

But Freud was mistaken in supposing that one's split self has a
structure which is primarily related to Oedipal objects and
formed in the patriarchal nuclear family. Though such structures
may indeed form some important aspects of self for most people,
there are other social crucibles which form personal identities and
their attendant sex/affective desires. Since there are a number of
social structures which act together to form the nexus of self/other
relations that constitute self identity, the self so formed may have
a number of conflicting aspects. The lack of unity of the self is
thus even more severe than Freud thought. Not only is the self
split between conscious (rational, calculating, instrumental) ego,
partly conscious norm-giving and valuating superego and the
repressed desires of the unconscious (the id), there are also
conflicting aspects of conscious ego and superego, as well as id, all
of which are aroused by participation in the various types of social
structures from which they derive.

Gender, kin-identity, economic class, racial and ethnic identities are all created in those ongoing social interactions which fix
and direct sex/affective energy flows (bonds) between a person
and groups of other people. In thinking about personal identity
from the political perspective of how people are likely to conform
to or resist existing social structures, it is helpful to distinguish
between two basic aspects of each self-identification, one of which
is oppositional and one of which is incorporative. The oppositional aspect of an individual is in some ways similar to Freud's
notion of the ego: that part of self which sees itself as potentially in
conflict with other humans in promoting his or her self-interest,

immediate wants or goals. Unlike Freud's notion of ego, however, the oppositional aspect of self does not solely use rationality, calculation or instrumental thinking to promote its goals. Rather, the oppositional aspect of self may be expressed either through instrumental activity or through symbolic activity which expresses a sense of self as an individual in opposition to some relevant group. Furthermore, the oppositional aspect of self is not always fully conscious: an individual may 'act out' oppositional elements of personality in ways of which she or he is not conscious.

The incorporative aspect of self is that part of an individual through which he or she feels identified as a part of one or more human groups – a nationality, kinship, a family household, an ethnic or racial identity, a gender, an economic class. Through this aspect an individual identifies self-interest as merged with the general interests of the group. This aspect of self may be expressed both instrumentally and symbolically: a wageworker joining a union strike may both promote the collective interests of fellow workers and also express a symbolic identification with workers as opposed to management. Incorporative aspects of self-identity may also not always be conscious. A person may consciously have rejected a certain group identity, as in a 'male-identified' woman or a 'white-identified' person of colour, yet still unconsciously have incorporative aspects of self that are arousable in certain conditions, as when a blatant instance of sexism or racism forces one to identify with the group belittled.

Oppositional and incorporative aspects of self may be more or less developed in one's personality, depending on one's social relations. A housewife immersed in family and kin networks may have weak oppositional aspects of self compared to wage labourers constantly exposed to structural oppositions of interests between management policies and workers' interests. Hence, Chodorow's analysis that there is a difference in content between masculine and feminine gender in that the former has more 'rigid' (or oppositional) and the latter more 'permeable' ego boundaries may get its plausibility from the fact that in capitalist private patriarchies the private/public split between women's family labour and men's wage labour will tend to develop the incorporative rather than the oppositional aspects of women's personalities. This is a situation which may now be changing in capitalist public patriarchies where most women must expect to work in wage labour as well as in household labour.

Emphasising these two aspects of personal identity and their relational definition suggests a way that countercultural incorporative peer identifications can create a 'culture of resistance' in which conservatising incorporative aspects of self can be countered by radical redefinitions of self. For example, the contemporary lesbian-feminist community and the wider networks of the autonomous Women's Movement create a countercultural community of peers among whom one's incorporative gender and sexual identities can be redefined in ways not mandated in the patriarchal nuclear family. The de-Oedipalising of sex/affective desire which occurs can create a gender identity in conflict with that childhood incorporative aspect of self defined through the nuclear family. Thus, a mode of sex/affective production, while it produces specific sexualities, social bonds, and aspects of self-identity, may be an internal process fraught with conflicting tendencies.

In positing modes of sex/affective production which organise gender, sexuality, parenting, friendships and the production of babies a relational and aspectival theory of self is assumed. That is, one's gender identity is formed not merely through the bare awareness of one's physical body but also through gender roles, in work and other social relations, in which one engages. Furthermore, in systems of sex/affective production with conflicting tendencies, a person may have conflicting aspects of self which are both connected to gender identity. For example, a woman involved in women's wage labour that is unionised may have an oppositional sense of gender identity because she defines her interests as woman worker in opposition to the male bosses. At home, however, she may have an incorporative gender identity in so far as her social practices there define her interests as wife and mother as identified with the interests of her family. Furthermore, her racial and class identity may sometimes pit her against other women and sometimes be overruled by a sex/class incorporative solidarity with women in other classes and races (cf. Ferguson, 1985, unpub., 1986b, 1987).

On the aspect theory of self, there is no automatic process by which a person's overall sense of social identity comes to be. Where social practices allow sex/affective energy to flow unimpeded, a person's identity-aspect will be defined incorporatively with others.[1] Where social processes block off the flow of sex/affective energy because of adversarial relations, however, a person's identity-aspect will be defined oppositionally. Aspects of self, defined, for example, in relation to gender or racial processes of social interaction, may create specific skills and interests. Those radical feminists, sectarian Marxists or Black nationalists who attempt to deduce a common political identity as a base for a separatist political practice from only one aspect of self are, therefore, in error. A personal political identity is always to some degree an existential project, as are the bonding political practices in which people attempt to create a self-conscious political community with others.

A socialist-feminist tri-systems theory

The main reason to apply the language of 'caste' in preference to 'class' to refer to the social opposition of races, genders, families and individuals (e.g. race class, sex class, family class and economic class) in US society today is to insist that narrow Marxist characterisations of class in capitalist society to refer to an individual's relation to production obscure a number of other social oppositions that turn on one's relation to production in other ways than simply whether one is a wage labourer or an owner. Other ways that groups may have their material interests socially structured in opposition to each other are ignored.

Consider the puzzle of defining an individual's economic class solely by relation to his/her individual relation to capitalist production. On this criterion, someone is a member of the working class if s/he works for wages and a member of the capitalist class if his/her income is gained primarily from returns on private ownership of the means of production. But not all members of society have an individual economic class: for example, full-time housewives are defined by their husband's relation to production, and minors are defined by their parent's relation to production.

Whether or not a person has an individual economic class, they do at least, and in addition, have a family class, that is a position in a family whose individual wage earners bear certain relations to production. One of the confusions about class identity comes from the situation where an individual's family class as defined by the father's work is different from their individual economic class as an adult, or their new family class if they marry a man with a different economic class position than their father's. This puzzle can be resolved by defining two separate relations – individual economic and family economic class. We must realise that the historical and cultural self-identity relevant for political organising will depend as importantly on the latter as on the former. That is, as one's self-identified class depends importantly on education, life-style, social identification and social bonds, we cannot simply see family class as an additive function of the individual economic relations of husband and wife. A man may own a small grocery store and his wife may work part-time in a factory, or she may be a full-time housewife. In either case, because of the cultural implications of the man's position and money, the family class of the couple would likely be petit bourgeois.

In an analogous way, we can see the sexual and racial divisions of labour in wage labour, family-households and community-living situations as aspects of the productive organisation of our society that create an opposition of material interests between men and women, whites and non-whites. The structural likelihood that women and minorities, no matter what individual or family class they come from, will be in less rewarded types of work than males and whites and that minorities will be in less privileged neighbourhoods suggests that racial and gender identities should be seen as economic oppositions in a racist and sexist society that create gender and race as oppositional classes. Gender and race-segregated labour and the lower relative income available to minorities and women benefit the white male working class, thus challenging Marx's idea that capitalism homogenises labour. By conceptualising racism, sexism and capitalism as semi-autonomous systems of social domination we see that it is not just the capitalist class which exploits the working class; rather, the white male working class can also be said to exploit women and minorities (Bowles and Gintis, 1977).

There are three key overlapping systems of social domination, capitalism, racism and sexism, which define an individual's material interests in our society. It is the developing contradictions between these class positions that define individuals (due to changes in the family and the economy) that create the potential for women to become a new revolutionary class in the US. It is to be hoped that this analysis provides a methodological framework for socialist-feminist intuitions that male control in the family and in wage labour is just as important as capitalist control of economic production for the persistence of male domination.

Furthermore, we must take into account the racial division of families into segregated communities to understand the material base of race class and the semi-independent dynamic of racism in our society. The historically developing contradictions between race, sex, family and economic class are instabilities around which it is important to focus our political organising as feminists.

Part of what it means to claim that the systems of racism, patriarchy and capitalism are semi-autonomous is that the tendencies of one system may undermine the stability of another. For example, though capitalism institutionalises forms of sexism and racism in the sexual and racial divisions of labour it promotes, it undermines sexism and racism in other ways, for example by creating wage labour jobs for women which allow them some economic independence. Thus, though group bonding with dominant/subordinate coding functions to support hierarchical systems, there may be dynamic processes at work which undermine any strict functionalist connection between domination systems. This lack of strict functional connection between domination systems means that a constant adjudication and negotiation must go on between members dominant in one social bonding but subordinate in another.

Since sex/affective energy is maintained not merely in familial but in other social interactions, the specific symbolic codes and, consequently, the historical contents of gender and other social identities – whether sexual, racial, ethnic or economic – may be shaped differently by different forms of the family, different systems of schooling and different economic, race or ethnic positions. As discussed above, any social identity may be composed of conflicting aspects. The gender process of the male breadwinner, female housewife bourgeois family in a capitalist society may produce women with a gender identity designed to serve men in the private sphere of the family, sexuality and romance. But a public school system operating on the principles of individualism and meritocracy for all regardless of biological or social origins may encourage women to compete with men in the public sphere of careers.

Analogously, minorities may internalise a racial or ethnic identity of inferiority, due to inferior schools and social segregation in poor communities. But state Affirmative Action programmes and the public schools' attempts at instilling an ethic of meritocracy may create the contradictory idea that colour, race and ethnic background are irrelevant to individual success in the United States. Thus, individual Black Americans may find themselves at once empowered by the ideology of equality to compete with white Americans yet oppressed by psychological feelings of inferiority and economic lack of resources.

Thus, the conflicting tendencies of racist capitalist public patriarchy create possibilities for those in oppressed classes – women, minorities, the working classes – to come to define themselves in collective networks of resistance to challenge the existing system.

The Marxist concept of class

The claim that women can come to identify ourselves as a radical group to challenge the system implies that women as a sex class can be a revolutionary class in the Marxist sense of the term. But are women, or can we be, a class in this sense?

In order to answer this question we must first define and clarify the concept of class. One of the strengths of the Marxist approach to understanding society is its ability to explain revolutionary change. Marx and Engels justify their theory that class struggle is the moving force of history by using a class analysis to explain the transition from feudalism to capitalism, and such events as the French Revolution and the Paris Commune. The concept of economic class that they develop is not simply an intellectual starting point which must be assumed in order to accept the rest of their theory. Rather, they show us the use of their concept by applying it in a way that helps us make sense out of a period of revolutionary change. And not only does their concept seem to work to explain past historical change, it is in addition a political concept, that is it gives us a method for identifying those groups which may be key political agents for revolutionary change in present society.

A problem with applying the Marxist concept of class to analyse new developments in advanced capitalism is that the cluster of criteria which are associated with the applications Marx and Engels made of the concept to understand feudalism and early capitalism now may no longer identify one unambiguous group in the social relations of production. We need, therefore, to unpack the Marxist concept of economic class in order to see which of the traditional criteria still apply.

The common core of the concept of economic class is a group defined in both political and economic terms: that is, a class is a group of people who because of the kind of work they do and the power relations involved in that work have, with other groups, a common interest either in maintaining the system or in over-throwing it. Class, then, has to be specified in terms of certain relations to production which individuals bear to each other in a given mode of production.

We need to specify more clearly what the relevant relation to production is and what sort of power relations are involved in order to make the concept of class concrete. We can isolate at least five different criteria of class which have been given or assumed by Marxists in their discussions of class differences. The first three criteria are clearly part of the basic conceptual apparatus of the classical Marxist theorists: Marx and Engels, Lenin and Stalin.

Criterion 1: exploitation relations

According to this criterion, an exploiting class in a society is one which owns and/or controls the means of production in that society in a way which allows it to expropriate the social surplus of a society. Whether that is defined in terms of surplus labour time or surplus value will depend on what specific mode of production, for example, feudalism or capitalism, is involved. The other classes of society are then defined in contrast to the exploiting class: that is, producers who have rights to appropriate part of their product, e.g. the peasantry, or producers who sell their labour as a commodity, e.g. the proletariat. This criterion is called here the economic criterion of class.

Criterion 2: political relations

Central to the classical Marxist conception of history is the idea that class conflict is the moving force for social revolution. Classes thought of as political entities are defined in terms of their potential as a cohesive reactionary or revolutionary force; that is, groups which because of their economic relation to production as defined in criterion 1 are expected to develop cohesive interests and a common self-consciousness. The four thinkers mentioned above all seem to have held an inevitability thesis with respect to the relations between criterions 1 and 2 for certain key classes. That is, certain groups of individuals with objectively similar exploited positions in production, a 'class in itself' would come to be a class 'for itself', a group which is conscious of its common situation and which comes to identify itself as a political group fighting for a common interest.[2] Not all economic classes would come to be political classes: as we shall see, for example, Marx did not think that peasants could become a political class. Hence peasants by themselves could not come to be a revolutionary class. The key to whether an economic group will come to be a political group seems to depend on the existence of historical and social conditions which give the group historical cohesiveness. This we can call the third criterion of class.

Criterion 3: historical cohesiveness

This criterion stesses the point that classes are not simply abstract collections of individuals who fit under certain labels because social scientists find it helpful to so describe them. Rather, they are groups of people who share a common historical background, a common culture, common values, and therefore in one way or another some collective self-consciousness of themselves as members of a group sharing a common identity and common interests.[3] The way I see it, there may be both structural and accidental reasons why an economic class does not develop the historical cohesiveness which is a necessary condition for further development into a political class 'for itself'. Marx appears to be giving some structural arguments why peasants do not form a class, according to criteria 2 and 3, in this quote from *The Eighteenth Brumaire*:

> The small-holding peasants form a vast mass, the members of which live in similar conditions but without entering into manifold relations with one another. Their mode of production isolates them from one another instead of bringing them into mutual intercourse. The isolation is increased by France's bad means of communication and by the poverty of the peasants. In so far as there is merely local interconnection among these small-holding peasants, and the identity of their interests begets no community, no national bond and no political organization among them, they do not form a class. They are con-

sequently incapable of enforcing their class interests in their own name, whether through parliament or through a convention. They cannot represent themselves, they must be represented. (Marx, 1972: 123–4)

There are plausible historical reasons why the US working class has not developed the class unity necessary to meet criteria 2 and 3: these are ethnic differences due to successive waves of immigration from different cultures, racism caused by the historical presence of slavery in the US; work patterns of noise and isolation which make it difficult for workers to communicate on the job, suburbanisation which fragments workers' sense of common social community with each other; and elitist trade unions which, dividing skilled from unskilled workers, have defused the trade union movement to the point where less than 15 per cent of American workers are represented by trade unions.

The second set of criteria for class has been developed by neo-Marxists out of the criteria that may have been implicit in some of the classical writers, but were never spelled out. It seems fair to summarise the historical function of these criteria for Marxist theory by saying that they all attempt to account for the failure of the working classes in the advanced capitalist countries to become a unified revolutionary class. Either they stress the relations of political domination and submission between capitalist and working classes due to the growth of the state and ideological institutions like the mass media. Or they isolate some new class which has a privileged position in the new social relations of production by virtue of its control and autonomy and whose ideological and social function perpetuate the status quo (Ehrenreich, 1979; Gorz, 1967; Poulantzas, 1975; Wright, 1978).

Criterion 4: domination relations

This criterion for making distinctions between classes is based on relations of domination and submission, primarily tied to authority and control of the process of work. Those who control the labour power of others are in one class, while those who do not are in another. People who are supervisors, managers or foremen are obvious examples of those who control other workers. Less obvious examples are doctors' control of nurses, teachers' control over their students who can be seen as 'workers in training', welfare officials' control of recipients' 'work' in childraising, men's control of women's work in the home, and parents' control of children, the future workers.

Some of these examples would be disputed by those Marxists who still hold that exploitation relations are the only way to distinguish classes. They would deny that work in the home or work in learning at school fits into the category of 'productive work': work which produces surplus value. They would conclude that such domination relations cannot be seen to be 'exploitative' in the important sense which constitutes a class distinction. Others would call them classes but relegate them to a secondary status in any revolutionary process. For example, Resnick and Wolff distinguish between 'fundamental' and 'subsumed' classes: only the former can be dynamic movers and changers of a society while the latter serve to reproduce status quo domination relations (Wolff and Resnick, 1987).

Another aspect of work relations closely related to domination/submission is autonomy, i.e. how much autonomy a worker has in producing his/her product and shaping the work process relative to other workers. This suggests a fifth criterion.

Criterion 5: autonomy

We might want to maintain that those who control their own labour and the product of their labour are in one class while those who are controlled are in another class.[4]

This group overlaps but is not quite co-extensive with the dominating as opposed to dominated class covered by criterion 4. Individuals might control their own labour, e.g. a free-lance photographer, yet not control the labour power of others. Conversely, a person might be a dominator, e.g. a foreman or policeman, but yet not be autonomous in his/her work if in turn controlled by bosses.

Women as a sex class today

Feminists have argued that our contemporary patriarchy involves unequal and exploitative relations between men and women in domestic maintenance and sex/affective work in the family. This generalisation remains true overall, even though the amount of power the man has in relation to the woman in the family will vary with their relation to the dominant mode of production. So, if the woman has an individual economic class, that is, if she is working for wage labour, or has an independent income, and if she is making equal wages, it will be harder for the man to appropriate the surplus in wages after basic family needs are met. In general the typical nuclear family in the US is less patriarchal than in earlier periods, and there are a substantial minority of households which are woman-headed. Nonetheless, the historical prevalence of the patriarchal family and a sexual division of labour have created a male-dominated sexual division of wage labour in which women's work is paid less, is usually part-time, and has less job security than men's.

Though women-headed households give women more inde-pendence than their sisters in patriarchal nuclear families, such households cannot be said to be matriarchal: not only do the women typically not have more power than the men they relate to, but the fact that the majority of them live below the poverty line and that more than a third must depend on the federal government for welfare payments to survive suggests that the fact of male domination has not changed so much as the mechanisms by which it is reinforced (cf. Delphy, 1984; and chapter five above).

I maintain that men and women are in sex classes in capitalist society today, classes which are defined by the sexual division of labour in the family (in both the male-headed nuclear family and the mother-headed family) and reinforced by sexual division of wage labour. In this section arguments are presented to show that women are exploited relative to men in most contemporary forms of the family, that they are dominated and have little autonomy. They thus meet criteria 1, 4, and 5 for class identity discussed above. In the following section the historical cohesiveness of the class (criterion 3) and the implications of whether women can become a 'class for itself' (criterion 2) are discussed.

By the capitalist patriarchal nuclear family (CPNF) I under-stand an economic unit of man, woman and possibly children, in which the man works full-time in wage labour and is thus the main breadwinner, while the woman works as the primary dom-estic and childcare worker in the home. If she is employed in wage labour, she is not employed more than part-time.

How then do men exploit women in the CPNF? There are four

goods produced in sex/affective production in the family: domestic maintenance, children, nurturance and sexuality. Since a sex/affective productive system is a system of exchange of goods and labour, we can classify such systems in terms of the power relations involved. That is, is there an equal exchange between producers? If not, who controls the exchange? Patriarchal sex/affective production is characterised by unequal exchange between men and women: women receive less of the goods produced than men, and typically work harder, that is, spend more time producing them. The relations between men and women can be considered exploitative because the man is able to appropriate more of the woman's labour time for his own use than she is of his, and also he gets more of the goods produced (cf. also Delphy, 1984; Folbre, 1982, 1983).[5] It is oppressive because the sex/gender roles taught to boys and girls to perpetuate the sexual division of labour develop a female personality structure which internalises the goal to produce more for men and to accept less for herself (cf. also Barrett, 1980).

What evidence is there for the view that men exploit women in sex/affective production? There is clear evidence that women spend more time on housework than men do on wage labour. The figure given by the Chase Manhattan Bank survey is that a full-time housewife puts in an average 99.6 hours of housework a week (Girard, 1968). We also know that the inequality in relation to hours of work a week put in by husband and wife persists even when the wife is working in wage labour as well, for in that situation, studies have shown that the wife still puts in roughly 44 hours of housework a week in addition to her wage work, while the husband only puts in 11 hours of housework in addition to his wage work (Ryan, 1975).

There is a problem with a simple time comparison of gender work in family sex/affective production as a way to measure exploitation. What is exchanged is use values not exchange values. It could be argued that housework is less alienating than wage work: that the relatively greater control and autonomy the woman has over her work day at home makes longer hours of this work a reasonable exchange for less hours of alienating wage work. After all, the husband is not like the capitalist or foreman who attempts to increase the rate of exploitation of his wife's labour power by speed-ups, reduced pay, etc. and the man in the CPNF is subject to a greater percentage of his work being done under conditions of capitalist exploitation.[6] (This point of course excludes nuclear families of the capitalist class.)[7]

To answer this objection it can be maintained that although housewives may seem to have more autonomy than wage earning husbands, they in fact have less autonomy overall: less control, less 'job security', and a lesser amount of the human goods that the sexual division of labour for domestic maintenance is designed to provide. The evidence for this inequality is based on three arguments.

The economic argument is that men, as the dominant wage earners, control the family income and have more power to dispose of any surplus as they wish. Connected to this is the relative economic dependence of women. Given that women overall can make only 60 per cent of what men can make in wage labour, it follows that women are not equal to men in their options: they are less able to protest male choices for the use of surplus income because the possible break-up of the marriage contract or living agreement would disadvantage them much more than the man. They often stand to lose their family class.

The sexual argument and the nurturance argument are similar: that women receive less sexual satisfaction and less nurturance from men than they give in patriarchal sex/affective productive systems. Women's inequality in sexual exchange and in receiving nurturance has one common cause: the 'woman as nurturer' sex gender ideal. This in turn is based on one of the key material bases of patriarchy: that women are the primary childrearers.[8] The sexual division of labour in which women are responsible for the major care of children under six teaches children that women are nurturers (mothers) and men are achievers. Girls learn as part of their sense of self-identity that they are successful as people primarily because they are good wives and mothers: and good wives and mothers are those who are able to manage harmonious relationships for their husbands and children in the family. They are taught to find satisfaction in the satisfaction of others, and to place their needs second in the case of a conflict. Boys, on the contrary, learn that it is only if they are successful achievers that they can be successful men. They learn that the needs of others (wives, children) depend on their achievement, and to be a successful achiever they must be aggressive, competitive, put themselves first at school and later in business. In sexuality men are taught to be the initiators, women the receivers. Sexual success and work success are so much part of the gender ideal taught to men that women as the nurturers have a large incentive to fake orgasm and to ignore sexual incompatibilities, in order to nurture a man's sense of self. No wonder, then, that the two Hite Reports, although clearly unsuccessful as statistical samples because of their middle-class bias, give evidence that 80 per cent of women do not regularly experience orgasms in sexual activity with men and that women remain unsatisfied with their sex/affective ties to men (Hite, 1977, 1987).

There are two other causes for the sexual inequality between women and men. These are 'double standard monogamy', also incorporated with sex gender training, and women's role in pro-creation. The fact that women are the biological childbearers and not men puts women on an unequal footing in any system of sexual exchange in which they cannot control their bodies and the unwanted costs of pregnancy. Though capitalist public patriarchy has increased the availability of birth control and abortions, the prohibitive cost of abortion to many working-class women, the refusal of many men to use birth control, and the possibility of failures in birth control techniques still make women more subject to unwanted consequences of sex than men.

The points made above about the exploitation and control by men of women in the CPNF apply as well to most other types of family household in the US today. Although many families are not of the CPNF structure, for instance, female-headed households or families where both husband and wife work full-time, most other families which have children involve exploitation of the mother's work by the father. This result is partly structural and partly due to social pressure on the mother to accept an unequal sexual division of labour. After all the CPNF is the legitimised arrange-ment to which schools, wage labour jobs and many social services are co-ordinated (Barrett and McIntosh, 1982). Those who do not live in a patriarchal nuclear family are not only inconvenienced but suffer a loss of status. Schools and older kin make full time wage-earning mothers feel guilty for time not spent with their children. The absence of affordable childcare and the relatively better pay of husbands makes it plausible for mothers not fathers to work jobs which are low in pay but whose flexible hours allow mothers to do childcare. Thus mothers not fathers tend to suffer the 'second shift' problem of a full shift of wage work added to another shift at home of childcare and housework.

With respect to single mother-headed families, Delphy (1984) argues that women in such families continue to be exploited by the absent fathers: for women now must do two full-time jobs without much help: being the breadwinner, and doing the housework and childcare.

Let us sum up these points presented about the inequalities between men and women in patriarchal capitalism in relation to the criteria for class identity in order to show why it can be maintained that women and men form sex classes.

Use of the first criterion, exploitation relations, usually assumes that exploitation involves ownership and/or control of production. It has been argued here that men in capitalist patriarchies (whether or not they are actually present in the family household) own the wage and thus control sex/affective production in such a way as to be able to expropriate the surplus: surplus wages, surplus nurturance and sexuality. Though the CPNF is no longer the dominant union of domestic maintenance and sex/affective production in the United States, its historical impact on the sexual division of wage labour, welfare state provisions and the legal structures of child support continues to create a situation of exploitative sex/affective exchange between men and women, whether it be in other family households, in wage labour, in politics or in the courts.[9]

The fourth and fifth criteria, domination and autonomy relations, can be shown to apply to men and women as sex classes, both in the family and in other spheres of social life. If we remember that we are comparing power relations not only in the spheres of housework *vs* wage work but also the sex/affective work of sexuality and nurturance, it becomes clearer how the analogy holds. After all, the type of work women do in wage labour is primarily gendered sex/affective labour: that is, it involves women doing physical maintenance (nursing, health care), providing nurturance and sexuality (waitressing and other service work with sexual overtones) in which men as clients, bosses and customers control the exchange.[10]

In this section it has been argued that three out of the five criteria Marxists have put forward to pick out class identity apply to women and men as sex classes. In the next section we shall consider whether women as a group have the sort of political potential Marx and Engels originally foresaw for the working class in capitalism. Are women a revolutionary class? Do we have historical cohesiveness (criterion 3)? And can we become a 'class for itself' (criterion 2)?

Women as a revolutionary class

The theoretical framework I have advanced here allows individuals to be members of overlapping classes: family class, sex class, race class[11] and individual economic class. We need to know what class an individual will be likely to identify with if s/he is a member of several classes whose interests are in contradiction to each other. Are there laws of motion of advanced capitalist patriarchal social formations that can indicate where key contradictions will develop that allow for membership in one class to supersede in political importance membership in another class? One of the advantages of restricting the Marxist concept of class to exploitation relations in wage labour (criterion 1) is that those who are exploited are also those who play a key role in the capital accumulation process. Therefore the implications of the laws of value and capitalist development seem to indicate why this class is of key political importance. Can we do something analogous with the analysis of sex class and family class in our society?

I maintain that we can. The task is to show that women are unlike Marx's characterisation of peasants and like his characterisation of the working class. Women have to be able to identify with sex class over family class, to be aware of ourselves as a historically cohesive group, with a common culture and common interests by virtue of our position in the sexual division of labour in the family and in society. We need evidence of the existence of different men's and women's cultures, as well as some understanding of how growing contradictions between sex class and family class identification for women will tend to push women to identify with the first.

There is certainly evidence of separate men's and women's cultures which is more distinctive the more patriarchal the society. By 'culture', I have in mind a very broad concept that includes accepted patterns of acting, ways of treating each other, values, aesthetic and expressive forms, preferences for friendships, etc. The evidence presented by conservative writers such as Tiger (1969) about male bonding supports the idea that men act as a sex class, and there is also evidence that women bond (Leis,

1974), although in strongly patriarchal societies this tends to be restricted to female kin and bound up with the family.

Historically, however, there are few occasions in which sex class bonding has taken precedence to family class bonding, and these exceptions have often occurred, as in the first wave Women's Movement in the nineteenth-century United States, when family class positions as well as gender roles were in a state of transition because of changes in the mode of material economic production (cf. Rossi, 1974). That movement failed to sustain the connection between middle-class and working-class women, or between Northern white and Southern Black women because the family class identification of the middle-class women (primarily petty bourgeois and wealthy farmers) prevented them from challenging either the economic or the racial class structure of American racist capitalism (Aptheker, 1983; Davis, 1981; Kraditor, 1965).

This is not surprising, for the family is a key economic, sexual, procreative and nurturant unit in capitalist patriarchal modes of sex/affective production. Men and women within families have seen as basic their common interests in raising children together, satisfying their material, nurturant and sexual needs together, and amassing property that is used as collective security though it is usually controlled by the man. Thus each individual tends to define his or her individual interests as those which promote the family's interests (cf. Humphries, 1977).

For woman this tendency is even stronger, given her gender identity which is bound up with family tasks. The sexual division of labour in patriarchal sex/affective production reinforces this identification of individual with family interests. In previous social formations it was not economically and socially feasible for individuals to live outside of families and expect to get their material, nurturant and sexual needs securely met. It is not then surprising that both men and women have identified themselves primarily with a common family class, defined typically by the male's relation to material production, with a common culture, values and interests connected to other families in the same position.

The situation is changing, however, in advanced capitalist societies. There are increasing contradictions developing between the social relations of capitalist production and the social relations of patriarchal sex/affective production in the family. The economic

material conditions for these developments are 1) the existence of
wage labour jobs for women which pay a subsistence wage; 2) the
existence of state welfare which will support women and children
without a husband/father, coupled with 3) the availability of
mass-produced contraceptives which allow women more control
over their fertility; and 4) inflationary pressures on family income
which cause women to seek part- or full-time wage work to
supplement their husbands' income.

What results from these conditions is an increasingly high rate
of instability in patriarchal nuclear families: more divorce, less
communal moral sanctions about 'keeping the family together for
the children', and more of an emphasis on the individual happiness of each partner. US individualism, which always encouraged
men to 'do their own thing' is now increasingly an acceptable
value system for women unhappy in marriage. This shift in
morality parallels the change in material conditions that allow for
the possibility that women can support themselves outside of the
patriarchal family. Inequalities in capitalist patriarchal sex/
affective production have historically been maintained because
most women have not had many viable alternatives outside the
nuclear family except prostitution. But the increasing number of
state sector, clerical and service jobs defined as 'women's work'
has now provided women with such options. Even those women
who are not seeking to stay single or to break out of unhappy
marriages can become caught up in the contradiction that occurs
between the wage labour job they take to increase their family's
income, and the strain that subsequently occurs in family relations because of the increase in the unequal sexual division of
labour this causes. Is the husband now going to shoulder more
housework? Are the kids? How will all of them deal with less
attention from wife and mom?

It is not only the new available options for work outside the
family that are relevant to women's changing position. The fact is
that with the increased instability of nuclear families, women can
no longer count on being maintained in families as non-wage
earning housewives, and thus achieve the old 'wife-mother'
gender ideal.[12] This makes it more likely that women will relate to
sex class rather than family class as their prime source of identity.
As wage workers women are thrown into proximity with other
women not in their family. Due to the sexual segregation of the
work force into men's and women's jobs, women can come to

identify with other women and put sex class identification as primary.

Another reason that women are forced to rely more on their sex class identity than their family class identity these days is that many women have to face the likelihood that they will lose their family class. Most wage labour possibilities for women are working-class jobs. If a woman remains single, she must either take a working-class job or be 'poor' by going on welfare, an option open primarily to single mothers. If a woman marries, it is likely that she will be divorced at least once in her lifetime, in which case she faces the same possibilities. Many single and divorced women whose family class was professional-managerial now are members of the working class as defined by their individual economic class (Sidel, 1986); and increasing numbers of women whose original family class was working-class have moved downward to the poor (are on welfare).[13]

Alimony and child support do not cushion women from these hazards of being a woman in US society today. Only 14 per cent of divorced women in the US in 1976 were even awarded alimony by the courts and only one half that number collect it regularly. As for child support, a full one half of the men ordered to pay child support are paying 'practically nothing', and 90 per cent of women receiving child support do not receive it regularly (Women's Agenda, 1976b). 'No fault' divorce legislation has not improved matters either. A recent study of the effects of the California 'no fault' legislation discovered that women's incomes dropped 45 per cent, while men's increased 73 per cent as the result of divorce (Weitzman, 1985). Furthermore, a homemaker is not entitled to social security benefits if divorced, so she has no prospects of a pension to support her in old age. A middle-aged divorcee is often a person thrown on the streets after years of homemaking with no marketable skills and not the energy or sense of self to start from the beginning to make a new life for herself.

Not only can women not count on wifehood and motherhood as a life concentration that will allow for a secure economic future but they cannot count on an easy way to care for their children. There is a contradiction between capitalist production demands and the existing patriarchal sex/affective production system for handling child care. Inflation requires many women to supplement the husband's income by wage labour, yet there is little available child care for children under six. In 1976 wage working

mothers had 27.6 million children under six (public school age), yet
there were only one million licensed day care slots for these children
(Women's Agenda, 1976a). Sadly, the situation has not improved
eleven years later in 1987. Both single and married working
mothers thus can identify around the sex class issue of child care.

There are other contradictions present in such important institutions in society as the schools and media. These institutions are
undermining the reproduction of patriarchal social relations by
encouraging contradictory patterns and values. Two of the most
important are the educational training of women and the emphasis on sexual consumerism by the media. The educational system
is sexist in many ways, but it does encourage the idea that women
too may develop skills through education that can prepare them
for a career independent of the family related goals of wife and
motherhood. It thus allows an alternative gender ego ideal for
some women, typically women whose family class is petit bourgeois or professional-managerial. These women go to better high
schools and their families can afford to send them to good
colleges. Access to an alternative gender ideal is extremely important as a tool to allow women to challenge the system. It should
come as no surprise that the majority of those involved in the
current Women's Movement are college educated women.

There has been an increased emphasis on sexual pleasure by
the media as a way to sell products. And the pornography industry has grown to a mammoth $8 billion in recent years. There are
two negative effects of commodifying sex. These are, first, what
Marcuse calls 'repressive de-sublimation' – pacifying people by
more superficial sex (Marcuse, 1964), and second, the increasing
sexual objectification of women's bodies. But there is also a
positive effect: an increasing acceptance of the idea that women
have a right to equal sexual freedom and satisfaction. This suggests a modification of the gender ideal of women as passive
dependents of men and is thus a challenge to the social relations of
patriarchal family sex/affective production.

These contradictions in education and the media tend to
weaken women's allegiance to family rather than to sex class when
a conflict arises between the two. For example, women are more
likely to leave husbands who do not satisfy them emotionally and
sexually than they were in the past. And the recent sex debate in
the Women's Movement over whether pornography should be
censored and what are appropriate sexual lifestyles for feminists

show that women are demanding the right as independent agents
to define our own sexuality, and what gives us pleasure, even if we
cannot always agree as feminists what that is or ought to be! (cf.
Ferguson, 1986a.)

Reasons have been given above to believe that women are a sex
class which is developing historical cohesiveness cutting across
family and race class lines because of contradictions appearing in
the social relations of material and sex/affective production. But is
this enough to make women a radical class?

Yes! Because women are a pivotal class in terms of the work we
perform in reproducing both capitalist and patriarchal relations of
production. Women are the 'culture-bearers' of family class *and*
sex class values. We teach children expectations and goals, train
them in rules of obedience to authority, acting as their first and
most important role models in this area, and in general as the
major child rearers do essential work in child socialisation necessary to continuing capitalist and patriarchal culture. Second, men
depend on women for the reproduction of their labour power by
continued women's work in domestic maintenance, nurturance
and sexuality.

Women as a sex class, then, do have potential disruptive power
in the interconnected systems of capitalist and patriarchal sex/
affective production. If women refuse to do their work as
presently organised, neither capitalism nor patriarchy could continue to function.

Though women are a sex class which cuts across family, individual economic and race class, most women (all but those in the
capitalist class) are a potentially radical class because we have no
objective interests as a sex class in maintaining the present
system. Thus when women organise with other women in sex
class identification, we can use the pivotal power gained by the
importance of our social function in reproducing capitalist patriarchy to challenge the continuance of the patriarchal family and to
raise the progressive aspects involved in family class identification
for members of the professional-managerial class, working class
or poor. The fact that women as a sex class cut across the divisions
of professional-managerial, working class and poor, as well as
across race class, can be a key to organising progressive class
alliances between these groups. In the United States, feminist
connections across these lines have been important in local coalitions of Jesse Jackson's Rainbow Coalition. Progressive feminists

have effectively communicated to many members of the autonomous Women's Movement that the objective conditions for women's liberation require the overthrow not only of male domination but of capitalism and racism as well. There has also been some effective consciousness-raising about the issues of economic class and race: how race, family and individual economic class distinctions continue to divide women from each other and from true sisterhood.[14] There are some indications that the increasing consciousness of economic class and race issues have allowed the Women's Movement to correct some of its earlier middle-class approach; for example, broadening such demands as the right to abortion and birth control to include opposition to forced sterilisation and demands for state and federal funds for abortion. The development of working women's unions is another way to connect feminism with working-class women, for example, the organisation for secretaries called Nine to Five on the US East Coast, the Coalition of Labor Union Women (CLUW), a national organisation, and a group called Union WAGE (Women and Gender Equality) in California.

Two further points about the strategic position of women. First, the breakdown of the family has an increasing tendency to cause new women from middle and working family class positions to enter the working class and poor. These women are usually angry because of defeated expectations, and can be an important group for raising both sex class and family class issues: the right to affordable quality child care and state subsidised health care, welfare payments to all women for housework, affirmative action and comparable worth salaries, etc. But many of the members of this group as single women and single mothers need economic and cultural support outside of the patriarchal nuclear family. In this context the cultural and material support systems of the autonomous Women's Movement are important. Communal households for women, battered women's shelters, show the falsity of the idea that a feminist cultural revolution must wait until after an economic revolution occurs.

Another point about the strategic position of women concerns women whose individual economic class is professional-managerial and whose wage work thus directly involves them in the reproduction of capitalist relations. If such women are feminists, and even better, socialist-feminists, they can use their relative autonomy and position of authority to undermine capitalist rela-

tions. They can make conscious efforts to overcome the hierarchical relations between themselves and their poor, working- or
middle-class students, clients or patients and can challenge
elitism and other attitudes that continue to debilitate working-
class and poor people and set them against those of the professional-managerial class. The contradictory position of such
women in capitalist patriarchy (a situation I know well from my
own case!) – for example, discrimination on the job and problems
with the sexual division of labour at home – make us likely
candidates for effective political work.

Before this chapter is concluded, a word should be said about
the evidence that the Women's Movement is losing steam;
indeed, that the younger generation of women with feminist
mothers are a 'post-feminist' generation, and thus no longer have
the same motivation to challenge male dominance as those of us
who became feminists in the 1960s and early seventies. A recent
article by Judith Stacey (Stacey, 1987) is instructive on this
question. Through her two case studies of the post-feminist
generation, she suggests that the daughters of sixties' feminists
may be post-feminist not in the sense of being anti-feminist but in
the sense of accepting feminist goals but not feminist politics. The
women she studied attempt to combine career and resurrect a
stable family life in a way that assumes feminist goals of equality
in gender roles while at the same time eschewing feminist activism. Though her data are clearly not sufficient to establish the
point, it could be that the cultural activism of the Women's
Movement, based as it was on informal networks of consciousness-raising and solidarity among women friends, has
not yet been established in the younger generation. If this is so, it
clearly is a problem for feminist politics. But it does not show that
feminism is either dead or has lost the potential for continued
radical challenges to male dominance in the future. Instead, it
shows that feminist organisers need to find new ways to raise the
consciousness and activism level of nascent feminists. Just as the
working class in the US can be seen as a potentially radical class
even though its consciousness and activism are very low right
now, so women are a radical class waiting to arouse ourselves and
be aroused by the right set of catalysts and the right organising
strategies.

The argument does not imply there is any inevitability about
women becoming radicalised in the United States today. Indeed,

the rise of the New Right shows that some women, aware of their inequality with men due to sex class, will attempt to hold on to their family class and race class by conservative attempts to preserve the paternalistic and racist aspects of white supremacist capitalist patriarchy.

What follows from this should not be a defeatist attitude, but a coalitionist one: if the radicalised elements of the civil rights movement, the Women's Movement and the working-class movement can find a way to unite their demands, there is an important potential for radical change toward a democratic feminist socialist society. But this cannot happen by a reduction of all the class movements' demands to simply those of the white male working class. Only a many issued race, sex and economic class coalition stands a chance of defeating the tendencies toward conservatism in each of the class positions taken separately.

Conclusion

It has been argued that women are a radical class and capable of revolutionary agency in the US today. But we are not the only such class. The working class is potentially radical, as are minority races and elements of the professional-managerial class. Indeed, because of the complicated objective contradictions between the professional-managerial and working classes, and between sex class, family class, race class and individual economic class, a socialist and feminist revolution is not possible in this country without class alliances of progressive people who identify the tri-system social formation of capitalism, patriarchy and racism as the enemy. Working-class women will not trust middle-class women until the latter are willing to forfeit some of their family class privilege to fight for working-class issues, nor will minority women trust white women enough to unite around issues of sexism until white women are willing to fight against their own and institutional racism. Furthermore, different people are likely to take different issues as their primary focus for organising – some prioritising the working class, some women's issues, some racism, and some focusing on the environment, the arms race or US imperialism and foreign policy. It is unclear at this point what kinds of structure – coalitions, a party, grass root organisations, caucuses – are needed to produce the ideal alliance.

The practical implication of this book is that only an analysis which takes into account objective contradictions between classes in the US today and the diverse class positions occupied by women and men can provide us with the understanding necessary to engage in the kind of practice that will teach us how and who to organise in the fight against racism, capitalism and patriarchy.

7

Sexual alienation and liberation

What is sexual liberation? What is the connection between the social control of sexuality and systems of social domination? And what relationship, if any, is there between women's liberation and sexual liberation? The answers to these questions are more complicated and controversial than they might at first seem, and disagreements on answers are at the base of the current polarisation of feminists around such questions as pornography, adult/child sex and consensual S/M sex.

> For sexuality is by its nature an experience that benefits from a stance that anything goes, that any avenue may (but not 'must') be explored. Erotic pleasure mushrooms when there are no musts. But this accessibility means that sexual experience can be affected by anything. Sexual intimacy is too generous an experience to exclude anything, including the forces of the unconscious and the forces of hierarchy. When you get into bed with someone, you bring all of you: your past, remembered or forgotten; your present, including parts of it which you think your rational mind can keep out; your hopes for the future. Sexual intimacy is therefore particularly resistant to rules of political correctness, or, rather, when it succumbs to rules, passion disappears. Its very non-rationality allows the politically incorrect to enter. (Dimen, 1982: 142)

This libertarian or pluralist feminist approach to sex implies that any consensual sex is acceptable sex.[1] It can be contrasted with a radical feminist view which stresses the sexual alienation in our society:

> The erotic has often been misnamed by men and used against women. It has been made into the confused, the trivial, the psychotic, the plasticized sensation. For this reason, we have often turned away from the exploration and consideration of

the erotic as a source of power and information, confusing it with its opposite, the pornographic. But pornography is a direct denial of the power of the erotic, for it represents the suppression of true feeling. Pornography emphasizes sensation without feeling. (Lorde, 1978: 296)

Very simply put, the poles of the feminist sex debate divide on the issue of whether consensual sexual pleasure empowers women. Since radical feminists hold a structuralist view of the social construction of male dominance through all the institutions of compulsory heterosexuality (e.g. marriage, mainstream pornography, the capitalist patriarchal nuclear family, prostitution), consensual pleasure appears at best irrelevant or at worst a co-optation of women into sexual slavery.

Though there is no one pluralist feminist analysis of male dominance and sexuality to contrast to the radical feminist view, most tend to assume that consensual pleasure is liberating for women, and thus to argue that feminists ought to condone any consensual sexual activity. Though pluralist feminists do not all share the same theory of sexuality, there is a pragmatic agreement that a feminist sexual morality must support the right to consensual sex for pleasure in order to oppose New Right morality whose positions on censoring pornography and opposing both adult consensual S/M and adult/child sex are uncomfortably close to radical feminism.

The problem with choosing sides in the sex debate is that both poles have valuable insights but important limitations. The pluralist feminist camp is correct to place importance on valorising consensual sexual activity, for only such an approach legitimises the freedom of experimentation necessary for individuals to discover what is sexually pleasurable, and by so doing, develop a sense of self as sexual subject. However, radical feminists are also correct to point beyond consent to the problematic domination relations built into the gender dualised roles in mainstream pornography, marriage, prostitution and the male breadwinner, female housewife nuclear family. How then can we create an alternative position in the feminist sex debate which can act as a corrective to the oversimplifications of the poles of the debate?

In this chapter it is argued that there is a way to reconcile both of these views, but only by providing an historical perspective on the contemporary form of US capitalist patriarchal sexuality. I shall offer an historical characterisation of sexual alienation in US society which bypasses the implausible universalities of both radical and pluralist feminism. My view stresses both the contradictions in sexual ideology and the relative empowerment of women today that explain why increasing numbers of women (and some men) are resisting prevalent sexual codes which embed male dominance. I shall also outline a vision of sexual liberation based on our contemporary values and historical possibilities that can act as a goal toward which to strive in challenging our present sexual norms and institutions. In chapter nine an attempt will be made to build on this historical perspective in order to understand our contemporary sexual identities and desires in a way which goes beyond the ahistorical picture presented by the present poles of the feminist sex debate on the relation of lesbian-feminism to feminism. And in chapters eight, ten and eleven we can address the more particular moral and political issues dividing feminists: motherhood, sexual identities, pornography, S/M sex, marriage, prostitution, adult/child sex, and general visions of sexual and human liberation.

Radical *vs* pluralist feminism

The division between radical and pluralist feminists in the sex debate involves some basic disagreements: first, a disagreement as to whether consensual sexual pleasure is inherently empowering; second, a disagreement as to what sexuality is, and thus, what, if any, are the 'authentic' goals of female sexuality. It will be helpful to give a summary here of the two frameworks in order to show how my own view enables us to avoid the essentialisms of both poles of the debate, and to draw a more complicated historical picture of the social construction of sex and gender.

Radical feminism

Radical feminism can be said to hold the following four views on sexuality:

1 Heterosexual sexual relations generally are characterised by an ideology of sexual objectification (men as subjects/masters; women as objects/slaves) which supports male sexual violence against women. Thus, standard heterosexual sex involves a danger for women.

1   She answers back.

2 Mother and bride, San Francisco, California, 1984.

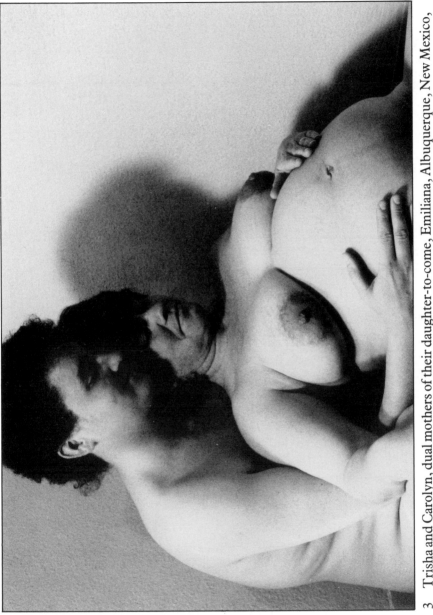

3   Trisha and Carolyn, dual mothers of their daughter-to-come, Emiliana, Albuquerque, New Mexico, 1986.

4 Sue and Angela are a mother and daughter from Granger, in Washington State's Yakima Valley.

5 Black Mother Woman.

6 Mother dressing her daughter, Seattle, Washington.

7 Some five hundred yards from the Honduran border, these women in San Pedro Norte live in constant fear of contra shelling.

8   Mother and daughter, San Pedro Norte, Nicaragua, 1983.

2   Feminists should repudiate any sexual practices or enjoyments which support or 'normalise' male sexual violence.
3   Feminists should reclaim control over female sexuality by developing a concern with our own sexual priorities, which differ from men's: i.e. more concern with process and commitment and less with performance involving compulsive genital sex with attention primarily on male orgasm.
4   The ideal sexual relationship is between fully consenting, equal partners who identify with each other and fully share emotional involvements; no double standard monogamy for example, no involvement in strongly polarised roles such as butch/femme, and the sharing of physical pleasures.

From these four aspects of radical feminist sexual morality, we can abstract the following theoretical assumptions about sexuality, social power and sexual freedom:

1   Human sexuality is a form of expression between people that is a way of bonding and communicating emotion (the 'primacy of intimacy' theory).
2   Theory of Social Power: in patriarchal societies sexuality becomes a tool of male domination by the phenomenon of sexual objectification. This is a social mechanism which operates through the institution of masculine and feminine roles in the patriarchal nuclear family. The attendant ideology of sexual objectification is sado-masochism; masculinity as sadistic control over women and femininity as submission to the male will. (Barry, 1979; Dworkin, 1974, 1981; Griffin, 1981). This ideology is supported and perpetuated through all the institutions of compulsory heterosexuality: marriage, pornography, sexual advertising, prostitution, unreconstructed heterosexual relations and sexual role playing, particularly butch-femme roles and S/M sexuality.
3   Sexual freedom requires sexual equality of partners, equal control as agents in the sexual exchange and equal respect for each other both as subject and as body. Sexual freedom requires the elimination of all patriarchal institutions: the pornography industry, for example, the patriarchal family, prostitution, compulsory heterosexuality, and sexual practices such as S/M, cruising, adult/child relationships and butch/femme roles in which sexual objectification occurs.

Pluralist feminism

The pluralist feminist framework can be summarised in a manner which brings out the sharp opposition in emphasis to the radical feminist paradigm:

1 Standard heterosexual sexual practices are characterised by sexual repression. The norms of patriarchal bourgeois sexuality repress sexual minorities (i.e. anyone not committed to married heterosexual sex), thus keeping the 'normals' pure and under control.

2 Feminists should repudiate any theoretical analyses, legal restrictions or moral judgements which stigmatise sexual minorities and thus restrict the freedom of all.

3 Feminists should reclaim control over female sexuality by demanding the right to practise whatever gives us pleasure and satisfaction, whether or not they be sexual practices (S/M, cruising, adult/child sexuality, non-monogamy) traditionally identified with male sexuality. The emphasis is on the importance of sexual pleasure.

4 The ideal sexual relationship is between fully consenting partners who negotiate to maximise each other's sexual pleasure and satisfaction by any means they choose.

The theoretical assumptions about sexuality, social power and sexual freedom they draw from the above sexual morality are:

1 Human sexuality concerns the exchange of physical, erotic and genital bodily pleasures (the primacy of pleasure theory). Sexuality may be conceived either on the model of the drive or energy theories explained in chapter four. In either case the goal of sex is held to be bodily pleasure (English, Hollibaugh and Rubin, 1984; Rubin, 1984; Vance, 1984; Webster, 1981; Willis, 1982, 1984).

2 Theory of Social Power: sexual energy is directed to objects by social institutions, interactions and discourses which distinguish the normal/legitimate/healthy from the abnormal/illegitimate/unhealthy. This institutionalises sexual repression and creates a hierarchy of social power and sexual identities. Pluralist theorists differ on whether they believe there is a real distinction between healthy and unhealthy sex, depending on

whether the paradigm of sex is a drive or social naming (energy) theory. Social naming pluralist theorists tend to hold that there is no ground for any distinction between healthy and unhealthy sex (the 'social relativity of sexual values').

3 Sexual freedom requires oppositional practices, i.e. the transgression of socially respectable categories of sexuality. This means refusing to draw the line on what çounts as 'politically correct' sexuality, except the minimal condition that it be consensual.

Comparison and critique of the two feminist poles

The radical feminist assumptions about sexuality are similar to the social energy theory of sexuality put forward in chapter four in the emphasis placed on the erotic as centred on the social connection between the individuals involved. But radical feminism differs from my view in that it is sexual romanticism, i.e. it assumes the only authentic and unalienated goal of sexuality is to deepen the emotional intimacy of those involved. On the contrary, I would argue that though sexuality involves a physical energy directed toward social union with others, the specific goals of sexuality are not inherent to it but are themselves socially constructed. Thus, both radical and pluralist feminism can be criticised for insisting that sex is primarily about emotional intimacy or bodily pleasure. Neither claim can be made in the abstract. Rather, in specific social and historical contexts, sexual interaction which prioritises either pleasure or intimacy, or which uses heterosexual intercourse as a functional tool to conceive children, can all be unalienated uses of sex/affective energy.

I maintain that both radical and pluralist feminists have too simplistic theories of social power. Radical feminists don't see that the patriarchal nuclear family has been undermined as the main site for the perpetuation of male dominance because of the way that advanced capitalism has displaced it as the main household form. Nor do radical feminists take account of the conflicting tendencies in the mass media and schools which undercut male dominance even though other tendencies still reinforce it.

Pluralist feminists, on the other hand, tend to overemphasise the way that sexual repression is due to sexual symbolic codes which stigmatise certain people and certain sexual practices. As a result, many pluralist feminists reject the idea of any legitimate distinction between healthy and unhealthy sex other than the distinction between consensual and non-consensual sex.

In my view, on the contrary, feminists must reject the idea that there is no distinction between healthy and unhealthy sex. Though the line should be drawn in a different place from where sexual puritans and male chauvinists draw it, we must look at the qualitative aspects of sexual interactions, and not just rely on the problematic notion of consent in order to decide whether they are healthy from a feminist perspective. The degree of social equality of the participants must be considered in order to determine whether the sexual exchange is a reciprocal rather than a hierarchical flow of energy.

With regard to sexual freedom, though radical feminists are surely correct that sexual liberation is not merely a matter of expanding the sphere of legitimated consensual relations, we disagree as to what sort of radical changes are required – both in terms of our visions and our transformative strategies. A socialist-feminist revision of the economy, family and sexual practices of the sort outlined in chapter eleven goes beyond vague radical feminist views of matriarchal society or alternative feminist communities which prioritise female friendships over sexuality. Thinking about how to get there from here requires a transitional feminist sexual morality and a strategy of coalitionism that acknowledges the possibility of an empowering aspect to some countercultural feminist practices in certain historical and specific contexts, such as lesbian butch/femme roles and heterosexual co-parenting, without simply rejecting them as examples of compulsory heterosexuality, as does the standard radical feminist line.

Our transitional feminist sexual morality cannot romanticise, as pluralist feminists tend to do, the oppositional practices of sexual minorities without regard to the content of what they do. Pluralist feminist strategy assumes that consensual sexuality is, in and of itself, empowering or liberating. This ignores the issue of structural inequalities between participants (e.g. man/boy love) that makes consent no guarantee of non-coercion. Though radical feminists may be mistaken to assume that heterosexual relationships can never be reciprocal, pluralist feminists are also mistaken to ignore the way that gender roles, when structured into sexual exchanges (whether in so-called 'vanilla' heterosexual sex, or gay or straight S/M or butch/femme sex roles) are risky because they

tend to constrain those in the feminine role from equal or reciprocal sex.

An historical concept of sexual alienation

An historical look at the conflicts in our contemporary mode of
organising sexuality, and sex/affective energy more generally, will
allow us to bypass the simplistic aspects of both poles of the
feminist sex debate and develop a feminist sexual morality appropriate to our place and time.

Before we do this, however, we must fulfil the promise made in
chapter three, and that is to supply an historical concept of sexual
alienation which saves us from the relativism which plagues the
theories of symbolic interactionism and Foucault, while not
requiring the universal (and thus essentialist) claims about human
nature of Reich and Marcuse. The hope is to develop a concept of
sexual alienation which is historically specific to our time and
place and yet gives us a way to critique our own social relations of
sexuality.

A key feature of contemporary US society is that women are
relatively empowered, in sex as in other areas of social lives,
compared to women in previous periods of our social formation.
Neither radical nor pluralist feminism really has a theory of
sexuality, social power or sexual freedom which allows us to
explain this fact. Our concept of sexual alienation and the consequent analysis we develop from it will only be adequate if it
allows us to explain this fact. It thus must explain the contradictory aspects of contemporary sexual codes and practices, both
those that relatively empower us, compared to past ages, and
those that continue to undermine women's possibilities of reciprocity in sex. We need to be able to target specific disempowering sexual structures, whose impact can be lessened or minimised
by those who manage to avoid those contexts. Our theory must
allow us to understand how some women have taken advantage of
the empowering aspects of contemporary sex/affective production
to escape the oppressive impact it has had on other women as well
as many men.

My historical framework for alienation allows a mode of sex/
affective production to be described as alienated if 1) there are
contradictory values built into the social construction of its sexual

symbolic codes; 2) sexual roles require an either/or choice of sexual values which an alternative social construction of sex (one which is historically possible to achieve) would make unnecessary; and 3) social structures in the present social formation make it impossible to achieve all the aims and objects of sexuality as socially constructed (thus implying the need for radical changes in the structure in order to achieve values promised by the society).

Just as capitalism may be seen to be a system with conflicting tendencies, some of which undermine its own ability to reproduce itself, so our contemporary capitalist public patriarchal sex/affective production system may be seen to produce expectations and sex/affective needs and desires that it cannot satisfy, thus undermining its own ability to reproduce itself.

A close examination of the material and symbolic possibilities for women in the US today reveals a set of structures with contradictory implications. For one thing, the increased possibility of divorce and availability of birth control have made possible the separation of sexuality from procreation. This empowers women, not merely to have less fear of unwanted pregnancies, but also to value the pleasurable aspects of sex and to demand more reciprocity as sexual subjects – including the possibility of lesbian sexuality. Though the interest in sex for pleasure has led to sexual consumerism, it has also relatively empowered women in the sense that women as sexual consumers can objectify men. This means that, increasingly, women can use men for pleasure in a way that only men were able to do with women in the past. Thus, though aspects of our sexual practices are still alienated, we as women still have greater sexual negotiating power than we used to.

The mass media have supported both genders' sexual consumerism by creating contradictory sexual images. Thus, radical feminists are mistaken to pick out merely violent pornography and passive housewife examples of the mass media's presentation of femininity, when it also presents strong feminist images in rock stars like Tina Turner and movies such as 'Alien', and androgynous, non-patriarchal masculine role models like rock star Michael Jackson. Indeed, the New Right's attempts to censor pornography can be seen as an attempt to challenge the newer images of sexually autonomous and demanding women by reverting to the Victorian asexual image of women.

In short, capitalist public patriarchal images of sexuality and love are a contradictory blend of a notion of romantic, egalitarian love and consensual sexual exchanges characteristic of possessive individualism and a patriarchal natural complement theory of men as sexual masters, women as sexual servers. These two ideologies cannot ultimately be reconciled with each other. But their coexistence in capitalist public patriarchy shows the possibility of an alternative socialist-feminist vision of sexual morality and sexual liberation which would eliminate the patriarchal aspects of the sexual code and create the social and material conditions to realise its egalitarian aspects.

Sexual alienation in all patriarchal sex/affective production systems is due in part to gender dualism; i.e. that the genders are socially created with different needs, desires and skills to achieve these needs. Though all known human societies have created some form of gender dualism because of the institution of the sexual division of labour, gender dualism involves a special form of alienation in capitalist public patriarchy because the material and social rationales for the sexual division of labour have disappeared. In advanced industrial societies scarcity is no longer a necessary feature of human life and childrearing practices need not be tied for efficiency to a sexual division of labour that has negative emotional and sexual side effects for heterosexual sex/affective interactions.

Furthermore, as shall be developed further below, our society possesses an ideal of human development which emphasises both a consumerist right to amass pleasures and a romantic ideal of deep emotional connections to others. But gender dualism, in continuing to perpetuate the learned split between emotion and pleasure, channels those involved with masculine roles to prioritise the search for and the skills appropriate to sexual pleasure and those involved with feminine roles to prioritise the search for, and skills to promote, emotional intimacy. Thus, persons of both genders are alienated because socialisation has taught all of us, women and men, the value of both goals yet nonetheless has forced individuals to develop the search for one in a way that excludes or makes difficult the potential for the other.

In addition to the gendered emotion/pleasure split, sexual alienation is manifest in the gap between romantic egalitarian ideology and the reality of the continued absence of conditions for such a reciprocal sexuality. Interestingly, this ideology/reality gap is due both to the continuing lack of material equality for women (particularly those who are mothers and engaged in the 'second shift' problem) as well as the internal contradiction in sexual desires socially constructed in capitalist patriarchy, that is, that both man and woman want equality yet have been taught to want the masculine subject to be dominant and the feminine subject to be submissive.

What follows from this brief analysis of how sexuality as a social energy is both constructed yet frustrated (*viz.* historically alienated), is that neither radical feminist nor pluralist feminist strategies for connecting sexual liberation with women's liberation are completely satisfactory. We cannot further feminist goals merely by validating consensual sex as the pluralist feminists suggest, for this ignores the structural inequalities present in standard sexual practices which makes reciprocal sexual exchanges between men and women difficult. But in a society that teaches conflicting sexual ideals to both men and women, we cannot appeal to an authentic feminine sexuality as a way of escaping these contradictions as the radical feminist position suggests, for feminine sexuality is itself an alienated social construction. Rather, we must develop a more sophisticated transitional feminist sexual morality based on an assessment of risks in the particular context in which acts take place. We will attempt such an analysis of concrete acts and their risks in our contemporary historical situation in chapter nine.

The dialectic of pleasure *vs* the dialectic of intimacy

It is time to sketch in greater detail the historical dynamic in contemporary capitalist public patriarchal sex/affective production which has created both our current sexual alienation and yet has empowered many women to conscious resistance to it.

Two conflicting dialectics of sexuality, the dialectic of pleasure and the dialectic of love/intimacy, are at work in contemporary society. These two dialectics involve the changing relations of women and men in sexual practices on the one hand and marriage and parenting practices on the other. Together they demonstrate the way we are alienated by our sex/affective production system, since it subjects us to a conflicting code of love and sexuality that cannot be satisfied.

Our contemporary social meanings for sexual pleasure and

emotional intimacy have a history tied to the development of the public/private split engendered by capitalist production. Pre-capitalist society organised sexuality to emphasise neither the possibilities of sexual pleasure nor emotional intimacy, but simply to regulate biological reproduction so as to strengthen the extended kinship networks through which economic production was organised.

The father patriarchies characteristic of early capitalist states involved a nuclearisation of the family which had two important effects in developing the modern structure of public/private spheres. On the one hand, acknowledging men as patriarchal heads of households allowed the emerging state to undermine the extended kin ties of the aristocracy which challenged its hege-mony. On the other hand, the creation of the private domestic sphere for bourgeois women and children set the stage for the eroticisation and intimisation of nuclear family relations (the 'sentimental family', cf. Nicolson, 1986; Stone, 1977; Shorter, 1975).

As argued in chapter five, the transition from father to husband family patriarchies in the first two phases of Western European and American capitalist development carried with it three impor-tant shifts in sex/affective production: 1) the emphasis on the maternal affectionate bond; 2) the development of the concept of romantic love as a base for marriage; and 3) (with the help of the bourgeois sexology of the late nineteenth and early twentieth centuries) a developing emphasis on sexual pleasure between husbands and wives as an important goal of marriage.

Contemporary capitalist patriarchal sex/affective production continues these emphases of husband patriarchy with some important developments. Husband patriarchy had a clear gender double standard for intimacy and sexual pleasure: that is, mothers but not fathers were expected to be emotionally intimate with children, wives but not husbands were expected to be emotionally nurturant to their mates, and the sexual pleasure relevant in marriage was generally assumed to be the man's and not the woman's.[2]

In the contemporary middle class, however, there is increas-ingly social support for an elimination of the sex/affective double standard; that is, for the rights of women and children to emotional nurturance by men and the rights of women to recipro-cal sexual pleasure from men or other women partners. Recent

studies (Ehrenreich, Hess and Jacobs, 1986; Hunt, 1974; Pietropinto and Simenauer, 1977; Seidman, 1987) have suggested
not only that many men value love and intimacy more highly
than casual sexual pleasure but also that women are increasingly demanding physical satisfaction in their relations with
men.

But this egalitarian tendency is countered by the continuing
gender dualism of our society which teaches girls but not boys to
value and develop skills for producing emotional intimacy and
teaches boys to treat egoistic sexual performance as a mark of
successful masculinity.

There are both material and symbolic supports for this gender
dualism. Materially, heterosexual sex is still dangerous for women
in the sense that it involves greater risks: pregnancy, single mother
poverty, reproductive diseases and complications. Furthermore,
the wage labour inequalities of men and women make an
economic connection to a man more important for a woman than
the reverse and make it an instrumental asset for women to learn
how to meet men's emotional needs.

The sexual symbolic code of our system of gender dualism
teaches boys and girls different gender messages about the
legitimacy of searching for bodily pleasures that can in any way
be construed as leading to orgasm. Boys are generally encouraged to think it manly to be assertive, if not aggressive, in
pushing to achieve their own bodily pleasure. Furthermore, a
man is assumed to be more masculine to the degree that he is
able to sustain more erections and to achieve more orgasms.
This normative assumption of male performance is coupled
with the assumption of male seduction: men are more masculine to the degree that they can influence women to acquiesce
to genital intercourse which results in orgiastic pleasure for the
man.

Most girls, on the contrary, are taught to be wary of sexuality
on the one hand, yet to aspire to be sexually attractive to men on
the other. Achieving sexual pleasure is not in any way part of the
norm of successful femininity – to the contrary, successful femininity still involves to some degree resisting casual heterosexual
intercourse in order to guarantee achieving a committed heterosexual partnership which allows the woman the social and
economic situation to mother.[3] Though pre-marital sex and living
together without marriage are increasingly tolerated by the

middle class and some subcultures of the working class, there is still the assumption that marriage is the ultimate requirement for a woman to have achieved social success.

The gender dualism of this sexual symbolic code leads to different goals in sexual interactions. For one thing, women will tend to gain more satisfaction from developing emotional intimacy than men. Men brought up by mother-centred childcare in the male breadwinner, female housewife nuclear family will tend, as Chodorow suggests, to achieve a separate sense of self from mother by denying their intimacy needs and hence will lack practice in the personal sharing and drawing out of feelings of those they are involved with. On the other hand, women from these families will tend to value close intimate relationships and to have much experience in learning how to supportively draw out and advise others in these areas.

This difference in intimacy skills and priorities will tend to create a lack of reciprocity in achieving their goals for each gender. Since men tend to derive personal self-esteem from successful genital orgasms, while woman's self-esteem tends to be based on the ability to understand and satisfy the emotional and physical needs of her partner, women will be more motivated to meet men's needs at the sacrifice of their own. Because of this frustrating situation, those women who are mothers may decide to focus more sex/affective energy into their relations with their children than with their mates which in turn may encourage men to turn elsewhere: to affairs or prostitutes for the satisfaction of their sexual needs.

The dialectic of pleasure presents a further complication in understanding contemporary sexual mores. For though girls by and large are still taught as children to favour sexual intimacy over sexual pleasure, the development of a sexual consumerist society is increasingly encouraging women to take our own sexual pleasure seriously and to challenge the sexual double standard. In keeping with the tendency of capitalism to commoditise as many objects and activities as possible in order to create and expand markets, the media not only sell products by sexually objectifying women for men but also increasingly sexually objectify men for women's consumption as well.

Looking at the whole contemporary system of ideological sexual communications, we can recognise five principles which make up the distinctive blend of the liberal individualism of capitalism and the 'natural complement' theory of our present patriarchal thought:

1 A voluntary love partnership (i.e. a love between equals) is an important human value (*principle of romantic love*).
2 Everyone, both male and female, has an equal right to sexual pleasures and the right to consensual interactions (*principle of sexual equality and freedom*).
3 Since men and women are different, they ought to engage in complementary gender roles in sex (*the natural complement gender principle*).
4 The masculine gender role is to initiate, while the feminine role is to submit (*the male seducer/female submission principle*).
5 Men generate sexual desire while women generate responsiveness (*the male performance/female responsiveness principle*).

The first two beliefs, the right to consent and equality, develop from market principles of capitalist production. However, they cannot be achieved in a capitalist patriarchal system which rests on a gender division of labour in the economy, family and personal life. The last three principles are modifications of the earlier gender ideology of family patriarchal societies. Principle 3, the natural complement principle, is a constant through different male dominant modes of sex/affective production. However, the last two principles are somewhat different from their analogues in family patriarchy.

The family patriarchy analogues could be described as the male seducer/female resister and male performance/female passivity principles. That is, in kin-organised family patriarchies, men are expected to try to seduce women while women's role is to resist sexual response to men in order to preserve their virginity, marital chastity and/or attention to the emotional rather than explicitly sexual interests of the family. If men succeed in overcoming female resistance, women are expected not to be responsive but to be passively acquiescent. These earlier patriarchal principles still operate in many contexts in society today, creating an explicit sexual conflict between men and women. Indeed, in male breadwinner/female housewife social formations, legitimised female sexual resistance is a source of sexual power for women over men that may explain 1950s pornography's fascination with the shrewish dominant woman/wimpy man stereotype.

Unfortunately, with the development of sexual consumerism the elimination of the 'female resister' aspect of the male seducer principle does not lead to an equalisation of gender roles, but on the contrary to the contemporary male seducer/female submission and male performance/female responsiveness principles outlined above. And these principles, though they continue to eroticise the subordination of women to men, are in increasing conflict with the second principle, the principle of sexual equality and freedom, which has gained increasing legitimacy as sexual consumerism has developed.

The dialectic of pleasure developed in advanced capitalism is based on a sexual consumerism that assumes both women and men are sexual consumers and, thus, sexual subjects. This suggests that women and men who engage in sex together should be equal negotiators of sexual pleasure for themselves. But the continuing assumptions of male dominance in gender roles hold that both women and men, or those in feminine and masculine roles in same sex relations, will want the masculine partner to be in control of sexual practices, to be the initiator and the dictator of the parameters of sexual pleasure possible for both partners.

It is increasingly true that men are sexually objectified by the mass media. But since men in general have more social power than women, as a sex/class men still think of themselves as sexual subjects. Thus sexual objectification is not as degrading to men as women since it does not imply men's loss of personhood and independent powers of will in the way it does for women.

Nonetheless, as the legitimacy of pleasure as a goal for both sexes increases, feminism, lesbian and gay liberation challenge the natural complement, male seducer, and male performance theses thus creating a dialectic of pleasure. These conflicting tendencies are handled in the mass media by a division of the images of sexual fantasy into three separate arenas; harlequin romances for 'good women' (Snitow, 1983), pornography for men and some erotica geared to a mixed audience of men and 'bad' women, feminists and other deviants. While harlequin romances and regular porn for men tend each in their own way to perpetuate the three patriarchal principles, the mixed erotica presents images of women demanding our own pleasure and sexually objectifying men. As well, the increased production of sex manuals for both men and women and the tendency of women's popular magazines (especially *Viva*, *Ms* and *Cosmopolitan*) which assume women's right to sexual pleasure provide a middle-ground discourse legitimising the goal of female sex for pleasure.

The other dialectic, the dialectic of love intimacy, is created by the continuing sexual division of labour in parenting which organises more of women's sex/affective energy, cross race and economic class divisions, into mothering and nurturing priorities than into sexual physical orgiastic pleasure. Though the increased social legitimacy and economic possibility of divorce allows women a greater option to leave emotionally and sexually unsatisfying marriages, the fact that the overwhelming number of children of divorced parents live with their mothers not only creates a continuity of unremunerated childrearing for women (Delphy, 1984) but also reinforces the prioritising for women of love and intimacy forms of sex/affective energy over those of genital pleasure (Modleski, 1982). Even women who are lesbians tend to prioritise love and intimacy over auto-erotic pleasure in their sex/affective relations, in part because of gender priorities most mothers communicate to their girls.

A standard consequence of the love/intimacy dialectic for women is to support the three patriarchal principles of the sex/affective code discussed above, thus disempowering women *vis-à-vis* men. Since women tend to prioritise love and intimacy over physical pleasure when there is a conflict between them in a relationship, they tend to accept the assumptions of the patriarchal principles when men insist on them in sexual practices in exchange for attempting to develop the intimacy connections in the relationship. Though not all women succumb to this way of resolving the conflicts between pleasure and intimacy, those who choose pleasure over intimacy continue to be labelled 'bad girls', even by other women – since such women may be promiscuous, refuse marriages or take jobs as prostitutes, pornographic models or other jobs in the sex industry.

In short, capitalist public patriarchal images of sexuality and love are a contradictory blend of a notion of romantic, egalitarian love and consensual sexual exchanges characteristic of possessive individualism, and a patriarchal natural complement theory of men as sexual masters, women as sexual servers. These two ideologies cannot ultimately be reconciled with each other. But their co-existence in capitalist patriarchy shows the possibility of an alternative socialist-feminist vision of sexual morality and sexual liberation.

A socialist-feminist vision of sexual liberation

The social energy theory of sexuality presented in chapter three implies that sexual repression is not simply a matter of damming up a natural sexual drive and using this energy for social domination. Rather, systems of male domination work through a process which produces sex/affective energies focused and intensified in different forms in men and women and creates a sex/affective male bonding through this sexual division of labour that gives men a material interest in preserving the system. In our contemporary mode of sex/affective production, sexual repression is a result of the sexual alienation which results from the gap between the historically conditioned needs for intimacy, pleasure and reciprocity and the gender-divided reality that makes it difficult for either men or women to achieve these goals.

This view of sexual liberation implies a much more complicated process than that conceived by Reich or Marcuse. For it does not involve simply freeing individuals from psycho-physical blocks to full bodily sexual expression. Undeniably individual psycho-body therapy is a part of the process since sexual alienation has built contradictory needs into the aims of our bodily sex/affective energies. But the overall process must also involve altering the structure of all of people's sex/affective practices. Sexual liberation, that is, requires recoding all symbolically charged sex/affective practices. And in our historical moment sexual liberation does imply gay and women's liberation. Women's liberation in turn implies the elimination of the gender division of labour wherever it occurs, not simply in explicit sexual practices but also in parenting, domestic labour, and wage labour, i.e. all gendered forms of sex/affective labour as discussed in chapter four.

Thus, a socialist-feminist vision of sexual liberation must demand an elimination of structures which mandate gender dualism in sex/affective work and sexuality. This is an historically based vision which suggests a way to achieve both the goals of pleasure and love/intimacy without being forced to choose to prioritise one or the other as women and men are at present. Family, sexual relations and social divisions of labour in the economy must be organised so that the values and skills of emotional intimacy and nurturance, on the one hand, and the knowledge of many and diverse erotic pleasures, on the other, are equally valued by, and possible for, both men and women.

Such a reorganisation cannot be achieved in a capitalist patriarchal society: only a socialist-feminist transformation of all aspects of social life could achieve this re-organisation. Only in this way can the equalising tendency of capitalist sexual consumerism for women be expanded into a fully non-alienated sexuality. The transformation to a democratic socialism would retain the emphasis on individual sexual choice while eliminating the gendered structures that perpetuate sexual inequality.

Though a programme of sexual liberation must defend rights to same sex relationships, a radical vision must question the gender dualism that assumes that sexual identities are fixed around the preference for one or the other genders (heterosexuality *vs* homosexuality). A vision which challenges existing gender priorities in sex/affective production would conceive of an alternative structure in which individuals retain the right to be sexually ambiguous: for example to relate to women as sexual partners for one segment of our life then switch to men; to stay with one sex or partner; or to alternate sexual preference regularly. In short, such a vision attacks the dominant Freudian power/ knowledge which supposes that our personal identity is essentially connected with one fixed sexual identity.

Until we have a socialist-feminist transformation of social life we will not be able to say for all of Freud's 'polymorphously perverse' forms of non-reproductive sexuality (e.g. homosexuality, exhibitionism, S/M sex, etc.) which can be truly reciprocal practices. This is because these forms usually involve roled sex (with the exception of homosexual relationships which need not do so), and it is not clear how much they owe their interest and excitement to male dominant systems of gender dualism in sex/ affective production.

Conclusion

I have argued that our society is sexually alienated because it has created a mix of possessive individualist and patriarchal expectations about sexuality which are inconsistent, as well as a gender dualism of sexual personalities and material social structures which partially empower yet also oppress women. No wonder there is increasing social crisis around marriage and divorce, premarital sex, pornography and sexual preference. Parenting also is in crisis, as we shall explore in the next chapter.

PART THREE

Feminist Politics

8

Contemporary motherhood

Oh baby, come, flop onto my warm belly-beach. Come,
creep into the crook of my arm-tree. Climb higher. Nuzzle
me. There's wet fruit to eat. Don't stop. Come closer. Eye to
eye, soul to soul. Come say hello to your new born Mother.
(Phyllis Chesler, 1979: 118)

I would like to affirm the rejection of motherhood on the
grounds that motherhood is dangerous to women. If woman,
in patriarchy, is she who exists as the womb and wife of man,
every woman is by definition a mother: she who produces for
the sake of men. A mother is she whose body is used as a
resource to reproduce men and the world of men, understood both as the biological children of patriarchy and as the
ideas and material goods of patriarchal culture. Motherhood
is dangerous to women because it continues the structure
within which females must be women and mothers and,
conversely, because it denies to females the creation of a
subjectivity and world that is open and free. (Jeffner Allen,
1984: 315)

Feminist theorists, like contemporary American mothers, have a
love-hate relationship with motherhood. We can't decide whether
motherhood is good or bad for women! Part of the confusion on
this question stems from universalist and static thinking about the
motherhood question on the one hand, and misguided historical
thinking on the other.
  While feminist motherhood theorists like Nancy Chodorow
(1974, 1978a, 1978b, 1979a, 1979b) and Adrienne Rich (1976)
approach motherhood as an institution of asymmetrical infant
care that universally has been appropriated by patriarchy, historians like Elizabeth Badinter (1981) argue that no generalisations can be made about motherhood, for even our notion of
mother-centred infant 'care' is a product of the bourgeois family

of European eighteenth-century development. Similarly such diverse writings on racial and class differences between women as those by Carol Stack (1974) and Gloria Joseph and Jill Lewis (1981) suggest that the tendency of neo-Freudian feminists to generalise greater separation problems (and hence greater ambivalences) between mothers and daughters than mothers and sons (e.g. cf. Flax, 1978) are based on the middle-class white bourgeois family context and not that of Black and working-class family backgrounds. Thus, since generalisations about the production of different female gender personalities (permeable ego boundaries) from male gender personalities (rigid ego boundaries) in asymmetrical mothering are suspect, the institution of motherhood cannot be targeted as the cross-cultural perpetuator of male dominance.

But there is a way out of the apparent impasse in feminist theory between the universal motherhood theorists and those historical thinkers who, by emphasising context, downplay the effects of motherhood in the reproduction of male dominance. Whether women gain or lose power in relation to their involvement in mothering depends not only on particular parenting practices but also on the wider social contexts in which these practices are enmeshed: the economic system, the race/ethnic and economic class positions of the women concerned. But, as argued in chapter four, parenting and sexuality are social products that operate by some general principles of reproduction in different social formations. Systems of male dominance are materially based in the sexual division of sex/affective labour in a society, a division which has always included different parental labour for the two genders.[1] Thus, to understand how male dominance connects to mothering, we must examine parenting as it relates to particular modes of sex/affective production rather than to seek some general essence or constant underlying motherhood. In this chapter our present historical situation of mothering in the United States will be examined, both to outline its rewards and its liabilities and to consider some empowering parenting alternatives available to feminists today.

Historical socialist-feminist thinking has to reject such a universalistic radical feminist strategy as that suggested by Jeffner Allen's claim, quoted above, that feminists should renounce motherhood. Though such a strategy might make sense in advanced industrial societies where children are economic and social liabilities rather than assets, rejecting motherhood can never be a collectively accepted strategy because most women's psychological sense of gender is connected to motherhood. Furthermore, such a strategy is clearly utopian in contemporary underdeveloped societies such as in Latin America and much of Africa where peasant economies make children an economic necessity. Thus, feminists seeking to create solidarity networks with feminists in Central America, for example, would do better to support organisations like MADRE which send material aid to mothers and children, or to support the Nicaraguan women's organisation AMNLAE in its fight to extend full legal child support and custody rights to mothers to challenge the husband patriarchy that existed before the Sandinista revolution.

Mothering *per se* cannot not be touted as the base for a superior female ethic. Thus, the work by Chodorow, Gilligan and Ruddick is misleading because they assume there is some way, independent of economic and cultural context, to suppose that women are more likely to be pacifists or to oppose militarist, abstract thinking than men (Ruddick, 1984). But this conclusion is implausible since it must ignore the violence mothers are capable of in their relations with their children or in defending their children (Hooks, 1984). Similarly, mothering cannot be condemned as a mistaken choice by feminists in the US today even though it is, generally, an economic liability.[2] Mothering is a complicated reality in contemporary America because, although it is an economic liability for most women, it is also a psychological asset. In capitalist public patriarchal sex/affective production, as in many other patriarchal modes of sex/affective production, mothering symbolises successful womanhood, and as such allows women self-love: an unrepressed sex/affective satisfaction with self that involves a feeling of gender security.

The social status of motherhood is, of course, being eroded today by the fact that children are perceived to be luxuries rather than social assets or necessities. Consequently, sexual attractiveness currently vies with motherhood as a mark of successful femininity. But the ongoing importance of motherhood as a mark of gender identity for women is indicated by the fact that the vast majority of women still want to mother at least one child.

The conflict between the goal of economic independence (most fully achievable in advanced capitalist society by women who are not mothers) and the psychological gender and sex/affective rewards of mothering create a unique situation in advanced capitalist societies. Motherhood, that is, is both a benefit and a burden. It is precisely these contradictory aspects of mothering in our historical situation which feminists must understand and use to our strategic advantage in organising women.

The public/private split in which mothering labour is trapped in our society creates certain oppressive structures which cut across class and race lines. These are 1) the single motherhood problem and 2) the mediation problem. Both of these problems have material bases and psychological consequences that disadvantage women in seeking parity with men. Let us consider in more detail the economic liability and mediation problems of motherhood and the potential for a united political platform on mothering rights that could cut across other social divisions between feminists.

The economic liability of motherhood today

Though there are obvious privileges that white and middle- to upper-class women have in relation to mothering that should not be ignored, the instability of marriages in advanced capitalist societies creates a greater uncertainty for all married mothers that they will be able to maintain their economic class of origin for their lifetime. For example, Sidel in her insightful book *Women and Children First* (Sidel, 1986) argues that very few American women are really protected from poverty. Her examples include: a happily married New Hampshire mother of eight whose income drops from $70,000 a year to $7,000 when her husband leaves her for another woman; formerly affluent women who as widows must count pennies on a vastly reduced fixed income; a former welfare worker in the Bronx who finds herself a welfare mother of three when her husband becomes addicted to heroin and alcohol; and a Maine mother of two who is pregnant with her third child and must choose between a husband who threatens to kill her and destitution.

Though most Americans might guess that one out of every seven Americans is poor, few understand what a rising percentage of these people is women and children. The 'feminisation of poverty' phenomenon encompasses this change in the demography of the poor. Today two out of three poor adults are women, and one of five children is poor. Women head half of all poor families and over half the children in female-headed households are poor: 50 per cent of white children, 68 per cent of Black and Latin children. According to Ehrenreich, Stallard and Sklar (1983), 10,000 additional women with children fell below the poverty line each year from 1969 to 1978. In 1979 the number surged to 150,000 and was matched in 1980. Households headed by women – now 15 per cent of all households – are the fastest growing type of family in the US.

Though the sex-segmentation of wage labour and the generally lower pay for women's work is obviously a part of the explanation of why single-mother-headed and lesbian couple family households are poorer than male-headed and joint heterosexual family households, we need the theory of sex/affective labour to understand why women continue to choose motherhood (including retaining child custody after divorce) when it is such an economic liability.

Even though children are an economic liability in advanced capitalist societies, the asymmetrical division of sex/affective labour by mothers rather than fathers in childcare means that mothers generally have more sex/affective energy invested in children and see children more as their products than men do. But this greater emotional investment in children by women puts women at a bargaining disadvantage with men in most issues of economic distribution, both within the family during marriage and when the family is separated by divorce.[3]

In her recent work, Nancy Folbre has defended Delphy's insight about the unremunerated childcare of single mothers (Delphy, 1984) by arguing that in advanced capitalist societies children ought to be seen as public commodities, the future labour force for collective social use, and mothers compensated fairly for their child producing services by the state (Folbre, 1985). The fact that women are not adequately compensated by the state is evidence of the way that capitalism and male dominance have reorganised into capitalist public patriarchy.

The mediation problem

... My disappointments at times worked themselves out on her. There were days with guilt feelings when I became the doormat for both of them. He who sat in his study and wanted to own me alone. And she who could barely walk, and cried for me from the other end of the house. I rushed from one to the other, always with a bad conscience. (Ullman, 1977: 74)

Father is the stranger, loser of that share of mothering he had from 'his woman' before there was a child between them, is the alienated outsider and yet somehow, he keeps reminding himself, proprietor of all this. Bestirred by angers and jealousies he cannot understand, he closes his eyes. He has, for so long, been the teller of the story. (Bernikow, 1980: 43)

I have argued that mothering is a psychological asset in capitalist patriarchy because it provides a sense of gender success for women in a situation when the alternative route, a satisfactory adult sexual love relationship, is uncertain. Nonetheless, mothering in isolated couples, whether these are heterosexual or lesbian, involves the psychological hazard of what we might call 'the mediation problem'. The analysis that follows historicises Chodorow's insights concerning feminine and masculine gender to argue that the mediation problem is a consequence of the psychological gender structure of those parented in any coupled form of capitalist nuclear families, whether it be the capitalist patriarchal nuclear family or the joint wage earning nuclear family.

The mediation problem involves a family context in which mothers are more motivated to mediate conflicts of interest between those they are sex/affectively bonded with, i.e. children and mates, than are fathers or, in lesbian relationships, those who are not mothers. For women raised in such families, one aspect of their unconscious gender structure is a triangular gender identity. That is, ideal femininity as we learned it from our mothers and fathers is understood as a mediating relationship between children, mate and self. Such mothers tend to seek their sex/affective satisfaction by maintaining harmonious relations between the other members of the relationship.

By contrast, a heterosexual male raised in either of these parenting practices has a double dyadic gender structure.[4] That is, masculinity is defined by two independent relations: possessing a wife or lovers, and male bonding. Though having a child may be incorporated into the male bonding dynamic, for instance, in father/son relationships, the success of either his love ties and his male bonding sex/affective ties are most usually not defined in relation to each other.

Thus, in capitalist patriarchal nuclear families and joint wage earner families, fathers will tend to be more interested in the sex/affective connection to the woman than to the young child. This creates a conflict of interest, where the man is jealous of the mother's time with the child. In addition, the very young child is more interested in its sex/affective tie with the mother than with the father/mate. Consequently, the mother/mate is either constantly forced to adjudicate between the two or to prefer one member's claims over the other.

The emotional logic of this incorporative triangle usually creates a situation where women are led to sacrifice some of their self-interests which are not defined through the child/mate/self bond. Thus, the emotional role of mediator creates a bargaining imbalance for the mother which is one of the supports of contemporary male dominance.

The weakness of the woman's mediator role as a strategy for female personal power within the system of family relations is increased when there is a strong father/son sex/affective tie in which woman/mother deprecation is an important element. For an example of this, see the discussion below of the sex/affective triangle of Milkman, Ruth and Macon Dead in Toni Morrison's *Song of Solomon*.

Types of mothering practice today

The mediation problem operates in different ways in the four major parenting subcultures present in the social formation of capitalist patriarchy. These are the capitalist patriarchal nuclear family (male breadwinner, female housewife), the joint wage-earning 'second shift' family, the extended female-dominant kin/network family and the isolated single mother family.

Though mothers in all of these parenting subcultures are oppressed, they are oppressed in different ways. A housewife, for example, usually has less control over the joint economic resources of the family than the wage working wife. Nonetheless she is likely to have more leisure time than the wage working mother. Indeed the housewife is not oppressed by the second shift problem of wage work and housework/childcare in the way the latter is.

Women in the extended female-headed family situation may totally control the economic income of their families, since they are the primary wage earners, and the upbringing of their children, thus having more negotiating power with fathers and lovers. But, as with the isolated single mother family, this increased negotiating power comes at the cost of increased exploitation of their sex/affective labour by fathers and lovers who usually provide no or only token paternal economic and childcare support for the children. Thus single mothers often face the 'third shift' problem: they must either face dire poverty on welfare or work overtime in wage labour in addition to their unpaid housework and childcare to compensate for the lack of father's input into household expenses and domestic work. The frustration that this structurally unfair situation creates may be vented in maternal violence and child abuse.

Given that there are such differences in the structured situations that mothering involves in capitalist public patriarchy, why should we think of it as a system of organising male dominance at all? There are two answers to this question. First, even though the capitalist patriarchal family, the joint wage earning family and the single mother-headed family differ from each other in the amount of gender power they offer women, they are all a part of the overall system of nucleated families which tend to be both authoritarian and male dominant. That is, they all turn out human products that tend to be similar in terms of their desires to reproduce the conditions for male dominance: a sexual division of labour at work and home where men retain control, authority and any social surplus, parenting where women and not men mother, and a privatised nuclear family sex/affective focus.

Second, there are social contradictions in our contemporary social formation which allows alternative family subcultures to emerge, some of which involve more democratic forms of sex/affective production that undermine capitalism and male dominance. In spite of these emerging alternative forms, however, the male dominant sex/affective symbolic codes governing motherhood and sexuality (good *vs* bad motherhood; good *vs* bad sexuality) continue to control the social meaning attached to these subversive forms, that they are deviant, illegitimate, 'broken' or unhealthy.

Just as the classic distinction between marriage and prostitution serves as a way to divide and conquer female resistance to male dominance, so the male dominant social coding of mothering practices, in conjunction with race, ethnic and class differences, divide women from each other, thus perpetuating race, class and gender dominance.

In all male dominant systems of sex/affective production 'good' women are divided from 'bad' women with regard to their motherhood and sexual roles. We are all familiar with the image of the chaste single or monogamous married woman *vs* the whore. But the patriarchal control of motherhood has further divisive normative categories. Thus, women who are mothers and married are 'good', to be distinguished from single 'bad' or 'failed' women who are non-mothers. Furthermore 'good' mothers (married) are distinguished from 'bad' mothers (unmarried).

During the earlier periods of capitalism, there was a social stigma cast on wage-working mothers. For until recently, when the Women's Movement encouraged women to put together professional careers with motherhood (thus perpetuating the second shift problem), the assumption in husband patriarchal capitalist society was that mothers who do not work in wage labour (middle- or upper-class, white) are better than mothers who do (working-class, Black or non-white).

The social stigma of the normal/deviant split in categories of motherhood functions to inhibit women from creating conscious feminist networks across mothering subcultures to challenge the public/private split in contemporary society. And the material differences in power *vis-à-vis* men and the consequent differences in gender identity created by these four major types of parenting practice (and others which are more consciously countercultural, to be discussed below) tend to create differences in female strategies for gender equality. Let us make this more concrete by again turning to some examples of mothering from feminist literature.

A good example of the capitalist patriarchal nuclear family is that of the Deads in Toni Morrison's *Song of Solomon*. In this family the women are put in the classic mediator roles between patriarchal male relatives, thus losing some of their own autonomy in the process. Ruth, the mother, is the daughter of a doctor who never liked her husband Macon. Macon is jealous of his wife's affection for her father. Macon comes to interpret her sex/affective tie with her father as perverse. Ruth becomes the classic scapegoat as Macon feels justified in punishing her by violent and demeaning treatment.

Milkman, Ruth's son, gets his name because a neighbour sees him still being nursed by his mother at the age of four or five. So Ruth acquires a social stigma in the community for the 'sin' of seeking to prolong the unproblematic and joyous maternal sex/affective tie of breastfeeding. Ruth's special bond with Milkman in breastfeeding, in part a compensation for her husband's (and to some extent her father's) rejection of her, is abruptly terminated, leaving Milkman unsure of what happened, and weakening the mother/son relationship. Ruth thus loses the chance for personal power that a strong supportive mother/son bond can bring a woman in patriarchal society.

A second crisis in Ruth's and Milkman's sex/affective tie comes with the separation period of adolescence. Macon, having hitherto seen the young child Milkman as a rival in collusion with his mother (indeed, he tried to induce Ruth to have an abortion to prevent Milkman's birth), now attempts to appropriate Milkman to his side in this familial gender sex/affective war when the boy comes to work for him in his real estate business. Milkman comes to copy Macon in certain ways and seek his approval: ' . . . he couldn't help sharing with Macon his love of good shoes and fine thin socks. And he did try, as his father's employee, to do the work the way Macon wanted it done' (Morrison, 1977: 63). So Macon decides to take the boy on his side: 'Macon was delighted. His son belonged to him now and not to Ruth . . . ' (Morrison, 1977: 63).

The crisis is precipitated when Milkman, finding his father beating his mother, hits his father. Macon then presents his accumulated evidence to Milkman of the incestuous relation of Ruth to her father, and attempts to win his boy over to mother-hating. This strategy succeeds for a long period, thus weakening his mother's social power.

The way that single mother, capitalist patriarchal and joint wage earning family structures are connected in white working-class family life is illustrated in Tillie Olsen's story 'I Stand Here Ironing' (Olsen, 1960). The first person narrative of the mother provides us with reminiscences of herself from the time she was a single poor mother, deserted by her first husband and forced to work in wage labour full-time, to her present situation as a house-wife (or part-time worker: it is never made clear) and mother of four children. As a second shift working single mother, she was forced to neglect her daughter by leaving her home alone. She was then separated from her by well meaning social workers who placed her daughter in an oppressive home for under-privileged children where love and affection are denied the children. Daughter and mother lose the chance for a strong sex/affective tie by these restricting structures. The mother is so encumbered by her mothering work and domestic labour for all of the children (and what remains unspoken but is there by implication: sex/affective care for her second husband) that she cannot create the stronger bond that would have given both of them more gender power.

What is interesting about the Olsen story, in contrast to the Morrison novel, is that the oppression of the women is not due to direct exploitation or domination by men but is indirect. In an isolated working-class single mother-headed family, the father is absent, thus leaving women to the double shift of breadwinning and childrearing. Nonetheless the absent father continues to exploit the woman's childrearing labour by leaving her to do all of what should be half his responsibility.

The rise in divorce and remarriage statistics may have increased women's ability to escape from direct patriarchal oppression such as domestic battering. But women have not been shielded from the indirect oppression of single motherhood or the impersonal forms of male dominance that the public/private split forces on women's mothering work. Tillie Olsen's working-class mother has had her sense of personal power so diminished by the public/private split and by her guilt and hopelessness to remedy the lack of adequate mothering for her daughter that she is intimidated by the school's middle-class judgemental authority and cannot intervene with the school on her daughter's behalf.

It is not just working-class women who face disempowerment as mothers. Even though middle- and upper-class women may have economic resources to hire nannies that ease second shift problems in juggling career and mothering, we should not under-emphasise the psychological effect of the mediation problem in creating an unequal negotiating situation for such women to get fathers to make career sacrifices comparable to theirs in bringing up young children (Ehrensaft, 1980).

Another disempowerment that mothers face which is no respector of economic class or race is the danger of de-legitimation as mothers because of their love relationship with a mate considered unsatisfactory. Lesbian mothers are in constant legal jeopardy of having their rights to children awarded to fathers or

other kin because of their suspect sexual preference. Even heterosexual women whose ex-husbands are determined to gain child
custody are in danger of forfeiting their rights to children if they
choose a non-traditional relationship over marriage. A good
example of this is portrayed in Sue Miller's *The Good Mother*
(1986). Anna loses her daughter Molly in a child custody fight
because her ex-husband, playing on the suspicion of a patriarchal
court judge against unmarried lovers, is able to misconstrue a
scene between her lover Leo and her daughter as sexually abusive.

There are contexts in our society, however, in which mother/
child relationships are empowering for women. The extended
female-headed family household can be either empowering or
disempowering, depending on whether or not the mediation
problem pits the women in the family against each other, or unites
them in support of each other (either against abusive males or
forces in the outside world).

It is instructive to contrast the empowering mother/daughter
relationships depicted by Ntozake Shange in *Sassafras, Cypress
and Indigo* (1982) with the disempowered ones between Sula and
her female kin in Toni Morrison's *Sula* (1973). Shange's mama,
Hilda, is not an authoritarian mother, although she is authorita-
tive. She manages to establish a process of negotiation with each
of her very different daughters which allows for a democratic
mediation of conflicting mother/daughter values. Thus, Indigo is
allowed to play the violin but only if she takes lessons, while
Sassafras and Cypress are alternately critiqued and supported in
their artistic and bohemian lifestyles by their advice-giving,
recipe-sending mother.

By contrast, Morrison's Sula expresses both the potential
gender power of her upbringing in a negotiating power subculture
of extended maternal influence and the fragility of her chances for
personal power. Sula is denied a strong maternal role-model
relationship by her mother Hannah's indifference and her grand-
mother Eva's antagonism. As a consequence her only chance for
personal support comes from her friendship with Nel. Unfortunately this friendship is broken up by Sula's affair with Nel's
husband, an affair that to Sula, replicating her mother and grand-
mother's instrumental relationships with men, is of little
importance.

While Sula's story is a tragedy, it demonstrates the possibility
for gender negotiating power in extended female kin networks

where women support each other and in addition have strong friendships with other women who are non-kin. Though mothers' love for daughters in situations of poverty and racism may be 'hard love', these often create tighter mother/daughter bonds than in white middle-class nuclear families where the social contradictions for daughters of a liberal education geared toward preparation for professional work in contrast to one's mother's subservient role as housewife creates ambivalent mother/daughter bonds (Joseph and Lewis, 1981).

In short, there are some parenting subcultures even in capitalist public patriarchy in which women can gain power as mothers and can empower their daughters. We shall now turn to the question of feminist alternative family forms and mothering structures for feminists in contemporary society.

Countercultural forms, networks and visions: social (chosen) families

A chapter on mothering in contemporary society would not be complete without some discussion of those 'chosen families', to use Karen Lindsey's concept (Lindsey, 1981), which intentionally choose to create alternative forms of loving, bonding and parenting to promote feminist and egalitarian values in themselves and their children.

Lindsey's idea of a chosen family includes both honorary and fictive kin incorporated into a nuclear family or any of the alternative family types below. Such kin are friends of a family household which come to be treated as relatives and from which one can expect the same kind of material and emotional support (income sharing, aid in a crisis, etc.) as from biological or marriage-related family. Lindsey points out how many such bondings and liaisons go unacknowledged except in feminist histories, since they fall outside the socially legitimated sense of who is kin. The prevalence of such socially chosen extended kinlike liaisons has been particularly prevalent in the Black community in the United States (Gutman, 1977; Stack, 1974).

I am going to discuss the six types of countercultural families of which I have had personal experience, either from being involved with them myself or having close friends in them. The feminist use of such structures can provide negotiating power for women and children and/or dismantle the patriarchal sex/affective roles which trap men in more traditional family subcultures. Each of these alternative forms, used by feminists, can be part of a feminist countercultural mode of sex/affective production which creates different gender identities, sexualities and parenting priorities in its members. In conjunction with women's inter-familial networks with other women, always key to women's power, such family households can act both as bulwarks against male dominance and as ways to make concrete an alternative sex/affective egalitarian and democratic way of life.

The types of alternative family which will be discussed are 1) communal family households (persons, not all of whom are biologically or maritally related, sharing a household with some commitment to collective economic sharing and decision-making); 2) the 'reconstructed' nuclear family (i.e. a family created by an amalgamation of sexual mating partners and children from first marriages or liaisons: step-parenting); 3) the lesbian or gay couple with children; 4) the 'living together but not married' heterosexual couple with biological or adopted children; 5) the divorced/separated but co-parenting family; and 6) the 'revolutionary family-community' (a group of non-kin-related, separate family and/or communal households of any of the above sorts, living in geographical proximity, which have an ongoing collective commitment to material and social support for each other and for childrearing together which emphasises feminist and egalitarian values).[5]

The difference between traditionally unconventional families and these countercultural family types depends on the degree of self-conscious rebellion against the traditional capitalist patri-archal nuclear family. That is, a structure is 'countercultural' to the degree that the individuals involved are self-conscious of choosing family arrangements which go against the grain of tradi-tional assumptions. Such arrangements allow individuals to pool resources, income, domestic work and childrearing in a way that can mitigate the liability of motherhood in capitalist public patriarchy.

But for countercultural families to be fully feminist, they cannot merely create material support for their members. In addition, for the arrangements above to be feminist, their members must consciously intend by their participation to chal-lenge traditional patriarchal values. Though not all families which can be classified under the structures listed above are feminist in intention or results, each of these structures has importantly been used as a successful arena for feminist childrearing.

There were many countercultural experiments with heterosexual communal households in the late 1960s and early 1970s. Only a few of these communes still exist, in part because of the difficulty of setting up collective processing and decision-making structures that are at once democratic and effective in counteracting the unconscious hierarchical assumptions of those patriarchal family forms in which members had grown up. For example, in my first experience with a heterosexual commune, my husband and I, the oldest and most financially secure couple, became Daddy and Mommy figures to the other adults who then acted out various rebellions. The young children in the group were treated inconsistently by the various members and tended to develop strategies of manipulation to get their needs met.

The failures of many communal households do not imply that the structure cannot be developed for feminist purposes. In particular, the model of a feminist communal household for single mothers is an important solution to the motherhood liability problem of capitalist patriarchy. My own lesbian single mother communal household was a household of myself and another lesbian mother, each with one child, and a third lesbian, lover with my housemate and co-parenting with her. This household was an extremely important support to me as a single mother. Not only is it easier to communicate feminist values to one's children when backed up by one or more other mothers: it is also easier to practise what one preaches when children see women successfully alternating tasks traditionally thought to be masculine and feminine.

A major advantage for single mother communes over isolated single mother or heterosexual nuclear family households occurs during the teen-raising years. The mother-hating that our society encourages in teenagers as they struggle to develop their own adult personalities can be more successfully negotiated by a household democratic process of group sharing and self-conscious adjudication of conflicts than by an individual mom who attempts to pull rank on her children.

Another alternative family structure is the lesbian or gay co-parenting family. Though I have never lived together with a woman lover and my child, there are many examples of successful lesbian co-parenting situations in my area. For example, one lesbian couple has a joint family of four children, three of whom are adopted, and another has a joint family of four children, all of whom are their biological children. Both daughters and sons in these families get wonderful role models of strong women who are able to break down gender roles both in domestic and wage work.

A problematic issue in women-headed, particularly lesbian, households is how to provide boy children, and girls too, with male feminist role models. Some families deal with this problem by finding their boys, and girls too, a feminist 'big brother': high school or college students who want a way to have children in their lives.

Co-parenting with men, the Chodorowian solution, is neither possible nor desirable for these women in their particular situation. In general, the single mother household, whether lesbian or straight, faces a similar problem that the Women's Movement needs to address by encouraging its male allies to consider social parenting or big brother relations to those feminist households desiring such input for their sons and daughters.

Co-parenting with a husband, male lover or former husband can be a successful alternative parenting structure but only in certain contexts. In particular, both boys and girls can develop alternative conceptions of masculinity and femininity when heterosexual parents challenge the gender division of childrearing. When or if co-parents divorce, children need not experience that great loss of the sex/affective energy bond (usually with the father) that usually is acted out in rage against the mother who continues to be held responsible for the break-up by the children (another effect of the mediation problem!).

But there are serious problems with heterosexual co-parenting in a male dominant society (Ehrensaft, 1980). For one thing, co-parenting tends to create a more permanent family bond between the co-parents and the child than the traditional nuclear family did, since parents must agree on all aspects of childrearing to share the tasks interchangeably. Thus, in the case of divorce, it is even more difficult for subsequent love mates of the parents to be accepted by the child(ren). I have found from my own experience that this is especially difficult for all concerned when the subsequent love relation is a lesbian relationship.

A further problem is that co-parenting allows the father equal emotional authority with the children, even though the mother, because of her early childhood gender-training, is likely to be more involved in the mediation problem than the man. This puts the mother at a disadvantage in parental disagreements: she has given up her greater emotional authority in relation to the child in favour of democratic co-parenting, yet she has more to lose than the father since his gender personality ordinarily does not motivate him to egalitarian solutions of conflicts of interest.

It is essential to counteract this psychological disadvantage of heterosexual co-parenting by feminist ties to women, either in women's support groups or friendship networks. Some form of feminist therapy can be very helpful as well. Feminist family therapy, in particular, can allow both parents to counteract these unconscious family patterns.

There is an additional problem for children involved with co-parents who are no longer lovers. As more and more adults these days tend to be involved in serial relationships, this may create a problem of overload (too many co-parents!) for the children involved. It is important in such cases to work out a democratic process (which may require some family therapy) for deciding how to resolve the parenting issue. This process should be one in which children have some say. After all, it shouldn't be only parents who get to 'choose' their families!

Non-marriage as a solution to combat the patriarchal patterns of heterosexual coupledom is becoming increasingly common for couples without children, but it is still rare for those who decide to have children. At this point, the social stigma of parents and other relatives becomes so intense that it is only likely to be in ethnic subcultures where this is accepted (e.g. some Afro-American contexts) or for older established individualists, often with children from previous marriages.

The non-marriage/living together option as a feminist solution works well for those couples both of whom have jobs which allow them a modicum of economic independence. Otherwise, the sexist organisation of the workplace makes it difficult for wage earning fathers to take paternity leave or flexi-time to combine childcare and waged job, and the lesser pay the woman usually gets makes it more likely that the couple will fall into a sexist second shift pattern with the mother doing more domestic work and childcare than the father.

To conclude this discussion of countercultural family forms that can subvert capitalist patriarchy a brief sketch of an ambitious educational experiment in challenging racism, sexism and capitalist oppression will be provided. This was the Che-

Lumumba School, a parents' co-operative Third World, anti-racist, anti-imperialist and anti-sexist school. My ex-husband John, my daughter Kathy and I were members of this school from the time she was in second grade through the time she finished fifth. It established what could be called a 'revolutionary family-community', that is, 'a number of families and/or individuals who may live separately but who are united in a working network which constitutes for them a self-conscious resistance community; a community which deliberately creates values which run counter to the dominant values of capitalist patriarchal culture' (Ferguson, 1981a).

The Che-Lumumba school was an alternative school for elementary school children which developed out of models created in a graduate education class of Gloria Joseph at the University of Massachusetts in the early 1970s. It had a political philosophy that involved advocacy of Third World liberation struggles from a generally progressive or socialist viewpoint. It was a parent-teacher co-operatively run school. The founding parents were graduate students at the School of Education who wished to provide an Afro-American self-determined education for their children as an alternative to the cultural racism of the public schools. The school subsequently broadened its base to include Hispanic parents, white parents with Third World children, and a small number (no more than twenty per cent) of white children.

Che-Lumumba school politics represented a loose coalition of political interests (fighting imperialism, racism, capitalism, sexism) rather than a unified set of priorities or theory of social dominance. Since feminist issues were definitely of secondary concern to most of the other members of the group because they seemed too divisive, it was always a struggle to legitimate concerns with sexism and heterosexism.

The bi-weekly school pot-luck dinner get-togethers of parents and children for democratic input into the running of the school, and the regular rotational discussion of individual children and their problems by the group gave us a sense of being part of a countercultural kin network that was developing egalitarian values in our children. For the children, many of whom were in single parent and/or divorced and reconstituted parent households, having the peer network of similar others and other adult role models who cared for them was an essential support against the social alienation they were made to feel as non-white people, and/or as people from non-nuclear or 'different' families.

An alternative school or ongoing collective parent-child network (for example a consciousness-raising group of single mothers and children, or a rotating after school home childcare network) can be extremely important in creating the affirmative peer networks needed by both parents and children who are oppressed by social dominance structures. For my daughter, being non-white, adopted by white parents, and being a member of a lesbian single mother communal household were differences that stigmatised her in the public school. Though the Che-Lumumba school never dealt very well with its homophobia, having a school and community context which brought her parents together and which validated some of her differences was a very healthy, healing experience.

Conclusion

The aim in this chapter has been to show how women's mothering labour can be either a resource or a liability, depending on the particular context (traditional *vs* countercultural family/ household or practices) in which it is embedded. Though mothering is a liability for most women in capitalist public patri-archies, there are different parenting and sexual sex/affective practices which can empower women, even within our society. Furthermore, feminist countercultural family forms, since they can be democratic rather than authoritarian, can provide all of us with an alternative feminist and egalitarian mode of sex/affective production to contrast with capitalist and patriarchal sex/affective production. These forms can provide women with alternative power bases through which to challenge male dominance at the same time as they provide male allies with a way to create more egalitarian relations between themselves, women and children. Out of such feminist countercultural practices a new vision of egalitarian sex/affective production is rising. In the last chapter we shall discuss more fully what this vision is and what political strategies are necessary to work toward achieving it.

9

Sexual identity: lesbian and gay liberation

During the early 1970s, the American Women's Movement split on the issue of whether lesbian-feminism is the vanguard of feminism. Radical lesbians argued that lesbians exemplified the rage of all women against male dominance, that fighting heterosexism was necessary to counter the stigma of being lesbian that strong women fighting sexism otherwise encountered and that women-loving women could best counter sexism (Radicalesbians, 1970). Charlotte Bunch and the Furies Collective took the analysis one step further by arguing that since compulsory heterosexuality is the crosscultural social structure that perpetuates male dominance, feminists should become lesbians to resist this structure (Bunch, 1975; Myron and Bunch (eds), 1975). More recently, Adrienne Rich has argued that crosscultural feminism can be understood by positing what she calls a 'lesbian continuum' of women who have resisted the strictures of compulsory heterosexuality (Rich, 1980).

These theories and analyses of radical feminism led to a political separatism that, at its most virulent, held that lesbian-feminists should not do political work either with men, including gay men whom many lesbians had previously identified as allies in the fight for gay liberation, or with heterosexual women, since such women still enjoy 'heterosexual privilege' in our society and hence could not be trusted to be 'true' feminists.

Lesbian separatism led to the demise of the idea of androgyny, that is, the elimination of gender dualism as an immediate goal for a feminist and gay liberation counterculture. For if heterosexual and bisexual men and women still have heterosexual privilege, and gay men cannot be trusted to give up male privilege (Frye, 1983), the assumptions that feminist and gay liberation are natural allies and that bisexuality challenges compulsory heterosexuality are types of assimilationism that must be rejected.

The problem with the extreme separatist view is that it is based on a mistaken theory of male dominance and hence lacks a cogent theory of social change. Adrienne Rich attempts to heal the split between lesbian and heterosexual feminists by positing a lesbian continuum which allows a place to heterosexual women who have bonded with children and women against men. But her analysis merely confuses the issue because she, like the extreme separatists, maintains an ahistorical view of male dominance and sexual identity. In this chapter what are believed to be the flaws in the separatist theory of compulsory heterosexuality and lesbian existence will be pointed out. Second, an interpretation of the history of northern European and American homosexuality in the nineteenth and twentieth centuries will be given, using the concept of sex/affective production. Finally, some political implications will be drawn from this analysis about the connection between gay and lesbian liberation and feminism.

Compulsory heterosexuality

A key theoretical question in the lesbian-feminist dispute is whether it is plausible to assume, as do Rich, Bunch, Penelope and others[1] that compulsory heterosexuality is the central social structure crossculturally which perpetuates male domination.

My view is that lesbian-feminist theorists who use the term 'compulsory heterosexuality' are guilty of false universalism. That is, instead of seeing that the concept of compulsory heterosexuality as a general analytic concept analogous to the concept of an economic class society that has many specific modes, they assume that the historical features of such modes are irrelevant to understanding male dominance and only the general similarities need be understood.

An example of this way of thinking is the manner in which Rich appropriates Kathleen Gough's work (Gough, 1975). She cites Gough's list of eight characteristics of male power over women: to deny women sexuality, to force it upon them, to command or exploit their labour to control their produce, to control or rob them of their children, to confine them physically and prevent their movement, to use them as objects in male transactions, to cramp their creativeness and to withhold from them large areas of the society's knowledge and cultural attainments. But Rich's aim is not to demonstrate the diversity of the structures of male dominance by this list, for she uses it to argue that these constitute a 'pervasive cluster of forces' all of which serve a single purpose, namely to enforce heterosexuality. We are left with the implication that the historical variations in the use of these forces are irrelevant as are their specific purposes (e.g. economic exploitation), for, after all, the prime goal or *telos* is to control a woman's sexuality by forcing her to prioritise sexuality with men to her other emotional or sexual concerns such as children and friendships with women.

Such a construal of compulsory heterosexuality is dangerously teleological and ahistorical. For, while there can be little doubt that lesbian and male-male attractions tend to be suppressed crossculturally and that the resulting institutions of compulsory heterosexuality are indeed coercive, Rich is surely mistaken to imply that there is only one institution of compulsory heterosexuality crossculturally with one overriding purpose. For example, Meillasoux (1981) and Lerner (1986) may be correct to suppose that one of the origins of male dominant social systems was the need to control women's reproduction for the economic wellbeing of the group – not, as Rich seems to imply, simply so men could develop a monopoly on women's sexuality. Historical modes of compulsory heterosexuality have varied immensely: some had institutionalised forms of homosexuality while still being male dominant (ancient Greek society is an obvious example) while others, like Mohave society, institutionalised both heterosexuality and homosexuality in a way that was more gender egalitarian.[2]

Another problem with Rich and the separatist analysis is that compulsory heterosexuality is assumed to be the central, key (and sometimes the only) mechanism which perpetuates male dominance. This is mistaken, for though forms of compulsory heterosexuality are certainly some of the mechanisms that perpetuate male domination they surely are not the single or sufficient ones. Others, such as the control of female biological reproduction, male control of state and political power and economic systems involving discrimination on grounds of class and race (systems which divide women by other forms of social dominance, thus weakening the possibilities for unified resistance to male power) are analytically distinct from coercive heterosexuality yet are social structures which support and perpetuate male dominance.

Part of the problem with the concept of compulsory hetero-sexuality is that although separatists using it usually imply that heterosexual attraction is socially conditioned rather than innately biological, they also want to draw the conclusion that lesbianism is somehow a more 'natural' or authentic choice for women. Sometimes Rich too seems to imply that women are essentially or naturally lesbians who are coerced by the social mechanisms of the patriarchal family to 'turn to the father', hence to men. But if a girl's original love preference for her mother is due to the social fact that women, and not men, mother, then neither lesbian nor heterosexuality can be said to be women's natural (uncoerced) sexual preference. If humans are basically bisexual or pansexual at birth, it will not do to suggest that lesbianism is the more authentic sexual preference for feminists and that heterosexual feminists who do not change their sexual preference are simply lying to themselves about their true sexuality.

The notion that heterosexuality is central to women's oppres-sion is plausible only by a characterisation of the institution of compulsory heterosexuality that assumes that women's sexual and emotional (sex/affective) dependence on men (as lovers, in mar-riages, as mothers) allows an unequal economic exchange in which men can control women's bodies as instruments for their own purpose. But many heterosexual women (e.g. single mothers, economically self-supporting or equal wage-earning women, Black and white) may in their sexual relations with men escape or avoid these other mechanisms. From the fact that compulsory heterosexuality is oppressive, it does not, therefore, follow that all heterosexuality is oppressive, nor that hetero-sexuals cannot be true feminists!

Lesbian existence

Though compulsory heterosexuality does have different historical modes, these modes have in common a sexual division of labour and male-dominated heterosexual marriages which give women less economic, social and political power than men crosscultu-rally. This is what allows us to formulate it as a trans-historical analytic concept and to see how some common structures of male dominance have persisted in different societies. But what then is wrong with Rich's idea that there may be a common trait of feminists crossculturally, that they are, or approach being, lesbians in their resistance to compulsory heterosexuality? Why not define the search for lesbian history as co-extensive with the search for feminist history? As Rich says:

> I feel that the search for lesbian history needs to be understood *politically*, not simply as the search for exceptional women who were lesbians, but as the search for power, for nascent undefined feminism, for the ways that women-loving women have been nay-sayers to male possession and control of women. (Rich, quoted in Schwartz, 1979: 6).

To use such an approach as an aid to discover 'nascent undefined feminism' in any historical period, the feminist historian has to know what she is looking for. We need, in other words, a clearer understanding of what is involved in the concept lesbian so as to be able to identify such women. Rich introduces the concepts lesbian identity and lesbian continuum as substitutes for the limited and clinical sense of 'lesbian' commonly used. Her new concepts imply that genital sexual relations or sexual attractions between women are neither necessary nor sufficient conditions for someone to be a lesbian in the full sense of the term. If we were to present Rich's definition of lesbian identity it would therefore be somewhat as follows:

Lesbian identity is the sense of self of a woman bonded primarily to women who is sexually and emotionally independent of men. (Definition 1)

Her concept of lesbian continuum describes a wide range of 'woman-identified experience; not simply the fact that a woman has had or consciously desires genital sexual experience with another woman'. Instead we should 'expand it to embrace many more forms of primary intensity between and among women, including the sharing of a rich inner life, the bonding against male tyranny, the giving and receiving of practical and political support; if we can also hear in it such associations as marriage resistance ... we can begin to grasp breadths of female history and psychology which have lain out of reach as a consequence of limited, mostly clinical definitions of "lesbianism" ' (Rich, 1980: 648–9).

In her re-definition of the concept of lesbian, Rich is following the tactic of Radicalesbians who were the first lesbian-feminist theorists to suggest a reconstruction of the term (Radicalesbians, 1970). Their goal was not merely to locate some central characteristic of lesbianism but also to find a way to eliminate the standard, pejorative connotation of the term. They wanted, that is, to rid the term of the heterosexist implications that lesbians are sick, deviant and unhealthy beings – a task important not merely as a defence of the lesbian community but of the feminist community, and indeed, all women. The problem is that Radicalesbians as well as Rich do not clearly distinguish three different goals of definitional strategy: first, valorising the concept lesbian; second, giving a socio-political definition of the contemporary lesbian community; and finally, reconceptualising history from a lesbian and feminist perspective. These goals are conceptually distinct and are not achievable by one concept, namely, the lesbian continuum.

Rich and Radicalesbians conceive of lesbian identity as a transhistorical phenomenon, while I maintain, to the contrary, that the development of a distinctive homosexual (and specifically lesbian) identity is a historical phenomenon, not applicable to all societies and all periods of history.

Rich's idea that resistance to patriarchy can be measured by the degree to which a woman is sexually and emotionally independent of men while bonding with women oversimplifies and romanticises the notion of such resistance without defining the conditions that make for successful resistance rather than mere victimisation. Her model does not allow us to understand the collective and social nature of a lesbian identity as opposed to lesbian practices or behaviours. In many cultures and historical periods a woman who makes love to a woman or women may not think of herself nor may she be thought of as a lesbian in our contemporary sense of the term. Although Rich is surely correct that some of the clinical definitions of lesbian tend to create ways of viewing women's lives in which 'female friendships and comradeship have been set apart from the erotic: thus limiting the erotic itself', her view undervalues the important historical development of an explicit lesbian identity connected to a genital sexuality.

My own view is that the development of such an identity, and with it the development of a sexuality valued and accepted in a community of peers, extended women's life options and degree of independence from men. The concept of lesbian identity as distinct from lesbian practices seems to have arisen in advanced capitalist countries in Western Europe and the United States, in the late nineteenth and early twentieth centuries, from the conjunction of two forces. In part it was an ideological concept created by the sexologists who framed a changing patriarchal ideology of sexuality and the family; in part it was chosen by independent women and feminists who formed their own urban subcultures as an escape from the new, mystified form of patriarchal dominance that developed in the late 1920s; the companionate nuclear family (Foucault, 1978; McIntosh, 1968; Simons, 1979; Weeks, 1979).

It is important to note that both the commonsense definitions of lesbian and Rich's definition run into difficulties if taken independently of context and used for a trans-historical political purpose. Consider one ordinary definition of lesbian:

A lesbian is a woman who has sexual attractions toward and relationships with other women. (Definition 2)

Such a definition does not exclude practising bisexual women and thus cannot be used by lesbian separatists to define the perimeters of the contemporary lesbian community as they would want to.

The ambiguity of the ordinary concept of lesbian, that is that it does not clearly distinguish bisexual from exclusively lesbian women, suggests that homosexual practices by themselves are not sufficient or definitive constituents of a homosexual identity. A certain kind of political context is required. Therefore, when considering sexual identity, we should be wary of attempts to make oversimplified crosscultural parallels.

Many of the known societies which have institutionalised various forms of homosexual practice do not have our contemporary notion of homosexual identity, namely a quasi-ethnic identity with others who constitute a distinctive subculture. For example, in ancient Mohave society and some contemporary Latin American and Mediterranean cultures, homosexual couples engage in strictly defined gender (butch-femme) roles but society distinguishes between the partners in such a pair: the social but non-biological male or female is considered deviant, while the social and biological males and females are considered normal (though sometimes thought unfortunate) members of society. Thus, in Nicaragua and Cuba the active male homosexual role makes a man macho, not gay; and only the feminine homosexual role (*passivo*) gives a man a homosexual, and thus deviant, social identity (Adam, 1987). We could try to correct definition 2 while still seeking some ahistorical descriptive component of lesbian and say that:

A lesbian is a woman who is sexual exclusively in relation to women. (Definition 3)

This definition certainly captures one important use of the concept lesbian in contemporary lesbian politics, in that it describes identified members of contempoary lesbian subculture in such a way as to exclude women who engage in bisexual practices. But it also cuts from lesbian history many women, like Sappho, Vita Sackville-West, and Eleanor Roosevelt who were married yet had lesbian relationships. A strict distinction between lesbian, heterosexual and bisexual rules out many historical personages whose lives contained both heterosexual and homosexual practices that most lesbian-feminists would like to include in lesbian history. Yet should a bisexual woman be accepted as a lesbian only if she is an historical personage and is not presently demanding to be included in the lesbian community? Surely, this is rather *ad hoc*!

A definitional strategy from which Rich, Nancy Sahli (1979) and other recent writers take their cues is that suggested by Blanche Weisen Cook:

A lesbian is 'a woman who loves women, who chooses women to nurture and support and to create a living environment in which to work creatively and independently' (Cook, 1977), whether or not her relations with these women are sexual (my added phrase). (Definition 4)

Note that this definition, like Rich's definition 1, would eliminate genital sexual practices as relevant to the concept lesbian, thus avoiding the standard, pejorative connotations of the term and extending its meaning to include celibate women who are otherwise excluded by definition 3 from the lesbian sisterhood (cf. Yarborough, 1979).

My main criticism of definition 4 is a political one. This extension and reconstruction of the term lesbian would seem to eliminate women like Virginia Woolf, Gertrude Stein, and so on – in fact, all women who were sexually attracted to women but who worked with men or in a circle of mixed male and female friends such as the Bloomsbury group. When juxtaposed to Rich's idea of a lesbian continuum as an indicator of resistance to patriarchy, this definition suggests that female couples like Jane Addams and Mary Rozet Smith or women like Lillian Wald whose community of friends were almost entirely feminist are more important role models for lesbian-feminists than women like Gertrude Stein, Emma Goldman or Bessie Smith. Not only is this classist and racist but it is historically implausible.

This approach also leaves out the historical context in which women live. At certain historical periods where there is no large or visible oppositional women's culture, women who show that they can challenge the sexual division of labour – that is, who work with and perform as well as men – are just as important for questioning the male dominant ideology of inevitable sex roles, including compulsory heterosexuality, as are the women-identified women described by Cook or Rich. At certain periods even women who pass for men – such as those adventurers Dona Catalina De Erauso, Anny Bonny, and Mary Read – are just as important as models of resistance to male dominance as the celibate Emily Dickinson may have been in her time (Myron and Bunch, 1974b). For these reasons the political implication of radical feminist theory that there is some universal way to understand true as opposed to false acts of resistance to male dominance is rejected.

The final objection to the reconstruction of lesbian definitions 1 and 4 is that they ignore the ways in which the sexual revolution of the late nineteenth and early twentieth centuries was a positive advance for women. The ability to take one's own genital sexual needs seriously is a necessary component of an egalitarian love relation, whether it be with a man or a woman. Furthermore, the possibility of an acknowledged sexual relationship between women is an important challenge to the male dominant ideology of the patriarchal nuclear couple that assumes that women are dependent on men for sexual love and satisfaction.

Therefore, any definitional strategy which seeks to drop the sexual component of 'lesbian' in favour of an emotional commitment to, or preference for, women tends to lead feminists to downplay the historical importance of movements for sexual liberation. The negative results of these movements in the twentieth century, for example that the nineteenth-century patriarchal ideology of a woman as a 'womb on legs' is replaced by another objectifying concept, woman as a 'vagina on legs', do not justify dismissal of the real advances that were made for women, including the possibility of a lesbian identity in the sexual sense of the term.

An alternative approach which sidesteps the question of the importance of sexual identity for feminism is that of Jan Raymond in her recent book *A Passion for Friends* (Raymond, 1986). For Raymond, the true mark of a feminist is not whether she is a lesbian (in the sense of exclusive sexuality with women), but whether she prioritises her friendships with women (gyn/ affection) over relationships of all sorts (work, political, sexual) with men. Though Raymond avoids downplaying the sexual component of lesbian identity, her characterisation of feminism does ignore the way that women who challenge gender definitions of women (by passing for men and working with them) may also challenge male dominance in specific contexts.

None of the definitions given above succeeds in accomplishing the three tasks lesbian theorists have wanted to accomplish: first, freeing the concept lesbian from narrow clinical uses and pejorative connotations; second, aiding the development of contemporary feminist socio-political categories by drawing clear lines among sexual identities and feminist communities; and finally, illuminating women's history by developing trans-historical categories that give us a better understanding of women's historical resistance to male domination. This failure surely occurs because it is a mistake to try to define lesbian or a lesbian continuum in such a way as to achieve all these tasks simultaneously.

An alternative approach will have to be an historical one. It must recognise that since lesbian is a relatively recent historical concept, we may be able to give a contemporary socio-political definition of lesbian but by that move alone we will not eliminate its pejorative connotations in the dominant culture; only political organisation will accomplish this. Furthermore it is a mistake to elevate 'lesbian' to a trans-historical category for this eliminates its historical importance as a relatively recent sexual identity. In what follows, a socio-political definition of lesbian will be given to achieve the second task listed above without assuming it will achieve the first or third task.

Our contemporary sexual identities are predicated on two methodological pre-conditions. First, and tautologically, a person cannot be said to have a sexual identity that is not self-conscious.

That is, it is not meaningful to conjecture that someone is a lesbian who refuses to acknowledge herself as such. Taking identity concepts to be self-conscious commitments or decisions eliminates the plausibility of the medical establishment's use of categories to stigmatise individuals as having a deviant sexuality who have not made such a decision. Identity concepts are thus to be distinguished from social and biological categories which apply to persons simply because of their position in the social structure, for example their economic class, their gender, sexual practices or race.[3] For this reason, labelling theorists make a distinction between primary and secondary deviance: one can engage in deviant acts (primary deviance) without labelling oneself a deviant, but acquiring a personal identity as a deviant (secondary deviance) requires a self-conscious acceptance of the label as applying to oneself.

A second methodological precondition for a contemporary lesbian identity is that one live in a culture where the concept has relevance. For example, a person cannot have a Black identity unless the concept of blackness as a social status exists in the person's cultural environment. (Various shades of brown all get termed black in North American culture but not in Caribbean cultures, partly because of the greater racism in our culture.) Again, Third World peasant countries which lack the material conditions for the development of lesbian and gay subcultures – because kinship defined by marriage structures the peasant economy and no one can afford to live without the kin networks created by marriage – lack our contemporary concept of homosexual identity: same sex bonding for romantic love and sexual exchanges that may become economic partnerships.

Thus, the second precondition for a modern homosexual identity rests on a more general idea borrowed from Sartre's existentialism: a person cannot be anything unless others can identify him or her as such. Just as a person cannot be self-conscious about being Black unless there is a potentially self-conscious community of others prepared to accept the label for themselves, so a person cannot be said to have a sexual identity unless there is in his or her historical period and cultural environment a community of others who think of themselves as having the sexual identity in question. Notice that the condition does not require that a person actually 'come out' or be known to the self-conscious community of others in order to acquire the identity – only that doing so is a possible option.[4] In a period of human history where the distinctions between heterosexual, bisexual and homosexual identity are not present as culture categories (namely, until the twentieth century), people cannot correctly be said to have been lesbian, bisexual or heterosexual although they may be described as having been sexually normal or deviant according to the sexual mores of their period. This point is emphasised by Carol Smith-Rosenberg in her classic treatment of the particularly passionate and emotionally consuming friendships of nineteenth-century middle-class women (Smith-Rosenberg, 1975). Though a contemporary sexologist might label these lesbian relationships, the Victorian ideology that women are spiritual and asexual labelled these relationships normal not deviant (cf. also Faderman, 1981).

The definition of lesbian suggested here, one that conforms to the two methodological considerations above, is the following:

A lesbian is a woman who has sexual and erotic-emotional (i.e. sex/affective) ties primarily with women or who sees herself as centrally involved with a community of self-identified lesbians whose sexual and erotic-emotional ties are primarily with women; and who is herself a self-identified lesbian. (Definition 5)

This definition is a socio-political one; that is, it attempts to include in the term lesbian the contemporary sense that lesbianism is connected with a countercultural community which has a quasi-ethnic status (cf. Adam, 1987; Epstein, 1987). It also includes the contemporary group norm against individual members defining themselves as dependent on or subordinate to men. The definition allows both bisexual and celibate women to define themselves as lesbian as long as they identify themselves as such and have their primary emotional identification with a community of self-defined lesbians.

This more inclusive definition of lesbian is a matter of some contention among older lesbians who came out before the Women's Movement and who do not trust women who feel they have a choice as to whether to define themselves as lesbian or bisexual. But whether one believes one's lesbianism is innate or chosen is partly a question of the historical context in which one lives, and the material conditions which made it necessary for lesbians (but not gay men) a more defensive and restrictive understanding of who can count as lesbian/gay in the early and mid twentieth century are no longer applicable today. Women have many more economic options that allow independence from men, though still not economic equality. Since more women who hitherto would have got along as heterosexuals have the material option to consider a lesbian lifestyle, the lesbian community has the political option to decide to include them now.

Many lesbian-feminists may not agree with this inclusion. But it may be argued that to exclude lesbian bisexuals from the community on the grounds that 'they give energy to men' is overly defensive at this point. After all, a strong women's community does not have to operate on a scarcity theory of sex/affective energy! On feminist principles, the criterion for membership in the community should be a woman's commitment to giving positive erotic-emotional energy to women. Whether women who give such energy to women can also give energy to individual men (friends, fathers, sons, lovers) should not be the community's concern.

Some responses to the vanguardism of political lesbianism have suggested that we avoid altogether such labels as heterosexual, bisexual and lesbian and begin to frame a bisexual or pansexual politics (cf. Campbell, 1980). While we certainly need new ideas to get beyond existing labels, it would be utopian to ignore the ongoing strength of heterosexism which continues to stigmatise and deprive lesbians more than heterosexual women.

We need, then, a lesbian oppositional culture of resistance, but as feminists we also need to find ways to strengthen our women's community with other feminists as well as to recruit new members into the lesbian-feminist community. The inclusive definition of lesbian offered above (definition 5) allows us to broaden the community to include bisexual lesbians. Another approach is to form political coalitions such as the Lesbian/Gay/Bisexual Alliance at the University of Massachusetts/Amherst, a coalition which validates bisexuality but distinguishes it from lesbian and gay lifestyles.

Let us turn again to one of the initial questions we posed: what is the connection of lesbian liberation to women's liberation? If the present analysis is correct, women's liberation and lesbian liberation, though they mutually require each other, are not identical movements. Our historical analysis has yielded a rejection of the lesbian separatist argument that true feminists have in fact been or approached being lesbians. Conversely, not all lesbians are feminists. Just as many feminists in both waves of the American and European women's movements have been homophobic, so many lesbians have made their peace with a sexist society and have or are living apolitical, co-opted lives.

If there is no necessary overlap between a lesbian and a feminist consciousness, things are even worse with respect to feminist and gay male liberation. This is because there are actual conflicts between gay male liberation and feminism (cf. Frye, 1983; Jacobs, 1986), despite attempts by New Left theorists of gay and feminist liberation to insist on their linkage (cf. Altman, 1974). In order to understand more fully the possibilities for coalitions between lesbian and heterosexual feminists, and feminists and gay men, we must first sketch the historical development of contemporary homosexual identities. Following this we can analyse the stages of lesbian and gay liberation movements in America and Western Europe in the twentieth century.

Historical development of lesbian and gay identities

In chapter five it was argued that there have been three modes of sex/affective production in American history from the colonial period to the present: father patriarchy, husband patriarchy and public patriarchy. It is in the transition between husband patriarchy and public patriarchy that a distinctive homosexual identity arises. The preconditions for the development of such an identity are material, ideological and motivational.

In patriarchal sex/affective production systems the material base of male dominance is in the family and extended kin networks. Such kin systems of the social production of sexuality, nurturance and the babies that will be the future labour force of family and society operate by a sexual division of labour in which men control women's sexuality in order to control their reproduction and also to control and exploit women's labour in unequal work exchanges. Although patriarchal sex/affective production systems may institutionalise compulsory heterosexuality differently (some allowing some forms of homosexuality), they all require that adult men and women prioritise heterosexual marriage and a complementary set of gender roles in work and social life.

Ideologically, these systems support what Barbara Ponse (Ponse, 1978) has termed the principle of consistency. That is,

people are taught a sexual symbolic code that connects gender
identity (the awareness of self as biologically male or female),
gender role (learned behaviour expected of males or females) and
sexual object choice (a learned code which defines the proper
sexual object of desire as the opposite sex). Those who deviate
from their assigned gender role or object choice are assumed
deviant and repressed by society. Interestingly, so deeply held is
the principle of consistency that violators of one aspect of it who
uphold others may either not be believed to be violators at all, or
may assumed to be breaking all. For example, the ladies of
Llangollen who, living in the Victorian period in England,
eschewed marriage and lived as a couple together were not perceived as violating heterosexual object choice since, in not cross
dressing, they did not violate gender roles. Instead they were
thought to be asexual, quite in accord with the patriarchal ideology for nineteenth-century bourgeois women (Faderman, 1981).
Conversely, those who violated gender roles (e.g. butch women or
fem men) were considered sexual perverts and assumed by sexologists to be 'men in women's bodies or women in men's bodies'.
Such deviants were assumed to have homosexual object choices,
whether they did engage in homosexual behaviour or not, which
were then explained by the principle of consistency on a heterosexual model! (Adam, 1987; Escoffier, 1985).

The weakening of the patriarchal power of fathers over children caused by industrial capitalism and the development of wage
labour created urban areas that not only increased the life choices
of women, but allowed for the development of homosexual liaisons and homosexual networks for both gay men and lesbians
freed from patriarchal family control.

With the breakdown of the hegemony of the patriarchal nuclear
family in sex/affective production, the relative material freedom
that wage labour gave to adult men and women to forge their own
sexual lifestyle created a change in the sex and gender symbolic
code distinguishing capitalist public patriarchy from previous
family patriarchies. In the twentieth century in advanced capitalist countries there has been a tendency for gender identities and
roles to be separated from sexual identities, so that the principle
of consistency true of family patriarchies no longer holds (Escoffier, 1985). As Gayle Rubin has noted (Rubin, 1984), the separation of the social construction of gender from the social construction of sexuality in advanced capitalist societies accounts for the

increasingly problematic connection between women's liberation and sexual liberation movements of various sorts.

The development of a distinctive lesbian subculture took much longer than the development of gay male urban subcultures (Weeks, 1979). This is not surprising, since the relative gain in freedom for women that industrial capitalism provided was not an instant effect: not only were male day labourers recruited much earlier than women in England and Europe, but in the United States where women were the first factory workers, this early wage labour gave most women too little money to survive on their own. Hartmann has documented how the late nineteenth-century institution of the family wage for married union men was calculated to undercut the wage labour of wives (Hartmann, 1981a). Nonetheless, acquisition of an income gave women new options, for example, sharing boarding-house rooms with other women, and eventually some women's wages were sufficient for a modicum of economic independence from the family. The wide-scale development of prostitution with urbanisation was one source of economic support for a lesbian lifestyle: sexologist Magnus Hirshfeld speculated that a large percentage of late nineteenth- and early twentieth-century prostitutes were lesbians (Weeks, 1979). There is some evidence that this is still true today (cf. Delacoste and Alexander, 1987).

Yet as the patriarchal family's direct, personal control over women weakened, the institutions of public patriarchy were already developing. These included, first, the hegemony of a growing class of male professionals (physicians, therapists and social workers) over the physical and mental health of women (Ehrenreich and English, 1979) and second, the sex-segregated wage labour force which gives lesser pay to women and more power to male bosses and male workers.

Contrary to Ehrenreich and English who see the shift from family-centred to public systems of male dominance as merely a shift from one set of men (fathers and husbands) to another (professionals and bosses), my view is that this shift not only created the material conditions needed for the growth of lesbianism as a self-conscious cultural choice for women, but it also was a step toward freeing all women from an ideology that stressed their emotional, economic and sexual dependence on personal relations with men. Partly this is due to the implicit validation of sexual needs inherent in the work of such sexologists as Freud, Havelock Ellis and others. Even though they and other sexologists created the language of sexual normality and deviance that stigmatises contemporary gay and lesbian identity, they also created the possibility of a group identification which, in the social conditions available in advanced capitalist societies, could foster a gay/lesbian counter-culture of resistance. In this way, capitalist public patriarchy, though still a male dominant system, contains more possibilities of freedom for women than previous patriarchies.

There is some evidence that in both the United States and Western Europe the growth of lesbianism among middle- and upper-class women connected with the first wave of the Women's Movement was similar in some ways to the growth of lesbian-feminism in the second wave of the movement. Magnus Hirshfeld claimed that in Germany 10 per cent of feminists were lesbian. In England, Stella Browne, the British pioneer in birth control and abortion rights, defended lesbianism publicly. Upper-class women like Vita Sackville-West, Virginia Woolf and Natalie Barney involved themselves in lesbian relationships (Adam 1986; Weeks 1979). The fact that the lesbian subculture did not develop extensively until the 1930s in most countries, however, indicates how difficult it still was for most single women to be economically independent of men. With the rise of somewhat better wage labour positions for women in the 1920s and 1930s, and onward, the gradual rise of an independent subculture of self-defined lesbians can be seen as a pocket of resistance to marriage. The second wave Women's Movement of the 1960s and 1970s made possible a further extension of that subculture and a clearer definition of its feminist nature.

Lesbian and gay liberation movements

Jeff Escoffier (1985) argues that there are three historical moments which lead up to the gay liberation movements of the 1960s and 1970s. First, there are the ideological attacks on the prevailing repressive, sexist and heterosexist sexual norms initiated by Kinsey's empirical studies of actual sexual practices (Kinsey *et al.*, 1948, 1953) and followed by Marcuse's attacks on surplus sexual repression (Marcuse, 1955). The second is the creation of a consumerist society made possible by Keynesian economic politics which enlarged the provisions of the welfare state, thus raising cultural expectations of material fulfilment. Though the 1950s saw a swing to the right with McCarthyism, red-baiting, gay-hounding and the attempt to re-establish the male breadwinner, female housewife ethic that had been undermined by women working during the Second World War, Keynesianism and its concomitant expansion of consumer goods and growth of the mass media sowed the seeds for a sexual consumerism that would eventually reject the repressive patriarchal sexual ethic.

The third historical moment was the creation of politically self-affirming gay and lesbian subcultures. Though the Mattachine society for the defence of gay rights had been established in the late 1940s, it had chosen an 'assimilationist' line, i.e. to emphasise the commonalities gays had with straights rather than their differences, which led gay communities to try to hide their distinctive social and sexual features. The 'cultural minority' position which maintained that gays had the right to be different from the majority lost out and was not revived until the examples of the Black power, student New Left and women's liberation movements created the social context for a similar extension to gays of the concept of a distinctive and self-affirming counterculture.

Escoffier argues that the initial New Left-influenced gay liberation movement held that since gender dualism was responsible both for sexism and heterosexism, the gay liberation movement should act as a vanguard for androgyny and bisexuality, thus freeing the homosexual in all of us and eliminating the normal/deviant distinction between heterosexual and homosexual (cf. Altman, 1974). To this end, 'coming out' by lesbians and gays is a political act that will eventually liberate all of us from the patriarchal repressive symbolic sexual code.

Two key problems with this political perspective are, on the one hand, its utopianism, and on the other, its lack of historical understanding of how the politics of identity generate a politics of difference. As Adam (1987) notes, the unisex image of the 1960s' and early 1970s' hippie, lesbian and gay liberation movements was not able to end gender dualism in the larger society. On the contrary, some present tendencies in lesbian and gay subcultures create and/or revalidate sexual roles in some ways imitative of the dominant heterosexual ideology: the new macho gay male role, the return of the drag queen and the development of the gay leather S/M subculture. This is paralleled in the lesbian community by the rise of lesbian S/M and the revalidation of butch/ femme roles. What does this imply about lesbian and gay liberation as vanguards, either of feminism or of human sexual liberation and androgyny?

Political implications of lesbian and gay liberation

There are several important implications which can be drawn from the above historical analysis. First, that the consolidation of distinctive sexual lifestyles outside of the nuclear family structure in public patriarchy involves advances for women's liberation in some ways and is problematic in others. Indeed, conflicting progressive and reactionary tendencies are constantly vying in capitalist public patriarchy, composed as it is of partially atomised interest groups in which individuals are situated with conflicting identities and interests. On one hand, the existence of lesbian and gay communities allows women who choose a lesbian lifestyle a private life of sexual equality and the chance to form coalitions with gay men to defend this lifestyle. But on the other hand, gay men have interests as men in defending male privilege and many are not likely to be supportive on such feminist issues as publicly supported child care for single mothers, comparable worth, violence against women, etc. (Jacobs, 1986).

What this suggests is that we must take an historical and dialectical view of the political process necessary to achieve the co-ordination of feminist, lesbian, gay and human sexual liberation. The immediate political and material interests of each of these movements do not automatically coincide. Though we need to forge a vision of how to reorganise society that would reconstitute individual sexualities so as not to create conflicts in material and sex/affective interests between us, we must also create a practical politics of autonomous self-affirming networks and coalitions based on an understanding that those who are our allies in one aspect of their identities may be adversaries in another (Laclau and Mouffe, 1985).

In the context of identity coalition politics the lesbian, gay and women's movements are similar to the Black civil rights movement: they require a separatist/nationalist wing (to defend the vanguard aspects of the cultural minority or oppressed group position), an integrationist/assimilationist wing (to negotiate for the reconstruction of the interests of the majority so they are not perceived to be in conflict with this minority or oppressed group), and those in the middle who act as coalitionists, both within and without the movement in question.

A coalitionist position must be able to balance the partial truths of both wings of the movement and to find a way to defend and redefine the interests of the whole in confrontation with the adversarial forces outside the movement. For example, a coalitionist position in the contemporary feminist sex debate must be able to acknowledge the pluralist feminist argument that butch-femme roles in the gay and lesbian subcultures are different from, and thus challenge, those in the dominant culture (e.g. the lesbian butch braves social ostracism and sets his/her first sexual task to pleasure the femme, unlike the heterosexual macho role). But the coalitionist must also find the partial truth in the radical feminist critique of butch/femme roles as being too assimilationist, indeed too imitative of the dominant culture's male/female roles (e.g. butches/males as initiators, femmes/females as submittors). Only by such a process of internal critique can feminist, lesbian and gay communities self-consciously assess and progressively challenge those aspects of the subculture inevitably determined by negative aspects of the dominant culture.

But what of the rise of many diverse sexual minorities other than lesbians and gays who demand rights to consensual sex? What position should feminists take on these matters? It was maintained earlier that the logic of normal/deviant categories, in the appropriate material conditions, generates a logic of resistance whereby those dissatisfied in some way with that defined as normal, affirm themselves as deviant and band together in a defiant oppositional subculture.

This is happening today in the context of a consumerist society which ostensibly validates a 'do your thing' plurality of private lifestyles yet stigmatises some choices as deviant. So, we have witnessed in the 1970s and 1980s not only the birth of the lesbian and gay liberation movements but also, following them, the butch/femme liberation movement, the feminist 'bad girls' pornography-consuming subculture, consensual S/M subcultures and man/boy love subcultures – all claiming rights as sexual minorities to do their thing and all claiming to be oppressed by social stigmatisation, both of the dominant culture and of elements of the Women's Movement.

Just as not all aspects of gay male liberation can be understood as compatible with feminist goals, so the Women's Movement cannot adopt a blanket principle that any and all sexual minorities should be defended by feminists. Rather we need to develop a feminist sexual ethics which considers each particular sexual lifestyle in its context and makes a moral and political decision on its merits *vis-à-vis* feminist principles – a task taken up in the next chapter.

10

A transitional feminist sexual morality

In chapter seven, it was argued that our contemporary American society is sexually alienated because of its gender dualism and the conflict between the ideology of romantic individualism and the reality of eroticised gender subordination. An ideal vision of sexuality that would remove these inconsistencies could occur only by a socialist-feminist transformation of our political economy which espoused the elimination of gender dualism as a principle of erotic life.

But our contemporary society is far from such a socialist-feminist transformation. Thus it would be utopian to demand that such an ideal be adopted by feminists in their present sexual practices. Acknowledging this, many feminist theorists who first suggested androgyny as a feminist ideal for human development have abandoned it (e.g. Daly, 1973, 1978; Dworkin, 1974, 1987; Rubin, 1975, 1984). Although I too first advocated androgyny, I now suggest an alternative tack. We can still hold to the vision of an ideal human development suggested by androgyny (cf. Ferguson, 1977) if we make two distinctions. First, we should not describe the vision as 'androgyny' but 'gynandry'. The reversal of the two roots referring to masculine and feminine is not just word play, but points to the need for a feminist transformation of values that involves more than simply patching together the traditional qualities associated with masculinity and femininity.

Second, we must distinguish the vision question from the practical political question of what should be our feminist transitional ideal sexuality. Since feminism is a political social movement which challenges the values of contemporary male dominance, we must have some contrary values of our own that we stand for. We need an interim sexual morality to deal with contemporary questions of how to 'draw the line' between sexual practices which should be forbidden and those which are permissible from a feminist point of view.

Contrary to the extreme relativists in the feminist sex debate, feminists do need to be moralists in order to advocate a public policy of what activities are so exploitative of women and children as to require legal prohibition. We also require a transitional feminist sexual morality for moral guidance when we are engaged in creating countercultural values with feminist friends, creating sex education programmes for youth, or in advising our own children and those who see us as role models.

A key question for framing a transitional feminist sexual morality is this: how can we both support a consensual sexual ethics that promotes sexual experimentation for pleasure, and yet take account of the social domination structured into certain sorts of sexual practices in capitalist patriarchy? On the one hand, we must reject the moralistic idea supported by many radical feminists that every personal interaction must be subject to the judgement of the feminist community for its political correctness. On the other hand, we need to suppose, unlike some pluralist feminists, that there is a political import to many personal interactions which cannot help but be relevant to feminists since structures of domination may be present whether or not they are acknowledged by consenting partners.

One way to create a cushion of space for personal diversity that will allow for fringe practices to be acceptable areas for sexual experimentation by feminists is to use a three-part distinction between forbidden, basic and risky feminist sexual practices (Ferguson, 1983, 1984).

The difference between a forbidden and a risky practice is that the latter involves taking risks from a feminist perspective because the practices are suspected of leading to dominance/ subordination relationships. To say that they are risky implies that there is no final proof that they in fact must involve dominance/subordination relationships – rather, in fact they are contested precisely because there is conflicting evidence at present. Basic feminist practices, on the other hand, are those where there is nothing about the general features of the act or the social structures in which it is undertaken which suggests that it is risky in the above sense.

One effect of making a distinction between forbidden, risky and basic feminist practices is to provide for an area of disagreement between feminists on personal value choices that, though contested, is not a condition for excluding someone as a sister in the feminist community. Feminists should permit other feminists the right to take risks in many of their personal value choices without censuring them for being non-feminist if they disagree with their choices. Feminists will often disagree about which feminist sex/affective practices are basic and which risky. For example, a lesbian-feminist may perceive her straight friend's heterosexuality to be risky while this woman in turn may perceive the class or racial differences in her lesbian friend's relationship to be more risky! But having a three-way distinction allows us the space to disagree on where to draw the line without writing each other out of the feminist community, as long as we can agree on what practices are forbidden from a feminist perspective.

Forbidden sexual practices are ones which the majority of feminists think should be illegal. These would include rape and domestic battering. Included in the forbidden category of sexual practices should be those difficult cases where there is strong reason to think that consensual permission is not present given the extreme social inequalities of the partners; for instance, generational incest and adult/child sexuality. Since not all feminists agree on where to draw the line between risky and forbidden practices, we should look at these contested cases more carefully.

Incest

In the case of both incest and adult/child sex there are feminists who have defended the idea of dropping the sanctions against these practices.[1] While I agree that some forms of incest, for example, those involving adults, or children of comparable ages, should be acceptable to feminists, the sticky cases are those which involve major differences in age, power and status between the participants. Thus the incest cases that remain contested turn out to be special cases of adult/child sexuality.

Since Firestone's and Dworkin's early work, many feminists have done detailed studies of father/daughter incest which document the systematic way that male dominant society allows fathers to use their patriarchal power in the family to play off mothers against daughters, thus strengthening their own power (Herman, 1982; Rush, 1980). Furthermore, the near absence of mother/child incest suggests that the forms of sex/affective energy that tie mothers to children, though they are erotic, are not genitally sexualised, nor is this likely given the gender split between emotion and pleasure in capitalist patriarchal forms of sex/affective energy. Thus, the call to 'off the incest taboo' must be seen for what it is: a utopian and dangerous slogan that is likely merely to lead to the legitimation of male sexual abuse of children.

Adult/child sexuality

Adult/child sex should be forbidden in a transitional feminist morality. This is not because it is inconceivable that human adults and children should have reciprocal sex but because it is nearly impossible to achieve in our society as presently structured.

Some pluralist feminists have disagreed with the policy implications of such a stand on the grounds of the 'slippery slope' – that is, how can age of consent laws be formulated fairly so as to protect the very young from predatory adults yet not forbid sex between those very close in age but on different sides of an arbitrarily agreed line for adulthood, eighteen and sixteen year olds, for example?

Obviously it is not easy to draw the line between child and adult. In part this depends on the way a society institutionalises this line by when it permits economic independence of children from parents. Our society creates conflicting consciousness in teenagers by infantilising them through economic dependence and authoritarian prison-like schools at the same time as the media and market forces of sexual consumerism encourage them to think of themselves as sexual commodities. Such a situation creates youth who may want to consent to sex with an adult yet do not have the minimum economic independence to give them bargaining power. Thus, our transitional sexual morality must defend age of consent laws between adults and teenagers or children, even though the enforcement of these may be arbitrary in some cases.

One policy initiative that feminists could take with respect to age of consent laws is to frame laws which ban sexual relations between children under eighteen and anyone eighteen or older who is more than six years older than they. This would allow teen-agers to be sexual with their peers and with young adults. At the same time it would protect them from potentially exploitative sexual relationships until they reach a minimal maturity level.

Forbidden *vs* risky sex

Our feminist transitional sexual morality should be pluralist with respect to most adult consensual sex. We should not condemn as non-feminist those practices which may seem extremely risky to us in terms of suspected dominance/subordination dynamics, as long as they are engaged in in private. Thus, such practices as consensual S/M, male breadwinner/female housewife sex, and prostitution have been critiqued as practices that may involve dominance and subordination. But there is no final proof that roled sex can never be reciprocal even if it is patterned after the gender dualism of compulsory heterosexuality. And though, for example, economic dependence and the psychological role of server strongly suggest that housewives will not be in a position to have equal sexual bargaining power, there well may be mitigating circumstances which allow a woman in such a position emotional parity with a particular husband. Thus, though we may want to advise of the risks of such practices to our friends and young people under our care, we should not claim these practices to be morally forbidden.

Unsafe sex: the problem of AIDS and other sexually transmitted diseases

The AIDS epidemic has created a serious moral and political problem for feminists. On the one hand, the fact that AIDS is a fatal disease communicated through blood and sperm suggests that feminists ought to urge the adoption of safe sex practices (e.g. using condoms, etc.) which minimise the health risks of such practices. But, on the other hand, it would be dangerous to put physically unsafe sex practices on our list of legally forbidden practices, for this would suggest that the state should pass coercive legislation such as mandatory testing for AIDS for marriage licences and even coercive legislation forbidding certain kinds of sexual practice, for example, laws against sodomy.

Feminists need to balance the defence of the rights of sexual minorities against state intervention in their sexual practices with the right of individuals not to be exposed to fatal sexual diseases without their knowledge. In the case of AIDS and other sexually transmitted diseases, feminists might make a distinction between what is morally forbidden and what is legally forbidden: not everything that we may want to forbid morally is something we may want the state legally empowered to coerce. Thus, feminists ought to morally forbid unsafe sex practices but yet oppose legislation which would make such practices illegal because of the danger that the state could encroach on civil rights in their enforcement of the law. Vigorous sex education with respect to safe and unsafe sex practices is a better means to creating situations where people practise safe sex than making the practices illegal.

Feminists are coming to realise that the fight against AIDS is a crucial one, for if we do not become involved in demanding money for research and public education about AIDS, the New Right will continue to use the existence of AIDS in racist, sexist and heterosexist ways to encourage the public to react in moral panic which will scapegoat minorities and gay men and create the danger of restrictive anti-sex legislation which will restrict the sexual freedoms of all of us.

Consensual S/M among adults

Many radical feminists maintain that S/M relationships ought to be morally forbidden from a feminist perspective, both because they involve the infliction of physical pain (hence violence) against women and because they perpetuate the eroticising of dominance/subordination roles so as to perpetuate male dominance. To defend the view that feminists should judge consensual S/M sex risky rather than morally forbidden, we need to consider both aspects of these practices: their potentially physically unsafe aspect and their eroticisation of dominance aspect.

Feminist sex manuals like Pat Califia's *Sapphistry* (1980) attempt to delineate safe sex practices for those engaging in consensual S/M. But aside from the physical dangers of a sexual practice that uses physical pain as an inducement to physical pleasure, there is the more difficult question of the suspected eroticisation of domination that S/M involves. Though its feminist defenders argue that the roles and fantasies enacted by the role of sadist and masochist are pure theatre, there is no escaping the fact that much of such theatre involves the enactment of roles that are explicitly degrading: e.g. master and slave or servant or dog, a parent punishing a child, or other clearly hierarchical positions. Should we accept the view of the pluralists that 'anything goes' in fantasy life, and that individuals have the right to private choices in this area (cf. Samois, 1981)? Or are the radical feminists correct that there is no clear line between fantasy and reality *vis-à-vis* a person's ultimate values (Linden *et al* (eds), 1982)? Is it true that persons who get off on masochism in bed are by that practice perpetuating a vulnerable ego in other areas of their social life? Or is that person merely venting an unconscious (and possibly unchangeable) aspect of her emotional life thus expurgating its influence from the rest of her life? And might many of those engaged in so-called consensual S/M practices, especially those who are the masochists, actually be constrained into maintaining these practices (Jonel, 1982)?

Despite the heated claims by both proponents and opponents of S/M that it is empowering *vs* disempowering to the women who engage in it, there is no clear proof either way and therefore consensual S/M should be considered a risky but not a forbidden practice for feminists.[2] Since it is risky, I would not want to advise anyone to experiment with it, but if someone is determined to try it, they ought not to be morally censured from engaging in it, though they should perhaps be advised against physically unsafe practices that they might otherwise try.

There is one further difficult aspect of S/M which a feminist sexual morality must deal with, and this is the public display of S/M fantasy objects, e.g. chains, handcuffs, Nazi insignia and the like. Must feminist political coalitions, women's centres and other public organisations support the right of S/M practitioners to create a public S/M sexual identity with the appropriate paraphernalia in the same way that feminists have defended the right of homosexuals to wear public symbols which express their sexual preference?

There is surely a disanalogy between the support of public gayness and the support of public S/M insignia. In the case of the latter but not the former, feminists have a right to withhold such support. Consensual lesbian or gay relations do not carry the same danger of general negative effects to others as does the public display of S/M symbols or the adoption of S/M as a public sexual identity.

The danger in the full justification of consensual S/M with the right to all its public trappings is as follows. Consensual S/M is justified (if at all) by being a theatre of private meanings. But S/M feminists have no right to insist on being supported to wear symbols of their sexual fantasies in public. This is because feminists must make a strong public stand against non-consensual violence and hierarchical coercion. As Alice Walker argues (Walker, 1982b) there is no clear way for the general public to understand the distinction between feminists supporting consensual and non-consensual violence when self-avowed lesbian feminists (e.g. a white woman with a whip and a black woman wearing a collar and handcuffs) present themselves publicly as S/M lovers.

A second reason why public display of S/M in a feminist context is problematic is its effect on women who have suffered non-consensual violence: rape survivors and victims of domestic battering. Whips, chains, collars and handcuffs cannot help but have a negative emotional meaning to those who have suffered the non-consensual use of these instruments. Thus, it is not surprising that many who have suffered such violence or whose political work involves working with survivors of such violence may want to avoid the emotional upset to themselves or these women that public displays of explicit S/M symbols would involve.

In sum, public display of S/M symbols is problematic for two reasons: first, because the standard meaning of these symbols implies the negation of the equal and consensual relations that feminism stands for, and second, because such symbols (in their standard meaning) violate the ground rules (a feeling of safety and security) that victims of non-consensual violence have a right to expect from spaces controlled by feminists. For these reasons, feminists ought not to support the public display of S/M graphic sex roles, even though we should support the right of an adult feminist to practise consensual S/M in private if she wishes.[3]

In arguing that private S/M should be categorised as risky and graphic public symbols of S/M forbidden, a moral distinction has been made between public and private which feminists who believe that the personal is the political may question. The need for feminists to re-appropriate this distinction for certain uses will be defended further below.

Housewifery, marriage and prostitution

Putting housewifery and prostitution in the same camp, not as morally forbidden but morally risky from a feminist point of view, allows us to highlight the structural features of these practices which have been targetted by radical feminists in both waves of the American and European women's movements – the fact that women who are economically dependent on men are expected to trade economic support for sexual favours, and that this makes for an unequal negotiating relationship.

At the same time as feminists need to have a way to advise against housewife/marriage and prostitution as risky practices in many circumstances, we need to acknowledge that many working-class women may have no better alternatives to choose. Many women choose to be housewives because they wish to raise children with a man and cannot afford child care. And others become prostitutes because of economic and personal coercion.

Since housewifery and prostitution have the same structure, it is hypocritical to outlaw one and not the other. While our ideal socialist-feminist society hopefully would eliminate both, this is not a realistic possibility within capitalist patriarchy. Thus, feminist public policy in our society today should advocate the elimination of legal sanctions against prostitution. Such a move would spare the women involved the stigma of outlaws (Delacoste and Alexander (eds), 1987). However, this does not mean that feminists need to approve of prostitution, any more than socialist-feminists approve of capitalism! But just as our disapproval of capitalism does not imply that we want to outlaw feminist businesses under capitalist patriarchy, so it doesn't follow that we should outlaw prostitution even though in an ideal socialist-feminist society prostitution would not exist.

Our moral disapproval of prostitution should not be used to stigmatise prostitutes. Marriage, like prostitution, should be classified as risky but not forbidden for feminists. We should press for specific laws against procurement (pimping) and the various sorts of violence and economic coercion through which women are constrained into prostitution (cf. Barry, 1979). Such activities should be rigorously prosecuted in a way that is not now happening.

Another example of a problematic decision for feminists is heterosexual marriage. The legal institution of heterosexual mar-

riage still creates legal structural inequalities between men and
women: rape in marriage is still permissible in many American
states and homemakers are not eligible for their spouses' social
security benefits. It also legitimises economic and social privileges
for heterosexual couples that are not possible for homosexual
couples. Feminists ought, therefore, to eschew standard marriage
ceremonies in order not to perpetuate the public symbolic
meaning of heterosexism and women as legal possessions of men.

Private 'ceremonies of commitment' or legal contracts which
are not explicitly marriage contracts are permissible since they
don't carry the same patriarchal and heterosexist interpretation.
They also allow straight feminist, lesbian feminists and our male
allies the opportunity to create a counterculture of sex/affective
resistance to the sexual symbolic code of patriarchal heterosexual
marriage. Couple commitment is an important feature of countercultural communities. Public alternative ceremonies of commitment allow a social expression to a community that does not carry
the capitalist patriarchal meaning of legal marriage ceremonies.

Assuming a sphere of private activities where consenting adults
have the right to take risks in sexual experimentation does not
answer the more difficult question of what to do about those
public arenas in which sexual symbolic codes are reproduced, for
example, mass media images such as sexual advertising, movies,
pornographic material etc. We shall turn to these questions concerning the representation of sex in the media in the next few
sections.

The case of pornography

When the US Supreme Court ruled against the Dworkin/
MacKinnon anti-pornography ordinance, they set to rest one
burning issue between pluralist and radical feminists: whether
this ordinance was a feasible way to use the power of the state to
challenge pornography. The Dworkin/MacKinnon ordinance was
an ingenious attempt to carry the work of WAP (Women Against
Pornography) further by arguing that pornography violates the
civil rights of women (by demeaning us and inciting harm against
us) and setting up provisions to allow women to bring civil suits
against producers, distributors and users of specific pieces of
pornography that could be shown to have had these effects. The

pluralist feminist group FACT (Feminists Against Censorship Taskforce) developed an *amicus curiae* (friend of the court) brief against such an ordinance when it was introduced in Suffolk County, New York. Though many of the specific arguments of this brief now seem passé, some of them are still relevant to the general question of how feminists should organise to deal with pornography as a moral and political issue.

FACT's arguments and the Supreme Court decision against the ordinance do not imply anything about whether women should continue to use civil suits against pornographers where actual harm and coercion of women can be demonstrated. This is important feminist work. Though it may be unconstitutional to use prior restraint against violent pornography, this does not mean feminists can't judge this material morally forbidden and take political action against it. We can use economic boycotts and civil disobedience as our protest against particular instances of violent pornography. But to make this point plausible, we need to respond to the FACT arguments which object to such a feminist sexual politics *vis-à-vis* pornography.

One key problem is how to draw the line between erotica, sexually explicit material, and pornography, material that eroticises violence against women and/or is otherwise degrading. Dworkin and MacKinnon define pornography as 'the graphic sexually explicit subordination of women through pictures and/or words', and they list seven categories of depiction which constitute this subordination. FACT goes to town on the ambiguity of these categories, and questions whether there is any objective, context-free way to determine that any portrayal of sex necessarily degrades or subordinates women. For example, though many women find the graphic depiction of women performing fellatio on men degrading and disgusting, others, who enjoy the practice, do not. In short, FACT wants to know how to draw the line that separates pornography from sexually explicit yet non-degrading material (cf. also Duggan and Vance, 1985).

But from the radical feminist viewpoint, such a problem, far from being the *reductio ad absurdum* of the WAP view, simply shows that the patriarchal construction of images in our society is so weighted as to construct most sexually explicit material to vest a degrading meaning in women's naked bodies. The deciding factor is the continuing presence of compulsory heterosexuality as a system that subordinates women. The ideological component of this is the natural complement principle which allots initiation and possession to men and responsiveness and submission to women. In a real world where men are the main consumers of pornography and have economic and political power over women, a standard reading of women's naked bodies, however they are presented, is that they are for the use of men and hence imply the degradation of women.

From this fact, however, it does not follow that Catherine MacKinnon's strong line on the connection between gender identity and media images is correct. MacKinnon argues (1983, 1984) that gender domination and sexual desire are actually created, not just fantasised, in pornography. This implies that there is no line at all between fantasy and reality: what the media thinks of us is what we think of ourselves! As many of us know from our own rape fantasies, this claim seems too strong: fantasising rape as a way to get over sexual inhibitions in masturbation does not at all imply that one wants to be raped in reality! And though the degrading natural complement images in pornography are a part of the gendered sexual symbolic code of our society, they are certainly not all of it. Not only are there some images of dominant women as well as equally negotiating partners regardless of gender in mainstream pornography and the mass media, but there are increasing numbers of publications attempting feminist erotic images. Thus we may suppose that the contradictions in the social meanings of our contemporary set of images weaken the overall power of the patriarchal aspect of our symbolic sexual code.

But if some radical feminists go overboard in obliterating the line between fantasy and reality, some pluralist feminists mistakenly minimise the difficulty of drawing this line. In so doing, they assume a liberal 'rational economic man' theory of human agency – a unified self-interested agent who clearly separates his/her fantasies from 'real' projects. But I have argued that that conception of human agency cannot plausibly explain the persistence of social domination nor the types of resistance to it. Rather, our fantasies are aspects of our reality, of selves which may be disunified and contradictory, but whose aspects are always relevant to the total meaning of acts we perform.

In most capitalist patriarchies, the vast majority of women think most mainstream pornography is degrading to women. It is beside the point to argue that this reaction is a leftover from puritanical feminine training. Degradation, even though socially constituted and in the eye of the beholder, is nonetheless psychologically damaging – and in this case contributes to male dominance. Just to raise the spectre of the relativity of sexual meanings, or the anti-sex implications of the critique of pornography, or the need to prove direct harm, is not enough to weaken the radical rationale for using some state or collective action against pornography.

What practical consequences does this analysis lead to? To me it suggests that our political practice needs to demonstrate the lie of the natural complement theory. If women collectively refuse to accept offensive images of women's bodies wherever they appear publicly, in pornography and sexual advertising as well as movies which depict objectionable violence against women, we are challenging and changing our image from sexual object to sexual subject. Pickets, boycotts and sit-ins present us as public subjects not objects, thus undercutting the use of sexually explicit images of women as passive objects for male use. This is true even if the 'slippery slope' argument – where to draw the line between demeaning and acceptable sexually explicit images – still applies: we can disagree on where this line is in particular cases and yet have a radical pornography politics of the sort being suggested here. Not all of us, after all, need to engage in any particular boycott or sit-in to make it effective as an act of symbolic self-determination!

What about legal action? Although objections to some parts of the Dworkin/MacKinnon ordinance were justified, that doesn't mean that all of it should be totally scrapped. By deleting the problematic clause which allowed suits against 'traffickers' in degrading images, the remaining ordinance could serve as a prototype for laws which would avoid the censorship question. So altered, the law would create the right to sue anyone – lover, husband, employer or trafficker – for being involved in the production or use of a pornographic item which is actually used to coerce a woman. In this way, it is an actual harms suit, similar to a suit brought against a toy manufacturer or distributor that is shown to cause actual harm to children.

The FACT argument that sexual minorities' preferences for sexually explicit material might be restricted by any pornography ordinance does not apply to this version. Only if actual harm or coercion could be proved would the law apply. In such a case the

activity was not consensual and thus would fall under the forbidden category for feminists no matter what sort of minority sexual
practice is involved.

If this sort of modified ordinance were made law, some evidence could accrue on the contested issue of whether pornography does directly harm women, as radical feminists claim, is a
catharsis as some pluralists claim, or a side issue as others see it.

Another argument typically advanced by libertarians is the
'misplaced emphasis' argument: we should be working on challenging the other major mechanisms of male dominance, since
pornography is more a symptom than a cause (Duggan and
Vance, 1985). At its most simplistic, the logic of the misplaced
emphasis argument is that we cannot attack any one of a network
of mechanisms which collectively perpetuate male dominance
unless we attack them all at once. This is rather like the weak
ultra-leftist argument against the National Organisation of
Women (NOW) organising for the Equal Rights Amendment
(ERA) that since the ERA by itself will not change the sex-
segregated nature of wage labour, it is futile to work for its
passage. Such an argument severely underestimates the practical
effect of symbolic types of legislation such as the ERA, affirmative
action and anti-pornography ordinances. It also reflects a liberal
fear of use of the state to regulate or censure anything which
connects in any way to speech, on the ground that our right-wing
opposition can censure our publications if we get a strong law in
place.

Just as feminists must use the state to push for the ERA and
comparable worth legislation, even though such legislation is not
enough and may be co-opted in some ways to further male
dominance, so we must not hesitate to use the state to censure
those who use images to harm and degrade us. Of course we have
to be careful to write legislation which cannot easily be used
against us: hence the pluralists are correct to critique the original
trafficking in degrading images clause of the Dworkin/MacKin-
non ordinance as dangerous because it is something patriarchal
judges could easily use against feminist and progressive sexual
images.

For example, Dworkin and MacKinnon characterise images of
women's disconnected 'body parts' as degrading to women, hence
pornographic. But the specific prohibition against images of disconnected body parts could be used to censor Judy Chicago's

paintings of vaginas or Tee Corinne's pictures of lesbian lovemaking focusing on parts of bodies. In other words, images celebrating women's bodies, especially when used in lesbian publications, could be interpreted as degrading to women and censored.

Nonetheless, from the fact that we must be careful in framing our legislation, it does not follow that we should eschew any legal battles against pornography at all! This is like throwing out the baby with the bathwater.

One final objection often raised by opponents of the ordinance is the 'perilous coalition' argument: any position which allies us with the Right has to be suspect. Shouldn't we refuse to lend our tacit support to the stigmatisation of sexual minorities such as prostitutes, paedophiles, S/Mers, lesbians and gays and other 'perverts' whose sexual practices the New Right wants to curtail by censoring the sexually explicit material they enjoy?

But the praxis of coalition politics often involves joining with others who don't agree with you on all issues. Whom to ally with at any given historical moment is a tactical as well as a strategic question. Given the proper context, we can ally with New Right women to push for the civil rights of women against pornography. The proper context would have to include a mobilisation of the local feminist community such as, unfortunately, Catherine MacKinnon did not undertake in her work to institute the Dworkin/MacKinnon ordinance in Indianapolis, leaving her open to charges of merely colluding with the Right rather than strengthening grassroots feminist anti-pornography forces (Duggan, 1986). Grassroots feminist involvement in any coalition with right-wing women is key, for only then can the proper symbolic significance of the action be preserved.

Any anti-pornography action, whether a referendum on an anti-pornography ordinance or an economic boycott of a store selling objectionable pornography, must be conceived as an activity of self-determination by ordinary women. Its feminist overtones will be strengthened to the extent that the feminists in the coalition can convince individual conservative women to overcome some of their homophobic and puritanical feelings about sex.

Thus, FACT is wrong to dismiss the idea of using economic pressure, including civil suits, against pornography. Their objection perpetuates the flawed assumption of classical liberalism, namely that there exists an equal market-place where all ideas and images compete. But we know that oppressed groups cannot compete fairly to get our ideas across; those who have the money create the market for their ideas and refuse to publish ours.[4] This does not imply that feminist produced erotica is not important. It clearly is. But the limited material resources available for its production and distribution compared to the power of the mass media makes this strategy one of limited effectiveness. We continue to require other means, like economic boycotts, to make our own speech heard against the phallocratic images of the mass media.

Incidentally, while feminists should consider economic boycotts against non-feminist pornography-carrying stores, a distinction should be made between feminist and non-feminist stores in this respect. The symbolic context of a countercultural store is very different from a mainstream bookstore. The latter typically sells the products of large corporations, where the economic market-place has given an edge to those with money. Feminist stores, however, are typically much closer to the ideal of a market-place of ideas, where each voice is presented in a more equal setting for the consumer to consider on its merits. For this reason, feminists ought not to picket feminist stores for carrying pornography they find objectionable (e.g. such controversial magazines, produced by feminists, as *On Our Backs* and *Bad Attitudes*). How else are we to have exposure to this material to debate and discuss its content? Such a boycott does, it seems to me, violate feminists' right to the free development of opinion on controversial matters by denying them access to the material to make up their own minds.

The right to engage in radical economic actions against pornography does not answer the question of how feminists should treat disagreements among ourselves about feminists' consumption of pornographic material. I would argue that this is an issue that ought to be placed in the arena of risky rather than forbidden activities. Though a steady diet of violent pornography may well be damaging to the psychological health of the feminist who uses it, we should not curtail her right to take psychological risks any more than we should restrict her intake of sugar because we may feel that sugar consumption is unhealthy for humans. Objecting to the public sale of pornography, the public use of offensive sexual advertising or representations of explicit violence against women in the movies and media is different than morally censuring a feminist's private consumption of such material. One may have an obligation to express one's value disagreements with one's friends about such practices but, again, this is very different from concluding that such a disagreement implies one standard of political correctness for feminists about what one should privately allow oneself to 'turn on' to!

Men's liberation

The question of men's liberation is relevant to a feminist sexual morality because of the fact that the poles of the Women's Movement are divided in how to handle the question of male allies. On the one hand, lesbian separatists feel that as men are the enemies they cannot be trusted. Men benefit from sexism, no matter how much institutional sexism stifles their human potential. Thus feminists ought to work as little as possible with male allies to challenge sexism. On the other hand, liberal feminists argue that since sexism oppresses everyone, both men and women, by creating sexual alienation and denying human androgynous potential, we ought to work with men to overcome gender roles.

My view is neither a separatist nor an assimilation/integrationist position, though I think the Women's Movement needs both its separatist and its integrationist wings. Rather, mine is a coalitionist position: men are both potential allies and potential adversaries. Since they, like women, have both incorporative and oppositional aspects in their personalities, the most willing male feminist ally can be co-opted by his incorporative bonding with other men and can be tempted to use his oppositional aspect to aggrandise his material privileges against women. But men can also develop an incorporative identification with a progressive feminist community that can counter their oppressor identification.

In one sense, the vast majority of women, whether heterosexual or lesbian, have no choice but to struggle with individual men for women's and sexual liberation, since we must continue to relate to men in personal ways (as employers, relatives, politicians, etc.) whether or not we choose them as lovers. In this process, we must struggle to recodify the symbolic meanings of our sex/affective interactions with men.

All women must find creative ways to challenge the male subject/female server aspects of these practices, whether they involve sexual harassment at work, pornography on our newsstands, or laws inhibiting our reproductive and lifestyle choices. Though we can join mixed organisations (the National Organization of Women, the Rainbow Coalition, Democratic Socialists of America etc.) to challenge sexist and right-wing politicians, we also require autonomous women's networks that maintain women's independent leadership of the fight against male dominance. We also need to choose lifestyles which symbolise the independence of women from male service such as feminist communal living, co-habitation rather than marriage, gay/lesbian/bisexual lifestyles, artificial insemination and adoption, single parenting, and so forth.

But what about men's participation in feminist sexual liberation? How can the powerful same sex bonding that perpetuates male domination be undermined, challenged or used to promote feminist goals?

It is not surprising that the men's liberation movement is so small, given my analysis of sex/affective homosocial bonding among men. Men in the men's liberation movement are looked upon by many as 'failed men', 'sissies' and 'wimps'. In fact straight feminist men have even a lower status than gay men! After all, 'out' gay men are opposing their own oppression and thus challenging heterosexual dominance. In the context of a gay liberation movement, this can be seen as a courageous, 'manly' thing to do! Unfortunately, this status is often achieved because of the anti-feminist nature of much of gay male culture, much of which is explicitly woman-hating (Bryant, 1986; Frye, 1984). Thus, gay male and women's liberation do not necessarily go together.

The question is, then, how can straight and gay men still be 'men', 'masculine', and ally themselves with feminism? Two supportive countercultural networks seem to be required: 1) a progressive community of men and women which supports feminist recodifications of the gender sexual codes, and 2) men's support groups or networks which are feminist in terms of the self concepts and alternative values and skills (e.g. intimacy skills) they allow men to develop. Such groups as Men Against Violence Against Women are extremely important in spreading feminist education among men in a way that can effectively challenge status quo male bonding.

Conclusion

In this chapter an historical analysis of the dialectics of pleasure and intimacy/love as they structure our contemporary sexual practice has been presented in order to develop a socialist-feminist vision of sexual liberation. It has been argued that feminists require a transitional sexual morality to guide us in our choices of which sexual issues should become demands for changes in state public policy. In so doing stands have been taken which support radical feminists on some issues and pluralist feminists on others. In particular, support has been expressed for the idea of a pluralist feminist community in which we can experiment with the creation of alternative consensual sexualities. We can agree to disagree on personal choices of sexual lifestyles by distinguishing between basic, risky and morally forbidden sexual practices, only morally condemning those who practise the latter, while feeling free to disagree with, but not condemn, those who engage in risky practices.

The endorsement of the pluralist right to sexual experimentation within limits does not challenge the radical feminist view that feminists have the right to decide that certain particular examples of violent pornography and other public sexist and demeaning images of men and women (e.g. public S/M insignia, standard public marriage ceremonies and beauty contests, sexist sexual advertising) should be forbidden and to take political action against them. Public protests against such images are important because in capitalist patriarchy the contents of masculinity and femininity are importantly reproduced in such arenas. Such protests challenge sexual symbolic codes which present women as sexual objects not as sexual subjects and in this way advance both women's and sexual liberation.

11

A socialist-feminist vision and strategy for the future

Sexual pleasure, emotional commitment, democratic parenting and an egalitarian economy have all been mentioned in previous chapters as goals of a socialist-feminist vision of gender and sexual liberation. It is time to sum up this vision and to outline a strategy for achieving it.

General goals and ideals

The socialist-feminist goals and ideals set forth here are very much a product of the United States historical context. They are an attempt to synthesise a socialist model of human potential best achieved through social structures encouraging a sense of community and group solidarity with an anarchist/individualist value on individual autonomy. Goals of community and autonomy have been in tension in the US ever since the Puritans attempted to found a community based on conformity to a Calvinist reading of the Bible which emphasised the right of Protestant individual autonomy from Church of England doctrine. The tendency toward individualism in a context where group solidarity was needed to survive continued as successive waves of immigrants from different cultures found themselves in competition in wage labour. Nonetheless, these historical tensions in American values provide us with an opportunity to develop a particular socialist-feminist model of an ideal society. But first, we need to clarify what is involved in these values.

Group solidarity does not merely involve an intellectual or moral commitment to give the needs of the group and individuals within it a higher priority than one's own interests. Rather, it involves a desire to see the needs of the group and its individual members met. Thus, one's incorporative identification with the group involves a heightening of sex/affective energy both to oneself and others in the group when the needs of individual members or of the group as a whole are achieved.

Individual autonomy, on the other hand, may involve the setting of individual goals, values or needs that are in conflict with the group. For example, an interest in solitary mountain climbing may sometimes be at odds with the collective work necessary for the good of any group in which such a person is a member. Or, a person's sex/affective desires may be defined as risky or forbidden by the majority of the group.

It is clear that the values of community and of individual autonomy or freedom are in tension, and that therefore a balance must be struck between their conflicting claims. There is no *a priori* way to resolve such tension – no categorical imperative or Golden Rule which can guide us as to what the proper balance is. The best we can do is to work for a society in which the material conflicts between individuals are minimised by political structures which set individual civil rights as non-negotiable rules of the game. One such rule of the game should be the right to privacy with respect to sexual and personal lifestyles that do not harm others.

In areas not protected by civil rights statutes, a democratic decision-making process should be the rule. However, the democratic creation of group values does not guarantee for any one member of a group that her opinions will win out. Many of those who identified as radical feminists in the 1960s have become pluralist feminists in the 1980s in the participatory democratic process of forming the values of the Women's Movement. But a democratic process should at least guarantee that others incorporate with them as members of one sex/affective energy network not to exclude them as members of the group for 'political incorrectness' unless the disagreement is extreme. The priority of defending group solidarity without group autocracy is one reason for the theoretical strategy developed in the previous chapter of creating a middle category risky between the extremes of basic and forbidden practices when setting up a feminist morality.

Obviously, what is included in forbidden *vs* risky *vs* basic practices will be in part dependent on the changing historical reality in which such a feminist morality is used. For example, a society which guaranteed children over twelve economic independence and job security and which involved democratic parenting to give young people experience in making their own decisions might justify a very different line between acceptable, risky and forbidden adult/child sexuality than is acceptable in our present society.

A society maximising egalitarian and democratic values would, by that fact, tend to maximise reciprocal sex/affective energy and in so doing would increase the amount of sex/affective energy available to all. This would occur by minimising the repressive aspect of social hierarchies – husband/wife, parent/child, teacher/ student, boss/worker – which reduce the quantity and quality of sex/affective energy by one-way channelling and control. One strategy to accomplish this would be to encourage peer group sex/affective bonding (work groups, councils) for the purpose of collective decision-making with as many persons as possible whose decisions affect one's life. Those with expertise in various areas because of age or training would act more as advisors and less as top-down authorities in a society which would encourage participatory democracy: workers' control and children, student, client and patient input into educational, therapeutic and medical structures.

The model of such a democratic socialist society assumed here is council socialism. For elaboration on the specifics of this vision as it contrasts with other forms of socialism and anarchism, see Albert and Hahnel (1978, 1981a, 1981b) and Shalom (ed.), (1983).

There are six further values we should discuss in more detail in order to spell out what this socialist-feminist vision involves: first, eliminating gender dualism; second, setting up a democratic non-race/ethnicist socialist political economy; third, maximising democratic parenting; fourth, promoting sex for pleasure; fifth, promoting committed sexual relationships; and sixth, guaranteeing gay and lesbian rights.

The elimination of gender dualism

The Women's Movement in the late 1960s and early 1970s advocated the elimination of learned gender roles and posited androgyny as a goal for human development. An attempt to spell this out was made in a 1977 paper (Ferguson, 1977):

... the term *androgyny* has Greek roots: *andros* means man and *gyne*, woman. An androgynous person would combine some of each of characteristic traits, skills and interests that we now associate with the stereotypes of masculinity and femininity. It is not accurate to say that the ideal androgynous person would be both masculine and feminine, for there are negative and distorted personality characteristics associated in our mind with these ideas. A masculine person is active, independent, aggressive, more self-interested than altruistic, competent and interested in physical activities, rational, emotionally controlled, and self-disciplined. A feminine person, on the other hand, is passive, dependent, non-assertive, more altruistic than self-interested (supportive of others), neither physically competent nor interested in becoming so, intuitive but not rational, emotionally open, and impulsive rather than self-disciplined. Since our present conceptions of masculinity and femininity thus defined exclude each other, we must think of an ideal androgynous person as one to whom these categories do not apply – who is neither masculine nor feminine, but human: who transcends those old categories in such a way as to be able to develop positive human potentialities denied or only realized in an alienated fashion in the current stereotypes. (Ferguson: 45–6)

Since this 1977 paper, I have come to accept one of Jan Raymond's critiques of androgyny: historically and etymologically the word 'androgyny' puts the male aspect of human nature first, making it primary, and sees the female aspect welded to that as a secondary attribute. Thus, to signal feminist transcendence of old oppositional gender categories, as well as to indicate that our vision of an ideal human nature must be derived somehow from our historically based gender norms and skills, I now use the term gynandry to refer to the type of personal development I earlier called androgyny.[1]

As feminists we must seek collective ways to revalue the feminine. This means that many of the historical skills of most women's sex/affective labour – nurturance, emotional sensitivity, receptivity to the desires of others, skills in the healing arts – must be revalued and taught to men as well as to women. This will require not only a breakdown in the gender division of labour in the household and in wage labour, but also the acknowledgement that this type of work, as skilled work, should be given comparable worth in pay scales compared to other professional work. Child care workers, elementary school teachers, nurses, social workers – all deserve comparable pay to university professors, doctors and psychiatrists.

Feminists cannot develop a specific vision of a non-patriarchal human nature without grounding it in a specific historical contradiction in values of our present categories of masculinity and femininity. Some of these conflicts are brought out in the discussion of conflicts in our capitalist public patriarchal sexual symbolic code in chapter seven. More generally, the conflict between the value of social solidarity and personal autonomy presented above is an historical conflict typical of the values of capitalist patriarchies. As such, the specific gynandrous model that feminists will develop in our society is likely to be quite different from that which would develop in a society lacking the concept of individual freedom and democratic process.

A gynandrous person would be someone with a democratic rather than an authoritarian personality; one who desires as much as possible reciprocal rather than hierarchical sex/affective energy exchanges with others (including sexual, love, friendship, parenting and wage work interactions).

The elimination of gender dualism which would be necessary to allow gynandry to develop would require the elimination of the sexual division of labour and the rejection of a natural complement theory of gender roles in human social interactions. But it would not thereby preclude the choice of complementary roles by individuals, whether lesbian, gay or heterosexual, in sexual, love, parenting or household relationships. Since such roles would no longer be tied to gender or even to all aspects of individuals' interactions (Newton and Walton, 1984), they would not support hierarchical relationships between individuals such as male dominance or compulsory heterosexuality.[2]

But what are the social conditions necessary for the emergence of this new gynandric human? For this we must turn to our ideal visions of a democratic socialist economy as well as to how parenting and childhood might be organised in this society.

A democratic socialist political economy

In order to promote collective solidarity, individual autonomy and gynandrous individuals, the kind of economy envisaged has been called council socialism. The authors who have done the most to develop this vision in the US today are Michael Albert and Robin Hahnel. Theirs is a model of a planned, yet decentralised economy which emphasises participatory democracy as well as representative democracy in the regulating of the economy. The economy would aim to develop more regional and local self-sufficiency in terms of the planning and development of local industry, and would make economic blueprints for development based on an 'iterative' process of consultation and consensus between workers' and consumers' councils at the local, regional and national level.

Though this is not the place to do a sustained elaboration of a council socialist political economy, we can consider the general features of such a society which could further feminist goals. Thus, a brief discussion of the general goals of such a model is in order. A basic goal would be material security for all, including state provided free health care and schooling, job training, free public child care services, and a minimum income for all whether they are old enough or too old to do paid labour. Another would be ending racial and gender divisions of wage labour. Ending racial segmentation of jobs would require job training programmes, and programmes containing quotas of, or special consideration to, racial minority candidates for jobs and competitive higher education programmes (called 'affirmative action' in the US today). Finally, adequate resources for public education would have to replace inadequate ghetto schools and inferior educational programmes for minorities.

Ending gender dualism in wage labour requires programmes which recalibrate the standard wages for men's and women's work requiring comparable though not identical skills (called 'comparable worth' programmes in the States). It also requires public worker-controlled childcare at places of work, flexi-time jobs that would allow both male and female parents to work part-time to care for small children, and extended maternity and paternity leaves.

Ending the gender division of labour can be seen as part of a wider project of breaking down the rigid divisions that currently exist between mental and manual labour. A society that values allowing individuals their full potential development of skills cannot be satisfied with creating individuals who are forced to develop mental skills to the exclusion of manual skills or, conversely, develop manual skills at the sacrifice of the development of critical mental skills. Our goal should be to organise the economy and schooling so as to promote as far as possible the rotation of jobs, both those which are rewarding, such as decision-making and supervising, and those which are costly such as hazardous, boring or physically tiring jobs.

Thus, our model society must find ways to break down the class construction of our present society which is due to the mental/manual split. Our present advanced capitalist society includes, besides a capitalist class of owners, a professional class which specialises in mental skills, including greater training in critical thinking and decision-making, and a working class composed of two parts: the skilled manual workers who develop skills but for the most part are given little decision-making over what, how much and when things are produced, and an unskilled or 'de-skilled' working class which learns some boring, repetitive skill or service in order to fit into a mostly automated assembly line or service industry (Walker (ed.), 1979). And cutting across these classes, of course, is the sex class division between men who don't and women who do unpaid or unremunerated housework, health care for elder relatives and child care at home, often in addition to sex-segmented wage labour.

An economic organisation that would move toward breaking down both this class mental/manual labour split and the sex class paid/unpaid sex/affective labour split would have to break down the current public/private division of the economy. One plan that might accomplish these goals is the following. All workers would have a work week totalling thirty hours, divided into two fifteen-hour sections. One section would be in what we can call standard sector work: construction, factories, doctoring, teaching, skilled clerical and white-collar work. The other section would be service work. Service work would be rotating. It would consist of all the manual, unskilled and generally low status service work, whether this low status be due to objective considerations, such as that the work is boring, repetitive or unpleasant, or social considerations, such as that it is thought of as women's work or work for servants. These types of jobs would include garbage collection, recycling wastes, janitorial work, para-professional health care and school aides. Some of these jobs would be work now generally done by low status men such as racial minorities or immigrants. Others are women's sex/affective labour, including physical care of the elderly, sick and disabled in hospitals and retirement homes, and educational support work with infants, children and young adults in child care centres and schools.

With economic priorities in this ideal society tending toward production to meet human needs rather than profit, the turn away from defence spending and the reappropriation of the social surplus of the society away from the capitalist class, there could be a large upsurge in demand for unskilled construction work in the building of new clinics, day care centres and the dismantling of old inhumane housing structures. These might be jobs that many teenage boys and girls might want to do as part of their work/study programme in the schools or part of their year or two in the National or International Youth Service to be explained below.

Individuals would have their choice of service work for half their work week. They could join a work brigade to do the above mentioned construction work renovating their communities, work which would be guided by skilled workers and professional contractors working their standard sector jobs. Or they could do the other types of job mentioned above. A typical service job centre would have skilled co-ordinators doing their standard sector jobs (e.g. child care co-ordinators) and service sector volunteers who would receive job training from the co-ordinators and would contract to put in a minimum number of months in doing this kind of work. Those performing unsatisfactorily at these jobs could be asked to transfer to other work after a process of evaluation by the workers' council.

A very important component of the service work requirement would be a minimum commitment (say three hours a week) for all workers to participate in work in a child care centre for children ranging in age from infants to kindergarten. This would involve working regularly in a community or work centre doing childcare of one's own choice, and would be mandatory for both men and women, whether they are parents or single, and regardless of their sexual preference.

Socialising and communalising child care in this way would break down the parental roles of nurturant *vs* macho parent that most kids get in this society, and would give them a secure way to get ongoing nurturance from other adults besides their biological parents. Single people would have the opportunity and part of the responsibility for the care of the coming generation, thus acknowledging everyone's social responsibility for children. The issues of social parenting and children's rights will be discussed further in the next section.

Jobs in the standard sector could initially have quotas for women and minorities, disabled and older people, etc. This expansion of our present Affirmative Action programmes would serve to break down race and sex stereotypes and other oppressive social inequalities. Racism, ethnicism and sexism could be further broken down by a massive assault on White Anglo-Saxon Protestant (WASP) culture control. The schools, mass media and government-subsidised cultural groups (music, theatre, etc.) would re-educate all Americans to the richness of American and Third World ethnic and racial cultures. This would mean emphasising in particular Afro-American, native American, Asian, Latin American and Jewish music, languages, food and values. It would mean revitalising the remnants of non-Anglo-Saxon white immigrant cultures (Slavic, Irish, Polish, Mediterranean, etc.). As in Cuba, cultural workers' self-definition as artists would be re-oriented. No longer would they think of themselves as talented, special individuals out to express their own inner meanings with no clear responsibility to an audience or social group. Rather, they would think of themselves as teachers of the people, sharing their skills with them as part of their service work (e.g. doing after-work courses and workshops in factories and schools).

Classism and family class privilege could be attacked by free education through the university level and free adult education in the community and at people's workplaces. Education for self-development could be seen as a right that continues for a person's lifetime, not simply as a means to narrow job training as in our present system. Free health, maternity and birth control services would eliminate some of the material burdens of our present society that disproportionately fall on poor women. Unemployment would be eliminated by the vast increase of jobs like teaching and medical care and the material rebuilding of society with non-environmentally 'harmful' sources of energy (e.g. solar-heated buildings, low rent quality housing for all who need it, new schools and day care centres, etc.). To handle some of the past damage that our country and other First World countries have wrought on Third World countries through imperialism, there could be youth and adult brigades of workers sent to help in technical, economic and social development of the sort requested by the beneficiary countries themselves. Indeed, a mandatory one or two years of work in a National or International Youth Service corps could take the place of time spent in the armed services, and could involve various forms of service work, including if necessary, militia training for defence purposes (I assume the professional armed services would be replaced by civilian militias).

Parenting and childhood

Feminist parenting, like our socialist economy, ought to promote the goals of collective solidarity and individual autonomy, as well as suitable conditions for the development of gynandrous individuals. Since in my feminist vision the economy and public school system will be structured so as to allow both men and women to engage in infant and early child care and teaching, it does not require that one model of the ideal family, such as the heterosexual co-parenting family, be adopted in order to further the possibility of gynandrous children. Though heterosexual couples who raise children together would be expected to co-parent, people would also have the option to raise children in other households as well. As many have pointed out (cf. Joseph, 1983; Raymond, 1986), single mother families, lesbian families, extended families and communal households can also be non-sexist environments if supported by the appropriate external collective nurturance context (whether extended kin network, non-sexist schools and child care, community networks, etc.) which will provide children with a range of male and female role models, personalities and lifestyles. The important principle to keep in mind is that in this new society, no one would be socially or materially penalised, either as a child or adult, for living in a particular type of household (cf. Helmbold and Hollibaugh, 1983).

An important way the revolutionary government could facilitate the breakdown of patriarchal sex roles would be to pass a law similar to the Domestic Family Code in Cuba. The Cuban law makes both men and women equally responsible for housework and for the maintenance of minor children by wage work. Our adaptation of this code could place parental obligations equally on all adults of the same or opposite sex who cohabit with children. Both biological and chosen social family living would be acceptable. Any unrelated people and couples could live together, in any numbers, contrary to the local housing codes in many communities today.

Our model society would have to have a way to regulate the social responsibility for children of those who live in communal households in a way comparable, but superior, to that of patriarchal marriage arrangements. That is, there has to be some way to ensure that unrelated adults provide security to children who become incorporated with them by not just choosing to drop out of the child's life whenever they wish. Also, some rights to see former children housemates should be allowed to such social parents. And, on the other hand, children should have some choice as to which of possibly many adults who cohabit with them they want to continue to spend time with.

The notion of rights for children requires a change in our stultifying division between adulthood and childhood. We need to challenge the assumption of classical liberalism that there is a natural division between learners – those who are too immature or lack the rationality to be choosers and choosers – those who have full political and civil rights (cf. Bowles and Gintis, 1986). Such a dictum was used for centuries to deny women, slaves, immigrants and children any democratic input into social decision-making that affected their lives. As Howard Cohen points out, it is based on the erroneous assumption that individuals can only have rights if they are believed to have certain competencies (Cohen, 1980). But much as wealthy people in this society are assumed to have the right to hire agents (lawyers, etc.) to compensate for their lack of ability in certain areas, so a socialist-feminist society should assume that all human beings should have rights to participate (with the help of others if necessary) in the decision-making which affects their lives. Only in this way can we break the last vestiges of authoritarianism and encourage the development of the kind of democratic parenting practices that will create the most prepared citizens for a democratic life, namely those who have learned from an early age how to think critically and choose for themselves.

This would mean that children should be allowed to be

members of workers' and consumers' councils as well as family/
household councils to participate in political decision-making.
Children over seven should have the right to vote in national
elections, with schools supplying full political debates on the
issues and candidates to inform them of the issues in a manner
they can understand.

In terms of the issue of children's and adults' rights to live in or
leave a household, one way to provide for some security yet allow
individuals freedom is to substitute a new concept of a 'household
contract' for the present marriage contract. This would be a
voluntary arrangement that children over seven, couples and
single people would enter into to live together for a minimum
period of two years and to commit themselves to sex/affective and
economic support and household sharing of tasks. Anyone who
had lived with a child for a minimum of two years would have
child visitation rights, assuming the child consented. All children
would have personal counsellors, perhaps connected to the school
or community centre, who would help them think through
psychological problems with their household, and would mediate
between biological and social parents and a prospective new
household if the child expressed a desire to live elsewhere.

The division between productive adult members of society and
unproductive 'learners' subject to authoritarian learning processes is especially noticeable in the present social division
between school and wage labour. Teenagers in particular are
oppressed by this social organisation which keeps them in school
with no sense that their education is connected to productive
work benefiting the community. As economic dependents, they
have no independent material base from which to challenge wilful
and arbitrary school and parental power. In our new society all
children would receive an economic stipend that they could have
control over (in consultation with their counsellors). Work/study
programmes in the schools would be organised along similar lines
to those of adult production. Students could study for twenty
hours a week and do service work for ten hours a week. Included
in this service work could be apprentice work for future jobs in
the standard sector (as Cuba presently organises its work/study
programmes). Children over the age of ten would also be expected
to do regular work in child care collectives as a part of their service
work.

Pleasure sex and reproductive rights

A feminist egalitarian society should acknowledge the right of those who meet the minimum conditions for personal autonomy and maturity to consensual sex for pleasure. We have already indicated that the problem of adult/child sexuality remains a thorny issue which cannot be settled by a general principle but would depend on the depth of democratic participatory structures in the society as well as economic and social living options for children. If every household had a minimally democratic decision-making structure including house meetings in which children had a say, if children were expected to do socially productive work in school work/study programmes, if children had some options to leave households of origin that they found unsatisfactory and economic stipends from the state which would provide them with a minimum economic independence, then we could expect the issue of adult/child sex to be much more open for experimentation than it is today. But only when social conditions are egalitarian enough so that children themselves organise a sex-for-youth movement will the conditions be right for such a change.

In terms of heterosexual relations between men and women, the key material change that will have to occur to allow sex for pleasure to be a non-sexist goal is the guarantee of full reproductive rights for women: not only contraceptive and birth control information available in the schools together with non-sexist and non-heterosexist sex education, but also community-funded abortion services and living situations for pregnant women and single mothers. Full reproductive rights also have to include the right to homosexual sex with no social penalties, and the development of full rights to artificial reproduction techniques for gays and lesbians and non-coupled heterosexuals.

Pleasure sex as a valid goal has been given a large setback in our society by the development of AIDS and the fear this has created about casual, promiscuous sex. The New Right has taken advantage of this situation to whip up homophobic attitudes against gay male cruising lifestyles. We cannot allow such developments to detract from the right to seek consensual sex for pleasure, whether it be casual sex or the prelude to more committed relationships. Of course, promoting sex for pleasure will also require a commitment to public education about safe sex, as well as the availability of condoms and other contraceptives.

Many feminists find distasteful the idea of promoting sex for pleasure. They would argue that casual sex lifestyles, such as 'cruising', are male-identified, since they promote a focus on sex for physical pleasure rather than sex as a means to deepen emotional intimacy and affectionate connection. As such, they would argue that seeking sex only for physical pleasure is dehumanising, for it uses oneself and the other person as merely a sexual object and thus doesn't tap the deeper potential for sex which is to be used as a reciprocal deepening of an intimate knowledge of, connection and commitment to another human.

My view, on the contrary, is that we should defend a diversity strategy on the question of the uses of sex. Valuing sex for pleasure does not have to mean eschewing the value of sex for emotional intimacy and commitment. To the contrary, I would argue that a model society ought to promote committed sex and ought to set up material and social supports that make committed couple relationships possible. It is only in a patriarchal context where the male sex has been given the right to seek its own physical pleasure and to use the female sex as an object to this end that casual sex for pleasure has demeaning implications.

In a non-sexist context where sexual pleasure was given the social meaning that, say, skiing for pleasure now has, there would be nothing demeaning in heterosexuals and homosexuals seeking casual sex for pleasure. It is only where the promotion of sex for pleasure tends to undermine the search for committed sex that feminists need to worry about sexual objectification. The pre-AIDS gay cruising lifestyle may perhaps be criticised fairly for having encouraged this outlook in many men, with the deleterious consequences of setting up a competitive premium on youth and physique that mitigated against age and committed relationships (cf. Bryant, 1986).

A note on pornography and prostitution. Would such practices exist in a feminist ideal society? With regard to the first, part of the problem lies in definitions. In an advanced industrial society that has gone through a consumerist phase, sexually explicit images and writing designed to promote 'prurient' desires will be likely to continue to exist in some guise (Soble, 1986). It is also true that all images and descriptions will be objectifying to some degree, since they all abstract from the uniqueness of the individual imaged or described and in that sense make them an 'object' of fantasy for one or more of their physical characteristics.

I don't agree with those feminists who suppose that the interest in all such objectifications will dissipate when individuals are able to be in touch with their tender, emotional sexual sides. (This is implied if not actually stated by Griffin, 1981.)

On the other hand, if violent and sexist pornography is due to male dominance and sexual repression, we would expect that these images would no longer be desirable, as the material conditions creating fear and struggle between the sexes (mother-dominated parenting, compulsory heterosexuality, the sexual division of labour in gender) are eliminated. Our society could monitor such images as well as those involved in the mass media in general by elected community media boards, who would carry out public hearings on controversial publications, films, and other media programmes and images.

Prostitution is another debatable issue. Many socialists have supposed that prostitution would die away in a gender egalitarian society where women have equal economic and social power with men. Others suppose that there may always be individuals who cannot find consensual sex for pleasure without hiring other individuals to provide this service for them.

My view is that prostitution should be de-criminalised and that legal penalties should be properly enforced against pimps and organised crime's coercion of women into sex work, including pornography. Only then will we be able to see whether individuals will continue to choose to work as, and to hire, prostitutes. In such a different sex/affective setting, we would imagine either that prostitution would die out, or it would become gender neutral, i.e. there would be as many male as female prostitutes. In either case, just the removal of the stigma of prostitution would also remove the stigma against equal social options for the validation of female sexuality in comparison to male sexuality.

Committed sex and friendship

A couple relationship which is sexual, committed to deep emotional intimacy, trust and sharing is a value which until recently has been normatively restricted to those who are heterosexual and married in our society. Such couple relationships meet human needs for security and sex/affective connection and, as such, are of intrinsic value. When there are a number of such couples who are monogamous and who have community connections together (work, religious, place of residence, political identity, etc.), they tend to stabilise the community bonds as well. Thus, such coupling is valuable for intrinsic and extrinsic reasons.

Traditional marriage was a way of guaranteeing stable couples who would stabilise community bonds. Traditional marriage also regulated and minimised sexual rivalries so that sexual jealousies and conflicts over the rights and obligations to children would not interfere with productive life (cf. Freud, 1961). But traditional marriage was also patriarchal. Furthermore, the prioritising of couple relationships, particularly heterosexual relationships, tends to make women's friendships secondary. And as I and others have argued, prioritising women's friendships is a necessity if feminists are to alter the patriarchal sex/affective bonding system that keeps men's ties with each other strong while women's ties with each other are either weak or reactionary (e.g. in patriarchal kin networks).

What structures and practices would our model society have to substitute for marriage in order to encourage committed sexual coupling and yet also to support friendship networks? Ceremonies of commitment, which would be open to those of any sex, could supplant marriage ceremonies, and be based on a more limited time commitment (e.g. 5 years rather than life). Friendship networks could be encouraged by similar ceremonies honouring friends, or even community networks of friends. These later could be structurally supported by regular get-togethers that might involve consciousness-raising sharing of emotions and discussions. And of course, women's caucuses, gay caucuses and lesbian caucuses would be a regular feature of political life at the community, school and work site.

Heterosexuality/homosexuality

Proponents of androgyny often assume that the elimination of gender dualism with the elimination of the idea of the genders as 'natural complements' supposes the development of bisexuality (Ferguson, 1977). This does not necessarily follow, particularly in the near future, where the notion of the heterosexual couple raising at least one child together will probably continue to hold sway as a social value. As we have discussed above, sex can be used for pleasure, or for committed couple relationships. However, heterosexual intercourse can also be used to produce children. Thus, where a committed couple relationship and raising children are valued, heterosexuality will probably continue to be the preferred sexual identity of the majority of individuals, even where artificial reproductive techniques are available on demand regardless of sexual preference.

Thus, though the breakdown of compulsory heterosexuality and gender dualism will be likely to create a situation where many more people develop bisexual identities, it is not likely that everyone will do so. Thus, lesbian and gay caucuses will still be required to validate and politically defend the choice of same sex relationships both for pleasure sex and for committed sex.

How do we get there from here: feminist strategies

Assuming that the analysis of male dominance and the vision of an ideal socialist-feminist society presented here is accepted, the question then becomes, what are the possibilities and strategies of getting there from here?

There are two polar theoretical strategies in the American Women's Movement today which divide lesbian-feminists who are radical feminists, on the one hand, and liberal feminists, on the other, with socialist-feminists ranging somewhere in between. These two strategies can be termed the universalist *vs* the diversity strategies of achieving an egalitarian society. According to the universalist strategy, there is one preferred means or structure to use, or set up, to achieve social equality. For the diversity strategist on the other hand, what is necessary to break the hold of present social domination structures is a vision and practice which allows for multiple, rather than one, alternative personalities, sets of sexual practices, families, communities and economic structures.

Universalist strategies tend to assume that the way to challenge the gender dualism which supports male domination is to create another structure which gives power to those in the subordinate category, women, in order to eliminate the social dualism. For example, the lesbian-feminist separatist tendency adopts a universalist solution by advocating lesbian sexuality for all feminists, and a separatist community of women lovers to achieve this goal. But, as one diversity theorist, Foucault, would have argued, such a strategy does not eliminate the dualism: it just reverses it (Foucault, 1977). Women are now seen, implicitly or explicitly, to be superior to men. This way of revaluing the feminine creates problems, for example for lesbians with male children or women already in committed relationships to men who cannot choose a type of woman power which excludes an empowering of men willing to challenge male domination.

An alternate strategy is to break the dualism by creating multiple countercultural groups none of which clearly fits into the old dualist oppositions, thus breaking the hegemony of the categories. So, for example, while radical lesbian-feminists attempt to challenge compulsory heterosexuality by advocating that all heterosexual women become lesbians, a Foucauldian approach would validate a plethora of consensual sexual minorities – lesbians, gays, bi-sexuals, trans-sexuals, transvestites, cruisers, S/Ms, adult/child sex, casual sex, prostitution, etc. – in order to break the hold of the norm of adult, married, heterosexual intercourse (cf. also Rubin, 1984; Sawicki, 1986; Weeks, 1985).

The difference in strategy between universalists and diversity theorists usually connects with a different analysis of domination relations. Universalists tend to be structuralists: that is, they assume there are material structures and social practices which perpetuate social domination which cannot be eliminated by a simple change of attitude, language or belief. Thus, to begin to challenge social domination, we must refuse to engage in the roled relations of these structures. Foucault's diversity approach, to the contrary, holds that social domination is based on socially constructed symbolic codes which are importantly perpetuated by discourses. Thus, there is a kind of voluntarism in the Foucauldian approach: we can break the power that discourses have in perpetuating social domination simply by refusing to judge our social practices in accord with the norms of male/female, good/bad, normal/deviant characteristic of the dominant symbolic code.

In my view, social domination is based equally on material structures which create unequal material options for dominant and oppressed groups and on symbolic codes which regulate what is considered normal and deviant. Thus, in emphasising primarily material structures or primarily normative discourse, both the universalist and diversity strategies are based on assumptions which are too simplistic. However, as indicated in chapter nine, there is a third strategy: the restricted diversity strategy. This view accepts a diversity of means to a feminist vision, but does insist that this diversity be limited by a structural analysis which rules out certain options (forbidden) and labels others risky.

A way to apply the universality/restricted diversity/diversity trichotomy to the political tendencies in the Women's Movement could map them on to another trichotomy of categories. In the US the Black civil rights, women's and lesbian/gay liberation movements have had three conflicting tendencies which can be labelled separatist, assimilationist and coalitionist. Though the movement for workers' control is extremely weak in the United States, we could perhaps also characterise tendencies within it in these categories as well.[3]

The separatist wing sees itself as a vanguard group. It pursues the universalist strategy of defining the oppressor as the enemy, and organising the oppressed to separate and prioritise values endemic to their subculture. The assimilationist wing wishes to show that the oppressed group is equal to the oppressor group by struggling for educational and material reforms which allow the oppressed to be assimilated into the values and structures now controlled by the oppressors. It pursues a diversity strategy by encouraging many tacks: besides reforms, we should challenge good girl/bad girl dichotomies (e.g. support sex workers by pursuing the de-criminalisation of prostitution). We should also attempt to persuade the dominators that their own interests will be best served if they allow the oppressed into their ranks (e.g. women have potential talents that are underutilised, and white men are locked into cultural patterns and roles that limit their potential human development, e.g. don't know how to cry, express emotion, be more sensual, etc.).

Each of these wings (which are also tendencies in other social movements against domination) expresses a partial truth. Minority racial and ethnic movements, the Women's Movement, and lesbians and gays require strong sex/affective bonding to defend our countercultural values against those of the dominant culture. Those who are privileged in the present sex/affective production system are indeed enemies in the sense that they will not give up their control without a struggle. Thus a separate countercultural community is important to break the incorporative ties of oppressed with the privileged that keep us from maintaining the struggle for equality. But the separatist wing also tends to isolate itself, eventually, from those very masses for which it wants to be the vanguard, because its sex/affective practices separate it from the daily life of these masses.

On the other hand, the assimilationist wing is correct to emphasise the importance of finding ways to educate those who are dominators about the strengths of the cultures of subordinates that they are missing out on and to find ways to open up opportunities for members of oppressed groups to show they can satisfactorily develop those skills that in our society legitimate more options for dominants, namely more income, more work autonomy and more interesting jobs. But the assimilationist wing tends to become co-opted into individual careerism, thus neglecting the structural heterosexism, racism and classism that keep the majority of women from escaping from social domination.

The solution is to combine the insights of both these approaches into a coalitionist position which finds a way to make compatible the partial truths of both wings. To a coalitionist feminist, men are both enemies and potential allies, depending on the context. In other words, they are adversaries, with some self aspects that set their interests opposed to ours (enemies) and some aspects that allow overcoming such opposition (allies). To guard against their enemy aspect, it is important to retain women's autonomous political and social networks and caucuses in any wider political coalition. To guarantee this emphasis, a separatist lesbian and feminist subculture is important.

But though men's presently constructed sex/affective interests are in opposition to women's, there is an historically grounded way to reconstruct those interests so they are not in opposition to women's. The vision suggested above would resolve the current sex/affective contradictions of capitalist patriarchy and cure the sexual alienation both men and women currently suffer due to our conflicting set of sex/affective values. Thus, there are good reasons to work in coalitions with male allies to aim for a radical re-organisation of our social formation. But women also need to retain our autonomous networks, friendships and organisations. Our feminist coalitions must follow a restricted diversity strategy. We must use a structural analysis of contemporary society to decide which groups express a feminist transitional morality as discussed in chapter eight. Our coalitions need to be principled, not simply instrumental: we cannot work with those who refuse to challenge racism, heterosexism or class privilege.

Since a socialist-feminist vision is also anti-racist and anti-ethnicist as well as egalitarian, coalitions which respect the rights of independent caucuses of oppressed groups are necessary to organise those who are not initially feminist or pro-gay but who wish to fight racism and classism. An obvious place to start in the US today is with the Rainbow Coalition headed by Jesse Jackson. Though Jackson has made political errors in the past suggesting sexism and anti-Semitism, the Rainbow coalition has developed itself with autonomous community bases in many areas in ways that have allowed feminist and anti-ethnicist segments to challenge and change Jackson's political stands on these issues. This is good evidence that the Rainbow Coalition may turn out to be more than the organising base for one presidential candidate. The popularity of Jackson's populist and anti-capitalist positions is hopeful in a United States otherwise deeply suspicious, and ignorant, of socialist options.

There are other progressive groups and movements into which feminists can infuse feminist analysis and issues, e.g. lesbian/gay liberation, the peace and environmental movements, the anti-US interventionist movement supporting liberation struggles in the Third World, the Democratic Socialists of America (DSA), and rank and file trade union organising.

The American feminist movement must develop a coherent set of policy positions to demand support from candidates for political office, as well as endorsements from trades unions and other political groups. Such demands include reproductive rights, lesbian/gay rights, non-sexist public school education, and especially sex education, comparable worth, a minimum national income guaranteed by the federal government, affordable national health care and parent-controlled public day care, stiffer legislation against violence against women, de-criminalisation of prostitution, paid maternity and paternity leave, and legislation requiring corporations to reduce the work week and to adopt flexi-time work schedules as well as employee child care programmes.

Most of these policies have already been advocated by such national women's lobbying organisations in the US as the National Organization of Women and the National Women's Political Caucus. What is lacking is a comprehensive political, economic and sex/affective vision, like the one outlined above, of how the future could change so as to eliminate male dominance. We need to strengthen the feminist component of progressive coalitions like the Rainbow Coalition so as to expand our sex/affective networks out from our sometimes too-narrow circles into a broader base of countercultural resistance.

Feminist movements in all countries need to develop an historical analysis of their particular patriarchal social formation using the analytic concepts of class production, race and sex class, and sex/affective production, as well as a model of a feminist alternative which fits their historical circumstances. We need to understand and respect each other's differences if we are to develop a successful international feminist movement. Only in this way can the strengths of diverse women's cultures, based in the sex/affective labour of mothering and female sexuality as it cuts across national, racial, ethnic and economic class lines, be used as an effective challenge that will one day dismantle capitalist and state-socialist racist patriarchies and create the possibility of a world egalitarian order free of racial, ethnic, gender and sexual discrimination.

Footnotes

Chapter one

1 The first radical feminists of the second wave American Women's Movement were, by and large, women who before becoming feminists were humanists fighting for social justice for others different from themselves (whites supporting Blacks oppressed by racial segregation, women supporting male draft resisters, Americans opposing the American government's war against the Vietnamese people). The subsequent discovery of the contradiction between the New Left's theory of human freedom, social equality and self-determination and its sexist practice (cf. Evans, 1980) moved New Left feminists from a politics of humanist solidarity to a politics of self-interest: women could now picture ourselves as oppressed people even if we were white and middle-class.

The emphasis on women as the 'fourth world' (Barry *et al*, 1973), i.e. as a universally oppressed group hidden within the ranks of other oppressed groups (working-class, minority, Third World, etc.) was strengthened in those New Left feminists who had a chance to talk to North Vietnamese women about the sexism in their lives, and those of us whose studies of state socialist societies like Russia and China had indicated that despite important advances for women's liberation during socialist revolutions, male dominance still persisted in these countries. Since capitalism as we knew it didn't exist in these societies, the reductive Marxist line that sexism is only a feature of class-divided societies was thereby challenged.

2 Though O'Brien too claims to hold that the availability of contraception will change the gender relations of reproduction, her explanation of how this will occur is incoherent. This is because she implies that woman's ability to control her reproduction will allow her to socially 'alienate' herself from species continuity so as to be on a par with men's natural alienation from species continuity. But this explanation founders because women's increased freedom to control our reproduction does not eliminate the biological difference between women's ability to have species continuity through motherhood and men's inability to have that same type of relationship. Thus, contraception eliminates neither male womb envy nor the purported reason to control women's sexuality through patriarchy, namely the male need to be assured of his paternity (cf. Lazaro, 1986).

3 Andrea Dworkin also holds such a vision in early writings (cf. Dworkin, 1974).

4 Charlotte Bunch has since changed her lesbian-separatist views and now supports the importance of coalitions of international feminism (cf. Bunch, 1976).

5 Bowles and Gintis point out that on the classical Marxist assumption that labour is a commodity (hence homogeneous and of abstract equivalence in the capitalist market-place) we would expect racist and sexist pay discrimination to disappear gradually in capitalism. Capitalists will tend to take advantage of initially lower paid Black, other minority and women's labour to hire these workers rather than white men (cf. also Friedman, 1982). This practice would increase their profits, thus in the long run driving down the price of white male labour to meet that of women's and minority labour. That this has not occurred suggests that the exchange of labour does not follow the rules for the exchange of other commodities. Thus, if labour power is heterogeneous not homogeneous (i.e. has different exchange values depending on whether the same work is done by a woman or a man, or white or non-white), men and racial elites can be construed as being exploiters of women and non-whites because the former appropriate part of the surplus value of the work of the latter. This conclusion contradicts the classic Marxist idea that only capitalists exploit the labour power of workers.

6 This is not to say that individual thinkers of Third World and Black nationalist orientations have not attempted to expand Marxism to deal with racism. See Carmichael and Hamilton, 1967; du Bois, 1961; Fanon, 1967, 1968; Marable, 1980, 1981; Sartre, 1969; Said, 1978.

7 In political terms, Marxism in the United States has wavered back and forth between a 'unite and fight' strategy of incorporating Black workers in the vanguard communist party, and encouraging autonomous organisation of the Black community. This latter tendency was strong in the 1930s when the 'Black Nation' thesis was adopted from Stalin's writings on nationalism to imply that American Blacks should be treated as an oppressed nation trapped in colonialist relations with whites. The salutory efforts of the American communist party in challenging racism when it was ignored by all other political groups in the US (e.g. in defending Black men accused of rape in the South, as in the Scottsburo trial) should not be forgotten.

8 Iris Young criticises both the psychological and economic versions of dual systems theory (Young, 1981, 1984). She argues that either we end up positing too universalistic structures of patriarchy, based in a nuclear family structure which does not apply to women in all classes or races, or we are unable to give patriarchy equal historical and material weight with capitalism as a 'motor' of history. If we centre 'the production of people' in the family, we ignore the importance of the sexual division of wage labour and male control of strata as structures which equally oppress women and which have had an independent weight in the development of capitalism.

Young's rejection of dual systems theory is premature. The concept of sex/affective production systems does not have to presuppose that there is only one site for the production of sexuality and nurturance, the family or the economy. Rather, as I argue in chapters five and six, the material base of sex/affective production shifts from family to public patriarchy. Furthermore, the reactive powers of a male dominant sex/affective production system are just as active motors of adjustments in the capitalist system (e.g. the family wage) as is the initial motor of capitalism (wage labour) which challenges the power of men over women in the family.

9 Althusserian Marxism is the view that what is called in classical Marxism the 'superstructure' of society (the state, schools, prisons, unions, families) actually has more causal or material weight on social outcomes (overdetermination) than was ceded by classical Marxism (cf. Althusser, 1971).

Chapter two

1 The constancy principle is the view that the human organism operates on a biological economy of tension reduction. The libido, or the sexual drive, is perceived to be seeking to release tension so as to bring the body's energy system back to equilibrium. On this view, sexual pleasure (particularly orgasmic pleasure) is sought not merely for its own sake but because it accomplishes the biological purpose of tension reduction (Wollheim, 1971).

2 In such societies, it is just as plausible to posit that women do more mothering because this allows them to breast feed babies and is a more efficient way to divide up the socially necessary labour of the society.

Furthermore, in such societies, children are not merely commodities for individuals to enjoy in their leisure time but essential because of the labour power they provide to their family and kin networks. In these contexts, Chodorow's assumption that women have a greater need to mother than men have to father seems questionable. Rather, both genders want to be parents so that their children may provide for their material needs in old age.

Another material consideration Chodorow doesn't consider is reproductive coercion. In patriarchal societies where children's labour power is important legal and religious structures tend to limit a woman's ability (via contraceptives and abortion) to control her fertility. This means that women mother not out of choice but out of necessity. In short, Chodorow's account doesn't explain why we should take her proposed psychological considerations for the choice of parenting as more important in the cluster of explanatory variables than material considerations. Though psychological considerations may seem more primary to us, we are members of an advanced capitalist society where the material considerations of children's labour are no longer important. This should tip us off to the fact that an implausible crosscultural generalisation is being advanced.

3 A more technical way to put this point is to note that the notion of a feminine gender composed of a 'triangular object relational structure' *vs* a masculine gender with a 'dyadic object relational structure' are not, as Chodorow supposes, analytical concepts on the general level of

'forces *vs* relations of production' which can apply to different modes of economic production. Rather they are middle level concepts like 'capitalist class' and 'working class', which describe a certain gendered personality structure peculiar to our gender cultural practices; that is, to our capitalist patriarchal family/households and sexual communities.

4   In this respect Isaac Balbus's attempt to historicise Chodorow's and Dinnerstein's insights by connecting different types of mother/child dynamics to different modes of male dominance rests on a similar mistake. See Balbus, 1982.

5   As Irigaray says, 'The issue is not one of elaborating a new theory of which woman would be the *subject* or the *object* but of jamming the theoretical machinery itself' (Irigaray, 1977, 'The Power of Discourse': 78).

Chapter three

1   The ideology of 'malestream' sexuality instinct theory is an amalgam of leftovers from a Christian patriarchal ideology of sexuality and its scientific replacement: evolutionary theory. Christian thought stressed a dualist approach to sexuality which divided the Soul, and Reason, on the one hand, from bodily desires and passions, Lust, on the other. Will was the intermediary between the two realms, a faculty which allowed humans to decide whether or not to give in to the 'sins' of the body.

    Nineteenth-century evolutionary currents of thought recast the Christian view of sexuality (that its 'natural' end is reproduction) as an instinct for mating, serving the function of preserving the species by reproduction. Thus, male and female sexualities evolve different aims and characteristics because of their different biological functions in the reproductive process.

    Twentieth-century socio-biological thought continues this nineteenth-century idea that women's sexuality is essentially an expression of the maternal instinct for reproduction. Though twentieth-century socio-biologists do not go to the extremes of those in the nineteenth century who supposed that feminine biological health centres around successful motherhood, they share the view that passivity and nurturance are women's natural traits while an interest in sexuality simply for pleasure is not. Men on the other hand are thought to have evolved a different sexuality: as natural competitors for women male sexuality is posited to be egoistic, aggressive and promiscuous.

2   Marcuse never makes clear under what circumstances a social repression is necessary and where surplus. If, after all, increased sexual permissiveness in advanced industrial capitalist societies connects with a functional change in amassing capital that requires a consumerist rather than an abstemious life style, this suggests that less sexual repression is currently necessary to perpetuate capitalism than in nineteenth-century capitalist society. But in *One Dimensional Man* Marcuse begs the question by arguing that the phenomenon of sexual permissiveness is an example of 'repressive de-sublimation', indicating that

repressiveness has not become less necessary but instead has changed its form.

An implicit reference to this vague Freudo-Marxism concept of 'necessary sexual repression' is used in conservative ways by Adorno and Horkheimer (1972) and Lasch (1977, 1979) to argue that the weakening of the patriarchal nuclear family by advanced capitalism creates a narcissistic personality that is incapable of engaging in a strong left movement of resistance against any form of social domination. The attack on the Women's Movement critique of the patriarchal nuclear family that follows from this perspective shows that feminism needs an alternative theory of the self, ego development and sexuality that can explain male domination and sexual repression without supposing that patriarchy is necessary to create an ego structure capable of challenging capitalism!

In my opinion, feminist countercultural structures such as women's consciousness-raising groups, women's communes, ongoing feminist political caucuses, and even feminist female kinship networks, are all ways in which sex/affective energy can be organised so as to yield a feminine gender identity capable of challenging male domination. But such a theory of the self needs to be further developed.

3   Ethel Person (1980) points out that such theorists as Gagnon and Simon (1973) contrast men's greater interests in 'sex for its own sake', namely sex for pure pleasure (read, orgasmic sex) to the greater female interest in sex to promote emotional intimacy, and find women's interests wanting. That is, they tend to take the associated conditions of female masochism and greater 'asexuality' as a cultural 'problem' due to women's acculturation while the conditions associated with masculine gender sexuality, i.e. the male compulsive search for orgiastic sex and a sexual performance equated with successful masculinity, are not defined as 'problems' at all!

I share Ethel Person's two criticisms of this approach. First, it takes a culturally defined 'masculine' standard of the purpose for sexual activity (bodily orgasmic pleasure) as the underlying human (natural) standard of successful sex, thus typing women's interest in intimacy in sex as a social 'deviation' to be explained by socialisation.

4   For a wonderful case study in the Foucaultian vein, see Campioni and Gross's study of Freud's *Little Hans* (Campioni and Gross, 1978).

Chapter four

1   Nancy Hartsock (1983) conceives of sexuality in a somewhat similar way to mine. She sees sexuality as being a social construction of a more basic Eros which has three characteristics: the desire for fusion with social others, bodily sensuality, and the desire to engage in creativity and generation. Depending on the type of social construction of its objects, Eros may be expressed in liberatory or alienated ways. Though I agree with Hartsock that sexual energy both involves body pleasure and an interest in social fusion, I privilege the social union aspects of

sexuality in order to stress the continuity between explicitly bodily sexual energy and affectionate types of energy. Furthermore, I question the essentialist idea that there are universally certain social constructions of sex/affective energy which are liberatory and certain which are alienating. Rather, I would argue that such claims are historically based and can only be based on an analysis of conflicting tendencies within existing social constructions of affection and sexuality and a claim about an historically possible way to reconstruct sex/affective production so as to resolve these contradictions.

2 There are two points to keep in mind about this distinction between reciprocal and hierarchical sex/affective exchanges. First, the valuing of the former over the latter is very much tied to the historical values developed by democratic individualism and is not at all a universal human sexual ethic. Second, it may be empirically quite difficult to ascertain whether any given exchange is reciprocal or hierarchical. For example, one of the controversies between pro- and anti-S/M feminists concerns whether consensual sexual exchanges between sadists and masochists should be interpreted as reciprocal or hierarchical (cf. Linden, Pagano, Russell and Star (eds), 1982; Samois (ed.), 1981).

3 However, since sex/affective production is a dialectical process, there are always those deviants who resist this canalisation of their desires: those classified as deviant, sinful or perverted by their historically specific sexual symbolic code. Thus, as Foucault points out, power creates resistances. Unfortunately, except in periods of major social crisis and re-organisation of a mode of sex/affective production, even such resisters are caught in the logic of reversal: their desires and behaviour do not challenge the underlying dualities of the symbolic code as much as they simply insist on desiring what is defined in the case as forbidden. Gertrude Stein, in dressing as a man and treating Alice B. Toklas as a subservient woman, acted as the phallic woman but did not challenge the dichotomy between masculine and feminine *per se*.

4 Sometimes the transcultural approach is labelled essentialism by its opponents who want to emphasise the historical and cultural relativity of symbolic social codes. What is less emphasised is that the constructivist approach itself hides two different approaches: the symbolic interactionist approach and the historicist approach. The former tradition stems from the work of the American philosopher and sociologist G. H. Mead and Herbert Blumer, and some of its contemporary advocates in the field of sexology are Gagnon and Simon (1973) and Plummer (1975). This work emphasises the plasticity of human desires and identities to sexual scripts, which vary according to social context. The historicist tradition, stemming from the French post-structuralist context of Foucault and Derrida, (cf. Escoffier, 1985; Weeks, 1979, 1981) focuses on the history of shifting discourses of sexuality and self-identity as they arise in social institutions (psychiatry, public schools, the army, social services, etc.) which are themselves historical products. I have discussed these perspectives in more detail in chapter three above.

5 Capitalist-class women are usually exceptions to patriarchal exploitation because they retain enough independent control over their own capital

to pay others (maids, tutors, therapists, doctors and nurses) to provide the sex/affective labour to husband, children and other kin that would otherwise fall to them.

6   An objection could be raised concerning the notion that sexuality, affection and parenting are such universal needs as to always require a social system of production (even assuming that these forms are historically relative). For example, Aries (1962) and Shorter (1975) argue that affectionate interaction between children, kin and spouses is characteristic neither of peasant nor of aristocratic families in the medieval period. Badinter (1981) gives us a feminist historical critique of the idea that biological motherhood of necessity creates a stronger social bond between children and mothers than fathers. But she goes further to question the idea that parenting by particular others is a universal human need. These authors all suggest that the ideology that families must provide children with affection only arose with the consolidation of the bourgeois family in industrial capitalism.

What this example shows, I would argue, is not that children do not require affection but that different modes of sex/affective production provide for it in different ways (sometimes by wet nurses, as in aristocratic families, from older siblings in peasant families, from peers and others in the putting-out apprentice system of child labour). The dominant class-divided economy (feudalism, capitalism, etc.) and its mode of sex/affective production interact with patriarchal sex/affective production in important ways which shape both the content of work (e.g. the race or economic class-specific gender division of labour) and its meanings for the participants. The interpersonal dynamic between parents, children and mates will obviously be different when affectionate interactions are assumed to be central and when they are not presumed present.

7   Margery Davies (1979) has disputed the extension thesis by giving historical examples (e.g. initial male clerical workers displaced by female secretaries because of the introduction of the typewriter) which suggest that gender wage labour has more to do with the changing status of jobs than their actual content. But this point can be accepted as a caveat to the generality of the rule rather than a refutation of it. Where the extension thesis does not apply (as when men are doing work that was considered female in the house, e.g. male chefs, or, when men and women together are doing for wages what women are expected to do in the home, e.g. mixed sex waitpersons), there is usually an explanation of this counter-example by capitalist or male dominant logics. So, chefs tend to be male in high-class restaurants to give the place a higher status, thus increasing its profits. And non-sex segmented workplaces usually occur when men can be hired as cheaply as women (e.g. students in a college town), or perhaps the work has no exact counterpart in the domestic gender division of labour.

8   Batya Weinbaum's *Pictures of Patriarchy* (1983) is insightful in demonstrating how kin categories are reproduced in the workplace, thus reinforcing the power of patriarchy. However, the kin categories she chooses (daughter, father, wife and brother labour) contain several

notable lacunae since they don't conceptualise mother or sister labour, those kin categories that are potentially empowering to women. Hence Weinbaum's work tends to stress an overly functionalist and woman-as-victim vision of the connection between the capitalist workplace and male dominance rather than the more dialectical vision I suggest here.

Chapter five

1 The history of forms of the Afro-American family differs from these dominant family forms because of the institution of slavery and subsequent attempts by the Black family after slavery to cope with the effects of institutionalised racism in the wage labour force (Gutman, 1977). Though Afro-Americans certainly came from cultures with elements of male dominance, most of the West African cultures allowed women more power than white European societies. As Leghorn and Parker suggest, many of these tribes allowed women negotiating power, not mere token power as in European societies (Leghorn and Parker, 1981). Thus, it can be argued that since the Black family has always had a different and more egalitarian internal structure than white family forms, much of the sexism in the Afro-American community is a reflection of dominant white cultural forms (e.g. the sexual division of wage labour, macho images in the media).

2 Some have argued that even such a generalisation across hunting-gathering, agricultural, slave and feudal economies is ahistorical because it assumes a unified concept of 'family' which is not accurate. Rather, the concept of 'family' is a 'sliding signifier': that is, it means something quite different in different social and economic systems (Barrett and McIntosh, 1982; Donzelot, 1979; Flandrin, 1976; Nicolson, 1986). For example, Flandrin's work on aristocratic families in medieval Europe suggests that there has been a shift in the concept of family from a group connected by lineage and blood (an important concept in the marriage alliances of the aristocracy) to a group living in the same household. This shift more or less coincides with the shift from feudalism to capitalism.

3 To be more precise, when I speak in this chapter of 'public patriarchy' this will be a shorthand for 'capitalist public patriarchy'. Industrialised state socialist societies such as Russia, China, East Germany, also can be categorised as public patriarchy. However, these countries with centrally planned economies lack some features of capitalist patriarchies. For example, the media images of women are much less important in perpetuating sexism, since pornography and romance novels are minimal and sexual advertising is all but eliminated. Furthermore, state services for single mothers make their childrearing much less exploitative than in capitalist societies. Nonetheless these countries still do not allow autonomous women's organisations. As a result, the social and medical services necessary for women to have full reproductive freedom (available state childcare, abortions, birth control, flexi-time jobs, etc.) have varied, not through women's needs but through decisions by the

male political elite as to whether more or less labour power was needed to fuel the economy (Scott, 1974). And without a fully autonomous and institutionalised set of women's caucuses in economic decision-making, the position of women can revert from negotiating to mere token power due to a shift in policy from public to more market-oriented economic development, as seems to have happened since Mao in China (Leghorn and Parker, 1981). Thus, these countries can still be seen to have an institutionalised form of male dominance more vested in public arenas rather than family control (*viz.* state economic planning controlled by a male elite) and to be aptly described as public patriarchies. But due to space considerations I will not further consider them here.

4   Some authors have argued (Ryan, 1975) that the Puritan emphasis on women as helpmates to men, the absence of an ideology of romantic love, and a more egalitarian sexual ideology which posited sexual drives in both men and women were indications that women were more equal as sexual partners in the early colonial period than in the US of the 1840s. It certainly is true that there was less of a sexual double standard in the Puritan period than subsequently; men could be punished for raping wives or for fornication outside of marriage. Nonetheless, I think some authors overplay the egalitarian implications of sexual practices in Puritan society (Mitchell, 1972). After all, sexual double standards still persisted with respect to adultery, and a woman who became pregnant by rape outside of marriage could still be flogged or fined (Folbre, 1979).

5   If asymmetrical mothering, interrupted though it was by Puritan patri-archal 'breaking the will' practices, was minimally effective in estab-lishing a strong mother/child bond, one would expect that in the deviant practices of Puritan society there would be rebellious practices in which women claimed some of the affectionate bonding denied them by patriarchy. Erikson (1966) suggests that the practices of those accused of being witches may have been expressive of mother-daughter bonding that challenged patriarchy. Of the accusations of the teenage girls in the Salem trials he gives a more standard psychoanalytic reading: an hyster-ical denial of a tabooed bonding between mother-figures and daughters.

6   My explanation of the shift in motherhood and sexuality in the nine-teenth century differs from those theories (Benston, 1969; Douglas, 1977; Zaretsky, 1976) that suggest that moral motherhood ideology was a sentimental response that sought to hide from consciousness the actual devaluation of women's role with the developing split between home and commodity production. What is wrong with this sentimentalist hypothesis is the assumption that middle-class women were the victims of an ideology meant to hide their parasitical dependence on men. Rather, I would argue that the change was the result of a dialectical struggle between middle-class men, women and ministers/writers, i.e. social groups whose roles were in transition. The evangelical minis-ters involved in the Great Awakening spiritual revival movement made common cause with middle-class women who formed the majority of their congregations, to elevate both the Church (weakened by the constitution's separation of Church and State) and women within it.

Thus, middle-class women were partial agents in a reformation of bourgeois patriarchal sex/affective production in order to gain greater power as mothers than they had in the Puritan period, while they nonetheless acquiesced to the preservation of some aspects of men's power in the family as husbands.

7   The gradual transference of parental authority from fathers to mothers and the intensification of the mother-child relationship would seem to have had contradictory effects for middle-class children. On the one hand, children became economic dependents of the family, as the length of time spent in schooling increased while the practice of apprenticing children decreased. As mothers came to feel children to be their exclusive products, children may have felt at once powerless to escape mothers yet encouraged to develop some autonomy because of the new, more permissive childrearing practices. We can thus suppose that certain forbidden sexual practices (masturbation, homosexual play) actually increased among children, in part as a psychological distancing and resistance mechanism.

This is quite a different explanation for the increased attention to adolescent sexuality evinced by nineteenth-century writers than that provided by Foucault (1978). According to him, bourgeois sexual discourses (including religious confessional writing, sexual purity writers, and sexologists) created a new bourgeois concern with sexuality in a rather spontaneous fashion. My explanation assumes, on the contrary, that a material change in power relations between bourgeois children and parents created new sexual practices, including sexuality between mothers and children (Deleuze and Guattari, 1977) which then spurred new regulatory discourses which in turn increased parent/child sex/affective energy by forbidding it (Campioni and Gross, 1978).

8   It should be emphasised that the distinction between family-based patriarchies and public patriarchy is a matter of degree and primacy rather than an absolute dichotomy. But of course this is not surprising because the distinction between 'public' and 'private' is as well. For example, conservative defences of *laissez-faire* market economics claim that the state has no role in the economy in such a model. But this is misleading because the coercive power of the 'public' state in defending and legitimising private property is a key condition for the so-called 'private' sector to run by market rules. Similarly the role of the state in legitimating fathers' and husbands' control over women in marriage, divorce, property rights and child custody was a key condition for the power that men had over women in family-based patriarchies.

The point is a relative one, then, which is that in *laissez-faire* economies and family patriarchies, the state, having once set the rules of the game, is not an ongoing site for contestation and adjudication of economic or family decisions except in certain small areas (bankruptcy proceedings, marriage and divorce). In public patriarchies, to the contrary, state and economic decisions are much more overlapping. Public policy must regularly deal with the question of reproductive control (extending or denying civil rights to lesbians and gays, defending or denying women's access to abortions and contraceptives, funding or denying funding to childcare via entitlement programmes, etc.). This expansion of the role of the state creates the possibility of new sexist controls but also new collective action by women as citizens to challenge these public policies.

9   In neo-classical economic terms, they are now 'consumer commodities' rather than 'investments' since parents can no longer control children's labour power by having them do productive work around the farm or in wage labour to repay the time invested in them (cf. Friedman, 1982).

10 Most divorced fathers cop out not only on direct childcare work, but on financial contributions toward child support: 90 per cent of divorced women do not receive regular child support payments from fathers, and those that do do not receive the full payments the legal settlement entitled them to ('Women and Childcare', *Women's Agenda*, March/April 1976). Welfare mothers are subject to a male-headed bureaucracy whose interference in personal life and demeaning regulations attempt to reduce women to menial status. An important recent study on no-fault divorce legislation (Weitzman, 1985) concludes that this supposedly egalitarian arrangement ends up leaving women much worse off economically than the old alimony arrangements.

Chapter six

1   Since human sex/affective energy is a social energy, it will flow between those who identify collectively themselves and their interests. Those, however, who see their interests in conflict with, or different from, others will block the flow of such energy.

2   The failure of working classes in Western capitalist countries to become revolutionary classes seems to undermine this prediction, leading Lukacs to develop the concept of 'false consciousness' (Lukacs, 1968) and Gramsci the notion of cultural 'hegemony' (i.e. pervasiveness and power) of values and ideas defending the status quo and hence the interests of the capitalist class (Gramsci, 1971).

3   The classic emphasis on the importance of class culture in the formation of a class is E. P. Thompson's *History of the English Working Class*, 1966.

4   Gorz (1967) argues that technicians and professionals are a key strata of the new working class precisely because their autonomous work conditions create an expectation that they should make all decisions controlling their work process. This expectation is increasingly in conflict with the interests of the capitalist class to control production arbitrarily for profit considerations.

5   I reject other Marxist-feminist analyses because they do not draw this conclusion. For example, Margaret Benston (1969) holds a view similar to mine about household work (i.e. that it deprives women of social power), but she fails to draw the conclusion that men exploit women in the present social formation. She argues that historically the development of capitalist industrial production rearranged the sexual division of labour in the household so that the woman continues to produce use values in the home, while the man now works for exchange values,

working for a full-time wage outside the home. Since only wage work provides social power in capitalist social formations, the woman domestic-use producer loses power in relation to men. This argument fails to explain 1) why women continue to do use-value production in the home while men do not; and 2) it ignores the fact that men and women are social actors who struggle for power in relation to each other when there are shifts in the mode of production. Benston assumes that women lose power as an accidental result of the automatic process of commodification. But, as Hartmann points out (Hartmann, 1981a), even a cursory look at the way male-dominated unions have sought to exclude women from wage labour casts doubt on this assumption. Furthermore, given that capitalist production is difficult to organise around the needs of nursing and caring for infants, women too support the sexual division of wage labour in which fathers are the breadwinners and mothers the housewives.

Another example of a Marxist-feminist analysis of women's oppression in capitalism that ignores the active role of men to preserve male privilege is that of Maria Dalla Costa (1974). Her analysis emphasises woman's role in producing the commodity labour power (by bearing children, doing maintenance work, and nurturing children and husband in her role as family domestic worker), in order to claim that capitalists exploit housewives by not paying them for their work in producing labour power. Dalla Costa doesn't target the patriarchal features of household production. Thus, the husband is seen merely as a product of the system and not as an agent who gets benefits and power from the sexual division of labour in the family.

6   Since this is not commodity production, we can't talk of a rate of exploitation for there is no exact quantitative way to measure and compare the values of goods produced for use. Nor does it make sense to speak of the man 'building up capital' with his human goods. Nonetheless there is a way we can approximate quantitative measurements of the inequalities involved in the exchange, and that is by comparing the market commodity costs of the equivalent amounts of sexuality, child care, maintenance and nurturance that are done by men and women. For an economic model of this, see Nancy Folbre (1982).

7   It should be noted that this characterisation excludes most capitalist-class families for the male breadwinner is usually not working full-time, due to his unearned income from capital investments. Indeed, male/female relations are sufficiently different as to not have a material base for patriarchy. Neither men nor women have to work; they can hire nannies for the children and maintain separate houses for their lovers, so it is unclear that women in the capitalist class should be thought of as part of an exploited sex class. Divorced women from this class never lose their family class status, due to alimony and child-support, income from trust funds, etc. The men, on the other hand, are still members of the exploiter sex class, for their relation to the material means of production allows them the power to exploit women from subordinate family and economic class positions.

8   As chief nurturers, women have been the sex to which both boys and

girls have had to look for the satisfaction of their nurturance needs, and
the ones toward which anger and frustration have been directed when all
their needs cannot be met. Both anthropological and psychological
studies suggest that female and male personalities develop differently as a
result of this situation (cf. Chodorow, 1974, 1978b; Dinnerstein, 1976).
The anger toward the mother is turned against themselves in girls, who
identify with the mother, and thus develop masochistic, self-sacrificing
personalities; whereas the anger toward the mother is directed to women
by boys, who tend to develop misanthropic, narcissistic personalities.
Though these studies are too universalistic in their original claims, their
findings are plausible when limited to conclusions about masculine and
feminine personalities as they develop in the CPNF.

The material base of patriarchy in the CPNF implicated here is that
the sexual division of parenting sex/affective labour creates masculine
and feminine personalities in which the male receives more nurturance
because he has learned to expect and demand more, and the female gives
more nurturance and receives less because she also has learned to expect
less (Flax, 1978). The culturally developed difference between male and
female personalities and skills has become, in Wilhelm Reich's words, a
'material social power' which reproduces patriarchy in the family and in
the larger society (cf. Reich, 1974).

9   According to Bowles and Gintis (1977), different rates of exploitation
can be assigned to different types of labour within the wage labour
force. Once we can say some workers exploit others, we can go on to
argue either that these sectors of the working class occupy class-contra-
dictory positions (using Wright's approach in Wright, 1978), that they
occupy different classes (as do Ehrenreich, 1979 and Poulantzas, 1975),
or that people can occupy more than one class at a time and that sex class
is one of these and race class another. This latter is my position.

10   Other feminists of course have made these points. Those who come
closest to formulating the arguments presented here are Deming, 1973
and Tax, 1970.

11   The concept of race class needs to be further developed. Though the
sexual division of labour in the family tends to ensure that women's sex
class identity exists across family and economic class lines, the corresponding social divisions of race are not quite as hard and fast. Though
there is a racial division of wage labour, the Black and other minority
petit bourgeois and professionals have escaped that division. And
though there tends to be neighbourhood segregation of many minority
middle-class individuals similar to the ghettos of the Black and minority
working class, there are also integrated neighbourhoods for some which
break down that cultural identification. Some have taken this diffusion
of the racial distinctions in productive relations to indicate the declining
significance of race in the US today (Wilson, 1978). Others have
strongly disputed this (Marable, 1981). My own view is that race class is
still a meaningful concept, in part because the family class of most
middle- and even upper-class Black and minority people was working
class; hence racial identity due to racial labour and community segregation was a part of their childhood identity.

12 For some American subcultures, e.g. Black Americans, this has long been true (cf. Degler, 1980).
13 For an insightful analysis of the distinctions between the working class proper, the working poor and the poor, cf. Kollias, 1975.
14 Cf. for example, Bulkin, Smith and Pratt, 1984; Moraga and Anzaldua (eds), 1981; Myron and Bunch (eds), 1975.

Chapter seven

1 In earlier papers I characterise this pole of the feminist sex debate as 'libertarian feminism' (Ferguson, 1983, 1984b). And while I still think that most thinkers in this camp can so be characterised, there are some who find the implications of this term offensive, perhaps because they agree that there are aspects of sexual repression that cannot be countered by an insistence on validating consensual sex. In any case, since I don't wish to beg the question by characterising either pole in a way which they feel distorts their position, I here withdraw the term 'libertarian' in favour of 'pluralist', which seems to be more acceptable to those to whom I've talked.
2 Of course these sexual codes were not always practised. Carl Degler (1980) documents the existence of much mutual interest in sexual pleasure in marriage in nineteenth-century America in spite of the ideology of women's asexuality.
3 Some subcultures, such as Afro-American ghetto culture, may encourage a valuing of motherhood which connects to a more permissive attitude toward female teenage sexuality without marriage or male commitment. The difference between the sexual symbolic codes of this subculture and white working- and middle-class culture suggests that it may be helpful to construe Black ghetto culture as a different subordinate mode of sex/affective production than the dominant culture (cf. Caulfield, 1975; Myers, 1980; Stack, 1974).

Chapter eight

1 Alison Jaggar (Jaggar, 1983) argues that women's mothering labour has been downplayed in the Marxist tradition because Marx and Engels conceived of it as 'natural' and not historical and social. She characterises socialist-feminist attempts to broaden Marxist historical materialism as emphasising this neglected socially organised 'procreative labour' as one of the material bases of male dominance. I include procreative labour within the wider category of sex/affective labour. The advantage of doing this is that it allows us to see forms of sexual and nurturant servicing of adults as included in the same organisation of production as mothering. Procreative labour is a more restricted concept, for though the mothering of children is clearly procreative, the nurturant labour that wives give to husbands, or female employees to male colleagues and bosses, is only by analogy 'procreative' labour – yet

on my theory such sex/affective energy production is equally important as parenting proper in the perpetuation of male domination.

2 This generalisation is misleading in one way, for it doesn't acknowledge the situation of poor women, particularly Black women, for whom lack of jobs and skills may create motherhood as the only way to become economically more independent (given welfare payments) in relation to their families of origin. For these women, motherhood, though it may be a necessary condition to a minimal economic independence, is also a liability limiting social mobility and full economic negotiating power *vis-à-vis* men, since they also face 'the mediation problem', which will be discussed more fully in the text below.

3 In 1976 the Urban Institute calculated that 40 per cent of ex-husbands contributed nothing toward their children's support. The remaining 60 per cent pay less than $2000 a year, which drops off sharply after the first three years. A Californian study found that in 1977 only 13 per cent of mothers with pre-school children were awarded any spousal support and only 1/3 of the mothers sampled received the full amount of child support in the first year following divorce (Ehrenreich, Stallard and Sklar, 1983).

Lenore Weitzman's study of the effect of no-fault divorce legislation in California (Weitzman, 1985) is particularly depressing since no-fault divorce has been touted as a feminist solution to the inequities of the old alimony and child support legal system. However the incomes of fathers rose over 40 per cent while those of mothers dropped more than 70 per cent after no-fault divorce!

4 The mediation problem also occurs when the mate is a lesbian (raised in a capitalist patriarchal nuclear family) and has not chosen to co-parent the child(ren) of her lover. For, though she is a woman, her triangular feminine desires can only be activated in a situation in which she defines the child and mate to be related as 'my child' and 'my mate'. Otherwise her triangular feminine desires will tend to collapse into dyadic form: wanting her lover to play both mother and child roles in relation to herself. This obviously puts her into direct competition with her lover's child(ren) unless she chooses to take on a co-parenting role.

5 There is one important 'chosen family' type of relationship that Lindsey points out that is not included here. This is one's lifelong friends as family, i.e. that supportive friendship network of people who may or may not be in proximate geographical areas and may or may not know each other, who act as material and social points of continuity and security for an individual. Though I think such networks extremely important, my focus in discussing alternative family structures is on unconventional childrearing. Though some chosen friend networks do involve friends who get involved in childrearing for their friends (the famous friendship liaison of Elizabeth Cady Stanton, with seven children, and Susan B. Anthony, who was childless, come to mind here), friend childrearing which does not fall into one of the five types mentioned above is relatively rare and thus will not be discussed further here.

Chapter nine

1　It is important to note that Charlotte Bunch no longer holds the separatist positions she espoused in 1974. More contemporary spokeswomen for lesbian separatists are Julia Penelope (1985) and Mary Daly (1978, 1982).

2　Ancient Greek society allowed men of the wealthy classes homosexual liaisons as long as they were with boys, but this occurred in a society where heterosexual marriages were also required for property alliances. Some upper-class women were also allowed lesbian alliances (Sappho's practices on the isle of Lesbos come to mind) though this freedom most certainly did not extend to peasant women nor did it allow such women the freedom not to marry. Mohave society allowed homosexual liaisons on the condition that one member of the same sex-pair play the role of the opposite sex (by cross dressing, gender-typed work, etc.).

3　Class and sex are clear structural categories in the sense that one cannot simply choose to be a member of the group or not. Racial and ethnic categories involve a more slippery slope, for they may be structural in the sense that clear economic, social and legal privileges accrue to one side of an oppositional pair as opposed to the other (e.g. white *vs* Black, Gentile *vs* Jew), but they may be identity concepts for some in the group who may have the freedom to define themselves as one or the other (e.g. some who are initially defined as Blacks may be able to pass for white, some Americans may become Israelis and some Jews may choose to convert to Christianity). Different theories of homosexuality prevalent in different historical phases of twentieth-century gay liberation have disagreed as to whether having homosexual proclivities is more like being male or female (a given) or more like being a Catholic or a Protestant (a chosen) (cf. Adam, 1987; Boswell, 1980; Epstein, 1987).

4　I hope this answers one of Jackie Zita's objections to my characterisation of modern sexual identities that it excludes women who do not actually 'come out' (Zita, 1981). On the contrary, it is meant to exclude those women whose societies do not create the possibility of lesbian and gay countercultures.

Chapter ten

1　For example, Shulamith Firestone in *The Dialectic of Sex* and Andrea Dworkin in *Womanhating* suggest that feminists smash the incest taboo as a way to undercut the Oedipus complex and thus the power of patriarchy based on the sex/affective relations in the nuclear family. Gayle Rubin has argued that some forms of incest (e.g. brother/sister incest) be removed from stigmatised status and be accepted by feminists (Rubin, talk, Fall, 1986). Others have argued that consensual adult/child sex should be permissible in order to support children's right to be sexually active (cf. Tsang, 1981).

2　For more on the pro-S/M point of view, see Califia, 1981, Rubin and the other authors in Samois, 1981, and Rubin, 1984. For the anti-S/M argument see the authors in Barry, 1979, 1981; Linden *et al*, 1982; Raymond, 1986.

3   Pro S/M defenders may criticise this conclusion by the argument that a refusal by feminists to support public use of certain kinds of S/M symbols, e.g. in Lesbian/Gay Pride marches, or in other feminist-controlled spaces, has the danger of marginalising consensual S/Ms and rendering them more vulnerable to police attacks. The response to this is a balancing-of-harms argument: that when the risks of contributing to the emotional terrorising of previously traumatised women and of presenting symbols that may lead the public to misunderstand the goals of the Women's Movement are weighed against the possible gains to S/Ms of public legitimacy by the use of public symbols, the dangers of the former outweigh the benefits of the latter.

4   Cf. Louise Armstrong's interview with Andrea Dworkin in *The Women's Review of Books* (Armstrong, 1986) in which Dworkin discusses her difficulty in finding a publisher for her erotic novel *Fire and Ice*.

Chapter eleven

1   I prefer the ideal of gynandry, a women-empowering fusion and transcendence of our old notions of masculinity and femininity, to Jan Raymond's notion of integrity. As she describes it, this latter suggests a pre-social essential self (suspiciously similar to the Christian notion of soul or the philosopher's notion of the Cartesian self) which exists prior to social categories and on which social categories are imposed. It can also be used in the ambiguous way that Raymond's present book *A Passion for Friends* (1986) is, to imply that there is an authentic female self present prior to and metaphysically deeper than patriarchal socialisation to which we can only return if we emphasise gyn/affection between other similar selves, *viz.* other women.

While Raymond attempts to bypass this charge of essentialism by suggesting that the 'return' to the authentic self can also be seen as an existential process of creating new values, the whole import of her remarks (*viz.* that a woman cannot be truly 'for herself' rather than 'for men' if she does not prioritise her friendships with women over those with men) suggests she feels there is an essential female self whose wholeness can only be brought out by relations with others with the same female essence.

2   The notion of gynandry I have sketched is still too general to answer this question and the related one of whether it would be proper to characterise a society as gynandrous where individuals might exhibit a variety of personalities ranging from what today we would type as masculine and feminine. They would of course have to exclude the undesirable aspects of today's stereotypical masculinity, such as tendencies to authoritarianism and violence, and of today's femininity, such as weakness, foolishness or incompetence. There is an interesting distinction made by Joyce Trebilcot (1977) between monoandrogynism, an ideal of a society with homogeneous individuals combining aspects of

masculinity and femininity in a uniform way, and polyandrogynism, a society which would exhibit a range of personality types, some of which would approach our contemporary feminine personality and some the masculine personality, though not in the extreme ways of authoritarianism and self denigration which are features of patriarchal and phallocratic societies. My view of gynandry is a version of polyandrogynism.

3   Separatist tendencies are manifested in the various socialist and communist party factions. Assimilationists are those trade union elements which are co-opted into compromises with capitalist firms, and coalitionists are those like the democratic rank and file movements which want autonomous but bottom-up reforms within capitalism, hopefully to lead to socialism at a later date.

Bibliography

Adam, Barry D. (1978) *The Survival of Domination: Inferiorization and Everyday life*, New York, Elsevier
—— (1987a) 'Homosexuality without a gay world: the case of Nicaragua', unpublished mss
—— (1987b) *The Rise of a Gay and Lesbian Movement*, Boston, Twayne/G.K. Hall
Adorno, Theodor and Horkheimer, Max (1972) *Dialectic of Enlightenment*, trs. John Cumming, New York, Herder & Herder
Albert, Michael and Hahnel, Robin (1978) *Unorthodox Marxism: An Essay on Capitalism, Socialism and Revolution*, Boston, South End
—— (1981a) *Marxism and Socialist Theory*, Boston, South End
—— (1981b) *Socialism Today and Tomorrow*, Boston, South End
Alexander, David (1987) 'Gendered job traits and women's occupations', PhD thesis, Economics, Amherst, Ma., University of Massachusetts
Allen, Jeffner (1984) 'Motherhood: the annihilation of women', Joyce Trebilcot (ed.) 1984: 315–30
Althusser, Louis (1971) *Lenin and Philosophy*, New York, Monthly Review
Altman, Dennis (1974) *Homosexual Oppression and Liberation*, London, Allen Lane
—— (1983) *The Homosexualization of America*, Boston, Beacon
Amott, Teresa (1985) 'Race, class and the feminization of poverty', *Socialist Politics*, vol. 3, April
Aptheker, Bettina (1983) *Woman's Legacy: Essays on Race, Class and Gender*, Amherst, Ma., University of Massachusetts
Arcana, Judith (1976) *Our Mothers' Daughters*, London, The Women's Press
Aries, Philippe (1962) *Centuries of Childhood: A Social History of Family Life*, New York, Random House
Armstrong, Louise (1986) 'Publish and be damned', review, Dworkin's *Fire and Ice* (London, Secker & Warburg, 1986), *Women's Review of Books*, vol. 3, no. 8: 1–3
Atkinson, Ti-Grace (1974) *Amazon Odyssey*, New York, Links Press

Badinter, Elizabeth (1981) *Mother Love: Myth and Reality: Motherhood in Modern History*, New York, Macmillan
Balbus, Isaac (1982) *Marxism and Domination*, Princeton, NJ, Princeton University
—— (1987) 'Parental politics: gender struggle and the transformation of Western child rearing 1500–1950', unpublished mss
Bar On, Bat Ami (1982) 'Feminism and sado-masochism: self-critical notes', Robin Linden *et al.* (eds)

Barrett, Michelle (1980) *Women's Oppression Today*, London, Verso
—— and McIntosh, Mary (1982) *The Anti-Social Family*, London, Verso
Barry, Kathleen (1973) 'The fourth world manifesto', in Anne Koedt *et al.* (eds), 1973
—— (1979) *Female Sexual Slavery*, Englewood Cliffs, NJ, Prentice-Hall, Inc
—— (1982) 'Sadomasochism: the new backlash to feminism', *Trivia*, vol. 1, no. 1, Fall: 77–92
Bart, Pauline (1981) 'Review of Chodorow's *The Reproduction of Mothering* (Berkeley, Ca: University of California) *Off Our Backs*, vol. 11, no. 1, Jan; reprinted in Joyce Trebilcot (ed.), 1984: 147–52
Beauvoir, Simone de (1952) *The Second Sex*, New York, Knopf
Begus, Sarah (1987) 'The social relations of sexuality: ideology, consciousness, sexual practice and domination', Baltimore, Md., MA thesis, Johns Hopkins University
Benjamin, Jessica (1980) 'The bonds of love: rational violence and erotic domination', *Feminist Studies*, vol. 6, no. 1: 144–74; reprinted in Ann Snitow *et al.* (eds), 1983
Benston, Margaret (1969) 'The political economy of women's liberation', *Monthly Review*, September 1969
Bernikow, Louise (1980) *Among Women*, New York, Harmony Books
Blanchford, Gregg (1979) 'Looking at pornography: erotica and the socialist morality', *Radical America*, vol. 13, no. 1, Jan/Feb: 7–18
Black Scholar, The, (1978) 'The sexual revolution', vol. 9, no. 7, April
Boswell, John (1980) *Christianity, Social Tolerance and Homosexuality*, Chicago, Ill., University of Chicago
Bowles, Samuel and Gintis, Herbert (1977) 'Heterogeneous labor and the labor theory of value', *Cambridge Journal of Economics*, vol. 1, no. 2
—— (1986) *Democracy and Capitalism: Property, Community and the Contradictions of Modern Social Thought*, New York, Basic
Brown, Carol (1981) 'Mothers, fathers and children: from private to public patriarchy', Lydia Sargent (ed.), 1981: 239–68
Brownmiller, Susan (1976) *Against Our Will: Men, Women and Rape*, New York, Bantam
Bryant, Dorothy (1986) *A Day in San Francisco*, New York, Moon Books
Bulkin, Elly; Smith, Barbara and Pratt, Minnie Bruce (1984) *Yours in Struggle: Feminist Perspectives on Anti-semitism and Racism*, Brooklyn, NY, Long Haul Press
Bunch, Charlotte and Myron, Nancy (1974a), (1974b), (1975) See Myron and Bunch (eds), (1974a), (1974b), (1975)
Bunch, Charlotte (1975) 'Not for lesbians only', *Quest* (eds), 1981: 67–73
—— (1976) 'Beyond either/or: feminist options', *Quest (A Feminist Quarterly)*, vol. 3, no. 1, reprinted in *Quest* (eds), 1981: 44–56
Burstyn, Varda (ed.) (1985) *Women Against Censorship*, Vancouver, Toronto, Douglas & McIntyre
Butler, Judy (1982) 'S & M: the politics of disillusion', Robin Linden *et al.* (eds), 1982: 168–75

Califia, Pat (1980) *Sapphistry: The Book of Lesbian Sexuality*, Tallahasee, Fla., Naiad Press

—— (1981) 'Feminism and sado-masochism', *Heresies*, 12: 30–4

Campbell, Beatrix (1980) 'A feminist sexual politics', *Feminist Review*, 5

Campioni, Mia and Gross, Liz (1978) 'Little Hans: the production of Oedipus', P. Foss and M. Morris (eds.), *Sexuality and Subversion*, Darlington, Australia, Feral

Carby, Hazel V. (1985) 'On the threshold of woman's era: lynching, empire and sexuality in black feminist theory', *Critical Inquiry*, Autumn: 262–77

—— (1986) 'It just be's dat way sometime: the sexual politics of women's blues', *Radical America*, vol. 20, no. 4, June–July 1985: 9–24

Carmichael, Stokeley and Hamilton, Charles (1967) *Black Power*, New York, Random House

Caulfield, Mina Davis (1975) 'Imperialism, the family and cultures of resistance', *Socialist Revolution*, Issue 20, vol. 4, no. 2, Oct: 67–86

Cedar and Nelly (eds) (1979) *A Woman's Touch: An Anthology of Lesbian Eroticism and Sensuality for Women Only*, Eugene, Ore., Womanshare Books

Chesler, Phyllis (1979) *With Child: a Diary of Motherhood*, New York, Crowell Pubs

Chodorow, Nancy (1974) 'Family structure and feminine personality', Michelle Rosaldo and Louise Lamphere (eds), 1974: 43–66

—— (1978a) 'Mothering, object relations and the female Oedipal configuration', *Feminist Studies*, vol. 4, no. 1, Feb: 137–58

—— (1978b) *The Reproduction of Mothering*, Berkeley, Ca., University of California

—— (1979a) 'Mothering, male dominance and capitalism', Zillah Eisenstein, (ed.), 1979: 83–106

—— (1979b) 'Feminism and difference: gender relations and difference in psychoanalytic perspective', *Socialist Review*, July–Aug: 51–69

Cleaver, Eldridge (1968) *Soul on Ice*, New York, Delta

Cliff, Michelle (1980) *Claiming an Identity They Taught Me to Despise* Watertown, Ma., Persephone Press

Cohen, Howard (1980) *Equal Rights for Children*, Totowa, NJ, Littlefield Adams

Combahee River Collective (1979) 'A black feminist statement', Zillah Eisenstein (ed.), 1979: 362–72; also in Cherrie Moraga *et al.* (eds), 1981

Cook, Blanche (1977) 'Female support networks and political activism', *Chrysalis*, no. 3: 43–61

Coward, Rosalind (1983) *Patriarchal Precedents: Sexuality and Social Relations*, London, Routledge

Dalla Costa, Maria (1974) *The Power of Women and the Subversion of the Community*, Bristol, England, Falling Wall Press

Daly, Mary (1973) *Beyond God the Father*, Boston, Ma., Beacon

—— (1975) 'The qualitative leap beyond patriarchal religion', *Quest*, vol. 1, no. 4, Spring: 20–40

—— (1978) *Gyn/Ecology: The Meta-ethics of Radical Feminism*, Boston, Ma., Beacon

—— (1982) *Pure Lust: Elementary Feminist Philosophy*, Boston, Ma., Beacon

d'Amico, Robert (1981) *Marx and the Philosophy of Culture*, monographs, Humanities Issue 50, University of Florida

David-Menard, Monique (1982) 'Lacanians against Lacan', *Social Text*, Fall: 86–113

Davies, Margery (1979) 'Woman's place is at the typewriter: the feminization of the clerical labor force', Eisenstein (ed.), 1979: 248–71

Davis, Angela (1971) 'The black woman's role in the community of slaves', *The Black Scholar*, no. 2

—— (1981) *Women, Race and Class*, New York, Random House

Davis, Madeline and Kennedy, Elizabeth Lapovsky (1986) 'Oral history and the study of sexuality in the lesbian community: Buffalo, New York 1940–1960', *Feminist Studies*, vol. 12, no. 1, Spring: 7–26

Degler, Carl (1980) *At Odds: Women and the Family in America from the Revolution to the Present*, New York, Oxford University

Delacoste, Frederique and Alexander, Priscilla (eds), (1987) *Sex Work: Writings by Women in the Sex Industry*, Pittsburgh, Pa., Cleis Press

Deleuze, Giles and Guattari, Felix (1977) *Anti-Oedipus*, New York, Viking

Delphy, Christine (1984) *Close to Home; A Materialist Analysis of Women's Oppression*, Amherst, Ma., University of Massachusetts

d'Emilio, John (1983) 'Capitalism and gay identity, Ann Snitow *et al.* (eds), 1983: 100–16

Deming, Barbara (1973) 'Love has been exploited labor', *Liberation*, May

Demos, John (1970) *A Little Commonwealth: Family Life in Plymouth Colony*, New York, Oxford University

Diamond, Irene (1980) 'Pornography and repression: a reconsideration of "who" and "what"', Laura Lederer (ed.), 1980: 183–200

—— and Quinby, Lee (1984) 'American feminism in the age of the body', *Signs*, vol. 10, no. 1, Autumn: 119–25

Diary of a Conference on Sexuality (1980) Barnard College, New York, Faculty Press

Dimen, Muriel (1982) 'Seven notes for the reconstruction of sexuality', *Social Text*, no. 6: 22–30

Dinnerstein, Dorothy (1976) *The Mermaid and the Minotaur: Sexual Arrangements and Human Malaise*, New York, Harper

Donzelot, Jacques (1979) *The Policing of Families*, New York, Pantheon

Douglas, Ann (1977) *The Lady and the Minister: The 'Feminization' of American Culture*, New York, Knopf

Du Bois, Ellen Carol (1978) *Feminism and Suffrage*, Ithaca, NY, Cornell University

—— and Gordon, Linda (1982) 'Seeking ecstasy on a battlefield: danger and pleasure in 19th century feminist thought', in Carol Vance (ed.), 1984: 31–49

Du Bois, W.E.B. (1961) *The Souls of Black Folk*, New York, Dodd, Mead & Co.

Duggan, Lisa, Hunter, Nan and Vance, Carol (1985) 'False promises: feminist anti-pornography legislation in the US', Varda Burstyn (ed.), 1985: 130–51, also in FACT (eds), 1986

Duggan, Lisa (1986) 'Censorship in the name of feminism', FACT (eds), 1986

Dworkin, Andrea (1974) *Womanhating*, New York, Dutton
—— (1976) *Our Blood*, New York, Harper & Row
—— (1977) 'Why so-called radical men love and need porn', Laura Lederer (ed.), 1980: 141–7
—— (1978) 'Biological superiority: the world's most dangerous and deadly idea', *Heresies*, no. 6, Summer
—— (1981) *Pornography: Men Possessing Women*, New York, Perigee/ Putnam Sons
—— (1985) 'Against the male flood: censorship, pornography, and equality', *Harvard Women's Law Journal*, vol. 8: 1–29; reprinted in Andrea Dworkin and MacKinnon, 1985
—— (1987) *Intercourse*, New York, Free Press
—— and MacKinnon, Catherine (1985) *The Reasons Why*, Cambridge, Ma., Harvard Law School
—— and Armstrong, Louise (1986) 'Interview with Andrea Dworkin', *Women's Review of Books*, vol. 3, no. 8, May: 5–7

Easton, Barbara (1978) 'Feminism and the contemporary family', *Socialist Review*, Issue 39, vol. 8, no. 3, May–June: 11–36
Echols, Alice (1983) 'The new feminism of yin and yang', Ann Snitow *et al.* (eds), 1983: 439–54
Ehrenreich, Barbara (1983) *The Hearts of Men*, Garden City, NY, Anchor/ Doubleday
—— and John (1979) 'The professional-managerial class', Pat Walker (ed.) 1979
—— and English, Deirdre (1973a) *Witches, Midwives and Nurses: A History of Women Healers*, Old Westbury, NY, Feminist Press
—— (1973b) *Complaints and Disorders: The Sexual Politics of Sickness*, Old Westbury, NY, Feminist Press
—— (1979) *For Her Own Good: One Hundred Fifty Years of the Experts' Advice to Women*, Garden City, NJ, Anchor/Doubleday
—— Hess, Elizabeth and Jacobs, Gloria (1986) *Remaking Love: the Feminization of Sex*, New York, Doubleday
—— Stallard, Karin and Sklar, Holly (1983) *Poverty in the American Dream: Women and Children First*, Boston, South End
Ehrensaft, Diane (1980) 'When men and women mother', *Socialist Review*, Issue 49, vol. 10, no. 1, Jan/Feb. 1980, reprinted in Joyce Trebilcot (ed.), 1984: 41–61
Eisenstein, Zillah (ed.) (1979) *Capitalist Patriarchy and the Case for Socialist-feminism*, New York, *Monthly Review*
Ellis, John (1981) 'On pornography', *Screen*, vol. 21, no. 1, Spring
Ellis, Kate (1984) 'I'm black and blue from the Rolling Stones and I'm not sure how I feel about it: pornography and the feminist imagination', *Socialist Review*, Issue 75/6, vol. 14, no. 34, May–Aug: 103–25
Engels, Frederick (1972) *The Origin of the Family, Private Property and the State*, Eleanor Leacock (ed.), New York, International Publishers
—— and Marx, Karl (1976) *The German Ideology*, Moscow, Progress Publications

English, Deirdre; Hollibaugh, Amber and Rubin, Gayle (1981) 'Talking sex', *Socialist Review*, Issue 58, July–Aug.: 43–62

Epstein, Steve (1987) 'Gay politics, ethnic identity: the limits of social constructionism', *Socialist Review*, Issue 93/4, vol. 17, no. 3: 9–56

Erikson, Kai T. (1966) *The Wayward Puritans: A Study in the Sociology of Deviance*, New York, Wiley

Escoffier, Jeffrey (1985) 'Sexual revolution and the politics of gay identity', *Socialist Review*, Issue 82/3, vol. 15, no. 4/5, July/Oct: 119–54

Evans, Sara (1980) *Personal Politics*, New York, Random

Ewen, Stuart (1976) *Captains of Consciousness: Advertising and the Social Roots of Consumer Culture*, New York, Harper

FACT Book Committee (eds), (1986) *Caught Looking: Feminism, Pornography and Censorship*, New York, Caught Looking, Inc

Faderman, Lillian (1981) *Surpassing the Love of Men*, London, Junction

Fanon, Frantz (1967) *Black Skins, White Masks*, trs. Charles Markmann, New York, Grove

—— (1968) *The Wretched of the Earth*, New York, Grove

Faraday, Annabel (1981) 'Liberating lesbian research', Kenneth Plummer (ed.), 1981

Faust, Beatrice (1980) *Women, Sex and Pornography*, New York, Macmillan

Ferguson, Ann (1977) 'Androgyny as an ideal for human development', Mary Vetterling-Braggin *et al.* (eds), 1977: 45–69

—— (1979) 'Women as a new revolutionary class in the US', Pat Walker (ed.), 1979: 279–309

—— (1981a) 'The Che-Lumumba school: creating a revolutionary family-community', *Quest*, vol. 5, no. 3: 13–26

—— (1981b) 'Patriarchy, sexual identity and the sexual revolution', *Signs*, vol. 7, no. 1: 158–72

—— (1983) 'The sex debate in the women's movement: a socialist-feminist view', *Against the Current*, Sept/Oct: 10–17

—— (1984a) 'On conceiving motherhood and sexuality: a feminist materialist approach', Joyce Trebilcot (ed.) 1984: 153–84

—— (1984b) 'Sex war: the debate between radical and libertarian feminists', *Signs*, vol. 10, no. 1, Fall: 106–12

—— (1985) 'Public patriarchy and how to fight it: a tri-systems view', unpublished mss

—— (1986a) 'Pleasure, power and the porn wars', *Women's Review of Books*, vol. 3, no. 8, May: 9–13

—— (1986b) 'Motherhood and sexuality: some feminist questions', *Hypatia: Journal of Feminist Philosophy*, vol. 1, no. 2, Fall: 3–22

—— (1987) 'A feminist aspect theory of the self', supplementary vol. 13 of *Canadian Journal of Philosophy*, Marsha Hanen and Kai Nielsen (eds), *Science, Feminism and Morality*, Alberta, Canada, The University of Calgary: 339–56

—— (1987) 'Socialism, feminism and the sex debate', unpublished mss

—— and Folbre, Nancy (1981) 'The unhappy marriage of capitalism and patriarchy', Lydia Sargent (ed.), 1981: 313–38

Firestone, Shulamith (1970) *The Dialectic of Sex*, New York, Bantam

Flandrin, Jean Louis (1976) *Families in Former Times: Kinship, Household and Sexuality*, New York, Cambridge University

Flax, Jane (1976) 'Do feminists need Marxism?', *Quest*, vol. 3, no. 1, Summer, reprinted in *Quest*, (eds), 1981: 174–86

—— (1978) 'The conflict between nurturance and autonomy in mother–daughter relationships and within feminism', *Feminist Studies*, vol. 4, no. 2, June: 171–91

Folbre, Nancy (1979) *Patriarchy and Capitalism in New England 1620–1900*, PhD thesis, Economics, Amherst, Ma., University of Massachusetts

—— (1980) 'Patriarchy in colonial New England', *Review of Radical Political Economics*, vol. 12, no. 2, Summer: 4–13

—— (1982) 'Exploitation comes home: a critique of the Marxian theory of family labour', *Cambridge Journal of Economics*, no. 6: 317–29

—— (1983) 'Of patriarchy born: the political economy of fertility decisions', *Feminist Studies*, vol. 9, no. 2, Summer: 261–84

—— (1985) 'The pauperization of motherhood: patriarchy and public policy in the United States', *Review of Radical Political Economics*, vol. 16, no. 4, Winter: 72–88

—— (1987) 'Patriarchy as a mode of production', Randy Albelda, Christopher Gunn and William Walker (eds), *Alternatives to Economic Orthodoxy*, New York, M.E. Sharpe: 323–38

—— (1987) 'The nature and logic of patriarchal capitalism', unpublished mss

—— and Hartmann, Heidi (1986) 'The rhetoric of self interest and the ideology of gender', Arjo Klamer, Donald McClosky and Robert Solow (eds), *The Consequences of Economic Rhetoric*, New York, Cambridge University

Foner, Philip (1979) *Women and the American Labor Movement from Colonial Times to the Eve of World War I*, New York, Free Press

Foucault, Michel (1977a) *Discipline and Punish*, New York, Pantheon

—— (1977b) Colin Gordon (ed.), *Power/Knowledge: Selected Interviews and Essays*, New York, Pantheon

—— (1977c) John Bouchard (ed.), *Language, Countermemory, Practice*, Ithaca, NY, Cornell University

—— (1978) *The History of Sexuality, Volume 1: An Introduction: The Will to Know*, New York, Pantheon

—— (1985) *The History of Sexuality, Volume II: The Use of Pleasure*, New York, Pantheon

—— (1986) *The History of Sexuality, Volume III: The Care of the Self*, New York, Pantheon

Fraser, Nancy and Nicolson, Linda (1986) 'Toward a feminist postmodernism', unpublished mss

Freeland, Cynthia (1986) 'Woman: revealed or reveiled?', *Hypatia*, vol. 1, no. 2, Fall: 49–70

Freud, Sigmund (1918) 'The taboo of virginity', Sigmund Freud, 1963b

—— (1950) 'Female sexuality', Freud, *Collected Papers*, James Strachey, trs., vol. 5, London, Hogarth Press

—— (1961) *Civilization and its Discontents*, New York, W.W. Norton

—— (1963a) *Three Essays on the Theory of Sexuality*, New York, Basic

—— (1963b) *Sexuality and the Psychology of Love*, New York, Colliers
—— (1963c) *The Sexual Enlightenment of Children* (Little Hans), New York, Colliers
—— (1963d) *Dora: An Analysis of a Case of Hysteria*, New York, Colliers
—— (1964) 'Femininity', in *New Introductory Lectures in Psychoanalysis*, Freud, *Collected Papers*, vol. 22, London, Hogarth
—— (1965) *The Interpretation of Dreams*, New York, Basic
Friedan, Betty (1963) *The Feminine Mystique*, New York, Norton
Friedman, Milton (1982) *Capitalism and Freedom*, Chicago, University of Chicago
Frye, Marilyn (1983) *The Politics of Reality*, Trumansburg, NY, Crossing Press

Gagnon, John (1977) *Human Sexuality*, Glenville, Ill., Scott, Foresman
—— and Simon, Wm. (1973) *Sexual Conduct: The Social Sources of Human Sexuality*, Chicago, Aldine
Gallop, Jane (1982) *The Daughter's Seduction: Feminism and Psychoanalysis*, Ithaca, NY, Cornell University
Gilder, George (1973) *Sexual Suicide*, New York, Quadrangle
Gilligan, Carol (1982) *In a Different Voice: Psychological Theory and Women's Development*, Cambridge, Ma., Harvard University
Girard, Alain (1968) 'The time budget of married women in urban centers', *Population*
Goldberg, Steven (1974) *The Inevitability of Patriarchy*, New York, Wm. Morrow & Co.
Gordon, Linda (1976) *Woman's Body, Woman's Right: A Social History of Birth Control in America*, New York, Penguin
—— and Hunter, Allen (1977) 'Sexuality, the family and the New Right', *Radical America*, vol. 11, no. 6, Nov. 1977/Feb. 1978: 9–26
Gorz, Andre (1967) *Strategy for Labor*, Boston, Beacon
Gough, Kathleen (1975) 'The origin of the family', Rayna Reiter (ed.), 1975
Gramsci, Antonio (1971) *Selections from the Prison Notebooks*, Quinton Hoare and Geoffrey Newell (eds), New York, International Publishers
Griffin, Susan (1979) *Rape: The Power of Consciousness*, New York, Harper
—— (1980) 'Sadism and catharsis: the treatment is the disease', Laura Lederer (ed.), 1980: 133–40
—— (1981) *Pornography and Silence*, New York, Harper
Grimshaw, Jean (1986) *Philosophy and Feminist Thinking*, Minneapolis, University of Minnesota
Gutman, Herbert (1977) *The Black Family in Slavery and Freedom 1750–1925*, New York, Random House

Haraway, Donna (1985) 'A manifesto for cyborgs: science, technology and socialist-feminism in the 1980s, *Socialist Review*, vol. 15, no. 2, Mar/April: 65–107
Harding, Sandra (1981) 'What is the real material base of patriarchy and capital?', Lydia Sargent (ed.), 1981: 135–64
—— (1986) 'The curious coincidence of feminine and African moralities: challenges for feminist theory', Eva Kittay and Diana Meyers (eds), 1986

Harris, Marvin (1979) *Cultural Materialism: The Struggle for a Science of Culture*, New York, Random House

Hartmann, Heidi (1975) 'Capitalism and women's work in the home', New Haven, Yale University PhD thesis, Economics

—— (1979) 'Capitalism, patriarchy and job segregation by sex', Zillah Eisenstein (ed.), 1979: 206–47

—— (1981a) 'The unhappy marriage of Marxism and feminism', Lydia Sargent (ed.), 1981. 1–42

—— (1981b) 'The family as the locus of gender, class and political struggle: the example of housework', *Signs*, vol. 6, no. 3. Spring: 366–94

Hartmann, Mary and Banner, Lois (eds), (1974) *Clio's Consciousness Raised*, New York, Harper

Hartsock, Nancy (1983) *Sex, Money and Power*, New York, Longman

Hatem, Mervat (1986) 'The politics of sexuality and gender in segregated patriarchal systems: the case of eighteenth and nineteenth century Egypt', *Feminist Studies*, vol. 12, no. 2: 251–74

Hegel, G.W.F. (1894) *Philosophy of Mind*, Wm. Wallace, trs. Oxford, Oxford University

Heilbrun, Carolyn (1973) *Toward a Recognition of Androgyny*, New York, Harper

Helmbold, Lois and Hollibaugh, Amber (1983) 'The family: what holds us, what hurts us, the family in socialist America', Steve Rosskaum Shalom (ed.), 1983: 119–22

Heresies (1981) 'Sex Issue', Issue 12, vol. 3, no. 4

Herman, Judith (1982) *Father-daughter Incest*, Cambridge, Ma., Harvard University

Hite, Shere (1977) *The Hite Report*, New York, Dell

—— (1987) *Women and Love: The Hite Report II*, New York, Knopf

Hoch, Paul (1979) *White Hero, Black Beast: Racism, Sexism and the Myth of Masculinity*, London, Pluto

Hollibaugh, Amber and Moraga, Cherríe (1981) 'What we're rolling around in bed with', *Heresies*, Issue 12, vol. 3, no. 4: 58–62

Holliday, Laurel (1978) *The Violent Sex: Male Psychobiology and the Evolution of Consciousness*, Guerneville, CA, Bluestocking Press

hooks, bell (1981) *Ain't I a Woman? Black Women and Feminism*, Boston, South End

—— (1984) *Feminist Theory: From Margin to Center*, Boston, South End

Horney, Karen (1967) *Feminine Psychology*, New York, Norton

Hull, Gloria; Scott, Patricia and Smith, Barbara (eds) (1982) *All the Blacks are Men, All the Women are White but Some of Us Are Brave*, Old Westbury, NY, Feminist Press

Humphries, Jane (1977) 'Class struggle and the persistence of the working class family', *Cambridge Journal of Economics*, vol. 1, no. 3, Sept: 241–58

Hunt, Morton (1974) *Sexual Behavior in the 1970s*, New York, Playboy Press

Irigaray, Luce (1974) *Speculum de l'autre femme*, Paris, Editions de Minuit

—— (1977) *Ce sexe qui n'en est pas un*, Paris, Editions de Minuit

—— (1985) *The Sex Which Is Not One*, trs. Catherine Porter, Ithaca, NY, Cornell University

—— (1985) *Speculum of the Other Woman*, trs., Gillian Gill, Ithaca, NY, Cornell University

Jackson, Margaret (1983) 'Sexual liberation or social control?', *Women's Studies International Forum*, vol. 6, no. 1: 1–17

Jacobs, Michael (1986) 'The contradictory relationship of gay men to feminism', unpublished mss

Jaggar, Alison (1983) *Feminist Politics and Human Nature*, Totowa, NJ, Rowman & Allanheld

Jeffreys, Sheila (1985) *The Spinster and her Enemies: Feminism and Sexuality 1880–1930*, London, Routledge/Pandora

Jonel, Marissa (1982) 'Letter from a former Masochist', Robin Linden *et al.* (eds), 1982: 16–22

Joseph, Gloria (1981) 'The incompatible menage a trois: Marxism, feminism and racism', Lydia Sargent (ed.), 1981: 91–108

—— (1983) 'Black family structure: foundations for the future', Stephen Rosskamm Shalom (ed.), 1983: 231–9

—— and Lewis, Jill (1981) *Common Differences: Conflicts in Black and White Perspectives*, New York, Doubleday/Anchor

Justus, Joyce Bennett (1981) 'Women's role in West Indian society', Filomena Steady (ed.), 1981: 431–50

Katz, Jonathan (1978) *Gay American History: Lesbian and Gay Men in the USA*, New York, Avon

Kinsey, Alfred C.; Pomeroy, Wardell B. and Martin, Clyde E. (1948) *Sexual Behavior in the Human Male*, Philadelphia, Pa., Saunders

Kinsey, Alfred C. *et al.* (1953) *Sexual Behavior in the Human Female*, Philadelphia, Pa., Saunders

Kittay, Eva and Meyers, Diana (eds), (1986) *Women and Morality*, Totowa, NJ, Rowman & Allanheld

Koedt, Anne; Levine, Ellen and Rapone, Anita, (eds), (1973) *Radical Feminism*, New York, Quadrangle/New York Times

Kollias, Karen (1975) 'Class realities: create a new power base', *Quest*, vol. 1, no. 3: 125–38, reprinted in *Quest* (eds), 1981: 125–38

Kraditor, Aileen S. (1965) *The Ideas of the Women's Suffrage Movement 1890–1920*, New York, Columbia University

Krieger, Susan (1983) *The Mirror Dance: Identity in a Woman's Community*, Philadelphia, Pa., Temple University

Kristeva, Julia (1977) *About Chinese Women*, London, Marion Boyers

Kuhn, Annette and Wolpe, Ann Marie (eds), (1978) *Feminism and Materialism*, London, Routledge

Kuhn, Thomas (1970) *The Structure of Scientific Revolutions*, Chicago, University of Chicago

Lacan, Jacques (1982) Juliet Mitchell and Jacqueline Rose (eds), 1982

Laclau, Ernesto and Mouffe, Chantal (1985) *Hegemony and Socialist Strategy: Towards a Radical Democratic Politics*, London, Verso

Lasch, Christopher (1977) *Haven in a Heartless World: The Family Besieged*, New York, Basic

—— (1979) *The Culture of Narcissism: American Life in an Age of Diminishing Expectations*, New York, Norton

—— (1984) *The Minimal Self*, New York, Norton

Lazaro, Reyes (1986) 'Feminism and motherhood: O'Brien vs. Beauvoir', *Hypatia*, vol. 1, no. 2, Fall: 87–102

Lederer, Laura (ed.) (1980) *Take Back the Night: Women on Pornography*, New York, Wm. Morrow & Co.

Leeds Revolutionary Feminists (1981) *Love your Enemy? The Debate between Heterosexual Feminism and Political Lesbianism*, London, Onlywomen Press

Leghorn, Lisa and Parker, Katherine (1981) *Women's Worth: Sexual Economics and the World of Women*, London, Routledge

Leis, Nancy (1974) 'Women in groups: Ijaw women's associations', Michelle Rosaldo and Louise Lamphere (eds), 1974: 223–42

Lerner, Gerda (1986) *The Creation of Patriarchy*, New York, Oxford University

Levi-Strauss, Claude (1969) *The Elementary Structures of Kinship*, Boston, Beacon

—— (1971) 'The family', H. Shapiro (ed.), *Man, Culture and Society*, London, Oxford University

Lichtmann, Richard (1982) *The Production of Desire*, New York, Macmillan

Linden, Robin; Pagano, Darlene; Russell, Diane and Starr, Susan (eds), (1982) *Against Sado-masochism: A Radical Feminist Analysis*, East Palo Alto, Ca., Frog in the Well Press

Lindsey, Karen (1981) *Friends as Family*, Boston, Beacon

Lippert, Jon (1977) 'Sexuality as consumption', Jon Snodgrass (ed), 1977

Lorde, Audre (1972) 'Scratching the surface: some notes on barriers to women-loving', *The Black Scholar*, vol. 9, no. 7

—— (1978) 'Uses of the erotic: the erotic as power', Laura Lederer (ed.), 1980: 295–300

—— (1984) *Sister Outsider*, Trumansburg, NY, The Crossing Press

Loulan, Jo Ann (1984) *Lesbian Sex*, San Francisco, Spinsters Ink

Lukacs, Georg (1968) *History and Class Consciousness*, London, Merlin

McCrate, Elaine (1985) 'The growth of non-marriage among US women 1954–1983', Amherst, Ma., University of Massachusetts PhD thesis, Economics

McIntosh, Mary (1968) 'The homosexual role', *Social Problems*, vol. 16, no. 2, Fall: 182–92

MacKinnon, Catherine (1979) *Sexual Harassment of Working Women*, New Haven, Ct., Yale University

—— (1982) 'Feminism, Marxism, method and the state: an agenda for theory', *Signs*, vol. 7, no. 3, Spring: 515–44

—— (1983) 'Feminism, Marxism, method and the state: toward feminist jurisprudence', *Signs*, vol. 8, no. 4, Summer: 635–58

—— (1984) 'Pornography, civil rights and speech', *Harvard Women's Law Journal*, vol. 20: 1–70; reprinted in Andrea Dworkin and Catherine MacKinnon (eds), 1985

—— (1987) *Feminism Unmodified: Discourses on Life and the Law*, Cambridge, Ma., Harvard University

MacPherson, C.B. (1962) *The Political Theory of Possessive Individualism: Hobbs to Locke*, Oxford, Clarendon

Marable, Manning (1980) *From the Grassroots*, Boston, South End

—— (1981) 'The third reconstruction: Black nationalism and race in a revolutionary America', *Social Text*, no. 4, Fall: 3–27; reprinted in Shalom (ed.), 1983: 101–27

Marcus, Marcia (1981) *A Taste for Pain: On Masochism and Female Sexuality*, London, Souvenir Press

Marcuse, Herbert (1955) *Eros and Civilization*, Boston, Beacon

—— (1964) *One Dimensional Man*, Boston, Beacon

—— (1969) *Essay on Liberation*, Boston, Beacon

—— (1972) *Counter-revolution and Revolt*, Boston, Beacon

Marx, Karl (1978) 'Alienated Labor', Robert Tucker (ed.) *Marx-Engels Reader*, New York, W. W. Norton & Co: 66–135

—— (1972) *The Eighteenth Brumaire of Louis Bonaparte*, New York, International Publishers

—— (1977) David McLellan (ed.), *Karl Marx: Selected Writings*, Oxford, Oxford University

—— and Engels, Friedrich (1850) *The German Ideology*, New York, International Publishers

Masson, Jeffrey Moussaieff (1984) *The Assault on Truth: Freud's Suppression of the Seduction Theory*, New York, Farrar, Strauss & Giroux

Masters, Wm. H. and Johnson, Virginia (1974) *The Pleasure Bond: A New Look at Sexuality and Commitment*, Boston, Little, Brown & Co

Meillassoux, Claude (1981) *Maidens, Meal and Money: Capitalism and the Domestic Economy*, New York, Cambridge University

Meulenbelt, Anja; Outshoorn, Joyce; Sevenhuijsen, Selma and de Vries, Petra (eds), (1984) *A Creative Tension: Key Issues of Socialist-feminism*, Boston, South End

Miller, John and Richardson, Wm. (1982) *Lacan and Language*, New York, International Universities

Miller, Patricia Y. and Fowkles, Martha R. (1980) 'Social and behavioral constructions of sexuality', *Signs*, vol. 5, no. 4, Summer: 783–800

Miller, Sue (1986) *The Good Mother*, New York, Harper & Row

Millett, Kate (1970) *Sexual Politics*, Garden City, NJ, Doubleday

Mitchell, Juliet (1972) *Women's Estate*, New York, Random

—— (1974) *Psychoanalysis and Feminism*, New York, Pantheon

—— and Rose, Jacqueline (eds), (1982) *Feminine Sexuality: Jacques Lacan and the ecole freudienne*, New York, Norton

Modleski, Tania (1982) *Loving with a Vengeance: Mass-produced Fantasies for Women*, New York, Methuen

Money, John and Musaph, Herman (1978) *Handbook of Sexology*, New York, Elsevier

Moraga, Cherri and Anzaldua, Gloria (eds), (1981) *This Bridge Called My Back: Writings by Radical Women of Color*, Watertown, MA, Persephone

Morrison, Toni (1973) *Sula*, New York, Knopf

—— (1977) *Song of Solomon*, New York, Knopf

Myers, Lena Wright (1980) *Black Women: Do They Cope Better?*, Englewood Cliffs, NJ, Prentice-Hall

Myron, Nancy and Bunch, Charlotte (1974a) *Class and Feminism*, Baltimore, Md., Diana Press
—— (1974b) *Women Remembered: A Collection of Biographies*, Baltimore, Md., Diana Press
—— (1975) *Lesbianism and the Women's Movement*, Baltimore, Md., Diana Press

Nestle, Joan (1981) 'Butch/Femme relationships: sexual courage in the 1950s', *Heresies*, 12: 21–4
Newton, Esther and Walton, Shirley (1984) 'The misunderstanding: toward a more precise sexual vocabulary', Carol Vance (ed.), 1984: 242–50
Nicolson, Linda (1986) *Gender and History*, New York, Columbia University

O'Brien, Mary (1981) *The Politics of Reproduction*, London, Routledge
Olsen, Tillie (1960) *Tell Me A Riddle and Other Stories*, New York, Dell
Orlando, Lisa (1982) 'Bad girls and "good" politics', *Voice Literary Supplement*, no. 13, Dec: 1, 16–17
—— (1986) 'Politics and pleasures: sexual controversies in the women's and lesbian/gay movements', MA thesis, Amherst, Ma., University of Massachusetts, Political Science
Ortner, Sherry B. and Whitehead, Harriet (eds), (1982) *Sexual Meanings: The Cultural Construction of Gender and Sexuality*, New York, Cambridge University

Penelope, Julia (1985) 'The mystery of lesbians', Parts I, II, III, *Lesbian Ethics*, vol. 1, nos 1, 2 and 3
Perlo, Victor (1980) *Economics of Racism USA: Roots of Black Inequality*, New York, International Publishers
Person, Ethel (1980) 'Sexuality as the mainstay of identity: psychoanalytic perspectives', *Signs*, vol. 5, no. 4, Summer: 605–30; reprinted in Catherine Stimpson and Ethel Person (eds), 1980: 36–61
Phelps, Linda (1975) 'Patriarchy and capitalism', *Quest*, vol. 2, no. 2, Fall: 34–48
Philipson, Ilene (1984a) 'Beyond the virgin and the whore', *Socialist Review*, Issue 75/6, vol. 14, nos 3 and 4, May/Aug: 127–36
—— (1984b) 'The repression of history and gender: a critical perspective on the feminist sexuality debate', *Signs*, vol. 10, no. 1, Autumn: 113–18
Piercy, Marge (1974) *Woman on the Edge of Time*, New York, Fawcett
Pietropinto, Anthony and Simenauer, Jacqueline (1977) *Beyond the Male Myth*, New York, Times Books
Plummer, Kenneth (1975) *Sexual Stigma: An Interactionist Account*, London, Routledge
—— (ed.) (1981) *The Making of the Modern Homosexual*, London, Hutchinson
Ponse, Barbara (1978) *Identities in the Lesbian World: The Social Construction of Self*, Westport, Conn., Greenwood Press
Poster, Mark (1978) *Critical Theory of the Family*, London, Pluto
Poulantzas, Nicos (1975) *Classes in Contemporary Capitalism*, New York, Humanities Press

Quest (eds) (1981) *Building Feminist Theory: Essays from* Quest, New York, Longmans
Quintanales, Mirtha and Kerr, Barbara (1982) 'The complexity of desire: conversations on sexuality and difference', *Conditions*, 8: 52–89

Radicalesbians (1970) 'The woman-identified woman', Anne Koedt *et al.* (eds), 1973: 240–5
Raymond, Janice (1979) *The Transsexual Empire: The Making of the She-male*, Boston, Beacon
—— (1986) *A Passion for Friends*, Boston, Beacon
Reed, Evelyn (1973) *Women's Revolution from Matriarchal Clan to Patriarchal Family*, New York, Pathfinder Press
Reich, Michael (1981) *Racial Inequality*, Princeton, NJ, Princeton University
Reich, Wilhelm (1949) *Character Analysis*, New York, Farrar, Strauss & Giroux
—— (1970) *Mass Psychology of Fascism*, New York, Farrar, Strauss & Giroux
—— (1972) Lee Baxandall (ed.), *Sex-Pol: Essays 1929–1934*, New York, Random
—— (1973) *The Discovery of the Orgone: The Function of the Orgasm*, New York, Farrar, Strauss & Giroux
—— (1974) *The Sexual Revolution*, New York, Farrar, Strauss & Giroux
Reiter, Rayna (ed.) (1975) *Toward a New Anthropology of Women*, New York, *Monthly Review*
Rich, Adrienne (1976) *Of Woman Born: Motherhood as Experience and Institution*, New York, W. W. Norton
—— (1980) 'Compulsory heterosexuality and lesbian existence', *Signs*, vol. 5, no. 4, Summer: 631–60; reprinted in Stimpson and Person (eds), 1980
Root, Jane (1984) *Pictures of Women: Sexuality*, London, Routledge/Pandora
Rosaldo, Michelle and Lamphere, Louise (eds), (1974) *Women, Culture and Society*, Stanford, Ca., Stanford University
Rossi, Alice (1974) 'Social roots of the women's movement in America', Alice Rossi (ed.), 1974
—— (ed.) (1974) *Feminist Papers*, New York, Bantam
—— (1975) 'A biosocial perspective on parenting', *Daedalus*, vol. 106, no. 2, Spring: 11–32
Rowbotham, Sheila (1973) *Women's Consciousness, Man's World*, Baltimore, Penguin
Rubin, Gayle (1975) 'The traffic in women', Rayna Reiter (ed.), 1975: 157–210
—— (1978) 'Sexual politics: the New Right and the sexual fringe', *Leaping Lesbian*, vol. 2, no. 2; reprinted in Daniel Tsang, (ed.), 1981: 108–15
—— (1981) 'The leather menace: comments on politics and s/m', Samois (ed.), 1981: 192–225
—— (1984) 'Thinking sex: notes for a radical theory of the politics of sexuality', Carol Vance (ed.), 1984: 267–319
Rubin, Lillian (1976) *Worlds of Pain*, New York, Basic
Ruddick, Sara (1980) 'Maternal thinking', *Feminist Studies*, vol. 6, no. 2, Summer: 342–67
—— (1984) 'Preservative love and military destruction: some reflections on mothering and peace', Joyce Trebilcot (ed.), 1984: 231–62

Rush, Florence (1980) *Best Kept Secret: Sexual Abuses of Children*, Englewood Cliff, NJ, Prentice Hall, Inc.

Russell, Diana (1979) 'Pornography and violence: what does the new research say?', Laura Lederer (ed.), 1980: 216–36

Ryan, Mary (1975) *Womanhood in America*, New York, Watts, Inc.

Sahli, Nancy (1979) 'Smashing: women's relationships before the fall', *Chrysalis*, no. 8: 17–28

Said, Edward W. (1978) *Orientalism*, New York, Pantheon

Samois (ed.) (1979) *What Color Is Your Hankerchief: A Lesbian S/M Sexuality Reader*, Berkeley, Ca., Samois

—— (1981) *Coming to Power: Writings and Graphics on Lesbian S/M*, Berkeley, Ca., Samois

Sanday, Peggy Reeves (1981) *Female Power and Male Dominance: On The Origins of Sexual Inequality*, New York, Cambridge University

Sargent, Lydia (1981) *Women and Revolution*, Boston, South End

Sartre, Jean-Paul (1956) *Being and Nothingness*, New York, Philosophical Library

—— (1969) 'Black Orpheus', Jules Chametzky and Sidney Kaplan (eds), *Black and White in American Culture*, Amherst, Ma., University of Massachusetts: 415–50

Sawicki, Jana (1986) 'Foucault and feminism: toward a politics of difference', *Hypatia*, vol. 1, no. 2: 23–36

Sayers, Janet (1982) *Biological Politics: Feminist and Anti-feminist Perspectives*, New York, Tavistock

Schrim, Janet (1979) 'S/M and feminism', Cedar and Nelly (eds), 1979

Scott, Hilda (1974) *Does Socialism Liberate Women?* Boston, Beacon

Schwartz, Judith (1979) 'Questionnaire on issues in lesbian history', *Frontiers*, vol. 4, no. 3, Fall: 1–12

Seidman, Steven (1987) 'The feminist debates over female sexuality', unpublished mss

Shange, Ntozake (1982) *Sassafras, Cypress and Indigo*, New York, St Martins

Shalom, Stephen Rosskamm (ed.) (1983) *Socialist Visions*, Boston, South End

Shorter, Edward (1975) *The Making of the Modern Family*, New York, Basic

Sidel, Ruth (1986) *Women and Children Last: The Plight of Poor Women in Affluent America*, New York, Viking/Penguin

Silveira, Jeanette (1984) 'Why men oppress women', *Lesbian Ethics*, vol. 1, no. 1: 34–56

Simons, Christina (1979) 'Companionate marriage and the lesbian threat', *Frontiers*, vol. 4, no. 3, Fall: 54–9

Simons, Margaret A. (1979) 'Racism and feminism: a schism in the sisterhood', *Feminist Studies*, vol. 5, no. 2, Summer: 384–90

Small, Margaret (1974) 'Lesbians and the class position of women', Myron and Bunch (eds), 1974a

Smith, Daniel Scott (1974) 'Family limitation, sexual control and domestic feminism in Victorian America', Mary Hartmann and Lois Banner (eds), 1974

Smith-Rosenberg, Carol (1975) 'The female world of love and ritual: relations between women in nineteenth century America', *Signs*, vol. 1, no. 1, Autumn: 1–29

Snitow, Ann Barr (1983) 'Mass market romance: pornography for women is different', Snitow, *et al.* (eds), 1983: 245–63

Soble, Alan (1986) *Pornography*, New Haven, Yale University

Sokoloff, Natalie (1980) *Between Money and Love: The Dialectics of Women's Home and Market Work*, New York, Praeger

Snodgrass, Jon (ed.) (1977) *For Men Against Sexism*, New York, Times Change Press

Spelman, Elizabeth V. (1982) 'Theories of race and gender: the erasure of black women', *Quest*, vol. 5, no. 4: 36–62

Spillers, Hortense (1984) 'Interstices: a small drama of words', Carole Vance (ed.), 1984: 73–100

Stacey, Judith (1987) 'Sexism by a subtler name: postindustrial conditions and a postfeminist consciousness', *Socialist Review*, Issue 96, vol. 17, no. 6: 7–30

Stack, Carol (1974) *All Our Kin*, New York, Harper & Row

—— (1981) 'Sex roles and survival strategies in the urban black community', Filomena Steady (ed.), 1981: 346–68

Steady, Filomena Chioma (ed.) (1981) *The Black Woman Crossculturally*, Cambridge, Ma., Schenkman Publishing

Stember, Charles Herbert (1976) *Sexual Racism*, New York, Harper

Stewart, Katie (1981) 'The marriage of capitalist and patriarchal ideologies: meanings of male bonding and male ranking in US culture', Lydia Sargent (ed.), 1981: 269–312

Stimpson, Catherine and Person, Ethel Spector (eds) (1980) *Women, Sex and Sexuality*, Chicago, University of Chicago

Stoller, Robert (1979) *Sexual Excitement: Dynamics of Erotic Life*, New York, Simon & Schuster

Stoltenberg, John, with Ian Young, Lyn Rosen and Rose Jordan (1978) 'Forum on s/m', Karla Jay and Allen Young (eds), *Lavender Culture*, New York, Jove/HBJ: 83–117

Stone, Lawrence (1977) *The Family, Sex and Marriage in England 1500–1800*, London, Weidenfeld & Nicolson

Tax, Meredith (1970) *Woman and her mind: the story of everyday life*, Boston, New England Free Press

Thompson, E. P. (1966) *The Making of the English Working Class*, New York, Vintage

Tiger, Lionel (1969) *Men in Groups*, New York, Random

Tong, Rosemary (1984) *Women, Sex and the Law*, Totowa, NJ, Rowman & Allanheld

Trebilcot, Joyce (1977) 'Two forms of androgynism', Mary Vetterling-Braggin *et al.* (eds), 1977: 70–8

—— (ed.) (1984) *Mothering: Essays in Feminist Theory*, Totowa, NJ, Rowman & Allanheld

Tsang, Daniel (ed.) (1981) *The Age Taboo: Gay Male Sexuality, Power and Consent*, Boston, Alyson

Ullman, Liv (1977) *Changing*, New York, Knopf

Vance, Carole (ed.) (1984) *Pleasure and Danger: Exploring Female Sexuality*, London, Routledge
—— and Snitow, Ann Barr (1984) 'Toward a conversation about sex in feminism: a modest proposal', *Signs*, vol. 10, no. 1, Autumn: 126–35
Veblen, Thorstein (1973) *The Theory of the Leisure Class*, Boston, Houghton Mifflin
Vetterling-Braggin, Mary, Elliston, Frederick and English, Jane (eds) (1977) *Feminism and Philosophy*, Totowa, NJ, Littlefield, Adams
Vicinus, Martha (1982) 'Sexuality and power: a review of current work in the history of sexuality', *Feminist Studies*, vol. 8, no. 1, Spring: 133–53
Vogel, Lise (1983) *Marxism and the Oppression of Women: Toward a Unitary Theory*, New Brunswick, NJ, Rutgers University

Wagner, Sally Roesch (1982) 'Pornography and the sexual revolution: the backlash of sadomasochism', Robin Linden *et al.* (eds), 1982: 23–44
Walker, Alice (1982a) *The Color Purple*, New York, Harcourt Brace Jovanovich
—— (1982b) 'A letter of the times, or should this sadomasochism be saved?', Robin Linden *et al.* (eds), 1982: 205–9
Walker, Pat (ed.) (1979) *Between Labor and Capital*, Boston, South End
Wartenberg, Thomas (1987) 'Social movements and individual identity: a critique of Freud on the psychology of groups', unpublished mss
Webster, Paula (1981) 'Pornography and pleasure', *Heresies*, no. 12: 48–51
Weeks, Jeffrey (1979) *Coming Out: A History of Homosexuality from the Nineteenth Century to the Present*, London, Quartet Books
—— (1981) *Sex, Politics and Society*, New York, Longman
—— (1985) *Sexuality and its Discontents: Meanings, Myth and Modern Sexualities*, London, Routledge
—— (1986) *Sexuality*, Chichester, England, Ellis Horwood
Weinbaum, Batya (1978) *The Curious Courtship of Women's Liberation and Socialism*, Boston, South End
—— (1983) *Pictures of Patriarchy*, Boston, South End
Weir, Lorna and Casey, Leo (1984) 'Subverting power in sexuality', *Socialist Review*, Issue 75/6, vol. 14, no. 3, May/Aug: 139–55
Weisskopf, Susan Contratto (1980) 'Maternal sexuality and asexual motherhood', *Signs*, vol. 5, no. 4, Summer: 766–82
Weitzman, Lenore J. (1985) *The Divorce Revolution: The Unexpected Social and Economic Consequences for Women and Children*, New York, Free Press
White, Fran (1984) 'Listening to the voices of Black feminism', *Radical America*, vol. 18, no. 2: 7–26
Willis, Ellen (1982) 'Toward a feminist sexual revolution', *Social Text*, no. 6, Fall: 3–21
—— (1983) 'Feminism, moralism and pornography', Ann Snitow *et al.* (eds), 1983: 460–7; also in FACT (ed.), 1986: 54–9
—— (1984) 'Radical feminism and feminist radicalism', Kate Soper (ed.), *The Sixties Without Apology*, Minneapolis, Minn., University of Minnesota: 91–117

Wilson, Wm. J. (1978) *The Declining Significance of Race: Blacks and Changing American Institutions*, Chicago, Ill., University of Chicago

Winston, Henry (1977) *Class, Race and Black Liberation*, New York, International Publishers

Wolff, Richard and Resnick, Steven (1987) *Economics: Marxian vs. Neoclassical*, Baltimore, Md., Johns Hopkins University

Wollheim, Richard (1971) *Sigmund Freud*, New York, Cambridge University

Women's Studies Group CCCS (eds) (1978) *Women Take Issue*, London, Hutchinson

Women's Agenda (1976a) 'Women and childcare', March/April

Women's Agenda (1976b) 'Women and poverty', June

Wright, Erik Olin (1978) *Class, Crisis and the State*, London, New Left Books

Yarborough, Susan (1979) 'Lesbian celibacy', *Sinister Wisdom*, Fall: 24–9

Young, Iris (1981) 'Beyond the unhappy marriage: a critique of the dual systems theory', Lydia Sargent (ed.) 1981: 43–70

—— (1984) 'Is male gender identity the cause of male domination?', Joyce Trebilcot (ed.), 1984: 129–46

Zaretsky, Eli (1976) *Capitalism, the Family and Personal Life*, New York, Harper

Zita, Jacqueline (1981) 'Historical amnesia and the lesbian continuum', *Signs*, vol. 7, no. 1, Autumn: 172–87

Index

INFERTILITY

Women Speak Out About Their Experiences of Reproductive Medicine

Renate D. Klein

Reproductive medicine fails women. Disturbing evidence exists of medical malpractice and invasive technologies which violate women's bodies and take a heavy toll on their lives.

Here, for the first time, women from many countries tell their own stories – about the pain the stigma of infertility; the never-ending cycles of drugs and hormone injections; the trauma of the 'test tube baby' method (IVF); their thwarted hopes when technology fails them yet again; and their exploitation as so-called 'surrogate' mothers.

These shocking stories shatter the myths of benevolent doctors working in the interests of women.

The women who speak out in this book offer support and suggest alternative strategies for other people with fertility problems. Their experiences show that we urgently need to resist the false promise of reproductive technologies if *all* women are not to become test-sites for medical experimentation and scientific ambition.

0 04 440367 4 pbk

TEST TUBE WOMEN

What Future for Motherhood?

Second Edition

Edited by Rita Arditti, Renate D. Klein and Shelley Minden

'Should be read from cover to cover by all concerned professionally, politically and personally with procreation.' Bernard Dixon in *New Society*

First published in 1984, *Test Tube Women* was the first feminist investigation into the new reproductive technologies and their personal and political consequences for women – genetic engineering, sperm banks, test tube fertilisation, sex selection, surrogate mothering, experimentation in the third world, increased technological intervention in childbirth.

Reissued to accompany Renate Klein's new book *Infertility: Women Speak Out About Their Experiences of Reproductive Medicine*, this new edition has been updated with a comprehensive new introduction assessing the developments of the past five years.

0 04 440429 8 pbk

THE PAST IS BEFORE US

Feminism in Action since the 1960s

Sheila Rowbotham

Leading feminist historian Sheila Rowbotham brings the recent past into a new perspective, placing it 'before us' as a vital resource for the future.

This major new history of the ideas of the women's movement shows how feminism has redefined the scope of politics. It gets behind the slogans, bringing them to a new life and complexity as women express their feelings about whether to have children, how to combine a career with motherhood, and argue about men, pornography or fashion.

The Past is Before Us traces the ideas and actions of women who were involved in the equal pay disputes, abortion campaigns and 'reclaim the night' marches of the 1960s and '70s; women who have lobbied for better housing, childcare and housing conditions; women in the 1980s who have come to feminism through a variety of political causes. It also highlights the key issues which will determine the options open to women in the 1990s.

This is a book for every woman who has wondered whether maybe it is the world, not her, who is at fault. It shows that things can be different and better, and that *every* woman can contribute to change.

'. . . captures exactly the mood of the moment when women's liberation came into the lives of women in Britain.' Beatrix Campbell

0 04 440365 8 hbk

YOUR VALUES, YOUR CHILD

Autumn 1989

Sheila and Celia Kitzinger

Sheila Kitzinger, social anthropologist and writer about birth, babies
and female sexuality, and Celia Kitzinger, research psychologist and
writer about feminist issues and morality, explore with more than 500
women the values they believe are important to pass on to their
children.

They discuss the ways in which children learn about right and wrong,
what helps them and what doesn't, and compare this with what values
were taught in the past and in different cultures.

Sex, religion, violence, death, racism, poverty, famine, nuclear war –
even three year olds ask difficult questions about these subjects – and
the answers can't be shelved.

0 04 440362 3 pbk

DOES KHAKI BECOME YOU?

The Militarization of Women's Lives

Cynthia Enloe

This is a book about sexuality and about racism. It is about the family and about work. All spheres of woman's life can and have been militarized.

A lonely young officer's wife in Germany, a prostitute at a 'rest and relaxation' base in the Philippines or a nurse in Beirut – more and more women the world over, civilians as well as soldiers, are providing essential support for the military.

Cynthia Enloe analyses the army's use and abuse of women, in and out of uniform, in Vietnam and in the Falklands. In a new introductory essay for this edition, she shows how women are being used to contain the threat of AIDS and the Irangate scandal, and to support military activity in the Gulf and in Central America. She argues for urgent resistance to such military manoeuvres.

'A fine book which never loses contact with the touchstones of feminist scholarship ... the voices of the women who speak in her pages are very real.' – Teresa Amott in *The Women's Review of Books*

'... thoughtful and provocative ... a disturbingly convincing portrait of the manner in which the protaction of the male ego is regarded as paramount in most aspects of military life' – Jenny Gould in *New Society*

'... a fascinating book, very informative, very well-documented and very readable. There's no need for rousing polemic: the facts speak for themselves.' – Penny Strange in *Peace News*

'... a triumph of feminist analysis ... dizzyingly well-written' – Zoë Fairbairns in *Spare Rib*

0 86358 301 6 pbk

BANANAS, BEACHES AND BASES   Autumn 1989

Making Feminist Sense of International Politics

Cynthia Enloe

This radical new analysis of international politics reveals the crucial role of women in implementing governments' foreign policies – be it Soviet *Glasnost*, Britain's dealings in the EEC or the NATO alliance.

Cynthia Enloe pulls back the curtain on the familiar scenes – governments restricting imported goods, bankers negotiating foreign loans, soldiers serving overseas – and shows that the *real* landscape is less exclusively male.

She shows how thousands of women tailor their marriages to fit the demands of state secrecy; how foreign policy would grind to a halt without secretaries to handle money transfers or arms shipments; and how women are working in hotels and factories around the world in order to service their governments' debts.

Cynthia Enloe also challenges common assumptions about what constitutes 'international politics'. She explains, for example, how turning tacos and sushi into bland fast foods affects relations between affluent and developing countries, and why a multinational banana company needs the brothel outside its gates. And she argues that shopping at Benetton, wearing Levis, working as a nanny (or employing one) or booking a holiday are all examples of foreign policy in action.

Bananas, Beaches and Bases does not ignore our curiosity about arms dealers, the President's men or official secrets. But it shows why these conventional clues are not sufficient for understanding how the international political system works. In exposing policy makers' reliance on false notions of 'femininity' and 'masculinity', Cynthia Enloe dismantles a seemingly overwhelming world system, exposing it to be much more fragile and open to change than we are usually led to believe.

0 04 440368 2 pbk

AN OLIVE SCHREINER READER

Writings on Women and South Africa

Edited by Carol Barash

with an afterword by Nadine Gordimer

Olive Schreiner's *The Story of an African Farm* (1883) was famous in England and South Africa. Her writings on women were recited by suffragettes in jail and her scathing criticism of British colonial rule still rings true today.

This is the first collection to bring together Olive Schreiner's shorter writings on women and South Africa. It covers the full range of her political and imaginative works, and is arranged chronologically to trace her shifting alliances with both the feminist movement in England and the South African struggle for independence.

As a white woman in South Africa, Olive Schreiner was both coloniser and colonised, and, as Carol Barash shows in her introduction to this reader, sexual and racial oppression are crucially related throughout her work. Olive Schreiner's writing will not give us politically correct heroines; instead, it raises central questions about the interdependence of our attitudes towards gender and race.

0 86358 118 8 pbk

A FEMINIST DICTIONARY

In Our Own Words

Cheris Kramarae and Paula Treichler

with Assistance from Ann Russo

This is a dictionary with a difference. It places women at the centre of language and uses definition and quotation to take us on a fascinating journey through the development and use of the English language from diverse feminist perspectives. *A Feminist Dictionary* illustrates women's linguistic contributions: the ways in which women have sought to describe, reflect upon and theorize about women, language and the rest of the world. This is a unique source book that will serve as a valuable work of reference for many years to come.

'A truly superb job.' – Casey Miller and Kate Swift

'. . . does not deal in sterile signs, but the living, evolving language of feminism.' – Barbara Smith, *New Statesman*

'Finally we have our own dictionary. Whether you choose to read it as I did, slowly, from beginning to end, or keep it handy as a reference book, reading entires as your interest suits you, A Feminist Dictionary deserves a special place in our personal libraries.' – Julia Penelope, *Women's Review of Books*

0–86358–015–7 pbk